PRAISE FOR RACHELLE DEKKER

"The strong female heroine will appeal to teen readers, and adults and teens alike may also enjoy the themes of corruption and religion, absolute human power, and government as God. . . . Dekker's debut is worth choosing."

PUBLISHERS WEEKLY ON *THE CHOOSING*

"The story vacillates between the sweetness of a tender coming-of-age romance and moments that almost resemble a Dean Koontz thriller. . . . At times frightening but often beautiful, [*The Choosing*] will leave readers eager for the next book of this new series."

SERENA CHASE, *USA TODAY*

"[*The Choosing*] is an amazing debut novel full of heart, drama, and complex believable characters . . . with a detailed plot and gripping truths that pierced my heart."

THE BOOK CLUB NETWORK INC.

"A swiftly moving plot puts readers in the center of the action, and the well-described setting adds to the experience. Deeper themes of value and worth will appeal to both young adult and adult readers."

ROMANTIC TIMES ON *THE CHOOSING*

"Whatever expectations you have of debut author Rachelle Dekker, go ahead and put them aside. Rachelle, daughter to bestselling author Ted Dekker, is carving out a space of her own. Her debut novel, *The Choosing*, is a rich statement about the author's future and her impact on Christian fiction."

FAMILY FICTION

"Ripe for discussion, [*The Choosing*] may inspire some readers to open up about the social pressures that they feel both in and out of their faith community. Expect it to appeal to dystopian fans of all ages."

FOREWORD REVIEWS

"Readers will find Dekker's storyline somewhat akin to her father's works in terms of action, adventure, and unpredictability. *The Choosing*, though, explores more the inner workings of her characters and how they feel about their lot in life. I look forward to more dystopian titles from Dekker in the near future."

BOOKREPORTER.COM

"*The Choosing* is an inspiring tale that reaches in to the hearts of men and women, showing both the love and the darkness that can lurk within."

FRESH FICTION

"Marrying the themes of the popular Kiera Cass Selection novels with the action danger of *The Hunger Games*, Dekker asserts a strong imaginative voice that had me gulping down sentences and events as quickly as they were relayed on [the] page."

NOVEL CROSSING ON *THE CHOOSING*

"[*The Choosing*] is part adventure, part romance, part mystery, and it works. The writing is wonderful. It flows in such a way that it keeps the reader turning page after page . . . more than likely long into the night to find out what happens!"

RADIANT LIT

"In her stunning debut novel, Rachelle Dekker plunges readers into a unique yet familiar-feeling dystopian society, where one girl's longing for acceptance, identity, and purpose becomes a mind-bending, pulse-pounding journey that'll [leave] you breathless and reeling. A superb story!"

JOSH OLDS, LIFEISSTORY.COM

"This intense dystopian read was reminiscent of the Divergent series. Christian themes of God's love and forgiveness are woven throughout [*The Calling*]."

CBA RETAILERS + RESOURCES

"[Dekker's] strong storytelling voice and ability to convey her ideas comes through nicely in this book."

STRAIGHTOFFTHEPAGE.COM ON *THE CALLING*

"Dekker pens another striking science fiction thriller including a well-developed dystopian society and strong depictions of good versus evil that can be easily read as a standalone."

PUBLISHERS WEEKLY ON *THE RETURNING*

"Rachelle Dekker completes this series elegantly. . . . the perfect conclusion to the Seer series."

CHRISTIAN LIBRARY JOURNAL ON *THE RETURNING*

WHEN THROUGH DEEP WATERS

TYNDALE HOUSE PUBLISHERS, INC.
CAROL STREAM, ILLINOIS

RACHELLE DEKKER

Visit Tyndale online at www.tyndale.com.

Visit Rachelle Dekker's website at www.rachelledekker.com.

TYNDALE and Tyndale's quill logo are registered trademarks of Tyndale House Publishers, Inc.

When Through Deep Waters

Designed by Dean H. Renninger

Published in association with the literary agency of The Fedd Agency, Inc., P.O. Box 341973, Austin, TX 78734.

For information about special discounts for bulk purchases, please contact Tyndale House Publishers at csresponse@tyndale.com, or call 1-800-323-9400.

ISBN: 978-1-4964-1712-1 (hc)
ISBN: 978-1-4964-1713-8 (sc)

Printed in the United States of America

24 23 22 21 20 19 18
7 6 5 4 3 2 1

For my dad,

who was brave enough to dive deep,

walk on water, and befriend white bats.

I can feel the love I want, I can feel the love I need
But it's never gonna come the way I am
Could I change it if I wanted, can I rise above the flood?
Will it wash out in the water, or is it always in the blood?

JOHN MAYER, "IN THE BLOOD"

1

The California afternoon sun pierced down across Alicen McCaffrey's toes, and she slid them up the cushioned pool chair into the safety of shade. She had the Redyington Social dinner event tonight, and the last thing she needed was a funky tan line across her feet. Criticizing eyes would be out for blood, and her toes had done nothing but offer her adequate support her entire life. They didn't deserve to be led to slaughter.

Her stomach growled under her lightweight black sundress, and she glanced at the gold watch that hung loosely from her bony wrist. 3:15 p.m. Only a couple of hours till dinner. She thought of the Marc Jacobs hanging under its plastic sheeting in her closet. It hugged every inch of her slender frame and had been a stunning find. It was worth starving for.

"Mom, Mom, watch!"

Alicen turned her eyes to the bouncing blonde five-year-old beauty happily tiptoeing up to the side of their home pool. Her baby-blues shimmering in the light, her red one-piece bright against her sun-kissed skin.

"I'm watching," Alicen said and reached for her glass of red wine. It was her second, which was a bit much for midafternoon, but she shook off the warning voices in her brain. She would keep it to two. She was drinking her calories so as not to bring any shame to the Marc Jacobs.

The child gave a little squeal of excitement before squeezing her button nose closed with her fingers and launching herself into the crystal waters. The impact sent ripples across the oblong pool and produced tiny waves that lapped the stone edge. She disappeared under the surface for several long seconds before her tiny head popped back up and she took a deep, giggling breath.

"Did you see?" the girl yelled, wiping water from her face and frantically paddling to the edge.

The sliding-glass door behind Alicen creaked, and she diverted her attention to see Serra, the housekeeper, poking her head through. The middle-aged Colombian woman was small in stature with round, soft features and a welcoming smile. She had been with the McCaffrey family for the last couple of years, and Alicen considered the woman as close a thing to a friend as she was allowed to have in this sunny city of Santa Monica. Not that she would ever admit that out loud, of course.

"Your mother is on the phone," Serra said in her strong accent.

Alicen immediately felt her back straighten and her chest squeeze. An uncomfortable annoyance ticked inside her brain. She had no patience for that woman today.

"I thought she was in Costa Rica with Brad," Alicen said.

"Apparently there is some trouble in paradise," Serra said, a mocking gleam in her eye.

"Shock," Alicen said, downing the rest of the wine in her glass as Serra huffed. This was her mother's regular pattern. Find the man of her dreams, swear this time was different from the dozens before, run away with him to whatever corner of the earth he resided in, and then end up back at Alicen's door when the man of her dreams turned out to be just a man.

"Mom, did you see what I did?" her daughter said, plopping her wet figure down on the end of Alicen's chaise longue. Droplets of water splashed across Alicen's knees, and she brushed them away.

"Jane," Alicen scolded, "you're all wet, honey."

"Sorry," Jane said, popping off the seat. "But did you see?"

"See what?"

"My huge jump," Jane said, spreading her short arms toward the sky, eyes wide with her own wonder.

More water flung off the girl and touched down on Alicen's skin. "Jane, please—I'm trying not to get wet!"

"Mrs. McCaffrey, your mother is still waiting," Serra said.

"Grandma? Is she coming to visit again?"

"No. Now please step back. If you're done with the pool, then—"

"No, no, I'm not!" Jane said.

"We've been out here for over an hour; maybe it's time to go in," Alicen said.

"Mom, no. I never want to leave. I want to live in the water. I want to be a mermaid." Jane spun in a small circle and dragged her arms across the sky.

"You're not a mermaid; you're a girl, and all this chlorine isn't good for your beautiful hair."

"Evie says I can be whatever I want," Jane said.

Alicen bit her tongue and tried not to show her disapproval at the mention of Jane's longtime imaginary friend. She was going to be six in a couple of months, and Alicen thought maybe she was getting too old to still believe in such things.

The phone chirped inside, signaling that her mother was still on the line. One would think that after minutes of waiting she would have hung up, but Alicen's mother was nothing if not relentless.

Alicen turned to Serra. "Tell her I'll be right there."

Serra chuckled at Alicen's clear lack of enthusiasm and left to deliver the message.

"Jane, it's time to go in," Alicen said, unwrapping her legs and slipping them into the thin flip-flops that rested next to her chair.

"Please just a couple more minutes?" Jane begged, her blue eyes bright and occupying the majority of her tiny round face.

"Jane—"

The girl dropped to her knees and clamped her hands together, her face doused in agony. "Mom, please. I'll do anything!"

Alicen tried not to smile at her daughter's flair for the dramatic and reminded herself that it was a trait inherited from the woman waiting on the phone. It wasn't Jane's fault her grandmother didn't have any positive traits to hand down.

She sighed and shook her head slightly before giving in. "Ten minutes. Once I'm off the phone with Grandma, you're coming in."

Jane bounced up with glee and rushed toward the pool, her long blonde locks swinging damply behind her.

"Don't run; it's slippery," Alicen called and watched her daughter slow. Barely. She turned to head inside as Jane's voice filled the sky with a song about transforming into a mermaid. Clearly a self-made number. Alicen couldn't help but smile. They were going to have to cure that dramatic streak before it was too late and Jane became Alicen's mother.

She stopped just before stepping inside and glanced at the dark wood luxury poolside furniture perfectly placed throughout the backyard. An image of her husband's annoyed face flashed behind her eyes as she briefly recalled the fight it had taken to get what she wanted. A wide smile broke over her lips, and a shiver of satisfaction rumbled beneath her skin. Winning was always sweetest when she was battling her beloved. Active as Allen's wandering hands were, Alicen deserved ten sets of luxury furniture.

She stepped inside, leaving the glass door open just a bit so she could still hear Jane's sweet notes, and walked across the marble tile to where the phone rested on the small built-in desk just inside the kitchen. The red light on the device blinked every couple of seconds to signal someone was on hold.

Alicen took a deep breath before picking it up off the receiver. "Betty," Alicen said, forcing a mildly pleasant tone.

"Oh, Alicen, dear, how are you?" her mother asked.

Alicen knew from the fake delight laid over the older woman's words that the "trouble in paradise" was far past repair. "How's Costa Rica? I hear it's beautiful this time of year." She glanced over her shoulder at the half-empty wine bottle sitting atop the massive kitchen bar. A prick of conscience inside her head reminded her she'd made a vow, but if she was going to deal with her mother's endlessly failing love life, she could afford another glass.

"It's beautiful," Betty said. "I mean, some crazy downpours, but in a romantic sort of fashion, you understand."

"Right." Alicen crossed the large, beautifully tiled kitchen in a couple of long steps, bracing the phone between her shoulder and ear, and reached for the bottle.

"But you know I miss you all terribly. How is my favorite grandbaby?"

"She's decided she wants to be a mermaid." Alicen poured a healthy serving of red wine into her glass.

"Mermaid," Betty laughed. "She gets all that drama from you, you know."

"Oh please. We both know where it comes from."

"No, dear, you were just like that at her age. Thankfully, you had a strong mother who knew what was best for you."

Alicen ground her back molars and took a large swig from her glass. A moment of silence filled the phone line.

Her mother didn't do well with silence. "How is that lovely Allen?"

Alicen held back a cackle at the absurdity of the words *lovely* and *Allen* in the same statement.

"Alicen, don't rock the boat," Betty said.

"I didn't say anything."

"No, but I can hear your mind wandering."

"Things with Allen are the same," Alicen said.

"The same is perfect. The same is the life you deserve, the one I always wanted for you."

At this, Alicen did let a sharp chuckle escape her mouth.

"The same, child, gave you that sweet baby girl, and the same will make sure she never wants for anything. Don't you want that for her?"

Alicen closed her eyes for a moment and nodded to herself. Jane was the only reason Alicen continued to offer herself up to a man who saw her as just another thing he possessed. Jane was the only reason Alicen did anything. "You know I do," she said.

"Then keep that boat steady, dear," Betty said.

"Did you call me just to remind me of something I already knew?"

There was a beat of silence on the other end before her mother cleared her throat and continued. "I was thinking of coming by for a few days to see everyone."

"Oh yeah? Will Brad be joining you?" Alicen already

knew the answer, and mentioning him was cruel, but the wine was beginning to think for her.

"No, I think it'll just be me from now on."

"Betty, I'm not sure this is really a good time—" Alicen started.

"Alicen Ray, I am your mother. You just can't imagine what I've been through the last couple of days."

Alicen inhaled and took another large gulp from her glass.

"I'll be there tomorrow," Betty said.

Alicen knew there was nothing that could be done. She clenched her eyes, trying not to get lost prematurely in the pain she'd be forced to face with each motherly interaction.

"Alicen?" Betty said.

Alicen swallowed. "I'll have Serra fix up a room for you."

"Wonderful! Well, I have to run. Give kisses to that darling sweet girl of ours."

Alicen's mother's proclamation of joint ownership over Jane grated at her chest, but she bit her tongue and let it go. She just wanted to be finished with this conversation. "Mmm-hmm."

"Be good, dear," Betty said.

Alicen pulled the phone away from her ear and clicked it off. Betty ended all of their conversations with those three simple words. Words that no matter how Alicen tried she couldn't run away from. *"Be good, dear."* As if she were still a gangly, twelve-year-old, walking disappointment. As if that was all she'd ever be.

Alicen shook her head at the notion. She glanced around the large, sparkling kitchen with its pristine white cabinets, glistening marble countertops, and state-of-the-art appliances. More than anyone would ever need and all that anyone could ever want. She had done this, made this kind of life a reality. Not Betty.

The uncomfortable wave of self-doubt washed away, and she walked across the cool floor to place the phone back in its cradle. She took a small sip from her glass and calmly went back to where the sliding door stood open. She stepped out into the warm air. A breeze ruffled the large palm trees planted along the side of the yard. She was going to be fine, she told herself. She would handle Betty with ease. Everything would be fine.

Alicen walked to the edge of the outside covering, still under the safety of shade. "Jane, it's time to come in," she called.

She glanced down at her watch. 3:35 p.m. It was nearly time to start preparing for the evening's events. She glanced back at the pool and took a step forward. "Jane, I mean it. You've been out here long enough. Let's go."

Only the soothing rustle of trees and trickling pool water. Alicen stepped out onto the hot stone deck that surrounded the pool, using her free hand to shield her eyes. "Jane!"

A sliver of panic blossomed in her chest. Alicen looked back and forth across the yard, the manicured grass and well-kept flower beds. She spun around and scanned the large, covered sitting area, trying not to let her anxiety get the best of her. "Jane Ann, if you're hiding from me, you'd better come out now."

She moved farther out toward the water's edge, squinting

against the reflecting sun, heart thundering. The water was still, and Alicen tore her eyes across every corner, a frantic sense pressing into her bones. Something caught the edge of her vision, bobbing in the corner where the pool curved up to make a small rock waterfall, hard to see. Something still. Something red.

Alicen's breath froze. The world stilled. The glass from her hand crashed to the stone, shattering shards pricking her bare feet. Her lungs exploded her daughter's name. Then she was running. When she reached the corner, she collapsed to her knees, thrust her long arms into the water, and dragged the small body from its clutches.

"Jane! Jane!" Alicen could hear her voice but hardly felt the words. She twisted the girl skyward. Jane's face was pale, her lips slightly blue. "No, no, no! Jane!"

Alicen laid her daughter out and pressed both hands into her chest. She pulsed the heels of her hands with force over and over as Jane's body jerked with each compression. "No, no, baby, please." Hot tears blurred her vision. She swept away the stringy locks from Jane's face, placed her mouth over her child's, and exhaled. Rest. Exhale. Back to compressions.

Nothing.

"Help!" Alicen screamed, "Help! Oh, Jane, come on."

"Mrs. McCaffrey, did you—oh my, oh my gosh," Serra said, peering through the back door.

Alicen didn't have to say anything as Serra disappeared inside to call for help. She couldn't have formed words anyway. Her body was forgetting how to function. Her mind melded with a pain so sharp her vision dotted in and out.

She pressed Jane's chest hard, the small rib bones cracking from the pressure.

Alicen opened her mouth to beg her daughter to wake up, to plead with her not to leave her alone, but only cries of agony escaped. She leaned down again, exhaled into Jane's mouth. Rest. Exhale. Back to compressions, her hands shaking, her tears dotting her daughter's face.

Nothing.

The small body was limp and lifeless. A perfectly crafted baby doll. Her baby. Her dead baby.

Alicen's mind snapped and she began to scream at the sky. Her entire body shook with pain, the world around fading into darkness so only the broken image of her sweet girl remained.

No, no, no, no, her mind wailed against itself. Jane was everything, all she had, her reason for sanity. *No, no, no.* How was she supposed to function in this life where she'd sold her soul for acceptance and ended up in agony with only Jane to keep her from despair? *Oh no, no, baby, no.* Jane was her only salvation, her light, her center; she'd be lost without her.

"I'll be lost, I'll be—" Alicen choked out, beside herself.

Somewhere in the haze soft sirens punctured the air, but Alicen knew it was too late. She could feel Jane's absence already. As if a part of her own soul had been taken. She pulled the lifeless form into her arms and buried her head into the girl's neck. The darkness thickened, blocking out everything except the ravaging ache of loss. The ravaging ache that ensured nothing would ever be the same.

2

FOUR MONTHS LATER

Alicen watched through her side passenger window as the large antique home came into full view. It sat back among the overgrown foliage, several yards from the road, a wide gravel driveway stretching to connect the two. It looked nearly identical to how she remembered it. A massive structure with white wood-paneled walls and dark-gray roofing jutting toward the sky at several points. A large wraparound porch with dense white pillars holding up the awning over the front entrance. Thick oak trees stood rooted deeply with time along both sides, covering the mansion in wide lines of shade. The Watson family summer home.

The car pulled in, and a shiver rippled down Alicen's spine. The engine cut to a stop. Silence engulfed the vehicle. The woman in the driver's seat cleared her throat softly, drawing Alicen's attention.

Louise Watson met Alicen's glance, her long red hair tucked behind each ear, her face soft, her eyes warm but hesitant. The same way Louise had been looking at Alicen since she'd picked her up from the airport. As if she were afraid that at any moment Alicen might throw herself from the car, lose her grip on reality, cascade into a mess of tears, or snap. Alicen exhaled and dropped her eyes. Her friend wasn't wrong to worry.

"We don't have to go in yet," Louise said.

Alicen turned her attention back to the familiar house. "It looks the same."

"You think? It's harder to see from the road since Dave stopped taking care of the grounds."

"How long has it been since anyone lived here?"

"Oh, man," Louise said, "a decade maybe? Dave kept the place livable until he retired last spring, and my family has come for small visits over the years, but not consistently like we used to. Red Lodge just isn't what it used to be."

The name of the tiny Montana mountain town still made Alicen's chest warm. There had always been so much about this place she loved. The summers spent browsing through the small, eccentric shops that lined the single main road. The familiar faces and well-known voices of the same people who had been living here their entire lives. And the Watson summer home, a place more home to Alicen than her own had been.

"When was the last time you were here?" Alicen asked.

"Two years ago. Peter and Sarah got married and moved to Chicago, so it was just Mom, Dad, and me in Billings. I work a lot, and it gets harder for Dad with all this travel. This place just became part of the past."

Billings, Montana, did not spark comforting nostalgia; in fact the thought of her birthplace turned Alicen cold. Billings, located an hour north of Red Lodge, represented a part of Alicen's past that she'd worked very hard to forget. The only good thing that had come out of that city was Louise. Her oldest friend, connected during their early school years, bonded by their endless adventures, unfazed by the distance and passing of time. Alicen had always hoped they'd end up back in one another's lives permanently. Just not like this.

"Be forewarned: I'm not sure exactly what we're going to find in there," Louise said. "It'll be just like old times, huh?"

Alicen's nostalgia blurred with the pain that had taken up permanent residence in her mind, and suddenly the car felt three sizes too small. She forced a nod and opened the passenger door. She stepped out, gravel crunching beneath her shoes, the thin mountain air washing over her. There was a chill in the air and too many leaves overhead to let the sun's warmth through. Alicen shivered and grabbed her carry-on bag out of the backseat.

Louise popped the trunk and began to unload the rest of their things. Several large suitcases. They were going to be here awhile. Alicen watched Louise and considered helping, but her body was harder to operate these days. It was as if the synapses in her brain that helped her do everyday things had been fractured. Sometimes just remembering to breathe was all she could handle.

Alicen shook her head and swallowed. She took a step toward Louise as the tall, athletic woman swiftly shut the trunk. She glanced at Alicen for a long moment and smiled. "Help me get them up these steps?"

Alicen nodded and forced herself to be useful. It didn't take them long to be at the front door and pushing their way inside. Louise had explained on the drive up that she'd made sure the house had all its systems working even though it'd been dormant for a time, so when she flicked the inside wall switch, light cascaded across the entryway.

"Good—power," she said.

Louise carried and dragged several cases across the threshold, and Alicen followed suit. A layer of dust hung in the air and covered everything in sight. Cobwebs wavered with the new life being brought into the house, and Alicen imagined an exterminator would probably be necessary to rid the space of whatever had taken up shelter over the last few months.

The entryway was large and square, capped at the far end by a wide, winding staircase. To the right of the main foyer, the house swept into a front sitting room that led into the dining room and then the kitchen. To the left, a formal living room and study adjoined a large downstairs bedroom and bath. If Alicen remembered right, three more elaborate bedrooms and a library could be found on the second floor, with another shorter set of stairs that took you to a huge attic, which had been the place where Alicen and Louise had spent so much of their time as girls.

"Do you wanna be upstairs or down here?" Louise asked.

Alicen, lost in a memory of running around the old oak floors, hardly registered the question and gave Louise a strange look.

"I had Martha from across town come by and clean two rooms for us, one down here and one upstairs; just didn't know if you had a preference," Louise said.

Alicen shook her head, suddenly incapable of words. Another outcome of being broken.

A sad flicker crossed Louise's face, but she did well to shake it off quickly. She smiled. "I'll take the room down here; it's smaller." She paused, biting the inside of her lip to cover up her awkwardness. A bad habit she'd always had. "I'll take your stuff upstairs for you," Louise said.

Alicen shook her head. "No, I can—"

Louise grabbed Alicen's largest suitcase and waved her off. "I don't mind. Why don't you walk through the main level and flick on some lights, maybe make sure the water's running?"

Alicen thought about objecting again. She felt enough like a burden without having to have her stuff carried upstairs for her, but the strength to be stubborn escaped her. She nodded, and Louise hauled the heavy luggage up off the floor and started for the stairs.

Alicen turned and stepped into the sitting room to her right. She crossed the space, the wood floor creaking under her feet, and switched on both of the tall lamps. Their light drowned out the darkness in the spacious room, and Alicen let her eyes sweep the familiar space. The cream-and-gold couches with matching chairs, the dark wood end tables and etched crown molding, the lace curtains, the classic floral rug. It smelled the way she remembered, like wildflowers and lemon, even after all this time.

She pictured a smaller version of Louise—always called Lou back then—her short wavy flaming hair framing freckled cheeks, racing along, Alicen trailing behind, Louise's mother scolding them for running in the sitting room, which was for sitting and being still.

"We can't be still, Mom," Lou would say.

"Yeah," Alicen would agree. "We're being chased!"

"Oh yeah?" Louise's mother, Stephanie Watson, would remark. Then she'd lean in with a wink. "Who is it this time?"

The little girls would exchange a worried, knowing look of mischief, and then Lou would respond, "Pirates."

"Pirates? Oh my!"

"We stole their buried treasure," Alicen would say, bouncing with excitement.

"But only because they stole it first," Lou would explain.

"Yeah, from the mermaids," Alicen would add.

Mermaids.

Something banged upstairs, jarring Alicen from her memory.

"I'm all right," Louise yelled down.

Alicen barely heard her through the pounding in her head. Her eyes stung with tears, and she blinked them away hard. She shook her head and cleared her throat, washing away the images of her younger self. Walking into the next couple of rooms, she turned on all the lights she could find, killed a lone spider, shook a couple decorative pillows free of dust, and finally stopped in the kitchen.

The overhead light came to life with ease, yellow warmth casting illumination over the dirtied counters. Check the water, Louise had asked. The counters needed to be washed anyway. Alicen walked into the pantry and flipped the light to look for anything she could use. There wasn't much—a couple empty boxes on the floor, a couple loose screws, an old lightbulb, and a full bottle of whiskey.

Her heart slammed against the inside of her chest. One deep breath in and out as her palms moistened. Her mind ran in circles, the taste of what sat inside the unopened bottle forming in the back of her throat, the smell burning inside her nostrils. Another deep breath. She should tear her eyes away from it, but that was proving difficult. Instead she shut them, the memories of her incident rolling back.

The way the dark thoughts had finally pushed her over the edge, the way the thick liquid had so easily passed between her lips and down her throat like poison. The way the world had blurred. And wavered. And disappeared. And for a moment peace had seemed attainable. A peace that had been shattered when the world had returned.

Alicen spun around, flicked the light off, and shut the pantry door. Her hand still on the handle, she exhaled and let her head fall against the closed door as she forced the nightmares back into their cages.

She found a single roll of paper towels under the large double sink. She pulled softly on the copper handle and after a second of rumbling, water rushed from the faucet, slightly brown at first. Alicen let it run until it was clear. Then she dampened a handful of towels and began wiping the kitchen's surfaces. The stone-tiled counters, the front of the refrigerator, the stovetop, the cabinets, trying to keep her mind on the work.

She could feel her heart racing. Her breath short, her mind buzzing. She closed her eyes and remembered what her doctor had told her. *Deep breaths. This is normal. You are in control. Focus on something else.* Alicen scrubbed the same surfaces again, harder this time, the water running in the background. The sound echoed inside her ears. Capturing her mind, taking it somewhere she didn't want to go.

Alicen spun around and twisted the faucet handle harshly, the water vanishing. The kitchen went silent; only the sounds of her short breaths filled the space. The faucet dripped against the metal sink, and Alicen found her eyes glued to the droplets as another fell. And then another. In rhythm, leaking from the faucet's head. *Deep breaths. This is normal. You are in control. Focus on something else.* It was mesmerizing, deliberate, and enough to break her resolve.

Before she could stop herself, she was there. The sun kissing her skin, the California breeze scurrying up her arms and neck. Warm, perfect. The sun reflecting off the pool, forcing Alicen to shield her eyes, the muffled laughing of a child piercing her sanity. She turned her head and saw her. Skipping through the grass, her tiny figure glistening in the sun, her blonde curls a moppy mess down her back, her little red swimsuit.

Alicen smiled, tears filling her eyes, as Jane spun around,

giggling at the sky. The girl stopped twirling and turned to look directly at Alicen. Alicen's breath caught in her throat as Jane held her gaze. The girl tilted her head to the right, scrunched her nose, and smiled. She raised her hand over her mouth to catch her giggles before launching back into dancing circles.

The sight of it broke Alicen's heart. The sound of it cracked her bones. She opened her mouth to speak, but nothing came. Her bottom lip quivered as she searched for words.

As if a tremendous idea had dropped into her brain, Jane came to a stop and started rushing toward the pool.

Terror exploded through Alicen's mind. And her fear spoke. "No, baby—not the water."

The child didn't register Alicen's words and continued toward the edge. The clouds that only moments earlier had been white and full twisted to dark grays and rolled in over the backyard. The wind picked up speed and thrashed against Alicen's frame.

"Jane, stay away from the water," Alicen said, taking a step toward her. Loud warning sirens began to echo through the air. The same haunting shrill the ambulance had made. *No,* Alicen thought. "Jane!"

Jane didn't even turn her face toward Alicen as she reached the pool and leaped with all her might.

"No, Jane!" Alicen cried and tried to rush forward, but the wind was pressing against her too tightly, holding her in place.

One moment her precious daughter was there, and the

next the water was splashing over her head, covering any sight of her.

"Jane!" Alicen yelled against the storm. Leaves and grass swirled up around her. Thunder crashed overhead as she searched, willing her daughter to resurface.

"Jane!" But her cries were drowned out as Jane's body remained under the waves. *She won't be able to breathe there; she'll drown.* The thought materialized from thin air, slicing like knives down her spine.

"Baby, please come up!" Alicen pushed forward, her feet wobbling under the pressure of the wind, as lightning crossed the sky.

Alicen.

"Jane, please, baby. Please!" She fell to her knees and tried to crawl low under the storm, but it seemed to swallow her completely.

Alicen.

Sobs shook her shoulders, her words lost, her mind shattered. Sorrow devoured any sense of will she had, and she collapsed against the ground.

"Alicen?"

A touch snapped her back to reality, and she turned to see Louise's worried expression.

Alicen was back in the Watsons' kitchen, the storm gone, the pool a figment, Jane dead.

Louise dropped her hand from where it rested on Alicen's shoulder and with concern watched Alicen's face. Alicen wanted to swallow the fresh set of tears brimming in her eyes. She wanted to laugh off what Louise must be thinking. She wanted to ask if she'd been screaming Jane's name out loud again. She wanted to bury herself in a dark hole, she wanted to be alone, she wanted to be lost.

She wanted to be dead.

But before she could latch on to a single thought, Louise stepped forward and wrapped Alicen in an embrace. Without the strength to resist, Alicen fell into her friend's arms, her weight dragging both women to their knees. Silent sobs broke to mournful cries and echoed through the empty house. There, on the kitchen floor that Alicen's childhood feet had scampered across, she cried until she was numb and had nothing left to give.

3

Louise moved to take the teakettle off the stove as its cry signaled the water inside was boiling. Alicen sat at the kitchen table, her throat raw, her eyes swollen from losing control of her emotions only minutes earlier. She had made some lame promise to herself that she wouldn't do what she just had, not this soon after being reconnected with Louise. In her naiveté, she'd actually believed she could control the monster of loss eating away at her soul. But control was an illusion.

"Here you go," Louise said, setting a steaming cup of tea down in front of Alicen and taking the seat across from her.

"Thanks," Alicen mustered. Silence filled the room as Alicen kept her eyes off Louise and watched the swirling steam rise off the top of her mug.

Louise cleared her throat. "So, I got a text from Martha to confirm that she and her daughters will be by tomorrow to help us get this place cleaned up. I figure it'll be easier to start sorting through things after we've had all the dust removed."

Alicen nodded. "I can't believe your family is really selling this place." She was glad to be in conversation that didn't bring them back to her mental collapse.

"It feels a bit odd, but it's time."

"Seems strange to think your family won't have roots here anymore."

"Like I mentioned, Red Lodge isn't what it used to be. The population is declining, and tourism just doesn't bring people in like it used to. My dad doesn't think it's worth the cost to maintain our properties here anymore."

"And the bookstore is all you have left in town?"

Louise nodded. "Dad sold the apartment and drugstore about five years ago. The bookstore was the first property his great-grandfather built, so he had a harder time letting that one go. And of course this house."

"The Watsons are leaving Red Lodge for good."

Alicen watched sadness creep into Louise's eyes. "We tried to keep this town vibrant, but it just wasn't meant to be, I guess," Louise said. "Both sites will have to be swept, cataloged, packed up; we'll have plenty to do. I'm glad you're here to help."

"Yeah, it really puts a damper on all my big summer plans." Alicen heard the bite in her tone and instantly regretted it. She was being cold for no reason, to someone who didn't deserve it. To someone who had stuck by her and offered her comfort at every turn. Someone who had just held her while she'd released her violent agony. Logic told Alicen her cruelty was another unfortunate outcome of loss, and her doctor back in Santa Monica would say that all the outcomes of loss could be controlled. But then he had clearly been wrong.

Alicen exhaled and shook her head. "I'm sorry, I—"

"Don't be," Louise said. "I understand."

Alicen swallowed the hateful response forming in her mouth to counter Louise's false proclamation of understanding. The woman had never married, had no children, had lost nothing. She couldn't possibly understand.

"Also, Victoria Flowers is coming by tomorrow morning. I thought it best to get you all acquainted right away."

The reality Alicen had been avoiding hit her like a train. She bit her tongue to keep from screaming, a visceral reaction to what she knew lay before her.

"It'll be good, Alicen. I mean, I don't know Victoria that well, but the work they do at Clover Mountain Retreat Center comes highly recommended."

"You make it sound like a vacation resort instead of a mental institute," Alicen said. She remembered hearing about the place growing up. It sat back in the mountains, about ten miles outside the Red Lodge city limits. She'd never been there, and she didn't know much about the Flowers family who owned and ran the facility. She certainly never thought she'd be a member of the institute's unique clientele.

"It really is a beautiful facility." Louise paused before continuing. "And their Home-Away program is perfect for you. We talked about this."

"Right, I get to be a resident of the crazy house without actually living in the crazy house."

"Don't call it that."

"Isn't that what it is? A place for people who aren't completely sane? Who need special assistance because they can't be trusted with their own minds? People like me?"

Louise said nothing. What could she say? That Alicen's only treasure had been taken from her and she'd lost her sanity? The familiar darkness of loss filled Alicen's mind, and the dangerous thoughts that had placed her in this position rumbled around like marbles.

Louise hadn't brought up the incident. Not since Alicen had been released from the hospital a couple of months earlier. In fact, no one had brought it up. In the world she'd come from, people didn't talk about such things. They buried them with money or power or both. Before the incident people had looked at her like she was a lost puppy and spoken to her in hushed tones, as if they might rattle her crazy loose if their voices became too loud. After the incident, they looked at her like she was broken and diseased. And they'd stopped speaking to her altogether. She wasn't one of them anymore. They'd all jumped ship, a massive herd—one day there, the next day nowhere.

"Being a part of this program is why you're here," Louise said.

"I thought I was here to get some fresh air. You said come be with people who love you, and get out of that empty house marked with . . ." Alicen couldn't finish her sentence. She shook her head and moved on. "You said come spend the summer with me; I'll keep you busy and distracted; come clear your head, remember?"

Alicen could feel Louise's tender expression without looking at her face, and she wished for it to stop.

"Yes, and all of that is true. But what you suffered—you need more than to be kept busy, Alicen. You need to talk to someone. You lost your daughter, your husband, your life."

"The husband part wasn't so bad," Alicen joked.

"I'm being serious."

Alicen let out a short, muffled laugh. "Me too."

Louise tried to hide her concern, but it was too strong to mask.

"Oh, come on, Lou; you knew Allen. Our marriage was a complete facade. It wouldn't have survived Jane breaking her leg, much less her . . ." Again Alicen couldn't verbalize the actual words. *Dying,* she thought. *Because Jane is dead.*

Silence filled the kitchen, and Alicen sipped her tea to keep her face from showing Louise any more brokenness.

"He should have stayed with you," Louise said.

"Did you really think he would? He hardly wanted me when I was sane. How could anyone expect him to stay with me in this state?" An image of Allen washed behind her eyes, the way he'd barely looked at her in their last days together. The man she'd committed her life and love to, the one who'd helped her make their most beautiful gift. The same man who had become so cold and hateful. She hadn't expected him to be comforting, but his disgust had stung more than she cared to admit. He'd blamed her. She couldn't fault him for that. Alicen deserved to be blamed.

"That doesn't make what he did right," Louise said.

"When did Allen ever do the *right* thing?"

Louise shook her head, anger rolling across her eyes. "He always was such a tool."

The comment made Alicen laugh in spite of the pain, and that brought a smile from Louise. She raised her eyebrows as if to say, *Just stating the facts* and took a swig from her mug.

Alicen was suddenly swept up in her dear friend's kindness. Everyone else had abandoned her, but Louise, even though they hadn't lived close to each other in nearly two decades, hadn't hesitated to help. Emotion roiled inside Alicen's chest, and she smiled to keep it from exploding. The swing of sensations from happiness to anger, from thankfulness to depression, was a ride she'd like to get off. No wonder she was going mad.

"Thank you," Alicen said softly, "for letting me come here. I'm not sure what I would have done otherwise."

"We were basically sisters once," Louise said. "A bond like that doesn't change." She let her words hang for a moment before pressing on. "Please talk to Victoria tomorrow? Let her help you? Let *me* help you?"

Alicen dropped her eyes to her lap and took a deep breath.

"I just want you to get better," Louise said.

"As if losing a child is a sickness you can recover from," Alicen whispered.

Silence again encased the room.

"I don't want you to hurt yourself again," Louise said.

And there it was. The incident she would never be free of. A moment of weakness that would forever haunt her. But then she knew it was more than mere weakness. It had been strong, a desire she'd dreamed of, something she'd wanted. It had masked itself as an escape, but in the end her actions had only imprisoned her more.

Louise reached her hand across the table and laid it on top of Alicen's. Alicen glanced up from her lap and met Louise's eyes.

"I can't imagine the kind of pain you must have felt to get you to that place, but I do know that you can't heal from this on your own," Louise said and gave Alicen's hand a soft squeeze. "Or at least you shouldn't have to."

Louise's touch was warm and comforting, something Alicen hadn't experienced recently. It chipped away at some of the stone forming around her heart, and she found herself wanting to make Louise happy. So she gave a halfhearted smile and nodded. "I'll talk with her."

Louise's face broke with joy. "Good," she said, releasing Alicen's hand. "This *is* going to be good, Alicen. I can feel it."

Alicen didn't want to do anything more to upset Louise, so again she faked a smile, wishing she believed as much as Louise did.

Louise stood and grabbed both empty mugs. "Now the real question is what the heck are we going to eat. I'm starving."

"It's about time we get to the hard questions," Alicen teased, pleased when Louise bought her fake humor and chuckled. Alicen would meet with Victoria Flowers; she would help Louise around the house and at the bookstore; she would play her part, like she was supposed to. But it would be a role, not a reality. Because she already knew her reality was etched in stone. Jane was dead. Alicen had killed her. That's all there was now.

• • •

Alicen stayed in the sitting room as Louise went to the front door. The bell had announced Victoria Flowers's arrival a moment earlier, and Alicen had decided to wait while Louise greeted her. Louise knew Victoria from high-school days, the ones that happened after Alicen and her mother left Billings and moved to California. From what Alicen gathered, Victoria hadn't attended the local high school, but she and Louise had crossed paths several times during their Red Lodge summers. Victoria's uncle, Donald Flowers, had held a seat on the town board, alongside Mr. Watson. The two families had interacted from time to time.

The night before had ended with a frozen pizza, purchased at the small market in the middle of town. On a warm day, you could walk there from the Watson home. The girls hadn't walked. They'd driven the two and a half miles, picked up a load of essentials—food, cosmetics, toilet paper, cleaning supplies—and come back to spend the rest of the evening working on the house. They hadn't done much, just enough to walk through the main living spaces without collecting a trail of dust.

It had been a good distraction for Alicen, putting her mind to a task. The aftermath of one of her episodes, as she coined them, could be difficult. Flashes of Jane's face, whispers of her sweet voice. Alicen had deduced that she had in fact been screaming her dead daughter's name aloud again. She had a tendency to do that when her mind got lost in the past. It was usually followed by the dark thoughts that were heavy enough to drag her soul into depths painted with depression and no foreseeable freedom. The kind that had caused her to reach for a bottle of pills and wash them down with burning liquor. The kind of depths that had gotten her here. Posttraumatic stress, they called it.

Alicen exhaled calmly as new voices lofted through the air. She couldn't stop the tremor in her fingers, so she wrapped them tightly in her lap. The voices got louder and were matched with faces as Louise escorted a striking woman and an older male associate around the corner.

Alicen stood as the three entered. The woman turned her attention to Alicen immediately. She was porcelain-skinned with short black hair and dark caramel eyes. Her lips were painted red and stood out against the fitted black suit she wore. Her presence was overwhelming. Daunting, even—her stance brewing with power; dominance and control readable on her face.

"Alicen," Victoria said, extending her hand. "It's such a pleasure to finally make your acquaintance."

Alicen smiled, feeling less than comfortable, and took Victoria's hand. "It's nice to meet you."

Victoria released Alicen's hand and turned to her associate. "Alicen, I would like to introduce Dr. Cormack Wells."

In opposite fashion from Victoria, Dr. Wells was understated. At least twenty years her senior with warm skin tones, graying hair, and brown eyes, he wore simple blue slacks and a white button-down shirt. No tie or jacket, which Alicen found immediately appealing. Although his presence entering the room had been completely overshadowed by Victoria's commanding stature, he held a silent confidence, and his smile was kind. She shook his hand and tried to release more of the tension residing in her shoulders.

"Dr. Wells is a renowned psychiatrist who just recently joined our team at Clover Mountain. I thought you would benefit from having a couple familiar faces around campus, so I invited him to join us today. I think he will be a wonderful resource for you." Victoria motioned to the chairs around the room. "Shall we sit?"

All parties followed her instruction. Louise took the plush chair next to Alicen, while Victoria and Dr. Wells occupied the couch across the room. Alicen shifted awkwardly in her chair, crossing her legs and tucking her hands between her thighs to hide their shivering. It was really only a brief moment of silence, but it felt eternal.

"I trust you are settling in all right?" Victoria aimed her question at Alicen.

"Yes," Alicen said. She noticed the tightness in her tone and tried to relax her throat.

"I'm glad to hear it," Victoria said. "I want to first say that we all understand how uncomfortable this can be and that it is completely normal to feel a bit of hesitation toward the work we do at Clover Mountain."

Alicen collected her courage and made eye contact with the strong woman. She was chillingly confident, but her words and tone were kind. It helped Alicen settle deeper into her chair. She shifted her eyes to Dr. Wells, who wore an agreeable expression on his face. They both seemed calm; Alicen wasn't sure whether that should make her feel at ease or more nervous.

"I promise you that if you commit to this process, we will do everything we can to help you," Victoria said.

There was a brief pause before she continued. "I think maybe it's best to review how the Home-Away program works and go over the commitments we at Clover Mountain Retreat Center make with our program recipients, as well as the commitments we hope you will make in return."

She waited for Alicen to respond with a slight nod before continuing. "I won't bore you with too much history of the retreat center itself; we can review more of that when you visit. But there are a couple things I always believe are helpful for our residents to know. Clover Mountain was founded by my great-grandfather Earl Flowers in the early 1940s as a way of making up for the insufficient care he believed his wife, Lori Marie, was receiving during her battle with mental illness. I say that because I believe it's important all those participating in our programs know the retreat center was built on principles that strive to go beyond the norms of how mental, emotional, and psychological struggles are handled."

Alicen watched the way Victoria's painted-red lips moved with phrases like "mental illness" and "psychological struggles." Each syllable pounded like a hammer against her skull.

"The center was created so the woman Earl Flowers loved

could get the help she needed while resting in a place focused on tranquility and peace," Victoria continued, "a place where her physical comfort was just as important as her mental and emotional comfort. We strive to maintain those original principles with each new resident who joins one of our programs."

Victoria reached inside her large slick black shoulder bag and retrieved a neatly folded pamphlet. She scooted forward and held the brochure forward, toward Alicen, who leaned forward as well. Alicen grabbed the item and then sat back to review it. A picturesque image filled the front panel, a large stone structure with gray roofing and clean white shutters and large oak doors, met by rolling green lawns, tall sturdy pine trees, and beautifully manicured rosebushes.

"My great-grandfather wanted a location that was hidden away from the chaos of the city while being close enough that all participants could still interact with the community as part of their recovery programs. This made the mountains surrounding Red Lodge uniquely qualified."

"It's beautiful," Alicen said as she held the pamphlet firmly, focusing to keep her hands steady. She thought about opening the pamphlet and reviewing the information inside, but she couldn't bring herself to commit that much yet.

"Yes," Victoria said, "we believe so. The Home-Away program was introduced in the late nineties for people who required a different level of care and support. A program administered by Donald Flowers, my uncle. I'm sure Louise has explained the way the program works, but for the sake of clarity, let's verbally review, since all parties committing to the program are present."

Again she paused to get a verbal cue from Alicen and then proceeded. "The Home-Away program allows participants to live under the supervision of a loved one away from the Clover Mountain Retreat Center campus, giving you the ability to continue your normal living situation. You do, however, commit to a weekly on-campus support group meeting as well as weekly individual meetings with an assigned retreat center counselor." Victoria motioned to Dr. Wells, who had nearly disappeared into the background as Victoria had commanded all the attention in the room. "After reviewing your files, sent over by Dr. Warden in Santa Monica, I think Dr. Wells will be a perfect fit."

Alicen turned her gaze toward the doctor, who grabbed her eyes with his own. He held them for a moment and smiled. "Unfortunately," he said, "I won't be able to make every encounter we have as uncomfortable as this one. I'm just not that skilled." His voice was round and full, projecting a wise, aged feeling across the room that was hard not to enjoy.

Louise and Alicen both chuckled as he teased, and Victoria gave a soft smile that vanished nearly as immediately as it had appeared. She then reclaimed the attention and directed it back to Alicen. Alicen was thankful for the brief moment of humor inside this terrifying encounter and thought maybe she wouldn't try as hard to hate Dr. Wells as she had her last psychologist.

"The program has no specific time requirement," Victoria said. "The reports and observations made by Dr. Wells and myself, as well as your progress with your support group, will determine how long your membership with Clover Mountain will last. It's really up to you. We simply strive to assist you as you adjust to your life now."

Any ease Dr. Wells may have injected into the conversation vanished. Alicen swallowed the emotions clambering up the inside of her chest. *Adjust* to your daughter being dead. Can someone *adjust* to that?

Louise must have noticed the clear discomfort Victoria's words had created, and she reached over and laid a hand on Alicen's knee. "We're here for you, and we just want to help however we can," she said.

Alicen desperately wanted this meeting to be over and knew the best way to arrive there was to agree. She forced a half smile and nodded. "I know."

Louise offered a return smile, and Alicen stole another glance at Dr. Wells, who gave another comforting grin—thankfully without the *poor thing* look that Louise usually had.

"We are very proud of this program you're about to partake in," Victoria said. "My uncle ensured it was something to behold, and I have tried to do the same now that it's in my care." She paused, softened her tone, and continued. "I am very sorry for your loss. Know that you are in good hands with us. We want nothing but clarity for you."

Clarity. It seemed like a strange word to use, but maybe clarity was what she was missing.

"We'll leave you to finish getting settled in here," Victoria said. "We only wanted a brief face-to-face to ensure we're all on the same page."

"I believe we are," Louise said, looking to Alicen, who nodded.

Louise stood, as did Dr. Wells and Alicen. Alicen was relieved. The meeting had been quick, and it didn't appear she was going to have to sit through a session with the kind old doctor just yet.

Victoria slung her bag over her shoulder and took a step toward Alicen. "It was nice to meet you. I wish it were under better circumstances."

Alicen nodded.

Victoria reached out and softly placed her hand on Alicen's shoulder. "I'm looking forward to getting to know you better," she said, then let her hand fall away. Her touch lingered, tingling Alicen's skin. She shifted uncomfortably. Victoria turned to Louise as the two said their good-byes, and Dr. Wells stepped in front of Alicen.

His soft gaze pulled her from her frozen state, and she gave a small grin.

"I know this transition can be difficult," Dr. Wells said, "so we'll just take our time. There's no rush in recovery."

Recovery. There was that dreaded word, mocking her with a future she knew didn't exist. Alicen swallowed uncomfortably, not sure how to respond.

Dr. Wells read her easily. He was good at his job. "Don't worry about that now; we'll just take it one day at a time. Sound good?"

Alicen glanced up at him and tried to release some of her panic. "Sure."

"Like I said, no rush." Dr. Wells extended his hand, and

Alicen took it. Then, with a simple nod, he stepped around the corner after Louise and Victoria.

Alicen stood in the sitting room alone, their voices drifting in and out as the front door squeaked open, signaling they were really leaving. She would be free of them for now, and with the agony and distress buzzing inside her brain, *for now* was all she could handle.

4

Alicen felt the autumn leaves crunch beneath her purple rain boots. The boots came up high, nearly grazing the bottoms of her knees, and she'd tucked her dark-blue jeans down into the boots. Ellie Stewart had worn a red pair of rain boots to class a couple weeks ago, and ever since laying eyes on them Alicen had been begging for a pair.

Her mom had refused at first, even after Alicen had explained that being a third grader was hard enough; how could she be expected to be the only girl in class who didn't have rain boots? Even at eight, Alicen understood enough about money to know that they weren't the kind of family that just bought whatever they wanted—not like Louise Watson and her parents. So the answer had continued to be no.

Nothing felt as terrible as seeing another classmate walk in sporting a new pair of perfectly shimmering rain boots while Alicen was forced to wear her year-old tennis shoes. She must have cried about it a dozen times, unable to imagine a way her life could get worse. So when Grandma Joe had surprised her with a long rectangular box yesterday, Alicen had nearly died of excitement. And they were purple, her favorite color.

"Do they fit okay?" Grandma Joe asked.

Alicen smiled wide and turned around to face Grandma Joe, who was sitting on the bottom step of her back porch. The woman's short, light-brown hair with strands of silver laced through the top was being pulled this way and that by the chilly fall breeze. Her squat frame was wrapped in a sweater, jeans, the same worn white Keds she always wore, and the heavy cotton scarf Alicen had given her for Christmas last year. It was purple, of course.

The little girl twirled, showing off the functionality of her new treasures, and laughed. "Perfect," Alicen said after she didn't topple to the ground. "I'm never taking them off."

"Never? I'm not sure your mother would approve of you wearing those inside the house," Grandma Joe said.

Alicen pondered this for a moment. "Isn't it your house? You can change the rules so I can wear them inside." Her tiny eyes grew with excitement.

Grandma Joe's smile. "No, your mother makes the rules around here."

"But you're her mother, so shouldn't you make the rules around here?"

"I'm not very good at rule-making."

"Then let's just forget all the rules!" Alicen said, giggling and

bouncing. Grandma Joe chuckled and Alicen continued. "Forget no cartwheels in the house; I love cartwheels." Alicen threw herself through the acrobatic feat, her grandmother's laughter filling the sky.

"Forget no racing; I love racing," Alicen said and paused. "Bet I can outrace you," she teased, freezing in place and sending Grandma Joe a devilish gleam. The old woman held Alicen's gaze before jumping up and after her.

Alicen screeched and raced off toward the back fence, Grandma Joe right on her heels. Grandma Joe reached the little girl easily, sweeping her up into her arms and toward the clouds. Alicen's laughter bellowed across the open air as she wiggled against her grandmother's hold.

"Let me go, let me go," Alicen giggled.

"Never," Grandma Joe boomed, laughter in her voice. She flipped Alicen so that the child was cradled horizontally, her torso flat against Grandma Joe's chest, and twirled in circles, Alicen screaming with glee.

Grandma Joe bent her neck down and pretended to devour the child with kisses.

Alicen laughed so hard tears started to stream down her cheeks. "Stop, stop, stop—it tickles too much!" Alicen yelled. "I give up; you win. You are the fastest."

Grandma Joe pulled her face back and laughed at the sky in victory before carefully turning Alicen upright and placing her back on the ground. "Don't you ever forget it," she teased.

Alicen was still laughing, her throat sore, not caring. She loved playing with Grandma Joe; in fact, she loved it more than her purple boots.

Grandma Joe knelt in front of Alicen. "Wanna know my secret to being faster?"

Alicen nodded.

"Magic," Grandma Joe whispered.

Alicen felt a strange concern flood her small chest, and she saw Grandma Joe's eyes change slightly. "What is it, honey?" she asked.

Alicen shrugged. "Mom says magic isn't real. That it's made-up. Is that true?"

"I see," Grandma Joe said.

Alicen could tell the question had upset her. "I'm sorry; I didn't mean to make you sad," she said.

Grandma Joe smiled, her eyes relighting with fire. She brushed her palms softly across Alicen's disheveled hair. "You didn't make me sad. You make me so happy. Do you think magic is made-up?"

Alicen considered it and then shook her head. "No," she whispered, "I think it's real."

"Me too."

"Why doesn't Mom?"

"Because that's the journey we all get to take."

Alicen squinted, confused.

"Remember what Jesus taught: you are the light of the world. Every single person gets to decide if they believe in the light. That's what makes the magic strong; you have to choose to believe it. You have to switch your view and see the truth beyond what can be seen. Sometimes it takes people longer to believe, and sometimes, like for you and me, believing is easier."

"Why?" Alicen asked.

"When somebody already believes, that person can help others believe too."

"Like helping someone hunt for treasure in their, um . . ." Alicen paused, trying to remember the term she'd heard her grandmother say many times.

"Earthen vessel."

"Yes, that thing," Alicen said.

Her grandmother gave a soft chuckle. "Exactly. Do you understand?"

Alicen thought and shrugged again. "I don't think so, but I'm only eight."

Grandma Joe burst out laughing, which made Alicen giggle too. "Fair enough," she said. She suddenly glanced over her shoulder for a long moment, something she did sometimes, almost like getting lost somewhere else, and then turned back to Alicen with another wide smile. Alicen knew what it meant. Knew that Grandma Joe was hearing and seeing the others. Alicen's mom said it was only Grandma Joe's imagination. That it was because she was sick, though Grandma Joe never seemed sick to Alicen. How could she be sick and still be faster? Sick people were supposed to be slow.

"What do you say we go inside and make some—" Grandma Joe started.

Alicen cut in before she could finish. "Apple cider?" Thrill filled her little body. She loved apple cider almost as much as Grandma Joe and her purple boots.

Grandma Joe chuckled. "Yes, apple cider."

Alicen jumped and rushed toward the house in front of her grandmother, yelling with eight-year-old enthusiasm. "Apple cider, get in my belly!"

Grandma Joe's laughter echoed behind, and Alicen's entire world felt perfect.

• • •

Alicen's eyes snapped open, the morning light tiptoeing in through her bedroom shade. Grandma Joe's joy softly vibrated inside her mind as she turned from her side and pressed the back of her head deep into her pillow. She hadn't dreamed about her grandmother in years. Hadn't recalled a memory that clearly in nearly a decade. She used to pretty frequently, but the normal occurrence had died off as time passed.

It must be this place, she thought. Being so close to where she had lost her. Or maybe it was the constant sting of her new loss that brought back memories of the old. It didn't matter why, only that it was just another pain spot she would now have to endure. That was her life now—enduring aches that would never leave.

She closed her eyes and exhaled. A silent tear slipped down her cheek. She knew sleep wouldn't return, but she would lie here in the silence until she was called for. Until the boring, mundane routines of her new life gave her cause to move. If it were up to her, she'd just stay here until everything went dark and the world ceased to be.

• • •

The wind pulled lightly at the ends of Alicen's hair as Louise fiddled with the Watson Family Bookstore lock. Alicen glanced up and down the main street behind them and found it vacant. There were a couple of cars parked along the sides of the road, which stretched the length of the small downtown, but not another person in sight. It almost felt like she and Louise were the only people in Red Lodge at all. If she stared at the emptiness long enough, she could almost convince herself that the world had abandoned them altogether.

A loud click pulled Alicen back to the present as Louise let out a huff of victory and pushed the front door open. Alicen followed her inside.

Light from the overhead bulbs flooded the small, two-story shop. Much like in the Watson home, a thick layer of dust had taken up residence over the majority of the store, and motes fluttered along the streams of sunlight coming in through the windows.

Alicen took in the bottom floor of the bookstore with one easy sweep of her eyes. It was just like she remembered. A long, thin blue rug ran from the front door to the bottom of the winding staircase that led to the second story. The rest of the floor was a caramel wood, bleached in spots by traffic and sunlight. On either side of the rug sat rows of waist-high bookcases, novels stacked along their shelves. The far walls to both the right and left, as well as the back wall several feet behind the staircase, held floor-to-ceiling shelves also filled with bindings and literature. A small desk, which held a cash register, sat in the far left corner along with a small table and grouping of chairs for reading.

The entire place smelled of paper and cinnamon and

peppermint, which brought a smile to Alicen's face. Louise's mother had been fond of peppermint candies and always had them available for anyone passing through. Their ever-present existence had left a permanent olfactory stain. It made Alicen feel like she was being transported back to a time when she and Louise would come rushing in through the front door, having spent the last couple of hours racing the streets of Red Lodge, chasing adventures.

Stephanie Watson would be sitting on a stool behind the cash register or in one of the plush chairs, reading, sorting, or planning. She'd raise her eyes to the girls and smile. "How's it out in the streets today?" she'd ask.

"Well," Lou would start, "we barely escaped captors who were definitely going to have us hung for treason."

"Definitely," Alicen confirmed.

"Treason?" Stephanie asked.

"Yeah, but we didn't do it!" Lou said.

"We're being framed because we know too much," Alicen chimed in.

"Really? About what?" Stephanie inquired.

Lou and Alicen shared a knowing look. "We can't tell you," Alicen said.

"We don't want to get you involved, Mom," Lou said. "Then you would be at risk."

Stephanie worked hard to hide the smile from creeping across her lips and nodded as if she totally understood. Then Alicen grabbed a handful of peppermint candies and shoved them into the small pack that Lou always had strapped to her back. "We're on the run and need to refuel our energy," Lou explained when her mom gave her a warning look.

"I see; well, try not to ruin your dinner, okay?" Stephanie warned.

"Dinner? Mom, this is serious. If they catch us, we'll never eat dinner again!"

"Well then, you'd better get moving. You've wasted too much time here already."

Both girls nodded and head back out into the sun while a soft chuckle began to escape Stephanie's mouth.

"Alicen?" a voice called, puncturing through her memory.

She turned to see Louise standing behind the cash register, giving her a funny look.

"Sorry; did you say something?" Alicen asked.

Louise watched Alicen a moment, and Alicen could see the concern working its way into her friend's face.

"I was just thinking about your mom," Alicen said.

"My mom?" Louise said, the worry dissipating.

"Yeah, about how she always played along with our silly imagined games."

Louise chuckled. "Yeah, well, that was easier than trying to convince us none of it was real."

"She never seemed afraid that we'd lose sight of reality or end up spending too much time in our imaginations."

"Why would she? We were kids; kids do that. And look—we both ended up totally normal."

The second the words left Louise's mouth, Alicen could see that she wished she could take them back. An awkward silence fell across the store.

Alicen watched Louise searching for something to say but spoke first. "She was great with us, your mom. I wasn't as great as her with Jane." The words stung coming out, and Alicen moved her eyes from the pitying look she was getting from Louise. "I should have let her dream more. I worry sometimes that I was more like my mom than yours." Alicen shook her head. "The last thing I ever wanted was to be like my mom."

More silence filled the store, and Alicen felt her mind being dragged back to the past. The times she'd been worried Jane wasn't maturing fast enough. The concern she'd felt over Jane's blind faith in magic and make-believe. Had she caused Jane to feel shame like her own mother had done so often with her? The thought crept in and drilled into her brain.

"Alicen—" Louise started.

"Don't," Alicen said. "Don't say I wasn't like her; don't say I was a good mother; don't try and . . ." Alicen fell short of words and shook her head. She felt her heart start to ache and her throat burn. She needed to change directions before she was a fumbling puddle of insanity in front of Louise again. "Forget it," she said and forced a sharp laugh, as if the train of thought were nonsense. She exhaled and looked around the room. "So where do you want me to start?"

Louise knew better than to push and cleared her throat. "Well, we should divide and conquer. I was thinking you could start upstairs, and I'll tackle this floor."

Alicen nodded.

"My dad wants all the encyclopedias, dictionaries, and reference books, which are upstairs on the first couple of bookshelves. Pretty much everything else from there goes.

Boxes and tape are over there," Louise said, pointing. Alicen crossed the floor and reached for them.

"Just mark the boxes accordingly and bring them down here when you're finished," Louise said.

Alicen grabbed a stack of collapsed boxes, a roll of tape, and a black marker and headed for the stairs.

"Let me know if you need anything," Louise said.

Alicen glanced over her shoulder to smile but said nothing as she climbed the curved steel staircase. It twisted up and out of sight, leading to a top level that was half the size of the ground floor. Ten taller bookcases lined the space, each one dark oak, each one filled with books.

Soft, muffled music drifted up from downstairs, and Alicen was happy for the white noise. She placed the packing tools on the only uncluttered surface on this floor, an antique reading desk, and flicked on the glass lamp that sat on top of it. Warm yellow light filled part of the room, and Alicen walked toward the rear to open the closed drapes.

Dust enveloped the space around Alicen's head as she ripped the curtains open. She coughed through the floating particles and waved her hand back and forth to clear a spot for her to breathe. The room now illuminated enough to work, the dust settling to the floor, Alicen walked up and down the rows of shelves. The first couple were as Louise had said they'd be, stuffed with hundreds of encyclopedias, dictionaries, and reference volumes. They were dressed in different-colored bindings, published across the decades. It was an impressive collection.

Alicen folded together and taped a cardboard box. She then

began to sort through and collect all the dictionaries published in a specific date range, trying to keep them as organized as possible. She worked diligently and taped the first box closed when it was full. She labeled it and began another.

Something thunked toward the farthest-back bookshelves, and she lifted her head from her work to see what it was. She waited for a moment, but when there was nothing, she went back to the task at hand. Something knocked again, as if someone were pushing books off the shelf, and Alicen stood from where she had been kneeling. She looked toward the back of the room, tucked mostly in shadows, and listened.

The noise sounded once more, and Alicen's heart leapt ever so slightly. "Louise?" she called.

"Yeah?" came her friend's voice up the stairs from below.

No surprise there. Louise wouldn't have been able to get up here and past Alicen without being seen; the space wasn't that large. Alicen wasn't even sure why she'd called out.

"Do you need something?" Louise asked.

Alicen shook her head. "No, sorry; I thought I heard you call me," she lied. She then scolded herself for acting paranoid over what was probably nothing, capped her black marker, and started toward the back of the room. She reached the final row of shelves and turned her head down the thin aisle. At the end, lying on the floor in the middle of the row, were three books.

Alicen felt her breath catch, and she peered down the second-from-last aisle to see if there was something pressing against the back side that might have made the books fall.

Nothing. The aisle was clear. She moved her eyes back

down the last aisle and stared at the fallen volumes. She exhaled forcefully and again scolded herself.

She'd heard three thuds and here, right before her eyes, was the evidence of where the noise had come from. Why should that make her heart quiver? This was annoying and ridiculous. Anything could have caused the books to slip to the floor. A draft, movement, a mouse. Alicen bit her bottom lip and scrunched her nose. She hoped it wasn't a mouse. She let out another deep breath and walked the short distance to the books, squatted to grab them, and stood.

Nothing strange about a breeze knocking books off the bottom shelf. That's what she was going to tell herself it was, because if it was a mouse she was going to lose it. She thought about kneeling to double-check, then decided against it. She looked at the books in her hand. They were chapter books, aged by time, with familiar titles.

A Wrinkle in Time.

The Secret Garden.

Treasure Island.

Children's books. Alicen looked at the covers fondly. She had probably read these exact copies. Mrs. Watson had always encouraged her and Louise to read and often let them borrow books from the shop to take on their adventures. Alicen had been the better reader, so on more than one occasion as the girls perched somewhere in hiding, Alicen would read the stories out loud while Louise questioned every character motive and plot twist. Louise was convinced she could tell the story better and often made up her own version.

Alicen chuckled softly to herself. Louise's version usually

was more exciting. Something rustled behind her, and Alicen spun around. There was nothing but stillness, the shadows, the air, completely calm. Again something reached her ears, soft and muffled, like whispers above her, and she turned her head in all directions. The noise came and went, almost like static, but softer. Like whispered voices.

Alicen took a step away from the stuffy end of the aisle, and the noise stopped. Her heart beat against the inside of her chest, the three books clenched against the outside. The voices returned. Or maybe they weren't voices; maybe it was the music from downstairs. Maybe it was the wind. Suspense drifted over her shoulders like it was coming from the air itself.

She heard herself say "Hello?" out loud, as if she expected the whispery static to respond, and again the entire floor went still. She stood like stone, waiting, straining to listen. Nothing.

For the third time she scolded herself, cursing under her breath at the insanity she was falling prey to.

Behind her another something thunked, and she jumped, letting out a tiny squeal. She spun around. Another book lay where she had just gathered the other three. The cover faced upward, the colored cartoon picture clear.

Alice's Adventures in Wonderland.

Jane's favorite.

Alicen just stared, unable to drag her eyes away. How many times had she read chapters from the classic? How many times had her daughter begged to read just one more page? The whispers came again, this time accompanied by what sounded like soft, playful giggling, the kind only children made. Alicen's mind swirled as she took an instinctive step back from the newly fallen book.

Then a distinct voice, louder than the others, close enough and real enough that Alicen was sure she felt breath behind her ear, said her name.

Alicen.

She whipped around.

Nothing. The giggling faded until the entire floor was quiet again. Cold chills rushed through her body, even though sweat had begun to gather in her palms. Without another thought, she left the aisle, headed for the staircase, and climbed down. Her breaths were short and trembling. She reached the bottom, her eyes stinging with tears, her heart thundering. She started for the front door; she needed to escape the past that was haunting her mind.

"Hey," a voice called from behind, and Alicen did a full jump and screech, bumping a nearby bookshelf painfully. She cursed and grabbed the place where her hip had connected with the sharp wooden edge.

"Whoa," Louise said, rushing to Alicen's side. "You okay?"

Alicen pulled away from Louise's touch and winced in pain. She took a deep breath and nodded. "Yeah."

Louise stepped back. "You sure?"

Alicen looked at her worried friend, unsure what to say. Should she tell her she thought she'd heard strange whisperings and laughing children while an invisible hand pushed children's novels to the floor? Hearing her own thoughts made her feel as crazy as she would sound saying that sentence aloud. She opened her mouth to say anything else and was suddenly struck with the absurdity of it all.

Louise just stared at her as Alicen shook her head and then released a chuckle. "You startled me," Alicen said.

"Yeah," Louise replied, her eyes widening and her lips turning up into a mocking grin. "I picked up on that."

Alicen brought her free hand to her forehead, closed her eyes, and laughed. A moment later Louise joined her.

"Sorry—I don't know why I'm so jumpy," Alicen said.

"You see a ghost up there or something?" Louise teased.

Alicen shook her head. "No, but I think you may have a mouse problem."

"Great," Louise said, rolling her eyes. She glanced down at Alicen's chest and pointed. "What are those?"

Alicen followed her gaze and saw that she was still holding the three children's novels. She shrugged and handed the books to Louise, who took them and glanced them over.

"Oh, man," she said with a hint of wonder, "I haven't seen these in forever. They were up there?"

"Yeah, they fell off the back shelf—the reason I think you might have an unwelcome tenant."

Louise turned them over, a puzzled look on her face.

"What's wrong?" Alicen asked. She rubbed the spot on her hip that was still throbbing.

"It's just weird that they would be up there. All the rest of the children's books are over there in the corner. I was just sorting through them."

"So they got misplaced," Alicen said, ignoring the slight quickening in her pulse.

"Yeah, must have." Louise stared another moment before exhaling and walking the books back toward the corner where she was sorting their peers. Alicen took a steadying breath and chased away the ridiculous thoughts creeping into her mind. She carefully stole a glance back up toward the second floor, her body tensing, as if ready for something to spring from the darkness.

"You wanna take a break?" Louise asked.

Alicen released the tension in her shoulders and turned her eyes back to Louise. "Already?"

Louise laughed and nodded. "Yeah, I think the dust in here is giving me a headache, and I could really go for a burger."

Alicen smiled. "And fries?"

Louise looked taken aback and playfully placed her hand on her chest. "How long have we been friends? Have you ever known me to eat a burger without fries? I mean really, I'm offended."

Louise grabbed her purse as the two women headed for the exit, Alicen unable to stop herself from stealing one last glance at the upstairs floor, where there was nothing but shadows.

5

Alicen found herself riding shotgun as Louise pulled the car into a perfectly lined parking space outside Clover Mountain Retreat Center. Alicen stared out the front window at the beautifully constructed white buildings before her. Everything was just as the brochure had captured it. Rolling green lawns, trees that had been standing for decades, people walking the neat paths and sidewalks. It was stunning, well kept, and completely normal looking. Except for the large Clover Mountain Retreat Center sign than hung from the main building's center archway. Every time Alicen pulled into this parking lot, that sign would be a blinding reminder of where she was and how she had gotten here. Glorious.

Louise turned the engine off and exhaled loudly as she dropped back against her seat. "Here we are."

Here she was. Today Alicen was walking the grounds and meeting with her appointed support group. She assumed the point was to make connections with others suffering similarly, to be in a place where losing her mind wasn't uncommon, because everyone around her was also losing their sanity, and somehow their shared trauma would help them all recover. What a crock.

"Do you need a minute?" Louise asked.

Prolonging the inevitable was for children; Alicen knew there was no running from this. "No, I'm as ready as I'll ever be." She opened her door and stepped out just as a familiar face approached from across the lawn. Clad in a black ensemble similar to what she'd worn the last time they met, Victoria gave a small wave and smiled. Alicen ignored the discomfort of her turning stomach. Everything about this day was going to be uncomfortable.

Louise, now standing outside the car as well, waved back, then turned to give Alicen a reassuring grin. "I'll be back to get you in an hour."

"You aren't staying?" Alicen said, her voice tiny. A wash of nervous panic cascaded down her spine. She knew she sounded like a baby, knew that expecting Louise to accompany her while she sat through her support meetings was ridiculous, but some part of her mind had still believed she might.

"Do you need me to stay?" Louise asked. That concerned look of sympathy flashed across her face.

Alicen ground her molars and swallowed the resounding *yes* that wanted to echo from her lips. "No, that would be a waste of your time."

"I can stay—" Louise started.

Alicen forced a chuckle and shook her head. "No, that would be crazy. I'll just see you in an hour."

"Alicen—"

"Go, Lou; I'm a grown woman. I'll be fine," Alicen said. It came out harsher than she'd have liked, but she was frantically covering up her insecurities of being left here alone and needed Louise to leave before she lost control of her will and began begging the woman to hold her hand.

Louise shrugged slightly. "Okay, I'll see you soon. Try to play nice with the others."

It was a small jab, and Alicen deserved it. Louise wasn't wrong to warn Alicen against being mean. It was Alicen's first and only defense mechanism. Alicen turned toward Victoria and heard Louise's car roar to life behind her. This was it. A couple more steps and she'd be too far to turn back and run for cover. And Louise would be gone. Alicen would be facing her demons alone. A knot collected in her throat and she calmly tried to breathe through it. A couple more steps. Victoria's stare came into perfect view, and the knot tightened. Alicen felt like a kid being dropped off for her first day of school or summer camp, every comfort she was used to stripped, only the terrifying unknown ahead. A couple more steps. The tires from her only retreat squeaked against the pavement as they pulled farther away. A couple more steps.

"Glad to see you made it on time," Victoria said, closing the gap and extending a welcoming hand.

Alicen found herself sealing her fate as she shook Victoria's hand and forced a tiny grin. This was all there was now.

"It's good to finally have you on campus," Victoria said. "I know this process isn't easy, so we'll take it slow."

Alicen wanted to say, *Yep. Slow and miserable like the rest of my life is bound to be.* Instead she said, "It's beautiful here."

Victoria smiled and glanced around. "Yes, my family took a lot of pride in making things well. If you're ready, we'll begin today with a short tour of the facility, and then I'll take you to meet your network."

"Network?"

Victoria answered, "We try to avoid words or phrases that a guest, such as yourself, might have negative associations with."

"Like *support group*."

"Exactly. It's something my great-grandfather insisted on. We want people to have a different kind of experience with us. We want them to feel as comfortable as possible."

"Good luck," Alicen teased, but she knew it sounded more defensive than humorous. There had been a time when self-control and emotional deceptiveness were strengths she wielded with pride; now she could hardly fake a smile correctly.

Victoria's face didn't even flinch. Her manufactured smile stayed untouched. She was used to dealing with people of Alicen's kind, and Alicen wasn't sure if that should make her feel comforted or distressed.

"I think you'll find that all the facilities are as beautiful inside as they are out," Victoria said, turning her body toward the largest white building and beginning the trek forward across the lawn. Alicen swallowed another round of fear and followed.

"The center structure directly in front of us, we call the big house," Victoria began. "It is the focal point of the campus and the only original building still standing. Most everything else you see has been added as we grew, and modified to support the growing advancements in technology, medicine, and comfort. We ensure everything you could need you'll find on the property, while we limit things from the outside environment that may act as triggers." Victoria paused and turned back to face Alicen. "You'll find the campus can feel like an island unto itself. A safe space away from the evil of the world."

She smiled, and a strange quiver pulsed at the base of Alicen's spine.

"In reviewing your file, I think some separation from the world would be healthy. Some space to get clarity and perspective on who you are and perhaps how you got here."

The small quiver in Alicen's spine grew as Victoria held her stare and continued. "I sense you're too smart for some of the games we play with guests; you'd see through that, so I'll be transparent with you. I want to offer you help, but the first step to recovery is to recognize the missteps that you've taken thus far. Honesty is necessary. Acknowledgment of our—" Victoria paused as she searched for the proper word and then gave Alicen a slight smile—"*inadequacies* is where we begin."

Alicen again felt as if she had returned to childhood. A little girl waiting to be rebuked for all her mistakes. Standing before a disapproving mother, quick to remind Alicen that she had gotten here by her own faults. She felt the rise of tears sting her eyes.

"My uncle Donald, who raised me on this very campus, used to say, 'Only through the acknowledgment of our stains are we cleansed.' Better stated: all are troubled, Alicen. Here I offer you acceptance and perhaps peace with your trouble."

Alicen swallowed her building emotions as the wind seemed to whirl about her suddenly. Pulling at her hair, sending chilled ripples across her skin. Soft mumbling whispers rose with the breeze, drifting into her ears and tingling at the edges of her brain. Her heart jerked, and she instinctively glanced toward the tree line to her left, where the sound had come from.

Nothing but bark and branches. As was to be expected. Yet the peculiar sense remained that she'd almost thought she'd see more.

"Alicen," Victoria said, yanking Alicen out of her reverie. Alicen opened her mouth to apologize, but Victoria held up her hand and silenced her.

"It's all right," Victoria said. "Few come here willingly, but I assure you we can offer you something tangible, if you let us."

The soft whispers Alicen had heard before pricked behind her head and became a single word.

Run.

Her heart quickened.

Victoria gave a small nod. "Let's continue." She turned and started again toward the main building.

Alicen released the breath she'd trapped inside her throat, stole a quick glance to either side to confirm that she was in fact hearing nothing, and followed. Even though every nerve in her body told her not to.

• • •

Alicen sat in a padded folding chair and faced a circle of twelve strangers. Four men and eight women, none of whom she knew, none of whom she had any intention of getting to know. It had only been ten minutes, and Alicen was convinced that enduring these sessions wouldn't help clarify her mind but would, in fact, probably drive her to a state of insanity from which she could never return.

A plump, white-haired woman in her sixties named Gina had addressed the group to start. She was their network host, guiding them through the process of sharing and healing, she'd said with the type of tone one might use to address a classroom of preschool students. Alicen had immediately pictured the old woman baking apple pies and placing them on her stone cottage windowsill and beckoning for the animals of the forest to come and help her tidy up her kitchen.

Alicen already hated Gina.

Gina had then opened up the group discussion, and a man named Stew—"Spelled like the soup," he'd announced for Alicen's benefit—had started sharing about the dark rain cloud that followed him everywhere, soaking him through even though everyone else around him was dry. He was envious of others' ability to maintain their state of "not wet" and found himself constantly depressed.

Gina had listened intently and with great concern, which made Alicen like her even less, and then after some thought had suggested Stew remember to carry an umbrella with him at all times. The idea had been received well from the group, with nods of approval, which seemed to give Stew some peace.

Another woman, smaller in frame and younger, giggled awkwardly throughout Stew's sharing, and then apologized profusely. Apparently several hundred penguins lived inside her head and were making jokes. Someone asked her if the green penguins had returned, and the girl announced they had not, and the group seemed pleased. Gina told her this was great progress, and the giggling girl smiled shyly, apologized again, and then asked Stew to continue.

Alicen waited for someone to jump out from behind a wall and yell, "Gotcha," while the rest of the room laughed as though they had all been in on the joke, but no one ever did. Because Stew actually believed a rain cloud was following him, and the laughing girl actually heard the voices inside her head.

Alicen tried to wrangle her prickly defenses. She knew it was poor form to think so negatively of people around her. People who were truly trying to seek help because their brains worked differently than the world deemed normal. She wasn't trying to be nasty, but all she could keep thinking was how on earth had she ended up here? Yes, she had tried to kill herself, and yes, admittedly she had heard a couple strange things, all sure signs of PTSD, but she wasn't like Stew or the strange giggling girl who actually needed help. She just needed to be left alone with her suffering.

A couple others shared as Alicen took to watching the ticking hands on the clock. Ryan, a heavyset man with black hair and a matching mustache was sleeping better and yelling less at his nurse. Hooray. Bethany, a mild-mannered middle-aged woman with terribly bleached blonde hair, had gone an entire week without stealing any of her roommate's things and burying them in the garden. Huge plus. And Heather, a very pale woman with an English accent, was just thrilled that they were now serving white chocolate pudding instead of red Jell-O. Congrats to the kitchen staff.

Alicen took deep, calming breaths, working very hard to hide her discomfort and counting down the final moments before she was free.

"Well, we have a couple of minutes left," Gina said.

Alicen felt Gina's gaze shift toward her, and the entire room rose in temperature. Alicen stared sweating before her name left Gina's mouth.

"Alicen, I know it's your first meeting, but we always like to invite our new guests to share," Gina said.

Every eye turned toward her, and it made Alicen want to vomit. No way was she sharing; she wasn't even convinced she was in the right group.

Gina smiled brightly and waited.

"Um, no, I don't really have anything to say," Alicen said. She moved awkwardly in her seat and commanded her legs to keep still instead of jumping up and carrying her far away from here.

"Are you sure? It's customary to share at your first session. Maybe just something interesting about yourself," Gina said. The syrupy sound of her voice rattled inside Alicen's eardrums.

The space around Alicen's head began to fill with cotton. She'd felt something similar while touring with Victoria and earlier, in the bookstore. The feeling was beginning to seem familiar. She could hear the distant pounding of her heart through the muffled air and felt the prying gazes from her groupmates. They were all just sitting and staring and waiting.

A tiny giggle echoed around her, then another, then several. The noise tickled behind her ears and made the hair on her arms rise. The soft, eerie sound bounced off the walls, and Alicen glanced at the penguin girl, who was sitting completely still. And silent.

A gentle tap pressed against the back of her right shoulder, and simultaneously the giggling changed to a single voice.

Alicen.

Alicen whipped her head to the right to find nothing. She reached around to brush her shoulder while the voice echoed to her left.

Alicen, do you hear us?

She whipped her head left. Still nothing. The cotton thickened, the giggling muffled in the background, the child-like voice whispering through.

Do you hear us?

Alicen stood frantically, nearly knocking her chair over, causing the voice, the soft laughter, and the cotton to vanish. Her head cleared, but her panicked, heavy breathing and thundering heart rate pounded in her ears.

"It's okay, Alicen," said Gina, who had also stood, very calmly, and was extending a concerned hand toward Alicen in the middle of the circle. Everyone was still staring at her, watching to see what she would do next. She opened her mouth to defend herself, but her mouth was dry, and she was unable to think of anything past her terror.

"It's okay," Gina said again. "You don't have to share today. Why don't you just take a seat, and we'll try again next time."

Alicen felt her sanity start to drop back into place. *Yes, Alicen, sit down. You look like a fool, Alicen. You only suffer from PTSD, Alicen. Stop acting as crazy as those around you. Sit down before they think you're just like them, Alicen.*

"Sorry," Alicen said, glancing at Gina and then the rest of the group.

Gina smiled with ease, and the wrinkles around the corners of her eyes held such authentic kindness, it made Alicen feel terrible for thinking so cruelly of her before.

"It's okay," someone said behind her. Alicen turned to see a soft-featured, green-eyed woman smiling at her. It was the woman who had been sitting quietly beside Alicen during the meeting. "This is a safe place, away from the evil of the world."

The woman's words echoed those she'd heard from Victoria, and Alicen noticed others nodding, understanding and recognition in their expressions.

"Thank you, Shannon," Gina said. "She's right, Alicen; this is a safe place."

Alicen, unsure of what else to do, just nodded and returned to her seat. As the group session came to a close, Gina added some final remarks that Alicen couldn't have repeated, because she wasn't listening. She was too busy searching through the realms of her feeble sanity to hear anything. She avoided eye contact with anyone for fear that she'd see more understanding, which would mean that she wasn't as different from them as she believed. Hearing voices, sensing she wasn't alone, creating things that weren't there. Yes, she was suffering from a traumatic loss, but she wasn't insane. Was she?

Alicen bit her back teeth together hard enough for it to ache up behind her ears. She was at war with her mind, and she was losing; that was all. She would do her time, she would control her crazy, she would defeat the hysterical whims of her brain, and then she'd be free, left alone with her suffering. Jane was dead because of her. She didn't want to heal, didn't believe she could, and more importantly didn't believe she deserved to.

• • •

Victoria closed the door to her office and let her hand rest on the knob. A twitch pulled at her chin. An outcome of her day. An outcome of Alicen's presence here. She took a deep drag of air in with her lungs and then let it pass slowly out between her lips.

The tension in her shoulders began to ease. A second twitch tapped her chin, and she swallowed back the reality she was in. Letting them onto campus was always the hardest step. Seeing their faces, watching their pain, masking her disgust. It wasn't all of them, of course. No, most of them were simply sorry sacks needing release from their dirtied pasts. Victoria let them roll off her skin like dust.

It was the special cases that seeped through her flesh and attacked her bones. Cases like Alicen.

Alicen had committed a horrendous crime. She'd been given something precious and had taken it for granted. She hadn't been better than the world around her. She'd taken a life with her carelessness, and now she had the audacity to walk around victimized, as if something had been taken from her. She was worse than a sorry sack. She was an infection. Victoria knew infections needed to be monitored carefully, or they would spread and eventually kill.

No, no, no, Victoria thought. She knew how to deal with special cases. A handful had come through during her time as head administrator. Several lived here currently, all managed and contained. Alicen would be no different.

Careful, little Victoria. Best-laid plans often rot.

Her uncle Donald's familiar voice burned inside her brain like a match too often struck whose flame she could never fully douse. Her constant penance. A mix of friend and foe. Giver and thief. The veins in her wrists pulsed. She craved relief from her darkness and quivered at her own inability to be free from her dirty secrets.

Born from filth, full of weakness. Have you learned nothing?

"Enough," Victoria said out loud. The voice inside her mind stilled. For the moment. It never really left her, though. She wasn't even sure she wanted it to, for then she would be utterly alone, and loneliness was the cruelest of fates. Uncle Donald had saved her from such a fate. He continued to save her even after being buried in the ground.

Accuser and savior.

Victoria took another breath and released it before letting her hand fall from the doorknob. She moved across her office toward the desk. Outside the window, the sky was caught in twilight. Night was on its way.

Victoria used to be afraid of the dark. No matter how much time passed, she could still clearly see the double bed she had occupied as a girl. Her small square room on the upper floor, down the hall from her uncle's. Scratchy sheets and drafty windows. Moving shadows and walking nightmares. When it became too much, she'd imagine she was somewhere else. Someone else.

Vicky. Sweet. Innocent. Not cursed, born to a family filled with evil and filth. Loved and hopeful. Vicky was delusional about the world, ignorant. Victoria felt sad for Vicky yet longed to be her. She was jealous of her stupidity and would have traded places with her in a heartbeat.

They'd have quiet debates in the middle of the night.

Vicky: Life can be beautiful.

Victoria: Only when you are blind.

Vicky: Then let me be blind.

Victoria: He says only fools are blind.

Vicky: Then let me be a fool.

Victoria: You are a fool because you believe in stories.

Vicky: My parents tell me the greatest stories.

Victoria: Parents lie.

Vicky: My parents love me.

Victoria: My parents ruined me, because that's what parents do.

Vicky: Why?

Victoria: He says people are worms.

Vicky: Worms? No, my parents are lovely.

Victoria: Only because they aren't real.

Victoria's head twitched again. She smudged out the memory, silencing the character she'd conjured to survive dark, cruel nights. She'd been a child then. She wasn't a child now.

She sat back in her office chair and folded her hands in her lap. It had been a while since she'd thought of Vicky. Her mind could easily track the recurrence to Alicen. Not Alicen herself but rather what Alicen represented. A parent who had failed her child. As Victoria's parents had failed her.

So easily you've let her get under your skin, little Victoria.

"I'm controlling it," she replied.

Control? Another illusion you've conjured, I see.

"I am in control."

We will see.

"Don't forget where I am, and where you are."

Uncle Donald's full, dark chuckle echoed through the air around her head. It mocked her. Poked at her inadequacies, held her under her own fears.

Don't forget who you are. Where you come from.

"How could I forget?" Victoria whispered into the darkness.

Then you will show her, as you were shown.

"I must." Again, her wrists beckoned. She instinctively ran her fingers over the scars that lined her forearm. A beat of desire matched by disgust pulsed in her chest.

You reap what you sow, and life always comes to collect.

"Retribution is necessary for all who are troubled," Victoria repeated from memory, her fingers still tracing the lines of relief carved into her skin.

Alicen is troubled. Time to collect. Do not fail.

Victoria nodded and removed her fingers from her wrists. She wouldn't fail.

6

Alicen lay on the couch in the summer home's main living room. The fan overhead spun at a moderately slow pace, the blades cutting the air and sending down a gentle breeze that ruffled the stringy edges of the throw pillows around her. The sun was gone now; it had been headed toward the mountains when she'd lain down.

Its absence left the room dark, with only a corner lamp to cast shadows. Alicen watched those too. They almost seemed to move if she stared at them long enough, which drew her buzzing mind back to the mysterious whispers she'd heard in the bookstore and at Clover Mountain Retreat Center.

Her visit to the campus yesterday and the uneasy feeling

that had plastered itself to the inside of her chest cavity afterward had followed her into this morning, through the afternoon sorting at the bookstore, and sat with her still. A discomfort and panic she couldn't seem to shake. Her brain was usually good at compartmentalizing things, tying up all the wispy threads of thought and then shoving them into their appropriate boxes so she was no longer plagued by them.

But not with this. Not of late. She was broken, and the tools that had served her so well throughout her adulthood were failing her. What a terrible time for her mind to become so curious and distractible.

Louise hadn't asked much after picking Alicen up yesterday, and Alicen hadn't offered anything more than "It was fine." Thankfully, the topic hadn't come up today. Louise had announced a couple of hours ago that she had to drive into Billings to grab some necessary paperwork. She'd invited Alicen to join, but Alicen was happy for the space. She knew Louise wasn't trying to smother, but the concerned glances, the checking-in questions, the constant eye contact—it was enough to make her feel rather claustrophobic about this unusual situation.

Alicen's stomach growled, and she placed her palm over it. She should move to the kitchen and find something to eat, but the effort would involve more than staring at spinning blades, so she ignored her hunger. Loss brought about an array of circling reactions. At times Alicen needed to be moving, working, anything that required her not to be still for fear of getting trapped. And then other times the numbness of depression swallowed every cell in her body, and moving was out of the question. And then there were times like now, when a combination of the two was worse than either singularity. Numb through her body but active in her mind. The wheels of consciousness turning while she lay trapped in the deep stillness that overpowered her physical senses.

It was basically torture, but the only way out was . . . well, actually, there was no way out. Only less of it, or control of it. Right now Alicen had neither. Because behind every spinning thought wheel was her. Her golden curls, her soft face, her crystal eyes, her voice, her smell, her touch, her laugh, her tears, her memories.

Her.

Her.

Her.

Alicen closed her eyes and exhaled into the soundless room. It was moments like this that had driven her to swallow a bottle of pills, and the idea still felt more welcoming than she dared to admit.

Something creaked overhead, and Alicen's eyes shot open. She waited for another sound, but nothing came. The room stayed still. A soft, distant groaning echoed outside the window behind the couch, and she used her arms to prop her shoulders up off the cushions. Wind, she thought. It was just the howling of the wind. A storm was coming.

The floor above creaked again, twice, short spikes of pressure that filled the dark room. Alicen bit the inside of her cheek to distract her heart from its quickened pace. There was wind, and old wood floors creaked. The old floors creaked *from* the wind; that was the way old houses worked. No reason to let her nerves swan-dive into panic.

She pushed a small stream of air out through her lips and sat all the way up. She ran her slightly trembling hand down over her face, hoping to press out the insanity rooting in her brain. She stood, walked to the wall nearby, flipped the switch next to a large mounted painting, and flooded the room with light.

Alicen's eyes swept the room—its familiar edges and corners a time capsule of memories. Her eyes wandered to the painting, inches from where her fingers still lingered on the light switch. A beachside ocean scene. Alicen could remember a couple of downpours that forced her and Louise inside for long hours of boredom. Once Stephanie had walked in on her and Louise lying on the floor beneath this painting, their backsides pressed up against the wall's bottom trim, their legs extended up toward the artwork, their spines stretched out across the carpet.

"What are you girls doing in here?" Stephanie had asked.

"Imagining what it would be like to die from being bored," Lou had answered.

Alicen only shook her head in agreement.

"Oh, I see," Stephanie said, crossing her arms and gingerly leaning against the wall. "That seems a bit dramatic."

"Life's dramatic, Mom," Lou complained.

Stephanie tried to hide a smile. "It could be worse."

"How?" Lou asked.

"Yeah," Alicen chirped in. "This is pretty awful."

"You could be stuck on a ship, in the middle of the ocean,"

Stephanie pressed. She pointed to the beachside image hanging above the girls. "These waters stretch for boundless miles, and early on, crews aboard massive wooden ships were sent out for months at a time to try and discover what lay beyond the setting sun."

"So?" Lou asked.

"So you think being stuck inside this house during a little rain is tough? Imagine being stuck belowdecks."

Alicen shared a worried glance with Lou, who had pushed herself up onto her elbows.

Stephanie slid down to a graceful squat, her eyes wide with wonder. "The wind howling so loudly it sounds like it might crack through the ship's sturdy hull, the rain pelting down across the deck, soaking through to the hold below, the waves tossing the ship with ease, stoking fear that they may just swallow the whole thing and drag its men down to the bottom of the sea."

"I'd be outta there," Lou said.

"There's nowhere to go," Stephanie continued. "The sailors are trapped by the storm and the endless waters surrounding them."

Alicen shook her little head. "We'd have to escape; I get terrible motion sickness."

"We would," Lou bolstered.

"Many men before you haven't; are you sure you're up for the challenge?" Stephanie asked, a twinkle in the corner of her eye.

Lou lay back down, the same twinkle in hers. Like mother, like daughter, they said. "We've escaped worse."

Alicen shook with glee. "Good. I hate boats."

Stephanie smiled and stood.

"You think there's enough stuff around here to build a submarine?" Lou asked as she began searching the room with her eyes.

"Submarine? I just said I hated boats!" Alicen said.

"Alicen, sometimes you gotta do what you gotta do," Lou commanded.

Stephanie turned to leave the girls alone. "Good luck, you two," she tossed over her shoulder before disappearing.

Alicen hadn't understood what Stephanie was doing at the time, but thinking back to those times now, she couldn't help but chuckle.

Now Alicen reached out and ran her grown fingers over the painting, echoes of her childhood voice still lingering in her head. Had she ever encouraged Jane to dream the way Stephanie had prompted them to? Had she led her precious daughter to believe she could be anything she wanted, or had she robbed her of wonder? Had she ever been worthy of being called mother at all?

Tears found their way down Alicen's cheeks, and she felt the numbing sorrow begin to refill her bones. A thud sounded overhead, followed by movement from the far corner to the center of the room before it went silent. Footsteps.

The sorrow that had been working its way into her system was replaced by dread. That was not old-house creaking. She held her breath, frozen in place, waiting for whatever was up there to move again. Her eyes glued to the ceiling, the fan still turning, the room filled with a still sense of terror.

Alicen watched. Waited. Nothing. She took a breath and cursed silently. What was wrong with her? She peeled her eyes off the ceiling and forced her legs to leave the living room. She stopped at the bottom of the winding staircase and dared to glance up into the black shadows. Another breath. The dread still remained as she reached out and lightly touched the wooden railing. She took a step forward, her toes reaching the bottom stair, her eyes waiting for something to appear, something logic told her wasn't there.

Something shifted at the top of the stairs. More raps echoed, as the shape above darted back farther into the shadows, its movement again disturbing the house's stillness. Fear walloped inside Alicen's chest as she jumped back. Whispers fell from the dark upper corner, small, familiar.

No, she thought. She reached out across the entryway and rammed the light switch to illuminate the staircase. Her chest pulsed with short breaths as her eyes tore apart the top level. Empty. The muffled hum of voices vanished.

Of course it was empty. Her mind had wanted to see something in the darkness, so she had. She was tired, her control frazzled. Alicen closed her eyes and ordered her brain to get ahold of itself. Of course there was nothing.

The static of voices started again, but Alicen kept her eyes closed. *It's not real.* The whispers grew—nothing discernible, just louder noise pressing like slivers into her mind. She swallowed and clenched her eyes tighter, balling her fists against her fingers' terrified vibrating. *Nothing, nothing, nothing.*

More footsteps passed overhead. They were tiny and quick, the pitter-patter of children. Tiny whispers, like the mischief of kids. Fear like a bull rammed Alicen's resolve, and she pressed her palms into her eye sockets to keep them shut. *It's nothing. It's nothing.* She was in control of her mind; she would not let it win. Her palms soaked up the angry tears she couldn't hold back.

Alicen. Can you hear us?

Pressure started to pulse in the back of her head. Her shoulders shook. Her knees barely held her steady. "No," she said, more thought than actually spoken. "No."

Alicen.

"No!" she screamed. "No, I cannot hear you!"

Her voice echoed through the empty house, and everything became still. For a moment it was only her breathing. Her pounding skull. Her thundering heart. Her rattling bones. As the moment dragged on, Alicen began to believe she had actually conquered her delusion. She let the thought linger, and as her confidence in what she may have accomplished grew, Alicen dared to uncover her eyes.

She was met by an illuminated entryway. The wind howled outside, vibrations of falling rain tapping against the roof. The house was empty. She drew her eyes from one corner of what lay before her to the other, and then back.

Alicen saw her then. She may have missed her completely had she not shifted slightly. Standing at the end of the hallway beyond the entry was a child.

A girl.

A shadow really, but standing there, short in stature, hands folded in front of her knee-length dress, hair tied into long, low pigtails on either side of her neck. Alicen couldn't see her face, couldn't see her breathing. She was more silhouette than human, motionless enough to trick the eye into thinking she might be an illusion, and then Alicen's logic told her it couldn't possibly be anything else.

But Alicen's logic had betrayed her before, and without another thought she was stepping forward. "You . . . ," she started, her words falling off flat. The shadow looked so real. "You . . . what are you?" Alicen muttered.

The moment the words left her mouth, the girl vanished from view. Like a flame extinguished with a single breath. Impossible. A long moment of terror slowly dripped down, from the top of Alicen's skull to her feet, covering her whole being, blotting out all streams of thought except panic. Then she snapped. Fury mushed with fear turned her into a beast.

"Where are you?" she screamed. "I saw you!" Stomping forward, attacking every light switch, Alicen hastily moved from room to room. "I saw you!" Each room came up empty. The tiny voice in her head tried to warn against losing herself to such madness, but Alicen shut it off and strode into the kitchen. The room sprang to life under the golden lights and like the others contained only furniture.

The static voices wavered in and out of earshot. She was being followed. Haunted. She grasped her head with both hands as a deep tremor rolled down her spine.

Alicen, can you hear us?

Alicen.

Do you see us?

"I saw you, I saw you!" Alicen's voice wailed through the house.

Alicen.

She yanked at her hair and closed her eyes. This couldn't be real; she was yelling at air; she was losing her mind. *Get a grip, Alicen. Act like an adult, Alicen. What would your mother say, Alicen?*

The tiny pulses of feet running overhead cut through her mocking logic, and Alicen rushed from the kitchen toward the stairs. She raced upward two at a time, hitting the lights at the top. The hallway was empty, but the sound of laughter and running came from the far room.

Alicen stormed forward. "Get out—get out of my house!" she yelled.

Get a grip, Alicen. Act like an adult, Alicen, her mind taunted.

She threw open every door, switched on every light. Her legs pumped like machines. Empty. Empty. Empty. All the rooms were empty. More footsteps drifted from behind her. Skitter-scatter. Skitter-scatter.

More childish laughter reached her, now wafting up from the first floor. They were downstairs. How were they downstairs? Alicen rushed back toward the stairs and bounded down. The whispers and giggling stretched toward the back of the house. Alicen followed their trail.

Alicen. Do you see us?

"Where are you? I know you're here! Get out, get out!" she screamed.

What would your mother say, Alicen? her mind lashed.

Alicen moved, not stopping, until she was pushing open the back door and stepping out onto the porch. Rain poured from the sky, and she stumbled forward to the wooden patio's edge. She stopped, searching the long stretch of lawn, trying to make out any shadows through the sheets of water. Her breathing was ragged, her throat raw, her mind frazzled.

Get a grip, Alicen. Act like an adult, Alicen. A thick razor of lightning cut across the sky, casting a moment of illumination over the backyard, and Alicen saw her.

Same shadowy figure, same knee-length dress, same double pigtails. Standing at the far reaches of the lawn, more imagined than real, but there. Alicen stepped down off the porch and into the rain. Heavy drops smacked against her skull and drained down her face. She pushed them away. The shadow was gone, or it was too dark to see her.

Alicen's hands were trembling; cold was soaking through her clothes and into her skin. She felt a familiar fading begin in her mind. The yard vanished, and the rain and darkness disappeared. And she found herself standing beside her pool, warm sun touching her skin, a soft breeze rolling across her shoulders.

Jane.

Alicen turned and saw her across the pool. Her beautiful little girl, bright-red swimsuit, tight golden curls. Joy filled her being, and she took a step forward. "Baby."

Jane smiled and giggled, her hand moving up over her mouth. Like always. Sparkle in her eyes. Like always. And then her tiny dancing feet moving about in circles. Like always. Alicen knew where this living nightmare would take her, but she couldn't make it stop.

Alicen. Her name carried past her ears on the wind. The

familiar child's voice she couldn't get out of her head. *No, not here,* she thought. *Not in this place.* This was Jane's place.

Alicen.

Something phased into view behind her dancing girl. A shadowy figure. She was there, the haunting silhouette. The child from inside the house.

Fire rumbled inside Alicen's chest, and her rooted parental instincts roared. She rushed toward the pool, but Jane wasn't even aware of the shadow behind her. She was hurtling toward the water, getting ready to launch herself over the edge and below the surface. To drown. Like always.

"Jane!" Alicen yelled. "Stop!"

The storm had rolled in. The clouds were dark with rage, the sky heavy with sorrow. Alicen's words were ravaged by the wind. Her daughter leaped with gusto off the ledge and splashed into the brewing pool as the wind lapped waves out over the stone edging.

Alicen.

"No," Alicen cried. "No!" She ignored the figure, the fear, the insanity. And the same thought that always prevailed was *Save her. Save Jane. Don't let her die again.* Alicen pushed against the raging storm and was dragged to her knees.

"Jane!" she screamed. "Please don't leave me."

The little head had gone underwater and would not resurface. It was happening. Jane was dying, and Alicen couldn't get to her. She let out a full-throttled cry of anguish. Every time her daughter died, Alicen wanted to die. Dying would be easier than living with this pain.

Alicen.

"Alicen!" Her name echoed through the sky above her. Another, outside voice. Mature and familiar. Rain poured down around her, the wetness reregistering across her skin. She was shaking, the pool gone, her daughter nowhere, and the summer home's backyard in Red Lodge the only thing that existed.

"Alicen!" the voice screamed as a body dropped down beside her, and through the darkness she saw Louise's face. "What are you doing?"

Alicen dropped her gaze. Mud covered her knees and fingers. Her hair dripped down into her eyes. Her top was soaked, her bones chattering. She was in the backyard, in the pouring rain. There was no pool, there was no Jane, and there never would be.

7

Once again Alicen was tucked into a kitchen chair inside the Watsons' kitchen after being rescued by Louise because she had lost all sense of reality. Once again Louise had prepared her hot tea, had watched her with peering concern, and had tried to understand what was happening, but ultimately had left Alicen alone with her insanity.

Get a grip, Alicen. Act like an adult, Alicen. What would your mother say, Alicen? The torment was endless. It was almost humorous the way her mind could both betray her, shoving her into a realm of delusion, and then mock her for being pushed when she finally regained balance. Endless and cruel. But she deserved it.

Mud was caked under her fingernails. Her wet hair had been pulled up high on top of her head and was drying. She still had bouts of deep shivers from the soaking she'd endured. Her clothes had been changed, but the wetness still lingered. She placed both elbows on the table in front of her and pressed her forehead into the heels of her hands, forcing her eyebrows and eyelids to smush together, igniting a dull pulse behind her face.

She had been over it so many times. Yes, she understood that she was possibly suffering from PTSD and maybe hearing things. Yes, she knew people's eyes played tricks on them. Yes, she knew the mind conjured up shadows in the darkness.

But she had seen something, someone. She was certain of it. It didn't feel the same as when she got lost in the place where Jane was. It felt tangible. Real. *But it wasn't. It couldn't have been.*

Soft footsteps yanked Alicen from her pose, and her heart leapt. Louise walked into the kitchen, barefoot, dressed for bed, and offered Alicen a small smile. Alicen exhaled relief and let her head fall back against her palms.

A moment passed with nothing. Alicen opened her eyes and let her hands fall away from her face. Louise stood across the kitchen, leaning against the sink. Her arms were crossed over her waist, and she was staring down at the floor, but she clearly wanted to say something.

Louise raised her gaze from the floor and met Alicen's. She held it for a beat. "I put your jeans and T-shirt in the washer. Hopefully the mud will come out with a couple of cycles."

"I could have done that," Alicen replied.

For the first time since Alicen had moved in a week ago, anger pulsed across Louise's expression. "I want you to go see Dr. Wells tomorrow," she said.

"I have a session scheduled with him on Friday already. That's just a couple days away."

"But he might be free tomorrow—"

"I don't need to talk to him tomorrow. I'm fine."

Louise bit her lip but didn't try to hide her concern.

"I swear there was someone in this house, Lou," Alicen said.

Louise's lips parted as if she were going to speak, but Alicen continued.

"Wouldn't you have chased after someone if they had been in the house?"

"If there had *actually* been someone in the house, I would have called the police," Louise said.

"Right, because you don't believe there was anyone here."

"Do you?"

Alicen opened her mouth to respond but suddenly couldn't think of anything logical to say. Of course Louise was right to ask, to be worried. Of course Alicen didn't truly believe someone had been in the house. Did she?

"Even if someone was in the house, that doesn't explain what you were doing outside," Louise said.

"I was chasing—" Alicen started.

"You know what I mean," Louise said. Her tone wasn't harsh, but it was firm. She was referring to the fetal position she'd found Alicen in. Covered in mud, soaked, cold deep below her skin. Even if Alicen could miraculously convince

Louise someone had broken into their home, what was she supposed to say to rationalize away that moment? A moment when all rationality had been lost.

Silence engulfed the two friends, Alicen unable to find words, Louise waiting for her to try. The wind whistled outside the kitchen windows, raindrops still tapping against the glass. Every couple of beats the night sky was illuminated with another strike of lightning, followed by another wave of thunder. The storm didn't look to be letting up anytime soon.

"Listen," Louise said, "I'm not trying to push you. But I know you, Alicen. I know how tight to the chest you like to keep things. And I just . . ." She paused, considering her words.

Alicen knew what she was thinking. She wanted Alicen to be less broken. But Alicen couldn't be anything other than what she was, and she *was* broken. Completely broken. She stole a glance at the wheels working behind Louise's eyes. Her friend searching for the right thing to say, the words that would help. Again Alicen was reminded of all the kindness she'd been shown. Louise deserved to believe Alicen was trying, even if Alicen knew trying was futile.

"You're right," Alicen said.

"I just . . . ," Louise said again.

"I know," Alicen reassured her.

Another batch of silence cupped the room for a long moment.

"I'll talk to Dr. Wells, but not till Friday," Alicen said.

Louise gave her another worried glance.

"I already have an appointment, but I will talk to him. I promise," Alicen said.

Louise nodded. "I hope so." She exhaled, pushed herself away from the counter, and rubbed her temples in small circles. A quiet yawn escaped from her mouth. "You need anything else before I head to bed?" she asked.

Alicen shook her head, and Louise padded toward her. She reached her hand out and gave Alicen's shoulder a tiny squeeze. "Try and get some rest, okay?"

Alicen nodded, and Louise released her hold. Alicen sat there while she listened to Louise make her way across the house to her bedroom. Listened as the old house groaned from the ongoing storm, listened as Louise fell completely silent and asleep, listened as the night got deeper and the morning closer. Alicen sat there, thinking about Jane, thinking about the shadow, thinking about her sanity, thinking about her trouble. *"All are troubled,"* Victoria had said. Alicen swallowed the truth like a pill. Troubled indeed.

• • •

"Do you feel that, Alicen?" Grandma Joe asked.

"Feel what?" Alicen was watching her feet swing back and forth over the water below as her legs dangled from the side of the wooden bridge. The sun was warm on her back, and she was happy to have taken off her yellow windbreaker and tied it around her waist. Summer was almost here, which meant no more school and plenty of trips to Red Lodge with the Watson family. Alicen was so excited she could hardly keep still.

"The power in the water," Grandma Joe said.

Alicen watched the small river below flowing by at an easy pace. This was one of their favorite spots. When her mom picked up an extra shift at work, and when it was warm enough, Grandma Joe would bring her out into the forest to their bridge. Grandma Joe had told her once that if they got lucky, magical creatures could be spotted. White bats, the size of small children, with karate skills. Alicen was always on the lookout for one, but she'd never seen any. She wondered if that was another thing that lived only in Grandma Joe's imagination.

It didn't bother Alicen that some of the things Grandma Joe talked about she couldn't always see. She wasn't too concerned with whether or not they were real. Sometimes she saw things from her imagination too. She thought maybe all kids did, and then they became adults and forgot how. But not Grandma Joe. She was special, and she said Alicen was special too.

"It just looks like water to me," Alicen said.

"You aren't looking close enough," Grandma Joe said.

Alicen pulled her head closer to her knees and stared intently at the moving liquid. It was pretty clear for a river. You couldn't see all the way to the bottom—it was too deep for that—but you could make out fish swimming close to the surface and the rocks that ran along the edges.

Alicen stared for what felt like an eternity before huffing, annoyed, and sitting back upright. "I don't see anything," she said, frustrated.

"Hmm. Well, maybe it's your eyes," Grandma Joe said.

"My eyes?" Alicen asked, squinting up at her grandmother. "Is there something wrong with them?"

Grandma Joe smiled down at her and chuckled. She reached out and placed her hands carefully on both sides of Alicen's face, her thumbs close to the outer edges of Alicen's eyes. "Not these eyes," she said as she teasingly pulled down on Alicen's cheeks, making her bottom lids stretch out.

Alicen giggled and shaped her mouth into a scary growl to match her long face. Grandma Joe released Alicen's face and tapped a single finger to the middle of Alicen's chest. "These ones," she said.

Alicen dropped her eyes to where her grandmother was pointing and scrunched her nose. "My chest?" she said, confused.

"Your heart," Grandma Joe said.

"My heart has eyes?" Alicen asked as she raised her head back up to look at her grandmother for explanation.

"Of course; everyone's does. They're the most important part of you."

Alicen tried to imagine what the eyes on her heart might look like. "How is that possible?"

"They aren't like the eyes you know; they are stronger, and they see the world differently. They use your spirit. Free of fear and condemnation."

Alicen used to think the way Grandma Joe spoke was silly, but now she found it comforting. Like she was sharing secrets with Alicen, bonding them together forever. Alicen gave her grandma a skeptical look and then shook her head. "I don't know about that. How do they see through my skin?"

Grandma Joe smiled and scooted slightly so she was sitting nearly behind Alicen. She raised her hands and gently placed them over Alicen's eyes, blotting out the world.

Alicen laughed. Was this going to be one of her grandma's games? She loved Grandma Joe's games. She could feel her body fill with excitement, and she bounced a couple times in her seated position.

"Let's practice this. Practice is important, you know. Jesus said that the eye is the lamp of the body, so if your eye is clear, your whole body will be full of light."

"I don't know what that means," Alicen said.

"It's about the way you see yourself, about the perspective you have of who you are. And how the world around you should look. When you remember to see yourself as he taught, the world is captured in grace and light; when you forget, there will be shadows. Can you see it?"

"You're covering my eyes," Alicen said through a giggle. "I can't see anything."

"Use the eyes of your heart. Look deeper, beyond your earthly vision. Use what you feel. See with your spirit. Focus on that. You got it?"

Alicen nodded.

"Now, what do you see?" Grandma Joe asked.

Alicen searched hard, picturing the backs of her eyelids, though she didn't really know what they looked like. She listened to the sounds around her, felt the wind on her skin, the sun spreading across her knees. She wanted to see with her heart, wanted to believe in all her grandmother was talking about, so she strained harder, until something broke through. Alicen gasped, her little mouth expanding, as the corners pulled up with glee.

"Listen carefully, because you're going to need to remember

this many times as you grow," Grandma Joe said. "The warmth filling your heart right now, the light filling your vision, it comes from the perfect love that created you. A love that tells you who you are. A love the world has forgotten."

"I'll never forget," Alicen said.

Grandma Joe let her hands fall, and Alicen tilted her chin up to see tears filling her grandmother's eyes. Grandma Joe stroked Alicen's cheek and softly bopped the tip of her nose.

Concern filled Alicen's frame. She jumped up, spun toward Grandma Joe, and wrapped her arms around the old woman's neck. Grandma Joe pulled her close and placed a sweet kiss on Alicen's bare shoulder.

"I'll never forget," Alicen said again.

"I know, sweet girl," Grandma Joe whispered. "I know."

• • •

The bell dinged overhead as Alicen pushed open the glass entry to the small corner market. The smell of freshly baked cookies filled her senses, and she smiled. It always smelled like Christmas in this little store, no matter the time of year. When Alicen was young, she and Louise used to beg until Mrs. Watson gave each of them a dollar so they could come get whatever fresh-out-of-the-oven treat Mrs. Goldenberg, the store owner, had baked that morning. Her daughter now ran the place, but clearly Mrs. Goldenberg was still making warm treats, or maybe the walls had just absorbed the permanent delicious smell? Alicen knew she would have to investigate.

Corner Market, perfectly named without a trace of originality, was only a couple storefronts up from the Watsons' bookstore, and after working most of the morning, Alicen had offered to grab them something to eat while Louise finished up cataloging. The little shop didn't offer much selection, but the food was good and homemade. That was worth more than a whole menu full of options.

Alicen smiled at the middle-aged woman behind the checkout counter and started toward the deli. Some small subs and a salad to share sounded good. She took her time, glancing up and down the aisles at the couple of other faces in the store. Her mind wandered, remembering the way her sneakers used to screech across the tiled floor and the way Lou's eyes had always been bigger than her stomach.

The morning had found Louise and Alicen much more relaxed. Alicen had only gotten a couple hours of sleep, confronted with another strange dream of her grandmother, but she'd played it off and forced her most positive attitude so as not to conjure any more worry from Louise. They'd headed to the bookstore after breakfast and had been a solid, well-functioning team as they'd continued to divide and conquer. The sheer number of things stuffed into every corner of the bookstore was alarming. They were nowhere near finished, but it was good to be focused on something outside of herself.

"Alicen?" someone called from behind.

Alicen turned her head to see a dark-skinned, elderly woman, short, with silver hair and painted-on dark-purple lipstick smiling at her, a small wicker basket clutched in one hand. The woman wasn't familiar to Alicen, but she clearly knew who Alicen was and seemed surprised to see her.

"Oh my goodness, it is you. Alicen Reese—well, I'll be, and in Red Lodge, of all places," the woman said.

Alicen smiled politely. "I'm sorry; have we met?"

"Not in several decades. I'm Annie Beckered. I'm just in town for the day. I knew your grandmother back in Billings, before her . . ." The woman took a pause. "Before she changed."

Annie's direct statement stirred the pain brewing in Alicen's chest.

"You were so little then; I don't expect you to remember me. Why would you?" Annie asked with a slight laugh. "Silly of me to even consider it."

Alicen smiled again, unsure how to respond.

"What brings you back to this old place? I would have never in my wildest dreams imagined running into you here. Of all places," the old woman rambled. "How is your mother? You really do favor her, you know. I bet people tell you that all the time."

"She's fine," Alicen answered when the woman finally paused.

"Oh, good. I always liked that Betty Reese. Good head on her shoulders, especially all things considered."

Again, pain pinched at the insides of Alicen's ribs. She opened her mouth to interject before Annie continued, but the woman couldn't be stopped.

"It was an awful situation your mother got dealt, with Josephine and all. Can you imagine losing your mother to such a state? You know, before it all happened, your grandmother and I went to church together, so I tried to offer help to your mother where I could. It seemed like the least I could do. You being so young, and your mother all on her own. I don't know how she managed it all without losing all her own sanity."

Alicen tried once more to interrupt the intrusive woman's word vomit but to no avail.

"I was glad your mother kept you away from here after Josephine passed. My condolences, of course. Such a tragedy, the whole thing, and surprising. To see such a lovely Christian woman lose her mind in such a way. Terrible, really terrible."

Alicen had had enough. "Yes, thank you," she said. "I actually really need to get going, though, Mrs. Beckered."

Annie let out a shrill chuckle and raised her hand. "Of course you do, dear. Here I am rambling on about things of the past, holding you up. It's wonderful to have bumped into you. You know, I read somewhere that these situations affect the children most, so I'm thrilled to see you doing so well."

Alicen forced a smile and bit back her growing fear.

"You tell that wonderful mother of yours I said hello, will you?" Annie said.

"Of course."

Annie reached out and gave Alicen's forearm a squeeze. "It really is so good to see you, child. If you need anything while you're in town, you let me know."

Alicen nodded with another forced smile. Annie returned the gesture and released Alicen's arm. Alicen didn't hesitate; she pushed passed the elderly woman, desperate to leave the small store that suddenly seemed to be closing in around her.

8

Alicen left the small corner market empty-handed, brain on full cylinders. Against all her efforts, painful memories from the past were being dragged into the present. Alicen could still remember when Principal Higgins had knocked on her seventh-grade classroom door and announced he needed to see Alicen in his office.

As she had followed the principal down the hallway, somewhere in the back of her mind she'd sensed whatever was coming next would change her. Alicen had carried a strange sense of knowledge about it the days leading up to her grandmother's death. The two of them had been connected. In a way that was different than she'd experienced with anyone else. Until Jane.

Josephine Reese, known to most as Grandma Joe, had been sick according to the rest of the world. She saw things that weren't there, talked to herself, raved about being called to change the world. But she hadn't always been that way. It seemed to come on suddenly and then changed her completely. As if something had come to life in her that had been dormant before.

People whispered about what it might be. Schizophrenia. Delirium. Dementia. Nothing was ever confirmed. Grandma Joe refused medical attention, and without ever being a harm to herself or others, she couldn't be forced to seek treatment. That didn't stop the town from buzzing about her perceived insanity, though. People could be so cruel. Once a lively part of the community, Josephine was cast out and marked as a "nut."

It had been too much for Alicen's grandfather. After years of fighting with Josephine, he'd given up and left, forcing Betty, a single mother, to move back to her childhood home in Billings with four-year-old Alicen in tow.

Maybe it was because she was so young or because they had bonded so quickly, but Alicen never remembered thinking Grandma Joe was anything other than wonderful. She'd just felt the unconditional love of a grandmother, a love she lacked from her mother. Alicen thought the stars rose and fell with Josephine.

The schoolyard did a good job of reminding Alicen that Grandma Joe was different. Children could be mean, all too willing to repeat what they'd heard their parents whisper around the dinner table.

Alicen had always come to her grandmother's defense. People just didn't know her the way Alicen did. Not even her only daughter. Alicen had loved the old woman fiercely and so had felt a responsibility for her. They'd spend hours in the backyard, lying under the clouds, counting the stars, listening to the wind, searching for more.

Sometimes Louise joined them. Stephanie Watson was one of the only mothers in town who wasn't afraid Grandma Joe would infect her child. That was one of the reasons Lou and Alicen had become so close. There had been a time when Grandma Joe and Lou were Alicen's only friends, and they were enough for her.

Everything was different after Josephine died. Brain aneurysm. Sudden and swift. She was there and then she wasn't. Nobody said it, but you could see it in their eyes. *It was her crazy that got her in the end.* Alicen's mother had taken Josephine's sudden death poorly. Even with all their differences, it broke her heart.

A couple of months later, it was time for another change, and Betty had dragged Alicen away from everything she'd known to the great state of California to "start over." Alicen had been right to carry a sense of foreboding in the days leading up to her grandmother's death. Everything had changed after that; the magic of the world had been erased, and Alicen had been forced to grow up, to face reality.

A car rolled by slowly, yanking Alicen back to the lonely streets of Red Lodge. She tried to shake away the memories as the sun warmed her shoulders and the breeze tickled her cheeks. But the past was hard to lock back in its box.

A sound disrupted her efforts to regain control. Something was chirping, painfully it seemed, and close by. Alicen took a couple steps forward, following the noise. She thought it was echoing out from the narrow alleyway that stretched between the Watsons' bookstore and Gina's Gems, the jewelry store beside it.

Alicen crossed in front of Gina's Gems and turned her head down the alley. It was empty. The sound came again, surely from the small walkable space between the buildings, and Alicen searched for its source. Her eyes caught something twitching slightly, about halfway down, and Alicen stepped around the bricked corner toward it.

Her chest ballooned with sympathy as she got closer. A tiny bird, barely hopping away from her. It tried to move its wing, but only one opened; the other must have been broken. It chirped even louder as Alicen approached, and she slowed, not to scare it to death. Not that it had much chance at this point. The sight broke her heart. Death of something so innocent seemed cruel.

She was surprised by how affected she felt and inhaled deeply as tears dotted her vision. *Get a grip; birds die,* she thought. *That's just what happens.* She closed her eyes, the bird's sad cries ringing faintly against the sky, and tried to wash away what had happened to her in the last hour. Enough thinking about Grandma Joe, enough thinking about the past. Enough.

Alicen opened her eyes and her breath caught in her throat. A little girl stood at the end of the alleyway. A white dress hung just above her knees, a thin bow around her waist, her face bright, her eyes golden, with low pigtails tied at either side of her neck. She couldn't be older than ten. She was staring at Alicen, and a deep knowing sank into Alicen's mind. She had stared at Alicen before.

Several thoughts collided at once. She should run; she should call for help; she should scream at this child; she should drag her back to Louise to prove she wasn't crazy. She *wasn't* crazy—here the girl stood, the shadow that had lingered in the house during the storm.

Another thought dropped into the chaos: What if she was still just a lingering shadow? If someone else stepped into the alley, would they see the little girl too?

No, Alicen thought, she had to be real. She was only a yard in front of her, her dress being blown by the wind, her hair being tugged by the breeze, her eyes blinking. She was real, and she had been in Alicen's home.

A small sliver of anger pushed through the madness, enough that Alicen raised her finger and found her voice. "You . . . you broke into my house."

"It isn't your house," the little girl said.

Her voice carried to Alicen, and she felt her heart ram inside her chest. She spoke like she was real.

"But I live there, and I saw you," Alicen said.

The girl tilted her chin slightly and pressed forward onto her toes and then back to her heels. "Do you like living there?"

"What?"

"It's very pretty. I mean, I think so. Don't you think so?"

Alicen huffed in disbelief, and her anger grew. "Do your parents know you were out breaking into my house?"

"It's not your house."

Fury boiled up through Alicen's face and she took a step forward. The stilled bird scurried to life, chirping hastily and trying to flee.

"Stop," the little girl said and moved down the alley toward the pitiful creature. Alicen took a couple steps back as the child approached and felt embarrassed at how much her pulse increased. It was just a child, for goodness' sake. Then again, this particular child was clearly a delinquent. The girl slowed and approached the bird on tiptoes until she was standing over the tiny feathered beast.

"What is your name? Where are your parents?" Alicen barked. Again the bird panicked.

"Shh," the little girl said. "You're scaring him."

Alicen watched as the child dropped to a squat and reached out her hands toward the bird.

"No," Alicen said, stepping forward. "Don't touch it; it might hurt you."

The girl giggled, a sound too familiar for Alicen to ignore, and her heart began racing again.

"He won't hurt me," the child said. She scooped it into both hands and closed her palms around the small animal. "I'm going to fix him." She stood and kept her eyes on her clasped hands.

A chill ran the length of Alicen's skin as unease filled her. "What do you mean?"

"You're asking me all the wrong questions," the girl said,

lifting her eyes to meet Alicen's. Their golden color captured Alicen's ability to speak and rooted her heels to the cement.

"Who are you?" Alicen whispered.

The girl shook her head. "Wrong again. Not who am I. The question is: who are *you*?"

"What kind of question is that?" Alicen asked.

"The only one there is."

Dozens of faint whispers filled the air around their heads, coming seemingly from nowhere and everywhere at once. The girl glanced over her shoulder, listened, and then looked back to Alicen.

"I have to go," she said.

Alicen glanced to the place where the child had turned her eyes and saw nothing. So many questions whirled themselves at Alicen's skull, she wondered if she would have permanent bruises from the onslaught. The little girl turned and started away from Alicen, back down the alley. The choir of whispers faded as she walked away, the little bird still cupped in her hands.

The war raging inside Alicen's brain roared. *You should go after her, stop her, demand to see her parents, drag her to the corner market. This is a small town; someone will know her; you should admit this isn't real, that she's in your head. You're seeing things; you're losing your mind; this is your own private form of madness.*

"Alicen," the little girl called and silenced all the rambling thoughts in Alicen's head. She gazed at the girl, who was now at the opposite end of the alley.

"Remember: when the eye is clear, the whole body is full

of light," the girl said as she dropped to her knees, unclenched her hands, and placed the little bird on the ground. Then she stood and stepped around the corner and out of sight.

Alicen stood, watching after her, letting her words sink in. The bird hopped, drawing Alicen's attention. It shook all its feathers and then sprang up and took to the sky. Its wing anything but broken.

• • •

Dr. Wells's office was larger than Alicen had expected. It had warm burnt-orange walls, dark hardwood floors, three large bay windows that overlooked the long rolling lawn of the Clover Mountain Retreat Center, and wood furniture with light-tan cushions, comfortable and clean.

She'd been escorted in a couple of minutes ago, told by the sweet nurse that Dr. Wells was on his way from the other side of campus and would be here shortly. Alicen didn't mind waiting; she had been early anyway.

When she'd woken up this morning and realized it was Friday, a knot of dread had started forming in her gut. She'd battled it the only way she knew how, by letting herself succumb to numbness. She had been doing that often over the last thirty-six hours. Ever since a little girl had healed a dying bird in an alley.

Impossible. Just like that same little girl appearing in her house was impossible, and hearing little voices was impossible. Alicen had experienced more impossibilities in the last few weeks than she had in her entire lifetime. So either she was turning into a wizard, which seemed unlikely, or she really was losing her mind.

Alicen chuckled at her own joke just as Dr. Wells pushed open his office door.

"Something funny?" he said, walking in and shutting the door behind him.

Alicen jumped slightly at his sudden presence and moved her eyes to meet his. He was sporting a casual look similar to what he'd worn the first time they'd met: nice denim, light-blue button-down, no tie, simple black loafers. His dark gray hair was managed, his face clean-shaven. He looked approachable and easygoing. She wished his appearance would help her feel at ease, but the knot remained.

"Oh, it's nothing," Alicen said.

"Bummer," Dr. Wells replied, heading for his desk across the office to place the stack of folders he was carrying inside the top drawer. "I could use a good joke this morning."

"That makes two of us," Alicen said.

Dr. Wells smiled, walked over to where Alicen was sitting, and sat in the plush chair opposite her. She avoided eye contact and acted like she was searching the room, which she had already done. She cleared her throat and pointed to a framed photo perched on one of the bookshelves' panels. It was of a much younger Dr. Wells and two aged companions.

"Are those your parents?" she asked.

His eyes followed her finger and he nodded. "Yep."

"Are they from here?"

"No, Boston," he said. "My entire family has been there for generations."

"I've never been."

"It's cold."

Alicen gave an awkward laugh, followed by a strained cough. Her heart had started beating against her rib cage, her pulse ramming under her skin. She would rather be any place on earth than here.

"What brought you to Red Lodge?" Alicen asked. It was a stupid question, of course. She already knew the answer.

"I worked in the Boston area after school for many years before I heard about Clover Mountain Retreat Center through an old graduate-school classmate and decided to give it a try. I was looking for a change of scenery, and I've always loved the mountains."

"Do you miss Boston?" Alicen couldn't stop the questions from falling out of her mouth, and Dr. Wells continued to humor her.

"I miss the pizza and the Red Sox; otherwise, small-town life seems to suit me. What about you? Do you miss Santa Monica?"

And so the questions turned to her. Silence filled the room as Dr. Wells waited for Alicen to answer. What was she supposed to say? Yes, because she had given birth to Jane there. No, because she had killed her there too.

"Let's try something different," Dr. Wells said. "How's the transition back to Montana been going? Are you enjoying reconnecting with Louise?"

Alicen swallowed and nodded. "Yeah, it's been fine."

"You're helping her with the bookstore in town, right? How's that going?"

"Fine."

"The summer home as well?"

"Yep."

"Good; I'm sure having something to do is helpful."

Alicen nodded.

"And how are you sleeping?" Dr. Wells asked.

Alicen's mind betrayed her as it replayed the last several restless nights on repeat. Every time she was about to fade to sleep, her imagination, combined with her memories, haunted her into a wakeful state. Along with insanity, exhaustion was also putting down permanent roots.

"Where did your mind go just then?" Dr. Wells asked.

Alicen considered telling him the truth but quickly thought better of it. "I liked it better when we were talking about you," Alicen said.

Dr. Wells nodded. "Okay; is there something else you want to know?"

Alicen pondered his question before speaking. "Why this? Why pick this career?"

Dr. Wells paused and thoughtfully considered her question. "Because I believe in change," he said. "I believe in second chances, that peace is obtainable after tragedy."

Alicen could feel herself losing control of her emotions. "Have you ever faced tragedy, Dr. Wells?" Sorrow made her throat feel like it was closing, and she pushed a sharp breath past it.

"Not like you," he answered honestly. He let his words sit in the air for a moment before softening his tone and continuing. "The loss of a child is not a pain that I think can be erased. However, I do believe it can be survived. Maybe I can help you learn to survive."

He held Alicen's gaze, and she was captured by the honest hope his eyes reflected. More hope than she'd seen in a long time, and she could feel her soul longing for some of it. She suddenly wanted to pour her heart out to him, beg him to help her, believe that help was possible. But something held her back.

"You can't," Alicen said before she could stop herself. She knew his hope was wasted on her.

"And why is that?" Dr. Wells asked.

"I have nothing to survive for." The truth stung to say out loud, but again Alicen couldn't keep the words locked inside.

"Don't you believe *you're* worth surviving for?" Dr. Wells asked.

"You wouldn't be asking me that if you knew what I had done."

Dr. Wells pondered this for a moment. "Why don't you tell me, and then I'll decide if that's true or not."

The open floodgate of honesty slammed shut, the flow rushing to a halt. Alicen wanted to be done talking. She may be forced to endure these sessions, but she wasn't required to share. And she'd said too much already. Her prickly defense rose up to intercept whatever she may have said next, and she coughed instead. She crossed her arms over her chest and dropped her eyes from the kind doctor's face.

Uncomfortable silence filled the office for several long moments, and Alicen refused to be the first to break it. She could feel Dr. Wells's eyes but held fast to her conviction and continued to let her hard nature drive.

"Okay," Dr. Wells said. "We'll just leave it there for now."

He reached for the folded sheet of paper that rested on the small side table to the left of his chair. Alicen hadn't even noticed it until now. He unfolded it and glanced quickly across whatever he saw, then back to Alicen.

"What if we talk about your family?" Dr. Wells asked.

Another wave of ice filled Alicen's throat. *Why would he want to talk about that?* "What does that have to do with anything?" Alicen snapped. Her words rushed out sharper than she would have liked. Sharper than was probably appropriate for an adult.

"It's a good place to start when getting to know someone," he replied. "It'll give me a better picture of where you've been."

"In hopes of helping me discover how I got here?" Alicen mocked. Again her internal maturity scolded her. Responding like a rebellious teenager was not helping.

To her surprise, Dr. Wells let out a soft chuckle and nodded. "You've done this before. It's good to know you'll keep me on my toes, then."

Alicen dared to make eye contact with the doctor. He was watching her casually, waiting for her to make the next move, to open up, to get comfortable. He was going to be waiting for a while. Now that she'd let the cold demeanor seep in, she refused to budge.

Dr. Wells gave a knowing nod, as if Alicen's thought had been projected for him to see. "I think that's enough for today." He stood, and Alicen followed suit. Dr. Wells walked across the room to where the door was and opened it. A bit surprised he wasn't going to insist she share her every thought, Alicen crossed the office to exit. She felt obligated to pause before leaving, and she and Dr. Wells shared another moment of eye contact.

"Like I mentioned, we can take this as slow as you like," he said and then smiled. "I'll see you in a couple days."

Alicen wanted to argue, but she had nothing to say. She just nodded and left, listening to the click of the doctor's door shutting behind her.

9

Alicen didn't feel completely at ease until she was safely parked in front of the summer home. She had gotten away pretty much unscathed from her meeting with Dr. Wells. She'd managed to escape without crumbling into a pile of crazy. She'd kept her emotions in check. Yet she still felt irritatingly vulnerable. Up until she pulled into the driveway, she felt as though a piece of her was showing. A piece she had worked very hard to keep hidden.

The setting sun was darkening the sky, and Alicen thought the fatigue swimming under her skin was strong enough that sleep might actually find her tonight.

She got out, shut the car door, clicked the button on the

key to lock it, and headed up the steps to the front porch. She was hungry and relieved that all she had to do until the sun rose tomorrow was worry about trying to sleep. Louise had given her a key, and she used it to let herself in.

"Hello," Alicen called, shutting the door behind her. She twisted the lock, listening to it secure with a click, and tossed Louise's car keys into the small glass bowl on the front entry table. "Lou?"

"In the kitchen," Louise replied.

"Please tell me you're not cooking; I'm way too hungry for your cooking," Alicen teased, walking through the sitting room and toward the brightly lit kitchen. Louise was standing inside the room, a glass of water in hand, her face bearing a strange expression.

"I was just kidding," Alicen said. "With enough salt I'm sure it'll be fine." She smiled at her own wit, but Louise didn't respond in kind. Alicen stepped into the kitchen and opened her mouth to apologize, but someone else spoke first.

"Alicen," a voice called from the corner.

Alicen froze. She knew that voice. It always managed to make her feel like she was being scolded even before she had done anything. She turned and saw her mother standing up from the chair where she'd been sitting at the kitchen table. She stole a glance back at Louise, where a mixture of anger and sympathy were working their way across her friend's eyes.

"Betty," Alicen said.

"*Mom*, Alicen; at a time like this a daughter should call her mother *Mom*," Betty said.

It hadn't even taken ten seconds for the critiquing to

begin. Alicen wanted to run away and smack the woman at the same time, a reaction she'd become accustomed to over the years. "What are you doing here?" Alicen asked.

"I wanted to check on you. I was worried, dear."

"Worried?"

"Don't say that like you're surprised. I'm still your mother."

"Don't worry, *Mom*; I couldn't forget that." Alicen could feel her temper getting the best of her.

Her mother raised her eyebrows as if to say, *Watch your tone*, and Alicen regretted her words immediately. As good as it might feel to rake the woman over hot coals, she knew from experience that making Betty angry was never a good idea. It was incredible the way her mother could give her the smallest look and suddenly Alicen was ten years old again, striving for her mom's approval—approval that was impossible to obtain.

"You shouldn't worry," Alicen said.

"Of course I should worry. After everything you've been through the last four months."

"You could have just called; there was no reason to fly all the way here."

"I needed to see you for myself. Besides," Betty said, casting a glance around the kitchen, "I haven't been back here in decades. This place hasn't changed at all."

"I'm surprised you remember," Louise said. Her tone had a bite to it, and Alicen had to hide her glee. It wasn't a secret how Louise felt about Betty, and unlike Alicen, Louise couldn't care less about Betty's impossible approval. Alicen was happy she didn't have to face her mother alone.

If looks could kill, Louise would be choking on the kitchen floor, but Betty's expression didn't even seem to faze her. She smiled at Betty and took a sip from her glass, waiting for whatever catty response Betty whipped out.

Betty just smiled back. "Of course I remember. A beautiful house like this isn't soon forgotten. It'll be a real shame when they tear it down."

Alicen knew that one stung, but Louise kept it hidden well.

Betty let the barb linger for a moment before continuing. "Lou, would you mind getting me a glass of whiskey or red wine—anything with a kick? Flying always gives me the worst headaches, and would you believe, they refused to bump me to first class from Denver to Billings, so I flew coach, which I haven't done in years."

Alicen swallowed, trying to mask the tension building in her shoulders.

"Actually, this is a dry house. We don't have anything like that around," Louise said. "But I'd be happy to get you some iced tea, water, coffee?"

"Dry house?" Betty said, looking from Louise to Alicen. "Why on earth?"

Alicen could feel her face turning red and knew that Louise was mere moments away from coming over the counter at Betty.

Betty sensed the discomfort and gave Alicen a questioning look. "This is because of your tiny incident? Baby, you got help for that. Surely you don't have to be sober your whole life?"

"It was more than a tiny incident, Betty, which you would know, had you bothered to come to Santa Monica earlier this year," Louise said.

Betty cut her eyes at Louise and took a step toward Alicen. "Had my daughter needed me, I would have been there. But you," she said, turning the blame on Alicen, "told me you were fine."

Louise huffed in disbelief and grumbled to the sink, where she slammed her cup inside violently.

"Listen, Louise Watson—" Betty started.

Louise spun around, ready for whatever Betty had planned to hurl at her, and Alicen knew she had to intervene.

"Both of you, enough," Alicen said, stepping between them and into their line of sight. "This isn't helping." Alicen turned to her mother. "The doctor recommended that I stay completely sober for a while, so I'm taking his advice; that's all. But if you want to go get something to keep in the house, you are more than welcome to. I'm fine."

"Alicen—" Louise cautioned.

Alicen twisted her neck to send a sharp look to her friend. "Lou," she warned, "I'm fine."

Louise didn't look happy, but she left it alone.

Alicen turned back to her mother and waited.

"Doctors aren't always right, you know," Betty said, needing to validate herself. "But if it's helping you, then I can play by the rules."

"Thank you," Alicen said.

Thick silence filled the kitchen. Tension heavy enough to drag the three women to the floor hung in the air. On the rare occasion that Betty apologized first, it was only because it served her in some fashion. When she turned to Lou and said she was sorry for snapping, Alicen knew it was only to get back in their good graces because she needed a place to stay. There was a hotel in town, but it surely wasn't up to her mother's outlandish expectations.

Louise nodded to accept Betty's apology. "I assume you're not planning to drive back to Billings tonight," Louise said.

"No, I was hoping to stay in Red Lodge," Betty said.

Louise shared a look with Alicen, asking with her eyes if she was okay with her mother under the same roof as her, and Alicen nodded.

"I'll go fix up a bed in an upstairs guest room," Louise said and excused herself.

"Oh, that would be wonderful," Betty said as Louise stepped out of the kitchen, leaving mother and daughter alone.

"I'm sorry, Alicen," Betty said. "I didn't mean to cause such a scene right away."

"It's fine, Mom," Alicen said.

Betty stepped across the kitchen and reached for her daughter. She pulled her into her motherly embrace, and Alicen obliged. A quick hug and Betty was pulling back. She touched her daughter's cheek, then tucked a loose strand of hair behind Alicen's ear. A gesture she had done ever since Alicen was a little girl. An effort to make her more presentable. Polished. Alicen hated it.

She took in her mother's face. She really did favor her: same dirty-blonde hair, same blue eyes, same long face, same freckled nose. Both were average height and slim, because being slim was important. Alicen had learned that from her mother. Slim, pretty, and desirable. All were key in capturing the kind of life a woman deserved. A lot of good any of that had done Alicen.

"It really is good to see you, baby," Betty said.

Alicen smiled.

"Are you still talking to someone? Are you feeling okay?" Betty asked.

Daughters shouldn't have to lie to their mothers, but Alicen and Betty weren't like most. Betty didn't actually want the truth; she just wanted to hear what would make her feel best.

"I'm feeling good, and yes, I'm still talking to someone," Alicen said.

Betty's face broke out into a wide smile. "That's good." She brushed her fingers through the ends of Alicen's hair again. "You know, I just want you to move past this and on with your life. Find a good man, have more children—you know, be happy."

Each word felt like a slap across Alicen's face. And it was made worse by the fact that Betty wholeheartedly meant what she said. Alicen fought back tears and dropped her eyes from her mother's face. She nodded to appease the woman and tried not to cringe when Betty leaned forward and placed a kiss on her forehead.

Betty released her daughter and took a step back. "Now, I am exhausted. You know how traveling can be. I think I'll just go lie down for a bit."

"Do you want us to wait on you for dinner?" Alicen asked.

"No, I ate on the plane, but that is sweet of you to think of your mother. Will you help me with my bags, dear?"

"Of course," Alicen said. She had switched to autopilot, a function she reserved strictly for her mother. Being her daughter was a role that took more than it ever gave.

• • •

"Thank you, Dr. Wells," Victoria said. "That will be all."

The older man nodded and turned to head back down the hall toward his office. It was always a sensitive process, bringing on a new member to the Clover Mountain Retreat Center staff. There was a particular way of doing things, and Victoria didn't have patience for suggested adjustments. Thankfully, Dr. Wells had yet to make any such requests and was complying with all of hers. She didn't predict that he would be a problem, but it was still very early. He had only just had his first session with Alicen.

A small group of chatting nurses turned the corner, and their conversation fell hushed as they offered Victoria knowing, polite smiles. She didn't return the gesture. It wasn't a requirement that people like her, only that they respect her. That was the way her uncle Donald had run the facility when he was head administrator, and Victoria now mimicked his leading. The nurses' conversation picked back up after they had passed Victoria and put a safe distance between them.

There had been a time when she'd longed for companionship with those who lived and worked on campus. But that was before she'd learned her truth. She hadn't understood the reasons Uncle Donald had kept her separate from others until those reasons had made themselves crystal clear to her. One more thing her uncle had been right about. Turned out, he'd been right about everything.

Victoria glanced at her watch. It was time. She walked down the hallway, turned the corner, and stepped into a large, open common room. Patients dotted the area. Nurses and visitors accompanied some; others occupied space alone. She could feel how her presence drew eyes as she crossed the room and exited through the back door to the outstretching grassy landscape.

The air was still, the afternoon sun coming down from its high perch in the sky. Her feet moved down the path from memory. She'd grown up on these outside paths, knew every inch of the campus; every room was familiar to her. None more than the small, humble cabin that occupied the back left corner of the property. The home she'd been brought to live in with her uncle.

She had spotty memories of her life before Clover Mountain. None of them were pleasant; none of them she liked to dwell on. Her father, Donald's younger brother, and her mother had been trash. And they'd done what trash did: cluttered the earth and left their toxic mark on the planet even after their deaths. Victoria had been that stain, and she'd spent the last twenty-five years trying to clean up her space.

Everyone in town could tell the story of poor Victoria Flowers. The child whose abusive, drunken father had shot and killed his wife and teenage son before turning the gun on himself after a bender late one night in October. All that remained after the violent implosion was a trembling six-year-old girl hidden in her bedroom closet. A tragic story indeed.

People had often said how lucky Victoria was to have survived. Some luck, she thought. Her father had simply forgotten she was there to execute. An unfortunate side effect of being powerless and unseen. Traits that had followed her into her teenage years. Traits she'd finally destroyed. She wasn't powerless and unseen anymore. She'd made sure of that.

A couple minutes' walk now separated her from the large main building that stood in the center of campus as the small house she'd called home came into view. A shiver ran down her spine, and she bit back the twitch that threatened to claim her.

She could still remember the day she'd been brought to Clover Mountain. The pudgy social worker with frayed, graying hair and dull brown eyes had told Victoria she was fortunate as she'd driven her decaying tan car onto the campus.

"Having a family member willing to claim custody of ya," she'd said, "that makes you blessed in my world. Don't screw it up, kid."

If only you had taken her advice, little Victoria.

Victoria swallowed back her uncle's haunting voice and approached the cabin door. She dug for the key in her pocket. Her hand twitched. She paused before placing the key into its slot and let her conflicting emotions swirl through her chest. To be so drawn to a place—a place that had served as her only source of comfort—but also to fear it was deeply chilling. She took a breath and slipped the key into the dead bolt. *Click.*

The wooden door used to feel much heavier. She used to be much smaller. Weaker. Unable to defend against the darkness in the world. She'd gained some strength since then, and now the door pushed open with ease.

Victoria stepped inside and flicked a nearby switch, illuminating the open bottom floor. It was modest; a midsize kitchen that bled into a dining room and sitting area occupied most of the space on the first level. The upper floor, easily reached by the narrow staircase against the left wall, was composed of three bedrooms and a single bathroom. Normal, Victoria had assumed. Nothing unusual about the place she'd called home.

But then the things that made homes suspicious were never seen at first glance. People didn't usually set their dirty laundry out on the couch. They hid it in their closets and sheds. Sealed with locks and fake smiles. The real trouble was found in the lessons taught and punishments received away from the watchful eyes of the neighbors. Not that the neighbors were watching very often. They were too busy covering up their own secrets.

Trips down memory lane, I see.

Victoria huffed and shook off her uncle's voice.

She's bewitched you.

No, Victoria thought, *I've barely spoken to her.*

True, but you know her. You're the same. Your trouble is the same.

Victoria's chin twitched, and she walked deeper into the

cabin. She made her usual rounds. Checking to make sure everything was exactly as she'd left it. She didn't stay here most nights. In fact, she couldn't remember the last time she'd slept in this place.

She spent nights on the couch in her office, and the attached bathroom and closet served well enough for everything else. But she still came here daily. It was part of a sort of routine that had developed. The cabin had been left to her with the assumption that she would move in. Victoria had considered remodeling it a couple of times but never could pull the trigger. She didn't want it to change, but she couldn't stand to be here in the state it was in, either.

She took the stairs up to the second floor and without slowing turned the corner to the room at the end of the hall. The door was closed. It was always closed. She paused before opening it, something else she often did, as if preparing herself for him not to be there.

Some days she wished he would be. Others she was glad he wasn't. Victoria twisted the knob, opened the door, and was met with the same stale smell that always occupied her uncle's bedroom. She didn't step over the threshold; she was afraid to. A product of learning her place early. Even without him there, it felt like breaking a rule.

Following rules is for your benefit. Hate to become like your father, wouldn't you?

"I'm not my father," Victoria whispered.

I had such hopes that you wouldn't be.

"He was a worm, filth; both of them were."

Yes, and you came to me with their filth. I tried to make you clean.

"You failed."

No, little Victoria, you *failed.*

A pulse of guilt spiked through her chest. Flashes from her past flittered through the hallway behind her like holograms. She turned and watched as a smaller version of herself trembled under the vicious force of her uncle's wrath. He'd never needed to lay a violent hand on her; his words had been enough. They had drenched her soul and reminded her of what she was. He'd been trying to make her better. Trying to help her pay for the sins of her father.

And he'd succeeded. Just not in the way he'd thought.

He was right; she had failed, but she had fixed it. And she'd helped others fix their failures as well. Pay back their debts. She'd helped them make amends for their darkness. Deal with their trouble. Live out what was owed of them. A smile crept over her mouth, and she shut her uncle's bedroom door.

And you believe you can fix her?

Victoria swallowed as she moved toward the bedroom she no longer slept in. She opened the door without hesitation and stepped inside. It was dim, the light from outside barely piercing the shades as they swayed from the overhead air-conditioning vent.

"Why do you keep bringing her up?"

There was a pause before he returned. *Does she remind you of who you are?*

Victoria pushed back the painful memories that her uncle's voice was drawing to the surface.

Of what you've done?

Anger rolled in her chest. When she'd been a child, his verbal abuse had driven her to strive harder for his affection. She shuddered to think of it now in these dark familiar hallways and chased the memories away.

Then they'd committed their evil. Knowing what she was and what that meant, Victoria had destroyed any trace of it. And then she'd needed to destroy her uncle, too.

The love she longed for so desperately had changed to hate. The plan had come to her in the dark hours of morning, shifting and formulating. It took her a decade to build up the strength and set her plan into motion. Constantly reminding herself there was no other solution until she believed it. Patience had been key. Control, which gave her steady resolve and absolution.

Ethylene glycol, commonly found in antifreeze, was easy to extract, odorless, colorless, and sweet. Slipped into his tea, just enough so that it took months. Slowly metabolizing to razor crystals that sliced and diced his kidneys.

His death had been ruled kidney failure. Not uncommon in a man his age, and without the proper testing machinery, which the hospital in Red Lodge didn't have, there was no way to detect the poison. And no suspicion to press the matter. Her uncle had been a master at keeping dirty laundry hidden.

Victoria snapped closed the perfectly kept box of hidden secrets that lay in her brain and rolled her neck around, letting the motion press out the terror that had almost been unleashed. She was still in control. Even though the familiar spots of pain ached on her scarred wrists. She was still in control. Even as pictures of the sharp tools she kept hidden away in her dresser materialized behind her eyes. She was still in control. He was taunting her with her old weakness.

Her teacher and bully.

"She reminds me of what I'm capable of doing," Victoria said. "I'll fix her."

If you don't, there'll be hell to pay. And you'll be paying it.

"I will."

You're weak, little Victoria.

"I was strong enough to kill you and erase your stain."

Her uncle's voice fizzled out, and Victoria felt a familiar buzz of power circulate through her body. She inhaled and closed the door to her bedroom, moving back toward the stairs.

Yes, she thought, she was in control of everything.

10

Something tugged on Alicen's shoulder, shaking her softly and rousing her from sleep. She opened her eyes slowly. The room was covered in darkness except for a tiny sliver of moonlight piercing through a broken shade. Alicen lifted her head off the pillow and strained with tired eyes to gaze around the room.

Someone shifted out from the dark corner and into the single strand of silver light. The girl—same small white dress, same pigtails. She moved toward the bed on tiptoes as Alicen pushed herself up to a sitting position. Somewhere in her mind she thought maybe she should be afraid. But she wasn't. In fact, she didn't even feel surprised. *Odd,* she thought.

"What—?" Alicen started.

The little girl put a finger over her lips, and Alicen obeyed.

"Follow me," the girl whispered and started creeping toward the door.

"Where are we going?" Alicen whispered back.

The girl glanced over her shoulder, and even in the dark, Alicen could see the twinkle of adventure in the corner of her eye. "You have to follow to find out."

Alicen felt herself smiling and pulled back the sheets from her bed, placed her feet on the floor, and grabbed her sweater before tiptoeing after the child. Again, a tiny warning signaled somewhere in the caverns of her brain, but Alicen ignored it. She followed the girl carefully down the stairs, through the hallway, and out onto the back porch. Once outside, Alicen slipped into her sweater. Wearing nothing else but a long sleep shirt that hung to her knees, she stepped off the deck and into the grass.

She looked down, expecting the grass to be cold beneath her feet, but it wasn't. In fact, the chilly fall Montana mountain air should have been nearly unbearable in the middle of the night, but Alicen hardly felt chilled. *Strange,* she thought.

"Come on, Alicen," the girl called, already halfway across the lawn.

Alicen started after the girl, her quick walk turning into a run as the child raced to the edge of the lawn and then into the forest beyond. The stars and large full moon provided enough light to see by as they moved. Alicen never stopped to question where they might be going; she was just following. Again it felt odd but familiar as well.

"Come on; come on," the little girl cried. "We're almost there."

"How can you be so much faster than me?" Alicen asked.

The child laughed. "Magic."

She laughed again, and Alicen found this funny as well. She shook her head and pushed herself to try and keep up. They dodged the trees, maneuvered over the rocky ground, and moved like forest beasts. As if they had done this a hundred times before. It felt good to have the wind lapping at her face, to feel the freedom of running among the trees, the whispers of the night cooing inside her ears. Alicen smiled, warmth ballooning through her body.

After a couple more strides, she saw the small girl slow, and she followed suit. Neither of them were huffing the way they should be after running at such a pace, but Alicen barely gave it a thought. The oddity of the moment was beginning to feel normal.

"We're here," the girl said.

Alicen looked around. All she could see was more forest, but she heard bubbling water close by and noticed the girl ducking off to the right. Alicen followed and stepped beyond a cluster of thick trees to find a stream. Maybe only ten feet across, it extended in both directions as far as she could see in the dark. The moon reflected off its surface. Stars dotted its glassy top. The water ran smoothly downstream and lapped the edges in peaceful rhythm. It almost sounded like a song.

"It's beautiful," Alicen said.

"It's more than that," the little girl said. "It can help you see the truth."

"How? It's just a river," Alicen said.

"Maybe to some, like maybe to some you're just a woman."

"I am just a woman."

The child smiled as a little puff of laughter escaped her lips. "Are you sure about that?"

Alicen shook her head. "You're a funny little girl."

The child smiled wide enough to engulf the bottom half of her face. "Hear that?" she called out. "She thinks I'm funny."

"You're not funny," came another small voice.

Alicen gasped and turned to see a boy walking out from the trees. A little taller than the girl with pigtails, but they looked to be about the same age. His hair, even in the dim light, was a fiery red.

"We think *you're* funny," said another young, new voice, as two more girls appeared from the dark. These two were smaller than the others, clasped hand in hand, one talking, the other quiet as a mouse. Twins. Both with short black hair and tiny round faces.

Alicen gasped again, took a deep breath, and exhaled sharply. She stepped back, her eyes trying to understand what she was seeing. There were four of them. Four children standing in front of her, along the side of a river in the forest, in the middle of the night. All that had felt normal moments before was now being called into question. What was she doing out here? Had she really crawled out of bed willingly? Why wasn't she afraid?

Get a grip, Alicen. Act like an adult, Alicen. What would your mother say, Alicen?

"Do you really think she's funny?" the redheaded boy asked, turning his attention to Alicen. "And be honest."

All of them moved their gazes to Alicen, anticipation mingling among them, all four waiting for a response, but her mouth was stuck open in shock. She took a step back.

The children exchanged glances, and the pigtailed girl shrugged. "I told you," she said.

"Alicen," the talkative twin said, "do you see us?" Her voice seemed to echo through the trees and on the wind. As if it were only in Alicen's head but also coming from the tiny human standing before her.

"Of course she sees us," the boy said. "She's staring right at us." He looked at Alicen with concern. "She just doesn't know who we are."

"She's been brainwashed," Pigtails said.

"Her brain was washed?" the twin exclaimed. She reached out and touched Alicen's forehead, turning her gaze to her twin sister. "How do they even do that?"

Get a grip, Alicen.

"Her brain wasn't actually washed, Roxie," Redhead said. "That isn't possible."

Act like an adult, Alicen.

"You don't know everything about everything," the twin he called Roxie said.

What would your mother say, Alicen?

"I know this for sure," Redhead replied.

"Alicen?" Pigtails said, stepping forward with hesitation and causing the other children to become silent.

"Who are you?" Alicen said, her voice barely audible and

nearly lost to the wind. A chill swept down her spine, and she shivered.

"It's okay," Pigtails said. "Don't be afraid."

The sky around her buzzed with muffled laughter and whispers, but the children before her remained still. Were there others?

"You can call me Evie," Pigtails said.

Evie. Alicen shook her head. "I'm dreaming; I must be dreaming."

"The dream isn't in here," Redhead said. "It's out there, and it pretends to be real."

Alicen didn't understand and opened her mouth to say so, but she couldn't get the words out. Evie took a step closer. Her movement caused Alicen to take another step backward. She reached out and felt for a tree behind her.

"You aren't real. This isn't real," Alicen said.

"Don't we seem real?" the redheaded boy asked.

Alicen swallowed and felt her lips quiver.

"Beck," Evie warned the boy over her shoulder. "That isn't helpful."

Beck. The boy blew a fallen piece of red hair out of his eyes. Alicen turned back to Evie, her mind teetering on the edge of sanity.

"You." Alicen stared, pointing a finger at Evie. "You healed a bird. That's impossible."

The speaking twin giggled behind Evie and smiled.

Roxie.

"Nothing is impossible," she said. The other little girl, who'd been completely silent, stepped away from the trees, hand in hand with her sister. She leaned over and whispered something into her twin's ear.

Roxie listened, then nodded. She turned her eyes to Evie, an excited bouncing starting in her heels. "Tate wants to show her," Roxie said.

Tate.

"I know," Evie said. She turned to Alicen. "But she wouldn't be able to see it yet. She isn't ready."

Tate and Roxie. Alicen felt nauseous from the rate at which her mind was spinning. This was a dream, she kept telling herself. Just a dream. "See what?" Alicen asked.

"Who you are," Roxie whispered.

More popping laughter and static whispers filled the air around them, and the children exchanged glances. "We have to go now," Evie said.

"Why are you doing this to me?" Alicen cried.

"You're still asking the wrong questions," Beck said.

A dull pain pulsed at the nape of Alicen's neck as Evie took one last step forward and grabbed Alicen's eyes with her own golden stare. "You made a promise once. And then you forgot how to keep it." Her expression took on a serious shade as she continued. "When you are ready to remember that promise, everything will change."

"What?" Alicen asked. "I don't understand."

The wind howled through the trees, and the pain that had started pricking at Alicen's skull grew with great force. The chilling laughter that the air carried rose in volume. It blocked out all the other sounds of the forest and pressed deeply into Alicen's ear canals. The throbbing in her brain amplified enough to blur her vision. She grabbed the tree behind her to stabilize her trembling knees.

Evie said something to her, but Alicen's ears were filled with cotton, the pain now too intense to focus. She dropped to her knees, crying at the sky as the world beyond shifted and vanished.

Alicen flew upward, gasping for breath, her heart pounding relentlessly inside her chest. Her eyes tore open, and it took her a moment to register that she was in her room. In bed. The first signs of morning light were sneaking through the window shades.

Her heavy breathing filled the quiet space, and her stomach turned. She thought she might be sick and yanked the covers from her legs. She was drenched in sweat, the chilly morning air sweeping over her and causing goose pimples to spread out across her bare legs. She felt like she couldn't breathe through the stuffy air around her head. Shakily, she stood, wobbled toward the window, pulled up the shade, and threw open the bottom glass panel.

More cold air punched her in the face, and she took a deep breath. She stood there for a long moment, inhaling the freezing early air and letting her mind come back down from its spinning heights. She was in her room. She was safe. No children, no forest. It had been a dream. Just a dream.

She laid her forehead on the windowsill and let the breeze cool the hot tears slipping past the corners of her eyes. Her shoulders started to shake as the emotions of everything that had happened suddenly overwhelmed her. She grasped the edge of the sill with her hands and slid down the wall until she was sitting on the floor. Soft cries escaped her lips, and she bit down to keep them from ringing out loudly across the still-sleeping house.

It was just a dream. Get ahold of yourself, her mind ordered. She wanted this to end; she wanted everything to end.

Alicen wasn't sure how long she sat there, window open, cold air rushing in, tears dripping off her chin, but eventually her emotions calmed and her tears dried.

She swallowed, laid her skull against the wall, and extended her legs out along the floor. With her eyes closed, she forced her breathing back into a normal rhythm. In and out. Calm. Collected. The rest of the house would be up soon. Her mother would be up soon.

Alicen opened her eyes, the sun now fully lighting the room. She scanned the room as she worked up the mental strength it would require to push herself off the floor. Her eyes caught sight of her bare feet, and her heart stopped. In the chaos of raw emotional turmoil, she hadn't even noticed.

She forced a shaky breath out through her lips and tried to control the panic crawling up her legs. Her shoulders shook, her mind melting back into a place of uncertainty. She reached out her shivering fingers toward her toes, needing to touch what she saw to confirm her fear.

Dirt. Dried in the curves of her toenails and between her toes. Dirt that had once been mud. As if she'd been outside. As if she'd been running through the forest.

11

Eventually Alicen dragged herself off the bedroom floor and into the shower. She let the hot, steaming water numb her skin as disbelief numbed her thoughts. Sleepwalking was new for her. She scraped her mind for another explanation, but logic kept bringing her back to what was obvious. "Alicen McCaffrey is talking to, seeing, and sleepwalking with imaginary children."

Even as she said the sentence out loud, shutting the shower off, she snorted in astonishment. Amid the insanity of it all, one thing was starting to become clear. She couldn't control this anymore. It was more than just feeling afraid of losing her mind; Alicen was actually afraid of putting herself in danger. She needed help.

She finished getting ready for the day in a fog. She heard movement through the house and knew the others were up. She didn't know how long Betty was planning to stay around, but she had let them know she hadn't yet booked a return flight, which meant Alicen, Louise, and Betty were going to be spending some quality time together. It meant Alicen was going to have to try and keep a grip on her sanity. She couldn't lose her mind in front of her mother. That was the last thing she needed.

Moving downstairs and into the kitchen, she was greeted by the other two women. They exchanged pleasantries, poured coffee into large travel mugs, and agreed to head to the bookstore to work. The thought of Betty getting her hands dirty caused Alicen and Louise to share a stolen bemused grin, but it was better to have her close so they could keep an eye on her than to leave her to meddle.

The three were out of the house quickly and parked outside the bookstore minutes later. The morning passed easily enough. Louise's soft jazz playlist drifted through the store, but other than a couple of necessary questions between them, they kept to themselves. Which suited Alicen fine. The less they mingled, the less likely she was to expose herself.

Louise dropped a heavy cardboard box on the wooden floorboards with a thud. She had just taped it closed and marked it with a black Sharpie. Dust particles danced through the sun's rays streaming in through the open shades, and Louise waved them out of her face. She coughed dramatically and then flashed Alicen a silly grin. Alicen chuckled and shook her head.

"What's so funny down there?" Betty asked, peering over the upstairs railing.

"Nothing's funny," Alicen said.

"Speak for yourself," Louise said. "I'm hilarious."

Alicen rolled her eyes.

"And starving," Louise said.

"What? You, hungry?" Alicen teased.

A rolled chunk of packing tape came flying across the store, and Alicen barely evaded it. "Careful," Alicen said, pointing at her friend. "My revenge is swift and deadly." Louise let out one loud cackle, and Alicen shook her head, a smile playing on her lips. "You have been warned."

"Actually, if a break and some food are up for discussion, my vote is yes," Betty called as she taped up the box she was working on.

"This is a first," Louise said, "but I'm with Betty on this."

Betty gave a mocking huff and shook her head. Alicen just laughed. And for a moment, the world felt normal.

Louise stood and placed her hands on her hips. "I believe it's my turn to grab lunch today," she said. "Or we could all break and go?"

"I'm actually not really hungry yet," Alicen said. "Maybe just grab me something for later?"

Louise nodded and looked up toward Betty. "Betty?"

"Can you grab me something too? If Alicen is staying, I'll keep her company."

Louise glanced at Alicen to make sure that was okay, and Alicen nodded. She could handle her mother alone for a little while.

"Suit yourselves," Louise said, grabbing her wallet. "Any requests on lunch?"

"Something low-carb, dear," Betty said. The woman turned back to her task, and Louise rolled her eyes.

"Burgers and fries it is," she teased, and Alicen couldn't help but laugh.

"I won't eat that," Betty said, clearly missing the sarcasm in Louise's tone.

"Get Betty a salad, Lou," Alicen warned, but with a smile in her voice.

Louise flashed Alicen a final smile and was out the door before Betty could say anything else.

"That girl is very odd, Alicen. I never did understand you two," Betty said.

Alicen ignored her and went back to work.

Silence engulfed the store again, and Alicen would have been happy to keep it that way. Wishful thinking. Betty clunked down the twisting steel staircase, a taped-up box in hand, and set it against the wall with the others.

She let out a dramatic sigh. "I am getting too old for this kind of labor."

Alicen glanced up and with one look at Betty's expression, knew the woman had no plans of returning back upstairs to work. Betty casually walked over to where Alicen was working through the history book collection, categorizing by year and country, and leaned against the waist-high bookshelf.

There was a pause before Betty tried to fill the silence. "So, Louise mentioned that you're taking part in a special program of sorts? At that retreat center."

"Uh-huh," Alicen said.

"What's it like?"

Alicen gave her mother a bothered look, and Betty sighed. "What? You can't take a little break to have a conversation about your life with your mother?"

Alicen took a patient inhale and capped the marker in her hand. "What do you want to know?"

"How long is it for?"

"As long as I need."

"So you're still depressed, then?"

Alicen shrugged. "It's only been four months."

"I know, honey; don't get defensive. I was just asking." Betty took a beat and then reached out and tucked a loose hair behind Alicen's ear. "We miss you in Santa Monica. Couldn't you go back to seeing your doctor there?"

"We?" Alicen said. Betty let her hand fall away from Alicen's face, and Alicen felt a pocket of anger open up in her chest. "Who's *we*, Betty?"

Betty opened her mouth to rebuke Alicen for calling her by her first name, but before she could speak, her guilty eyes confirmed Alicen's collecting fear.

"You have got to be kidding me!"

"He made a mistake, and he knows he did," Betty said.

"Allen didn't make a mistake, Mom. Marrying him in the first place was the mistake. Getting divorced was the only good thing to come out of this mess."

"You don't believe that."

Alicen stood, anger seeping out through her pores. "Is that why you're here? Did he send you?"

"Of course not! I wanted to see you. You're my daughter."

"Then act like it. Allen is a total jerk!"

"Allen is a good man, Alicen."

Alicen could feel her mother's temper growing, but hers was fully lit. "No, Betty, he's a rich man. That doesn't automatically make him good!"

"He gave you everything and is the only reason you ever had that sweet girl."

"And the second she was gone, he abandoned me," Alicen spat.

"You were supposed to be watching her!" Betty yelled. She might as well have shot Alicen with an arrow.

Alicen sucked in a painfully sharp breath, tears blurring her vision and a tremor starting in her fingers. "You think I don't know that?"

"Alicen—" Betty started, her expression plagued with guilt.

"You think I don't feel that every moment of every day?"

"Honey, I—" Betty tried.

"Did you come all this way to remind me that this is my fault?" Hot tears streamed down Alicen's cheeks. "To make sure I didn't forget that Jane is dead because of me?"

A sob choked out Alicen's words, and she covered her mouth with her hand. She turned away from Betty, even now trying to hide her weakness, and stared out the bookstore window. And there, across the street, Alicen saw them.

Four children, standing shoulder to shoulder, across the road on the sidewalk, staring back at her. One with red hair, one with pigtails, and a set of twins. Their faces expressionless and haunting.

Not now, she thought, Not while she was here. A truck drove by, blocking them from view, and when the street was clear once more, the four were gone. Alicen let out the mouthful of air she'd been holding, and another sob escaped with it. She swallowed and tried to regain control.

Steps echoed across the ground, and Alicen could feel Betty approaching.

"I shouldn't have said that," Betty said.

"But you did," Alicen retorted. "Because you believe it."

"No, I was just angry," Betty said, reaching her hand out to touch Alicen's arm.

Alicen yanked away, turning to face her mother. "Don't," Alicen said. "You should believe it. It's the truth."

Betty dropped her hand, and there was a short pause. "Just come home, and everything will be fine."

"Everything is not fine. I am not fine," Alicen whispered.

Fear washed over Betty's expression. "Honey, don't say things like that."

Alicen saw genuine concern in her mother's face. The woman wasn't a monster. She hadn't been dealt the most favorable hand in life, and Alicen supposed Betty had simply done the best she could with what she had been given.

"Allen said he would take you back, baby. You can make this right," Betty said.

Alicen clenched her jaw as a wave of heat rushed to her cheeks, followed by a tinge of hope. Was Betty right? What if the only way to survive this was to go back to the scene of the crime and beg forgiveness for her sins? Could her old life give her redemption? If she tried hard enough, could she be free?

Alicen.

She glanced over her shoulder out the window and saw the four children had returned. If she left, would the demons she'd acquired here follow? Alicen didn't know the answer. What she did know was that going back meant facing the demons she'd left there. And as quickly as the ounce of hope had surfaced, it was drowned out by the reality that those demons would never let her be free.

"For now, I need to be here," Alicen said, looking directly at her mother to make sure the woman received the message clearly. "But you are free to leave whenever you'd like." Alicen let the words hang in the air, watching Betty's face twitch slightly, then walked back to where she had been working, not bothering to glance over her shoulder once.

• • •

Alicen stood on the large boulder and surveyed the forest around her. Grandma Joe was there, as always, standing in the sun and singing one of her songs. Alicen knew all the words by heart, even if they were funny and strange. It was one of Grandma Joe's favorites. The familiar tune filled Alicen's brain as Grandma Joe's soft, warm voice sang the words.

"'When through the deep waters I call thee to go, the rivers of sorrow shall not overflow. For I will be with thee, thy troubles to bless, and sanctify to thee thy deepest distress.'"

Grandma Joe turned and caught Alicen's eye. Now aware

of an audience, Grandma Joe's eyes grew with delight as she raised her volume and began to dance. "'When through fiery trials thy pathway shall lie,'" she sang with a spin, "'my grace, all-sufficient, shall be thy supply.'" She held out the last note, raising her arms into the air and curling them over her head to strike her ending pose.

Alicen giggled and began to tap her little feet as Grandma Joe continued to hum and dance over the forest floor. In one wide turn, she was at the rock, taking Alicen's hand in her own and spinning her around. Alicen laughed against the warm air, her entire body filling with pure joy. These moments with her grandmother were why their love was so strong. Grandma Joe made Alicen feel like she could fly if she just jumped high enough.

Grandma Joe's song came to an end, and she let out a soft laugh. Alicen heaved, out of breath from spinning and laughter, dropped to her seat, and rested atop the rock. Her grandmother plopped down next to her and wrapped her fingers inside Alicen's.

"Do you know why that song is one of my favorites?" Grandma Joe asked.

"I don't even know what that song means," Alicen admitted with a giggle.

"What do you think it means?"

Alicen thought about the familiar but confusing lyrics and bit the inside of her lip as she searched her mind for meaning. Nothing. "Wouldn't it be easier if you just told me?"

Grandma Joe chuckled and gave Alicen's side a loving pinch that caused the girl to laugh and squirm. "And since when have you ever done things the easy way?"

"I think I'll start today," Alicen said.

Grandma Joe gave Alicen a sweet smile. "I love that song because it reminds me of the greatest truth there is. 'My grace, all-sufficient, shall be thy supply.'"

"What does 'all-sufficient' mean?"

"I like to think of it as ever-present, or simply all there is. It's easy to get caught up in the illusion of the rest of the world, Alicen. The idea that what lies before you is more powerful than what lies within you. It's easy to get stuck believing we are trapped by the troubles of what lies ahead of us and forget the grace given to us from what lies beyond us."

Grandma Joe turned her face to the sky, losing herself in the warmth of the sun. Alicen watched as a moment of silence passed, and then a wide smile stretched Grandma Joe's lips. She was hearing them—the voices. It was a look Alicen knew well. It scared some people, but never her. Because she knew more than most people.

"Grace, sweet Alicen, is your greatest gift. And remembering that grace and the name given to you by the Father of grace is your most important journey."

Alicen mulled Grandma Joe's words over. She wanted to believe everything her grandmother said was true, but the world gave her questions that sometimes took control.

"You have your thinking face on," Grandma Joe said.

Alicen shrugged her shoulders. "How do you know for sure that you're right?" She looked up at Grandma Joe as she waited for an answer.

There was a pause, and then the old woman smiled. "I wasn't always so sure. Many times I questioned and turned away from the truth that was always within me. But for me, servants were sent to help remind my spirit of what it already knew."

Grandma Joe looked back out across the treetops. "'Don't forget to show hospitality to strangers, for some who have done this have entertained angels without realizing it.'" Grandma Joe gave a small huff of laughter. "I always thought that was an odd verse until I was saved by it."

"Angels?" Alicen questioned.

"Ministering spirits, helpers, sent to show me what my eyes alone could not see. I have no doubts now of the truth. My spirit and mind are in line with the truth of grace, the truth of Jesus, and I will never be the same." Grandma Joe closed her eyes, her face still turned toward the sun, and a tear slipped from the corner of her eye and down her cheek.

"Don't cry," Alicen said, concern lacing her tone.

Grandma Joe turned her gaze back to her granddaughter. "It's okay, honey; I'm only swept up in the beauty, is all."

Alicen shook her little head. "Crying because you're happy is a weird adult thing I'll never understand."

Grandma Joe burst out laughing and pulled Alicen close. "There are many weird adult things I could do without. It's much better to be like a child."

"Well, then I hope to never become an adult."

"Your body will grow; there's no stopping that, but your mind and heart can stay childlike, full of belief in who you really are. That is what is important."

Alicen thought about this and then laid her head against her grandmother's shoulder. "Is your mind childlike?"

"I hope so. The more time I spend listening to the voices of

truth and letting go of the world around me, the more my mind remembers its childlike nature. Your mother and others like her think I'm ill. I've wondered about it myself at times, to be honest. Surely some people who hear voices no one else can hear are ill. But me? No, I don't think so. I think I'm lucky. And I think you're lucky too. You know why?"

"Because of grace?" Alicen said. She thought maybe she was starting to understand.

Grandma Joe kissed Alicen's forehead. "Yes, my sweet girl, because of grace."

12

Dr. Wells was waiting for Alicen in his office when she arrived. The drive to Clover Mountain Retreat Center had taken her twice as long as it should have because she'd pulled over twice. Both times to throw up. Due to a mixture of nerves, anger, fear, exhaustion, and probably more dysfunctional emotions that Alicen just couldn't identify.

She hadn't eaten much yesterday, and nothing today, so vomiting had been painful. Like her mother not speaking to her since their fight was painful. Like the idea of sharing her secrets with Dr. Wells was painful. Like not being able to sleep for fear she might stumble into the woods again was painful. Once she'd arrived, it had taken her several long minutes to climb out of the car and cross the campus to the big house. But at this point Alicen was out of options.

And terrified.

She tried to get comfortable in one of the plush office chairs, even though she knew it was no use. Comfort was something she'd known once but had all but forgotten.

"Thanks for seeing me," Alicen said.

Dr. Wells smiled. "As cliché as it sounds, my door is always open."

A moment of silence passed. Alicen crossed her legs and tucked her hands between her thighs. She wasn't sure how to start.

"Tell me about Jane," Dr. Wells said.

Her name sounded so sweet echoing in the room. "Jane?" Alicen questioned.

Dr. Wells nodded. "I never had the pleasure. What was she like?"

Alicen was used to people purposefully not asking about Jane, for fear of being insensitive, so to have Dr. Wells so boldly ask was alarming. But also refreshing. She smiled in spite of herself, an image of her sweet girl dancing through her mind.

"She was funny," Alicen started, "and I don't know where she got it from because I'm not funny at all, but she could get a room of adults rolling."

"So she loved to entertain?"

Alicen laughed. "If she really loved a food, she'd make up a song about it on the spot and sing it for anyone who would listen. And they were good, or at least I always thought they were. She called them her 'Happy Meals' songs because they were all about the meals that made her happy enough to sing. Once, with complete serious intention, she asked me if I thought McDonald's would sue her if she made an album and it went platinum."

Dr. Wells chuckled, and Alicen shook her head.

"She was pretty dramatic; she got that from my mother. Everything was either the greatest thing to happen to her or the worst. And she was good with words. Always telling stories. She started talking young, reading young, the more adventure the better."

Alicen lovingly rolled her eyes. "Agh, that girl could be a handful. She would get lost in her imagination. And stubborn as they come. That she definitely got from me. It could be like pulling teeth to get her out of her own imagination sometimes. She'd lock herself in her room with Evie—" Alicen's words rammed to a halt and her heart leapt into her throat.

Evie. The air around her skull thinned and her vision hazed over. She felt like she might pass out, and she grabbed the plush chair's armrest to steady herself.

"Alicen?" Dr. Wells asked. "Are you all right?"

She lifted her eyes to him, tears dotting the world in her view. She shook her head, losing control of the raging emotions she was trying to keep at bay.

"Who's Evie?" Dr. Wells asked.

Alicen swallowed and licked her dried bottom lip. She cleared the shakiness from her voice and spoke. "Jane's imaginary friend."

"And why does that conjure up such a strong emotion?"

Again Alicen looked away from Dr. Wells's gaze. There was no turning back now. She let out an uncomfortable noise that was half laugh, half shriek, and pressed her palms to either side of her head. "Because I'm losing my mind."

Dr. Wells waited patiently, his expression warm, without judgment or concern. Just present and attentive.

"I've been hearing and seeing things that aren't there," Alicen said.

"What kind of things?"

Alicen kept her eyes on the floor. "Whispers, laughter . . . I've been hearing voices."

"And seeing?"

"Children," she whispered. "I've been seeing children."

"Jane?"

Alicen bit the inside of her cheek and nodded. "I see her in everything." She paused, another painful image of her daughter flittering across her mind. "But this is different—I'm seeing other children as well. One of them calls herself Evie."

"They talk to you?"

Alicen nodded. "I'm pretty sure the whispers and laughter I hear is them." Alicen's chin quivered as she tried to keep a sob contained in her throat. Several tears crossed over her bottom lids, and she reached up and brushed them away. "They're haunting me, and I don't know what to do." She barely got the words out as sorrow threatened to engulf her.

"It's okay, Alicen. Try and take a couple of deep breaths," Dr. Wells said.

Alicen did as he asked, and he gave her time to collect herself before continuing.

"When did this start?" he asked.

"A couple weeks ago."

"Before coming to Red Lodge?"

"No, not before. Does that mean something?"

"Perhaps. I wish I could say there was always an exact science to every situation such as this, but there is still so much we are learning about the brain. It's possible that your return to a familiar place, one already filled with memories, triggered this type of psychosis."

Psychosis. The word sounded dirty and made Alicen shrink farther into her chair.

"There is also your family history to consider," Dr. Wells said.

There it was. A truth Alicen knew she wasn't going to be able to escape. A thought that had been haunting her as long as the figment children. With the recent onslaught of memories of her grandmother, the similarities were impossible to ignore. Once again Alicen was at a loss for where to begin. Once again the room fell silent.

Dr. Wells held the same blank folder he'd had during their first session—one Alicen assumed contained a detailed history of her past, of her family's skeletons, of the dark secrets she'd avoided for more than a decade. Alicen wasn't ready to face that just yet. She was supposed to have PTSD. Depression. Not . . . She closed her mind off before another idea could fully surface.

"Is this normal for PTSD?" Alicen asked, desperate to stray away from the steep edge of that reality.

Dr. Wells played along. "Different minds react to tragedy

differently. Many people with PTSD suffer from hallucinations triggered by certain sounds or images. Are your recent experiences with these children tied to any sort of memories? Or do you see a pattern to their appearances?"

Alicen thought back through the times the children had visited her, then shook her head. "They just happen." She felt like her chest was being pumped full of hot, suffocating air. She raised her trembling hands and laid her face softly into her palms.

"It's all right," Dr. Wells said. "Take another deep breath."

"I'm afraid of my own mind," she said in a whisper.

"You don't have to be. We can help."

Anger flashed through Alicen's system. "Everybody keeps saying that to me," she said harshly and raised her head. "How are you going to help? My daughter died!" Like a water line, her control broke, and a flood of emotions devoured the room. "I lost . . ." Raw sorrow choked her words, and angry tears filled her eyes. She took a short breath, tried to swallow her pain, but it was too large and hard to force down.

"I lost everything," Alicen said, the tone of her voice controlled by emotion. "Are you going to give that back to me?" She knew she was being irrational, but she couldn't rein in her madness now.

Dr. Wells leaned back in his seat and let Alicen's emotional explosion happen without hindrance.

Alicen avoided making eye contact. She was struggling to breathe through the raging torment in her chest. "Louise, my mother, you: 'We just want you to get better, Alicen; we're here for you, Alicen; we're trying to help, Alicen.'" Her words fell out with violent, sharp edges, like knives slicing at her lips. "Don't I have to believe I can be helped for it to work? Isn't that how these things are done? The only good thing that ever happened to me was taken. I *let* her be taken! I did this to myself." Another batch of tears blurred her vision, and she blinked hard to chase them off.

The whispers that followed her like a shadow hissed around her head, and she closed her eyes against their sudden appearance.

Not now. Not here.

Alicen.

Do you hear us?

The tears she'd been trying to fight off overpowered her, and again she felt them break across her lower eyelids. She shook her head, sniffing and trying to gain even a small amount of control.

Do you hear us, Alicen?

"I'm losing my sanity," Alicen said. "I really am crazy. Just like she was."

"You're referring to your grandmother Josephine?" Dr. Wells asked.

Alicen didn't respond. Her silence was enough.

"Alicen, I think it is important we discuss her and her condition."

A wave of panic and nausea rolled through her body as her defense of the older woman sprang to action. "She was never diagnosed with a condition."

"You're right, but many people believed—"

"People believed all kinds of things about her that weren't true."

Dr. Wells paused and changed his approach. "What did you believe about her?"

Another wave of nausea washed through her. "I was so young," Alicen said, getting lost in memories from the past. Remembering her dream from just a couple hours ago. The older woman's beautiful tone washing through Alicen even now. Sitting in the forest, talking about grace, Alicen caught up in the confidence her grandmother had in what she believed. Alicen wasn't sure how to answer Dr. Wells's question.

"From what I've seen of her file," Dr. Wells continued, "it appears she may have suffered from some sort of schizophrenia or dementia."

Alicen shook her head. "No. She was never diagnosed."

"My understanding is that she refused to be. That doesn't mean she wasn't suffering from a disease."

"How is this helpful?" Alicen knew the answer to the question, but her mouth formed the words anyway.

"These kinds of psychoses can oftentimes be hereditary, and not unlikely triggered by your recent tragedy," he said.

"But she wasn't ever diagnosed. She was just . . ." Alicen's words lost steam as her mind fully grasped what Dr. Wells was suggesting.

"As scary as it feels," the doctor explained, "giving what is happening to you a name and definition may serve as a comfort. It gives us some understanding and opens the different routes we can take to help you cope."

Help her cope? With a mental disorder? Alicen's mind began to try to mold itself around the idea, but she just couldn't get it to maneuver properly. There had to be some other explanation.

The most recent memory of Grandma Joe floated across her mind again. Nagging at her. As if it wanted her to see something she was missing. Then a crazy thought blossomed, and her mouth spoke words before she could stop them. "Could it be more?"

"More how?" Dr. Wells replied.

Silence filled the office as Alicen's mind began to churn over ideas that would make her sound crazier than she already did. *"Helpers, sent to show me what my eyes alone could not see,"* Grandma Joe had said. The words rang through Alicen's brain like a bell.

She glanced up at Dr. Wells, who was patiently waiting for her to speak. "Is there ever any truth to it?" she asked, her voice barely a whisper. "Could they be real?"

Dr. Wells thought about his answer carefully. "By *they*, you mean the things you're seeing? You're asking me if I believe in spirits? If it's possible to be visited by something from beyond?"

Alicen dropped her eyes sheepishly. "I bet you get asked that often."

He nodded. "Many patients believe in what they're seeing."

"But you don't believe it's real?" Alicen asked.

"If you had asked me ten years ago, I would have said that placing your belief in anything but science was a waste. Now, although I still claim to be a man of science, I also concede that the mind finds healing in different ways. I had a cousin who was tormented by her mind for much of her life—depression, anxiety, dangerous mood swings. It wasn't until she was visited by angels a couple of years ago that she was able to find peace. She claims that God sent them to minister to her and care for her. I watched a woman I've known for forty years transform from being constantly miserable to being peaceful and happy. Now, do I think angels are real?" Dr. Wells smiled and shook his head. "No. Personally I've always found religion a bit far-fetched, but I can't deny the impact it had on her. She would say God saved her. I would say her mind found a way to heal itself by giving her what she needed when she needed it."

"And what would you say is happening to me?" Alicen asked.

"That's what we are here to figure out. Together." He let a beat of time pulse before plunging forward. "I would like to start you on an antipsychotic paired with a sleeping aid so we can get you rested."

Alicen shifted uncomfortably. "I was on an antipsychotic back in Santa Monica, and it only made me feel out of sorts."

"Adjusting to the medication can be uncomfortable, but since you're suffering active delusions, I believe it is the best course of action. And we'll take it slow. A mild grade to start with, just to give you some peace of mind."

Alicen swallowed, an unsure expression filling the lines in her face. Dr. Wells noticed and leaned toward her in his chair. "I'm here to help, Alicen, but only if you let me."

She bit the inside of her bottom lip and gave a small nod. Dr. Wells stood from his chair and walked to his desk. "I'll write these up for you, and I encourage you to get them filled today. Just so you have them, so you can take them when you're ready."

Nodding, she waited as Dr. Wells wrote up both prescriptions. Once finished, he crossed the room and handed them to Alicen as she stood. "You should have no problem getting these filled in town."

"Thanks," Alicen said, placing the small square scripts in her purse.

"We made progress today. Let's keep the lines of communication open and meet again in a couple of days, all right?"

Alicen forced a small grin. Dr. Wells returned her smile and gave her shoulder a soft pat. "Call me if you need anything," he said.

She nodded and left his office. Somewhere in her mind a delusional voice started saying maybe this had been what she needed. To just get it off her chest and start moving forward.

Alicen drove straight to the local pharmacy and picked up both prescriptions, as suggested, just to have them close. Her mind was starting to clear from her discussion with Dr. Wells. She was starting to rationalize her own insanity. She probably wouldn't even need the antipsychotic she now held in her hand. She just needed to get her mind back in check. Sleep would help, she thought. And with a sleeping aid in hand, she was surely on the road to recovery.

Yes, that was all she needed. To talk it out, as she'd done, and to sleep.

Yet her cynicism mocked the belief she was clutching. The belief that she could move forward. The belief that maybe things could get better. The belief that she was under no circumstance actually losing her mind.

• • •

Victoria stood inside the small bathroom that was attached to her office. The hallways outside her locked office door were quiet. Still. The residents of Clover Mountain tucked into their white sheets, minds dulled as necessary, nurses gone home, only the night staff remaining. She couldn't remember how long she'd been standing there. The small wooden box sat perched on the back ledge of the sink. A box she'd retrieved from the cabin earlier when she'd visited.

Worn from time and use, the box held her secrets. Secrets she'd thought she'd killed along with Uncle Donald. But here it sat. Whispering for her to open the lid and release her darkness. A tool she'd learned to use when she failed. When she'd tried but couldn't be better. When the filth in her began to show.

Only through the admittance of our stains can we be cleansed.

You reap what you sow, and life always comes to collect.

Inside the wooden lid was a form of payment. The pain, and blood. It was her skin in the game. Maybe she could obtain forgiveness for the sins of her parents. For her own. But forgiveness didn't come free.

She needs to be taught the truth.

Yes, Victoria thought as her uncle's voice filled her mind.

This sudden urge for penance was because of Alicen. The woman's stains were infiltrating Victoria's control. Alicen's filth, her darkness. They were calling forth the same in Victoria.

She is a worm.

"Yes, the worst kind," Victoria said.

Why do you hate her?

"I need to fix her."

Because you hate her?

"Because of what she did."

Ah, yes. It always does come back to the children.

Victoria backed away from the sink and ran her fingers through her hair, pushing against her scalp. "Children should be protected," she whispered and closed her eyes to block out the images threatening to stir. He was right. Those who inflicted harm on their children rattled her control. They crawled under the skin and planted seeds that grew, tormenting Victoria constantly.

Many had come, their mistakes paid for by those they were supposed to nurture, and Victoria had helped them amend. Controlled their true nature, dumbed down their ability to cause any more chaos, seen that they gave up their minds and wills as penance.

All her patients were trouble, but this particular kind of trouble needed to be eradicated. If she had it her way, they would be disposed of. But she couldn't go around killing patients. There were laws against such action. Yet blood still needed to be given for their sins. Metaphorically, of course.

Taking their minds, shoving them into a place of numbed

existence, became ample payment. Worse than death for some. And as she led each special case to a place of retribution, she found a sliver of her own. Their trouble became her trouble, and in fixing them, she healed herself.

Alicen was no different.

But then she *was* different, wasn't she, Victoria thought. No other patient had affected her so deeply. Reading through her file, staring at her photo, discussing her progress with Dr. Wells—each time Alicen seemed to burrow deeper into Victoria's mind. She couldn't shake the woman.

Weak—and foolish.

Victoria cursed her uncle under her breath and glanced back at the box sitting on the sink. A long stream of silence passed as she stared, the longing to be clean pulsing in her arms. With as much resolve as she could conjure, Victoria yanked herself away from the small object, flicked the light off, and left the bathroom behind.

She was neither weak nor foolish. She was in control. Victoria couldn't lose focus on what was needed here. It was critical that Alicen pay for her trouble. She was a stain, and stains were best dealt with directly. Accept what she was. Blood for blood. It was necessary so Victoria didn't have to pay with her own.

Careful, little Victoria, or you'll never be free.

She would be clean. Through their punishment. Blood for blood. Time to bring Alicen into the fold.

13

When Alicen finally came to from the strong sleeping aid she'd taken the night before, morning sun was washing across the wooden floors of her bedroom. She pushed herself up from her pillow and out from under the covers. It took her a moment to realize where she was, to recall yesterday, to remember why she felt so disoriented, and to shake off the last bit of medication swirling through her bloodstream.

Still a bit drowsy, she got ready for the day and made her way down to the kitchen, where Betty and Louise were already seated. They were being pleasant to one another, which Alicen found odd but ignored. She was coming out from the fog of her sleeping pill and found herself more refreshed than she'd been in a while.

Betty hardly acknowledged her daughter as she walked into the kitchen, and Alicen ignored that as well. She had slept like a rock for the first time in months, and that gave her a twinge of hope for her future. Alicen just wanted a hot cup of coffee and to bask in the single most evident moment of normality she'd experienced in ages. She wouldn't let her mother's grumpy disposition interfere with that.

The kitchen contained random pops of surface-level small talk before Louise announced they needed to make a stop at the grocery store before doing any work on the house or bookstore. They all decided to go together and rose to get ready. Again Betty made a solid effort at letting Alicen know she was ignoring her, but again Alicen managed not to let it get under her skin. The idea of experiencing the entire day with a clear and rested mind was just too lovely to allow Betty to ruin it.

The drive to the market was quiet and quick. Once inside, Louise decided they should divide and conquer. "I'll take half; you two take the other," she said, holding out a folded piece of paper.

Alicen had to fight hard not to audibly exhale her frustration at Louise's manipulated pairing. She glanced sideways at her mother, who only shrugged. Saying she was too angry to shop with her daughter would be giving up too much. They would just have to suffer together.

Betty snatched the list from Louise before Alicen could and turned to go grab a cart. Alicen shot a glare in Louise's direction, and her friend responded with a work-it-out look before heading off in the opposite direction. Alicen steeled herself, reexamined the smidge of peace she had spotted on the horizon of her life, and grasped it. Then she walked toward Betty.

"You push," Betty said, stepping away from the silver buggy, list in hand.

See the light at the end of the tunnel, Alicen, she thought.

They walked toward the produce section at the right-hand side of the store. Betty quickly began collecting items in wispy plastic bags and securing them with green wire ties. Apples, mushrooms, red peppers, jalapeños, avocados, potatoes, each one clunking into the metal cart after she had bagged them.

It was a risk to break the painful silence that had collected, knowing full well that an argument could ensue which might be even more unbearable, but Alicen knew it had to be done.

"Did you sleep all right last night?" Alicen asked. Starting small seemed like the best strategy to test the waters.

"Ha," Betty replied.

Clearly the waters were quite cold.

"Oh, come on, Betty," Alicen said, already losing her patience. If anyone had the right to be mad here, it was Alicen. Betty was at fault; she'd basically accused Alicen of killing her own daughter after suggesting that her sham of a marriage was worth saving. Betty should be groveling, not giving the cold shoulder.

"Why can't you just call me Mom?" Betty snapped, twisting her neck around violently to glare at Alicen.

"Sorry, *Mom*," Alicen fired back.

Betty huffed and turned away. "The way you say it, it's

like it tastes rotten. I get it. I see. I was a terrible mother, still am. Poor Alicen with the terrible mother."

Alicen wished she hadn't broken the silence. This was a typical pattern for Betty. Playing the victim, trying to get Alicen to admit fault. And it always worked.

"Mom, you're not terrible," Alicen said, focusing on keeping her voice even and soft, though heat was building on the back of her neck.

"Aren't I, though?" Betty asked, glancing back, tears collecting in the corners of her eyes. At the sight, Alicen softened without having to try. She had always hated to see her mother cry. She scrambled to think of something to ease Betty's mind, but the woman was already in a downward spiral.

"I can see the constant disappointment in your eyes," Betty said. She took small, hard steps forward and continued to grab the items they needed, her voice low and harsh. "I wasn't comforting enough. I wasn't present enough. I wasn't understanding enough."

"Mom, please," Alicen tried. She couldn't help but glance around to see if anyone was watching and judging. A nasty habit she'd learned in childhood. *Don't let them see your flaws; what will they think of you then?* Only a small elderly woman stood within earshot, but she looked as though she'd have trouble hearing an argument even if it were happening right beside her.

Betty sniffed and used the back of her hand to brush away escaped tears. "You're right; I was never good at those things," she said.

"I didn't say those things were a problem; you did," Alicen

said, but Betty ignored her. Alicen knew she had already lost the battle; nothing she could say would get through now. Betty was having a conversation with herself, and any chance for survival hung on Alicen's ability to just listen.

"At least I was better than *her*," Betty said, and Alicen knew she was talking about Grandma Joe. "At least I didn't lose my mind. I did better by you than she did by me, or at least I thought I had. That's all I ever wanted—to be better than her." Betty was hardly even speaking to Alicen at this point; she was caught up in herself.

Soft laughter ruffled through the air as if a sudden light breeze were carrying the noise through the store. Alicen cringed. *Not here, not today,* she thought.

Alicen.

The sound was becoming as familiar to her as her own voice. She bit down on the inside of her bottom lip and tried not to let the change show in her face. Not that Betty was paying any attention; she was too busy wallowing in her own self-inflicted misery.

"Have I failed at the only thing I ever tried to be?" Betty asked, suddenly turning to Alicen. "A better mother to you than the one I had?"

Alicen was distracted by the collecting whispers weaving in and out of her ear canals and paused long enough to give Betty the ammunition she needed to continue to fire shame-filled bullets at herself. She huffed and sniffed again, nodding to herself and letting her self-pity further consume her.

"Come on, Mom, don't do this to yourself, not here," Alicen said, trying to recover. "You weren't a terrible mother, not at all." But even as the words were leaving her mouth, she knew they weren't true.

Alicen. The whispers echoed.

Alicen fought for control over her mind. *It's not real,* she thought; *you just have to remember it's not real.* A flutter of laughter rushed behind her, and she instinctively twisted her neck to look. The ends of wavy blonde curls disappeared around the corner of a long food aisle. Agony pulsed inside her heart as haunting images of Jane filled her memory. For a split second her heels itched to follow, but then reality stole her focus. It wasn't Jane. Jane would never run through the aisle of a grocery store again.

"Alicen?" her mother called.

Alicen snapped her head back toward Betty. "Sorry," she said.

"You aren't even listening anymore," Betty said as she stepped away.

"Sorry, I just—"

"No," Betty said, raising her hands in defense. "I'm finished with this." She sniffed and started to scan the store behind Alicen until her eyes landed on her target. She thrust the list out toward Alicen, and Alicen hesitantly took hold of it.

Betty gave Alicen one last scolding look before storming off past her.

"Mom," Alicen called as the woman walked away.

"I'll find Louise and finish with her," Betty said over her shoulder, not stopping.

Alicen watched her mother make a beeline for the

bathrooms and then vanish through the wooden door marked with a little blue girl on the front. She exhaled deeply and considered going after her, but honestly, she wasn't sure she could handle another round of Betty.

Alicen. Do you hear us?

She clutched the handlebar that lay across the top of the metal shopping cart and closed her eyes. She wasn't sure she could handle any more of her own mental abuse either. She examined the cart to see what they had already gotten off the list and then set her focus on getting everything else quickly, so they could leave. She wanted to be home, she wanted to be in bed, she wanted another sleeping pill, and she wanted to go back a few hours to when she thought maybe this day would be different from the others.

Alicen pushed her buggy down one of the food aisles, grabbing items from the list. The aisle was still, except for her. The entire store seemed to have fallen eerily quiet. She moved to exit the row and head into the next when a chirp of laughter echoed behind her. She paused and turned. Her heart dropped into her stomach as her skin went cold. Jane was there, standing in the center of the vacant row, a yard away.

Right before her eyes, wearing a little red dress, a dress Alicen remembered buying her, the one Jane had insisted she needed because it was her favorite color. A yard away, blonde curls hanging past her chin, blue eyes blazing. Her daughter, standing inside the store, not in her dream, not a fluttering image caught on repeat in her nightmares, but Jane in her entirety.

Alicen.

Her knees shook. The small hole in her heart exploded into

a cavern. Her sanity screamed for attention, her rationality begged her to listen, but the bottomless cavern of agony swallowed them both whole, and Alicen slipped away from reality.

"Baby?" Alicen whispered, and stepped toward Jane.

"I thought you were going to leave me," Jane said. She stayed in place, her eyes glued to her mother, her voice sweet as ever.

"No, baby girl, I would never leave you," Alicen said. She was aware of the tears slipping down her cheeks and robotically brushed them away.

"You did leave me, though, once," Jane said, her tiny voice saddened.

Alicen wondered if she might collapse from the pain pressing against her airways. A wave of guilt raked across her vision, and the world dotted.

"Don't you remember, Mommy?" Jane asked. Her face seemed to fill with shadows, and Alicen could hardly stand under the weight of it.

Run, Alicen. Run.

"Do you remember what happened?" Jane asked. But it wasn't really Jane anymore, not the Jane that Alicen knew. Her shiny outlook on life, her joyous spirit, her constant optimism, her belief in magic and miracles—all gone. Replaced with the callousness of death, the pain of betrayal. Betrayal served to her by her own mother.

But that didn't stop Alicen from desperately wanting to rush forward and sweep the child into her arms. It didn't stop her from wanting to carry her home and tuck her into bed. It only amplified her desire to do what she'd been unable to do before. To save her. Shame poured down from the store's exposed rafters, as if the roof were collapsing upon her.

"Yes," Alicen managed to breathe out.

"Me, too," Jane said, the light draining from her eyes.

"I'm so sorry, baby," Alicen said.

"Too late for sorry, Mommy," Jane replied, her voice now carrying a haunted echo. "Too, too late."

"Jane, please, sweetheart—" Alicen stammered.

"Too, too late," Jane said, all her sweetness dissolving into anger. She turned then and started to walk away.

Alicen's heart felt like it was reaching out through her chest cavity. "Jane." Alicen found her feet and started to follow. "Jane, baby, stop."

No, Alicen. Alicen, run.

Somewhere buried beneath her pain, her brain was joining the whispered warnings, but Alicen was too far gone to yank herself back. Jane vanished around a corner, and desperation filled Alicen's legs with fuel. Determination to yank her child back from the fate Alicen had unwittingly forced her into became all-consuming.

"Jane," Alicen hollered. She abandoned her cart. Abandoned her reason. Jane was all that mattered.

She stepped around the corner after the child and caught sight of her sweet head, laced with a golden bounce, turning down the final aisle, back toward the produce. Alicen followed, doubling the small girl's stride.

She stepped into the aisle and reached Jane within a couple of steps. Alicen grabbed the girl's shoulder, turning her around and seeing that the light in her once-blue eyes was completely gone. Just black marbles filled her skull now. The sight caused Alicen's heart to break, but she remained steadfast. She had done this to Jane; she had caused this transformation. She was responsible, and now she had to save her. She was her mother; only a mother could save her child.

"Jane, baby, come with me, okay?" Alicen said.

The little girl yanked away from Alicen's hold and shook her head no, her small brow gathering with concern.

"Jane," Alicen said, reaching out and grabbing hold of her daughter's arm, "you need to come home with me. I can help you."

"No, let go of me," the child cried.

Run, Alicen. Run!

She ignored the ever-present words of the others. She ignored her wailing sanity. Saving Jane was all that mattered. "Stop it, Jane."

"No! You can't help me." The little girl wiggled under Alicen's grip, but Alicen wouldn't release her hold.

"That's enough, Jane!"

"Stop, stop! You can't help me. You killed me!"

Alicen eased her grip slightly as Jane's words smacked against her being. A small part of her wondered if Jane was right. Maybe she couldn't help her; maybe she could only harm her further?

No, she thought, *a daughter needs her mother.* She would do more for Jane than her own mother had ever done for her. She would not abandon her twice. With one sweeping motion, she lifted Jane off the ground and into her arms.

"No!" Jane cried, but Alicen ignored her.

"We are going home, baby," Alicen said. She started down the aisle, the sliding exit doors in view. Voices from somewhere else tried to break through, but Alicen was consumed with only one thought. Get Jane out, get her home. Save her.

"Put me down. Stop! Mom, mom!"

"It's okay, honey. I've got you. I'm going to help you." Alicen kept her eyes on the door. The child in her arms thrashed violently, and Alicen struggled to hold on.

"Alicen!" another familiar voice cried out. "Alicen, stop!"

But Alicen was too far down the rabbit hole to register the concern. She saw motion out of the corner of her eye, and she picked up her pace. They were going to try and take her baby from her. Because they knew she was a bad mother. But she wouldn't let them. She wouldn't let any of them.

"Mom!" the child cried, tears now streaming down her cheeks.

"Stop, stop!" an unfamiliar voice called. "Someone help!"

"Alicen, what are you—?"

"Alicen, stop!"

"Miss, miss, you can't—"

So many voices tried to shake her resolve, but Alicen was steadfast. The sliding doors opened, and the cold morning air rushed across her face. "We're going home, honey; we're almost there."

The child cried and shook. "I don't want to go home with you. I want my mommy."

"Jane, stop; I am your mommy."

"No," the child wailed. "No! I want my real mommy."

Angry voices were still hollering at her from behind, and

Alicen glanced down at the small child in her arms. Fear flooded her body, her face going numb. Dark-brown hair, brown eyes, a wail of terror distorting what should have been a crooked smile. This wasn't the way Jane should look.

Because it wasn't Jane at all. As if reality itself had materialized and grown a fist, it clocked her across the chin and rocked her back to consciousness. She gasped, terror filling her core and spreading out into every limb. Fear pulsed in the little girl's face. A face that wasn't Jane's.

As if the physical evidence weren't enough, as if her brain were lagging behind what was happening, Alicen sputtered, "Jane?"

The little girl shook her head, her eyes filled with tears.

"Oh no," Alicen whispered, the final blow of reality smashing against her skull.

"Let go of my daughter!" a woman cried.

Alicen turned and saw a handful of people rushing out of the grocery store after her. Frozen in confusion, she just stood there. Before she could react, a heavyset woman with a growl on her face reached out and yanked the little girl from Alicen's clutches. The woman clenched the girl close to her breast, consoling the frightened child and stroking her hair softly. "What is wrong with you?" she snapped at Alicen.

Still too dumbstruck to formulate words, Alicen just shook her head in disbelief.

"Alicen?" Louise asked, stepping up behind the woman and the strange child she was holding.

Alicen looked at Louise, terror and concern consuming her friend's face, and then caught sight of her mother, who was pale and nearly trembling at Louise's side. Several others were there too, people with faces she didn't know, a couple of them in store uniforms. A man in a white button-down shirt, tie, and store badge who was outraged himself was trying to reassure the furious mother that this sort of thing never happened at his store. The woman was hollering back, but Alicen wasn't listening anymore.

Alicen stumbled back a few steps, her mind a mushy mess between what she'd thought she was doing and the reality of what she had almost done. She stared at the little brown-haired girl in shock. She had been Jane. She had been Jane!

"Get your eyes off my daughter!" the mother yelled, and Alicen dropped her gaze.

Louise started to interject then. Stepping between the mother and Alicen, she tried to help the store owner calm her down and explain that there must have been a mistake. Alicen shut it all out then. She succumbed to the numbness that was spreading through her body. The defense she'd built up to protect herself. The world faded, except for Betty, who stepped around the others and closer to Alicen.

The two held one another's eyes for a long moment before tears broke through Alicen's wall and escaped down her face. Then Betty placed a comforting hand on her daughter's shoulder, and Alicen's face caved to the sorrow she felt.

"She was Jane," Alicen whispered. "I was trying to save her."

Betty didn't respond with words. She just pulled her daughter into her arms as the numbness that had collected across Alicen's senses evaporated, and she fell apart in her mother's embrace.

14

The clock on Alicen's nightstand ticked loudly against the quiet of her bedroom. She had been lying on her bed for hours, maybe days—time was hard to track when you were losing your sense of what was real. Louise and Betty checked on her periodically, probably to make sure she was still locked in her room, where she couldn't accidentally try to steal another person's child.

Alicen had tried to recall what had happened in the moments between breaking down in the grocery parking lot against her mother's shoulder and ending up in her bedroom, but it was all a haze with only small snippets filtering through. Getting in the car, driving home, walking up the stairs, Louise's voice assuring Betty she was certain that with the right explanation the store owner and the child's mother could be convinced not to press charges.

The right explanation. Alicen had let her own daughter drown four months ago, and in the wake had tried to kill herself, failed, decided instead to lose her mind, begun hallucinating little children everywhere, then believed a complete stranger's child was her own, and finally tried to steal said child. Surely anyone with a sound sense of reality could relate and would take pity on her.

If Alicen were that mother, she'd sue the pants off the crazy human who gave an explanation like that. She'd insist that person be checked into a psychiatric facility immediately. Well, the joke was on them if they pursued that route. Alicen was, technically, already a patient at a psychiatric facility. Maybe they'd try to get her moved onto the campus? Maybe she needed to be?

Someone knocked lightly at the door to her room, and when Alicen didn't respond, she let herself in. It was Betty. "Can I come in?" she asked.

Betty never really asked for anything; the words were just par for the course, a formality of being part of the human race. So without waiting for Alicen to reply, she walked in and shut the door behind her. Alicen didn't care, though. Eventually she was going to have to talk about this with her mother, now that her secret was out. It might as well be sooner rather than later.

Alicen pushed herself up from where she was curled against her comforter and sat cross-legged facing the sofa chair in the corner. She waited for Betty to cross the room and sit on the plush furniture, but she didn't. She waited for her to demand answers, to start popping off questions, but she didn't do that, either. Instead, she slowly walked to Alicen's bed and sat beside her.

Betty reached over and cradled Alicen's hand in her own. Alicen dropped her eyes to where her mother's aged hand sat in her lap. Her touch was warmer than Alicen would have expected it to be. And comforting. Tears from exhaustion, from desperation, from a sense of overwhelming helplessness settled into her bottom lids, and Alicen didn't even try to keep them hidden. She was too far gone to care anymore.

The two women sat there on Alicen's bed, encased in silence for a while. Betty stroking the top of her daughter's hand with her free thumb, and Alicen occasionally wiping away a fallen tear.

Finally Betty spoke. "I know why you didn't tell me this was happening to you." Her voice low and kind, an inflection Alicen didn't often hear. "I know why you kept this to yourself. I know, because I taught you how to be this way. It's my fault."

Alicen looked at Betty and shook her head. "No, Mom, this isn't your fault."

"Yes, it is. Yes . . ." Her mother's emotions interrupted her confession, and she took a hard swallow to manage herself. "Hiding flaws is a Betty Reese specialty. Something I learned in response to the way the world treated . . ." Betty's voice died off.

Grandma Joe, Alicen thought. She'd known it wouldn't be long before their conversation ended up there.

"Of all people, I should have seen this because I've seen it before," Betty started. Tears now rested in the pockets of Betty's eyes. She captured her daughter's gaze and placed her palm against Alicen's cheek. "You're sick, honey, like Grandma Joe was sick."

There it was, said out in the open. A thought that Alicen had been drowning out. An idea that had all too often crossed her mind but that she'd shoved into the darkness. Alicen moved her eyes away from her mother's and exhaled as reality revealed itself from the shadows of her mind. It had always been there; Alicen had just been ignoring it.

"I made a mistake with your grandma. I didn't push hard enough for her to get help. I failed her, but you are my daughter," Betty said. "I won't make the same mistakes with you. You need help, baby." Betty's cheeks were moistened with tears, and Alicen felt her own dripping off her chin.

"I thought I could control this," Alicen whispered through her emotion.

"I know," Betty said, using her thumbs to gently wipe Alicen's cheeks. "It's okay to admit you can't. It's okay."

It's okay. The words echoed inside Alicen's head like a warming calm in the midst of a raging, freezing rainstorm. A sense of release she never thought she'd receive from her mother. Permission to be broken, to be weak. Alicen lost any resolve she'd been maintaining and let her sorrow consume her. She collapsed into her mother's embrace for the second time that day. Betty pulled her close, whispering into her ear that everything was going to be all right. Mothers' words to ease troubled children's fears. Comfort Alicen longed for. Permission she hadn't even realized she needed.

Again the two women were caught up in a rare moment of oneness. Where just being together, playing the role of mother and daughter, was enough to make the world seem like it might not be such a terrible place. That maybe there was hope beyond the madness that had taken rule of their lives.

Again silence captured the room as Betty held her daughter and Alicen let the painful emotions that had built up inside of her drain from her chest. For several long, quiet minutes, they were still, until the moment started to become uncomfortable for Alicen. She wasn't used to being held, comforted, vulnerable. She could feel the uneasy twitch of needing separation tickle at the insides of her brain, and she softly pushed away from her mother's arms. Her mind repeated that she wasn't a child anymore, so she shouldn't act like one.

Even now, after succumbing to insanity, Alicen wanted to save face in front of the one woman who had judged her more than the rest of the world combined. She wasn't ready to let that go.

Alicen sniffed, ran her fingers across her nose, wiped her tears, and unfolded her legs. They ached as she stretched her feet toward the floor, another reminder that her youth was behind her. Betty shifted as well, Alicen having caused a disturbance in their connected flow.

Alicen.

The sound caused Alicen to twitch slightly, its sudden intrusion unexpected. The timing of her mental delusions was almost comical.

Alicen, can you hear us? Do you see us?

She closed her eyes and ran her tongue along the back side of her clenched teeth.

"Alicen?" Betty asked, concern registering in her tone.

"Sorry," Alicen said, pushing away the voices and turning back to her mother.

Betty's face exposed her worry as she studied Alicen's for a long moment and then reached into the pocket of her cardigan. She pulled out an orange pill bottle, one Alicen recognized, and held it in her lap.

Betty glanced down at the item and swallowed. "I found these in your bathroom earlier while you were resting. I know you haven't been taking them, because the bottle's full. I counted."

"Of course you did," Alicen said without thinking. Her natural defensive stance against her mother was always her first reaction and took no effort. It was the letting her guard down that took real work.

Alicen. Do you hear us?

Do you see us?

Alicen bit the inside of her cheek and ignored the temptation to scream out at the voices only she could hear.

"I only just picked them up," Alicen said. "I hate the way they'll make me feel; I . . ." She wasn't sure what else to say. She had thought she didn't actually need them, hadn't she? She had thought she could handle this on her own.

Betty held the bottle out toward Alicen. "I think maybe you should reconsider after . . ." She trailed off.

After Alicen had tried to steal a child from a public place? She didn't blame her mother for not being able to vocalize it. It still seemed like something that had happened to someone else. It still felt like a nightmare.

Alicen reached for the orange tube and took it from Betty's

hand. The long, off-white pills rattled inside as Alicen's hand moved.

"You need help," Betty said, placing her hand on Alicen's arm. Alicen didn't glance up; she didn't want to see the expression on her mother's face.

"Don't, Alicen," a small voice echoed. This caught Alicen's full attention, and she looked up to see Evie standing across the room, next to the plush chair in the corner.

Alicen's breath caught in her throat.

Evie spoke, looking and sounding as real as any human Alicen had ever encountered. "They'll cloud your body and fill it with shadows," Evie said. "Shadows make it hard to see." There was a startling clarity bleeding through the girl's eyes. There wasn't a hint of fear, only certainty.

"Alicen, honey, do you understand what I'm saying here?" Betty asked.

"We have so much more to show you," Evie said.

The two voices raked at the inside of Alicen's brain. Each sounding as legitimate as the other. Each pulling her in opposite directions. It disturbed her that Evie, the little girl who had been haunting her for weeks, could feel as real as the mother she'd known her entire life. Another wave of sorrow washed over her, rattling the ends of her already-fraying resolve, and she couldn't hold back the tears threatening to bring her to her knees.

"Alicen, baby, please. I really think this is the best thing for you," Betty said.

"She doesn't believe; she doesn't know," Evie countered. "But you know. You have always known."

The air in the room felt too thick for Alicen to breathe, and panic started to work its way through her veins. She closed her eyes, shook her head, and stood.

"Alicen, please hear reason," Betty pleaded.

"Don't you want to see clearly?" Evie asked.

"Stop," Alicen whispered, straining to take a deep breath.

"Honey?" Betty said somewhere in the chaos taking over Alicen's mind.

"You know the truth; you've touched it before. Don't you want to remember?" Evie asked.

"I said stop," Alicen said, stronger, her eyes still closed. She stepped back and forth, pacing, pressing against the side of her skull as if she could push the crazy out. The air felt hot and humid even though in reality it was thin and chilled.

"The rest is just shadows," Evie said.

"Enough!" Alicen screamed. She couldn't take it anymore. "Enough, enough, enough! Get out of my head!"

"Alicen," Betty said, stepping up from where she was sitting and grabbing her daughter's shoulder.

Alicen yanked away from Betty's touch and opened her eyes to see the spot that had hosted Evie's tiny body was now empty. The air had started to thin, and the heat began to drain. She glanced at her mother, who looked terrified, her face white as a sheet, her eyes glistening with fearful tears.

Again Alicen looked to where Evie had been standing and was relieved to see she was still gone. The door to her bedroom cracked open, and Louise poked her head inside. Another set of worried eyes to stare at the deranged Alicen.

"Everything okay?" Louise asked.

Betty didn't respond. Neither did Alicen. What could either of them say? No, everything was not okay. Things hadn't been okay for a while. Alicen felt something shift in her palm and looked down to see she was still holding the orange pill bottle filled with her prescribed antipsychotic. There was no more getting past the inevitable.

Alicen didn't glance back up at the two women who anxiously waited to see what she would do next. She took the five long steps to the small bathroom connected to her room, moved inside, flipped the faucet on without turning on the light, opened the bottle, dropped two pills into her hand, popped them into her mouth, and took a deep swig of water flowing from the head. They struggled to slide down her throat, as if even her body was in rebellion against her, but she firmly forced them down.

Alicen looked at herself in the mirror. She searched for something in her face that would remind her of reality. She searched for something that would look familiar, that would look sane, but all she saw was a hollowed-out reflection of a woman she might have known once. Cruel tragedy had taken what she loved most, and then her own mind had stolen everything else that remained.

What *was* familiar was the numbing depression that was spreading up her legs, into her waist, and through her gut. It would erase the pain, it would encase her with a sense of nothingness, and it would drag her into a dark hole where she could suffer alone. She just wanted to be alone, without her fearful mother, without her concerned friend, without her rambling delusions, without her logic. Completely alone to drown in the undeniable truth that she was more than broken. More than lost. She was totally ruined.

She caught sight of the sleeping pills, nestled in their case, sitting in the corner of the counter, and grabbed them.

"Alicen?" Louise said, opening the bathroom door wider and stepping inside.

"I'm fine," Alicen replied. An automatic response that tumbled out with ease. She popped open the second bottle and used her fingers to dig for two pills.

"Okay," Louise said. "Betty and I thought some hot tea might be nice. You want to come join us?"

"No, thank you," Alicen said and placed the two sleeping aids on her tongue. She swallowed them easily and replaced the bottle's lid. "I'm just tired, so I think I'll rest."

"Okay; if you need anything, you let us know," Louise said.

Alicen nodded, still looking in the mirror as she listened to Louise leave, Betty in tow. The door to her bedroom clicked closed.

With a final glance at herself, Alicen left the attached bathroom and walked out into her room. She yanked the curtains closed. The sleeping aid was already beginning to work its magic, or maybe that was the fogginess that came from the antipsychotic swimming in her bloodstream; she wasn't sure. Either way, it pulled her to the mattress, tugged her under the comforter, and blocked out all thoughts. The only things that lay down with her were the feeling of loss, the sorrow it created, and the tears it conjured. All else was lost.

15

Alicen sat in Dr. Wells's office, alone. A nurse had shown her in, asking her to have a seat and wait. She wasn't sure where Dr. Wells was but found herself hardly caring. Not because she didn't want to care or because caring would be out of character for her, but because she couldn't seem to. She was sure her antipsychotics could be blamed for that.

So she'd sat as asked and found herself staring at nothing. Even that felt exhausting. She wanted to drop her head into her hands, wanted to cross the room and curl up on the couch under the window, wanted to go home. The drugs she'd been taking constantly the last several days had found a comfy home within her system and had taken over. Her brain felt mushy, and her will to struggle against anything was gone. Her medications had driven her to a nearly frozen state. Like she'd been mummified, or zombified, or something-fied. Like she was living inside her body but not really in complete control. She hated it, but she hadn't had a delusion since starting the pills, and seeing ghostly children was worse than feeling like a vegetable. Right?

The door to the office suddenly came to life, and she watched as Dr. Wells walked in, followed closely by his superior, Victoria. The sight of the administrator jarred Alicen's senses, and even in her fogged state, a nervous tension tightened her chest. Since having control of her body was a thing of the past, Alicen felt her eyes latch themselves to the tall woman's face and follow her as she crossed into the space and sat on the couch under the window.

"Good afternoon, Alicen," Dr. Wells said.

Her response time was slowed, but she finally yanked her eyes from Victoria and turned to see Dr. Wells had taken his usual place across from her. His smile was comforting, his eyes warm.

She swallowed and tried to smile in return. She couldn't see her face, but it felt more like a grimace across her lips than a smile.

"You remember Victoria," he said, motioning to the place where she sat. "I thought it might be a good idea for her to be a part of our session today."

"You did?" Alicen said, finding her words.

"Actually, to be candid, I asked to join," Victoria said, her voice drawing Alicen's attention back toward her. Her tone was clear and bold but intentionally soft. Or at least that's how it felt. Maybe it was just the numbed sensation it had to push through to get to Alicen's brain that made it feel that way.

"Oh," Alicen said. Again she would rather have kept her eyes downward, but her body wasn't her own.

Victoria didn't shy away from Alicen's stare. "Is that all right with you?" she asked.

Alicen nodded, unsure what other option there was.

Victoria smiled and relaxed against the couch's back. Alicen felt a sudden cold chill, and she dropped her eyes from the stark woman. Victoria had asked to join? *Of course she asked to join,* her mind rambled. *You tried to steal a child, honey. They think you're insane.*

I'm not insane, Alicen mentally countered.

But aren't you?

Reality sank farther into her weary brain. *Yes,* she conceded, *yes, I am.* An inappropriate sputter of laughter rippled off her tongue, and she bit down on it to conceal the insanity that was threatening to pour out.

"What's going through your mind right now?" Dr. Wells asked.

Alicen looked up at him. "I was just thinking about how crazy I actually am. Crazy enough to need two psychiatrists because one probably isn't enough at this point."

"We prefer not to use the word *crazy* around here," Victoria said.

Alicen let out another soft chuckle. "I thought another child was my dead daughter; what would you call that?" Alicen could feel anger surfacing even through her drugged state. It was warm inside her belly, like a simmering firework waiting to explode.

Victoria held Alicen's stare without any hesitation.

"Broken, maybe?" Alicen continued, the heat rising. "Fractured? Unsettled? Incapable of emotional control or mental clarity!" Her words were sharper than they needed to be. Pushing past the numb sensation seemed to heighten her emotions. As if she were overcompensating for her own lack.

A moment of silence hung around them before Victoria calmly turned to Dr. Wells and spoke. "Can you give us a moment alone?" It was a question phrased like a command, and the doctor gave Victoria a hesitant glance. It seemed as though he wasn't sure how to respond.

"Dr. Wells," Victoria said. It was pretty clear she wasn't going to be happy if she had to ask again.

He gave a swift clearing of his throat, turned to Alicen, and spoke as he stood. "I'll be right outside." A couple seconds later he was gone.

Another moment of silence filled the space as Victoria moved her gaze back to Alicen. Her expression remained steadfast and impassive. There was no telling what the woman was thinking behind her eyes, and it made Alicen unsettled. Dr. Wells had only been gone a moment, and already Alicen wished he'd return.

"Dr. Wells is an excellent addition to our facility here, but he is different from us, from you and me," Victoria said. "He comes from a different background. He can't quite understand that part of you." Victoria held Alicen's gaze. "His demons are different."

"Demons?"

Victoria nodded. "We all have them. Everyone is troubled. Some more than others, though. You, for example. You let your daughter drown."

She didn't even hesitate as she said it, and Alicen felt the room press down upon her.

Victoria continued. "The guilt of it now follows you around in the form of children. Little walking demons. Reminding you of what you did and who you are. Correct?"

Alicen couldn't reply. She wanted to be furious. Offended. But she couldn't be either, because Victoria was right.

Victoria nodded. "Or at least that is what you believe. I know because I have similar demons. You and I are the same, Alicen. I see myself in you. I know your trouble. I know it because it is my trouble."

Alicen remained silent. What could she say?

"It's simple really," Victoria said. "We were both born into hereditary evil, both suffered tragic loss, both paid for the sins of our parents. Perhaps unfair are the cards we've been dealt, but they are, nonetheless, ours."

Victoria leaned forward from the couch and placed her elbows on her knees. A bell echoed somewhere deep inside Alicen's psyche, warning her to retreat, but instead she felt herself drawn deeper into Victoria's gaze.

"There is only one path from here," Victoria said. "People like to believe there are many options, but there is only one. Acceptance."

She paused, letting her words worm their way deep into Alicen's chest. The air was stuffy, and still a shiver presented itself under Alicen's flesh. Her heart raced, even as the world seemed to have stilled. She could feel the bitter tears collecting in her eyes but also the groggy numb of drugs running through her bloodstream.

"Alicen," Victoria said, dropping her tone low, "you have to accept who you are and where you come from. Then we may have a chance to help you atone for your mistakes. Pay what you owe, so you can be free of your debt. Wouldn't you like to be free?"

Warm tears traced Alicen's cheeks. "How could I possibly pay for what I've done?"

"I will help you," Victoria said, "as someone helped me."

"What if I can't be helped?" Alicen's voice was barely a whisper.

"The reasons you are here can be terrifying to come to terms with," Victoria said. "No one understands that better than I do. But it can be done." Victoria reached out and placed her hand on top of Alicen's knee. "Even for you."

Fresh tears spilled from Alicen's eyes as her gaze continued to intertwine with Victoria's. *Even for you* echoed through her brain. Even for a mother who let her daughter die—that's what she meant. Even for a person who failed at the only thing worth living for. Even for you, Alicen. Time to pay for your mistakes.

"The choice is yours," Victoria said, releasing Alicen from her touch and sitting back against the couch. "I'm offering you freedom from your mind, but we won't force you into recovery. You have to want it, because it doesn't come without a cost."

Alicen took a shaky breath and finally dropped her eyes from Victoria's magnetic hold. Could what Victoria was suggesting actually be obtainable? Could Alicen pay enough to be free?

"Let me help you, Alicen," Victoria said.

Tearstained, Alicen glanced up at Victoria and nodded.

A spark flashed across Victoria's gaze as a half smile pulled up the corner of her mouth. "I knew you were going to be special," she said. "As I help you, it's almost like I'll be helping myself."

She gave a soft pop of laughter, and all the tiny hairs on the back of Alicen's neck stood.

"I'll be heading up your treatment from here on out," Victoria said. "I take on very few cases personally, but I'd like to keep my eye on you. For starters, we'll change up your medication, give you something with a little bit more strength. Ease the fracturing in your psyche."

"I'm already—" Alicen started.

"I know," Victoria said. Her words had a sharp edge. "Something stronger will be better. We need to control your mind, Alicen. Remove the strong will that is fighting the reality of where you are. Trust me."

Yes, Alicen. She's going to help you obtain freedom. Maybe make you worth it. Act like an adult, Alicen.

"I think that's enough for today," Victoria said, standing. Alicen hesitantly followed suit as the cold woman gave her a forced smile. "We're going to do so much good together."

Alicen didn't know how to respond to such an odd statement, so she simply nodded.

"I look forward to the path before us," Victoria said.

All Alicen's nerve endings seemed to pulse in response. In

fear or in excitement, Alicen wasn't sure. Either way it was uncomfortable.

"I'll send in a nurse to see you out," the administrator said as she turned and left.

• • •

Alicen had just left her session, all of what Victoria had said still lingering in her brain, when it happened. She was nearly to the parking lot when suddenly the silent world around her was interrupted by the haunting laughter she'd hoped to never hear again. One moment she was alone, contemplating snippets from her hijacked session with Victoria; the next she was surrounded by the eerie sound of her worst nightmare.

Alicen, can you hear us?

It caught her so off guard at first that she nearly tumbled over her own feet. It couldn't be. She was doped up good and proper, the antipsychotics swimming through her bloodstream, invading her mind and controlling her thoughts. Doped up against her every desire so that she didn't have to hear them. Didn't have to see them. Didn't have to fight them off.

Alicen, we're here. We're here.

"No," Alicen said, her voice nearly lost in the whooshing of the wind around her. It whirled violently and picked up the fallen leaves from the ground, carrying them skyward before dropping them back to the earth. Alicen looked in every direction, the laughter tickling the back of her neck.

Alicen, we're here. Do you see us?

She wanted to burrow into the ground at her feet. Wanted

to disappear. Again she turned in a circle, the wind still howling, seemingly right at her, the scene around her vacant of the children even as their giggling continued to reverberate inside her ear canals.

Alicen.

Their whispers were getting closer, right on top of her. She shook her head, panic and fear crawling through her insides, erasing any numbness the drugs may have induced. She had to get out of here.

She turned back toward the parking lot; she could see the car sitting a couple yards away. If she could only make it inside, maybe she could regain control. She began walking forward, the wind pressing at her shoulders, the whispers and laughter relentless.

The ground at her feet was dry, only dying grass and fallen leaves, but moving forward felt like trudging through mud. Every step harder than the last. Her body was betraying her again, her mind divided into different parts. One yelling at her to run from the imaginary madness, the other yelling at her to stay and believe it was more than imaginary. To give in.

Alicen, we're here. Do you see us?

She tried to move faster, against whatever force was taking over her body and the half of her brain that was lost to insanity. The wind's intensity was growing. It was as if she were caught inside a tornado, though the rest of the world sat unaffected. Another delusion of her mind. Another delusion created by the sickness taking up residence in her brain.

"Alicen," the same voice materialized in more than a whisper. And it was close. Before she could stop herself, Alicen glanced up and saw her. Evie, with three more familiar little faces behind her.

She isn't real, Alicen. She isn't there, Alicen, her mind said. *None of them are real.*

"When through the deep waters," Evie said, her voice a whisper as the wind whirled around Alicen like an angry force and dragged her to her knees. Another voice joined the imaginary children, an older voice, one she knew well and longed for often these days. On the wind, a familiar song. Grandma Joe's angelic tones barely touching Alicen's ears but clear enough to be sure of.

"'When through fiery trials thy pathway shall lie, my grace, all-sufficient, shall be thy supply.'"

"Time to remember, Alicen," Evie said.

"No, no, no!" she screamed, but the wind stole the sound as it exited her lips. She refused to become victim to this. "You aren't real; you're just my demons."

Grandma Joe's singing voice echoed through her brain. Soft and kind. Tears drained down Alicen's face, her nerves already rattled and torn. She wanted to be free of this nightmare. She felt unsteady and reached out to grab a nearby tree. She took short, shaky breaths, her eyes closed, her knuckles aching and turning white as she held herself in place.

"Time to remember," Evie said again.

Alicen squeezed her eyes shut and reminded herself that this was only insanity. It wasn't real. It wasn't real.

Alicen.

The drugs weren't working. The numbness was gone, and she was trapped in the falsehood of her own mind, which was trying to kill her. Alicen turned and pressed her back against the tree trunk. She kept her eyes closed as she tried to release the hold the voices had on her mind. It wasn't real. It wasn't real.

She didn't notice the wind die down or the voices quiet; she was lost inside herself.

Something lightly tapped her shoulder, springing her from her darkened state, and she screamed. Her eyes opened to be met by someone she wasn't expecting. An older woman, who took a step back, her eyes wide with fear, even though she had been the one to startle Alicen. She recognized the woman but couldn't place where she had seen her before through the pudding that was her brain.

"Sorry, sorry, sorry," the older woman mumbled, as she tucked a disheveled strand of hair behind her ear. Her voice was tiny, mouselike. Also familiar. It struck Alicen then—this was one of the women in her support group. She grappled for a name, searching back through her memory as she pushed herself away from the tree.

"I didn't mean . . . I saw . . . I shouldn't have . . ." The woman took another step back as Alicen moved forward.

"It's okay," Alicen said, feeling uncomfortable by how shaken the woman appeared. Like a deer caught in headlights. Alicen was afraid the woman might rush off at any moment.

The woman nodded, her whole body trembling, and fiddled with the ends of the scarf wrapped around her neck. A name suddenly dropped into Alicen's mind. Shannon. This woman's name was Shannon.

"Shannon, right?" Alicen asked, hoping to ease her clear discomfort.

The woman's face lit a little, and she smiled at the ground. "You remembered me. That's nice."

"From group," Alicen said.

Shannon nodded. "Yeah. I saw you over here, and you looked like maybe you were in trouble, so I meddled. Sorry—I meddle. I shouldn't meddle."

"No, it's okay. I'm not in trouble," Alicen said. Shannon seemed too loose of a cannon, so Alicen wanted to appear stable for fear of the woman losing it.

"Right, right. Well, I saw you talking to them, and talking to them can cause trouble. I don't want you to get in trouble," Shannon said. She spoke so fast, Alicen nearly missed it.

"Saw me speaking to whom?" Alicen asked.

Shannon glanced down at the ground momentarily, but her gaze didn't linger there. She shook her head, her eyes twitching back and forth, as if she wasn't sure what to say.

"Shannon," Alicen said, stepping toward the woman, her own mind churning.

Shannon took another step back, her fingers frantically rubbing the stringy ends of her scarf. Alicen paused, not wanting to scare her off.

"I saw you," Shannon whispered. "I see everything."

"What?" Alicen asked, shock rising in waves.

"I'm not supposed to—we . . . we shouldn't talk about it. They were talking to you, I thought. Were they not talking to you?" Shannon said, her words tumbling out confused and jagged.

Alicen tried to catch her breath as her heart raced. "You see them?"

Shannon looked at her, sympathy and knowing filling her eyes. "I see everything." Something formed between them in that moment, a tether that made Alicen feel strangely connected to this woman. Shannon nodded, tears filling her eyes, then swallowed hard and dropped her gaze. "But we shouldn't see them," she said.

"How can you see them?" Alicen asked.

"I'm sorry; I shouldn't have said anything," Shannon said. "I meddle. I shouldn't meddle." She turned to walk away.

"No, wait," Alicen said, following her.

Shannon paused as Alicen caught up to her and walked to stand in front, facing the woman.

"I see them; I was talking to them. Who are they?" Alicen asked.

Shannon kept her voice low. "Your trouble. You reap what you sow."

Alicen shook her head. Shannon wasn't making sense.

"Bad parents reap what they sow. I know what you did," Shannon said.

Her words hit Alicen like a punch to the gut.

Suddenly Shannon's mind seemed to be in a different place, and Alicen watched as a small smile pulled at her mouth. "I never had a daughter," Shannon said. "I had a son, though." The smile vanished and was replaced with sorrow. "I don't anymore."

Alicen took a deep breath through the pain Shannon's words had opened in her chest. She wanted the woman to explain herself, but she couldn't seem to find the words she needed.

Shannon's mind shifted again, and a look of terror took

over. She began to shake her head. "You shouldn't see anything. Trouble, trouble, trouble, and I don't want any more trouble." She stepped away from Alicen, grabbed either side of her skull with her hands, her head still shaking, and began mumbling under her breath.

"Shannon, tell me how you—" Alicen started, finally finding words.

Before she could finish, Shannon stepped so close to Alicen that she could smell the chicken and corn Shannon had eaten for lunch on her breath. Her eyes were wide with terror, and she locked them onto Alicen's as she spoke. "Don't come back to this place. You're special. She hates special."

"She? I don't understand," Alicen said.

"It's not safe here," Shannon said. "She's not safe." Something grabbed the woman's attention, something only she heard, and her eyes shifted away from Alicen quickly. "I have to go," Shannon said.

"Wait," Alicen said.

Without another word, Shannon raced past Alicen and back toward campus. Alicen considered following, but shock filled her ankles with lead, rooting her in place. Her mind was chaos, running in circles, stumbling over hurdles, falling down black holes of impossibilities.

She wasn't the only one who saw them. One haunting question formed through the madness, more terrifying than any she'd encountered before. If her mind was creating delusions, how could anyone else see them too?

16

Alicen felt like her mind had been run through a wood chipper by the time she arrived back at the Watson summer home. She sat in the car, parked in the driveway, until nearly dark. The sun was setting, the sky turning a dark blue, before she found the will to drag herself from the car and go inside.

The onslaught of questions being hurled at her mind through time and space were threatening her ability to think clearly, so she decided heading straight to her bedroom for the night was probably best.

It took Louise and Betty a couple of minutes to realize Alicen was back. Both of them, on different occasions, tapped on her door to make sure she was all right. Alicen dismissed them and then immediately crawled under the covers and began working to block out the world. If either of them later poked their heads in to check on her, Alicen didn't notice. If either of them tried to inquire into the events leading up to her stuffing herself under her comforter, she didn't register it. Her brain didn't have enough space or power to accept any more information, not while being suffocated by the weight of what had happened between her and Shannon.

Eventually everything went quiet. Alicen's mind didn't slow; she only became numb to the continuous pounding of questions. As if her body were protecting her, an eerie calm started to flood her bones. There was a single moment where she considered trying to get a couple of sleeping pills to drown the night in slumber, but then she decided she probably didn't need them. Slipping away from reality, hiding in the darkness built by her mind, was all that was left. So slowly, and without warning, Alicen fell asleep.

She didn't dream under the influence of her sleeping aids and assumed the same would be true of her present state, but when she opened her eyes and saw the depths of the forest around her, she knew her assumptions had been wrong. Unless, of course, she wasn't dreaming.

She turned her head in either direction, taking in the familiar scene. It was dim but not dark. The sky was captured in twilight but also held a bright round moon and dozens of shimmering stars. *Odd,* she thought.

"Beautiful, isn't it?" a little voice asked.

Alicen turned without surprise. Evie stood there at her side, alone. Her face clear, her eyes bright.

"It reminds me of the place I used to go with my grandmother," Alicen said.

"I know," Evie said.

"How could you know that?"

Evie smiled sweetly. "I know many things, Alicen."

Evie lifted her small hand and extended her pointer finger past Alicen. "For example, you used to come to that bridge with Grandma Joe. She taught you so much truth there. Truth you've forgotten."

Alicen turned and saw for the first time a small wooden bridge that extended over a flowing river she hadn't noticed before either. Surely they had been there before, though; rivers and bridges didn't just appear. Unless this was a dream, of course. The thought caused Alicen to glance down at her feet and wonder if she'd wake up in bed with dirt caked on them again. Could you be in a dream and in reality at the same time?

Another thought broke through her consciousness. "This isn't the right bridge. That was in Billings; this is Red Lodge," she said, turning back to Evie, who was smiling again.

The little girl shrugged her shoulders slightly. "Those rules don't really apply here. Only in the world of form."

"That doesn't make any sense," Alicen said.

"That's because you're trying to wrap your mind around it, and the mind is limited. You're trying to see it with the wrong set of eyes."

Alicen recalled the memory of her and Grandma Joe sitting on the bridge, discussing how to see clearly. One of the moments Evie was claiming to know about. Alicen felt her gaze drawn back to the bridge, where flittering images of her younger self and her grandmother faded in and out. Seeing even a hazy memory of Grandma Joe opened a well of emotions Alicen had sealed closed long ago.

"You've been dreaming of her again," Evie said.

Alicen turned back to Evie in wonder.

Evie smiled and tilted her head playfully. "I told you; I know many things."

"So you know what's happening to me? That I'm going crazy?"

Evie's face took on a shade of seriousness. "Crazy isn't a very nice thing to say about yourself."

"You're the second person to tell me that," Alicen said.

"She will tell you many things; be careful of her, Alicen."

Alicen knew Evie was referring to Victoria. "What she's told me so far is true."

Evie shrugged. "If you believe something is true, then maybe you make that thing true."

"What does that even mean?"

Evie gave a silly grin. "It means belief is a powerful thing."

"So if I just believe I'm not crazy, I suddenly won't be crazy?" Alicen mocked.

Evie chuckled, clearly taking Alicen's mockery as humor, and shook her head. "Who says you're even crazy to begin with?"

Alicen huffed in frustration, and it turned into a harsh cackle of laughter. "Why am I even talking to you?" She knew she was actually talking to herself, not this small delusion in front of her. She captured Evie's gaze with her own. "You aren't real."

Evie didn't flinch.

"You're just my trouble."

Evie cocked her head to the side slightly. "More things that she's told you. Lies that are easy to believe when you're clouded."

"The way you say things is funny," Alicen said. "It almost makes you sound as crazy as me."

Evie smiled without offense. "Many great speakers of truth have been labeled crazy. The greatest of all time was called a madman. Yet his truth set people free. I long to be his kind of crazy." The child let out a small laugh, and a warm spot opened in Alicen's chest.

"I don't think I know who you're talking about," Alicen said.

"Your grandma knew him well. So did you, once."

Alicen shook her head. "No. I wouldn't forget someone like that."

"Yet here we are."

Alicen didn't understand and opened her mouth to say as much before she was cut off. A tiny singing voice sounded from behind. Soft and whimsical.

"'When through the deep waters I call thee to go,'" the small voice sang. Alicen turned to see the twins. Roxie, the one who talked, and Tate, the one who didn't. Arm in arm, little bounces filling their steps as they moved toward her. Humming the familiar tune, its strains opening Alicen's heart further.

They both looked up at Alicen with wonder-filled expressions. Roxie smiled and spoke. "You can sing with us if you want."

Alicen shook her head. "I don't remember the words."

Tate leaned close and whispered something in Roxie's ear.

Roxie listened and then continued. "Tate wants to know why adults forget so many things." Both twins looked at her with curious eyes and waited. Were they actually asking her how she'd forgotten lyrics to a song she hadn't heard in decades?

"I guess time," Alicen said. "Life happens, and you just forget things. It happens to everyone."

Roxie and Tate exchanged an excited glance, as if they had a secret they didn't want to share, and turned their attention back to Alicen. Tate let out a small giggle as Roxie spoke. "Maybe it isn't actually forgotten, just hidden in the shadows. Remove the shadows, and you'd see it again. Right?"

Alicen shrugged, a smile pulling at the corner of her mouth. These two were odd. Adorable but odd. "I suppose so."

"You are the light of the world, Alicen," Evie said. Alicen had almost forgotten she was there. "Shadows are only shadows."

Roxie let out a joyous squeal. "Shadows are only shadows! I could explode from happiness. Don't you feel like you could explode?" She threw her hands into the air and twirled around, laughter slipping past her lips.

Alicen shook her head, her mouth still gaping open. Her mind stuck. One part insisting this was nothing more than a dream. Another insisting it was so much more than she realized. All of it colliding and overwhelming her senses so that all she could do was wonder.

Something cooed across the river, and all the children turned their heads. Alicen did the same and spotted a piercingly white creature, small in stature, maybe two feet tall with wings that expanded from its body. It was perched at the bottom of a tree, looking at them all, cocking its head to the right and then to the left. A furry white bat. Alicen's mind whirled as memories of her grandmother exploded through her psyche.

This isn't real, something urged deep in the caverns of her brain.

Or is it? another thought whispered.

Roxie and Tate bounced in unison. "Oh—he's so cute!" Roxie said. "I want to catch one and keep him."

"You can't catch them," redheaded Beck said, stepping out from under the cover of trees. "And you definitely can't keep one as a pet. Besides, they talk too much."

Talk? Alicen heard the word but struggled to process its meaning.

"I think they're funny," Roxie said.

"You think everything is funny," Beck said. He walked over and joined the group, making the band of children complete.

The white creature shifted once more and then turned its head to look right at Alicen. For a moment Alicen held eye contact with the creature. Then it winked at her and launched itself off the ground and into the sky so quickly that it seemed to disappear into thin air. Just like that, it was gone.

A small hand tugged on Alicen's sleeve, drawing her out of her frozen state. Roxie smiled up. "He liked you; I can sense these kinds of things."

Alicen couldn't think, much less speak.

"Do you think if we caught one, he would teach us karate?" Roxie asked no one in particular.

Alicen returned her eyes to the sky that had a moment

earlier held a bat. A bat that had winked at her. "My grandma used to tell me if I searched hard enough, I would see one," she whispered, the insanity of her words echoing back to her. But it all seemed so real. "I never thought I would."

"Well, they aren't really from this place," Beck said.

Alicen looked back to the children, who had all now turned their eyes to her. They were staring at her with as much excitement as they had given the small white bat. "Where are they from?" she asked.

Beck smiled. "That's a story for another time."

"It's a great story," Roxie said.

A crack of thunder crashed overhead, shaking Alicen from her numbed state. Her treacherous mind turned angry and violent. She yanked away from the children and stepped back. *This isn't real,* she thought. *None of this is real.*

"Alicen," Evie said.

"No," Alicen replied. Wind whipped up around her, the air darkening as rain clouds appeared from nowhere and the sky opened up. Cold drops fell on her head, soft and slow at first. She took another step back as the rain began to quicken.

"Shadows are only shadows, Alicen," Evie said.

"That doesn't make any sense!" Alicen snapped. "Winking bats, imaginary children, and magic water." She shook her head.

Get a grip, Alicen.

Act like an adult, Alicen.

What would your mother say, Alicen?

"You can see behind the shadows," Roxie said through the howling wind. "If you want to, you can see."

"Stop," Alicen said. "This isn't real. You aren't real."

"Alicen," Evie said, stepping forward and extending her hand.

"No!" Alicen held her own hands out in defense. "I'm sick, and you're my trouble. You're my trouble for what I've done." The rain overhead became weighted, as if it had turned to mud, as the realization of her situation pressed into her shoulders. Shame for who she was and the pain she had caused. The life she'd stolen.

"Don't, Alicen. Remember, you are—" Evie started, but Alicen was finished with this nonsense.

"Enough! Enough! You aren't real. I'm sick. You're my trouble." Alicen pressed her hands over her eyes. The rain fell harder, the wind harsh as it thrashed against her body. She sank to her knees and repeated, "You aren't real. I'm sick. You're my trouble." Her face was damp, rain and tears combined.

Alicen.

The children's voices had returned to the air, swimming around her head, tempting her to fall back under their spell. But she wouldn't. This was just a dream, and she needed to wake up.

Get a grip, Alicen.

Act like an adult, Alicen.

What would your mother say, Alicen?

"Wake up, Alicen," she said under her breath. "Wake up."

Alicen, do you hear us?

She could see the lightning streaks through her closed eyes. The heavy rain still pelting her skin. The thunder rolling in waves.

Alicen, can you see us?

"You're sick, Alicen; this is your trouble," she said. "Wake up."

Alicen.

"Wake up wake up wake up wake up!"

Alicen's eyes snapped open inside her dark bedroom, her vision hazy, her head throbbing as her breaths came in shaky waves. Her face was pressed against something hard, but her arms were free, and she used them to push herself up. Her eyes began to adjust to her familiar surroundings, and it only took her a moment to realize she was lying on the floor. In her bedroom, fully clothed, boots on, shivering and wet.

She pushed herself all the way up to standing, her muscles aching and stiff. A soft tapping was echoing against her windowsill. Alicen moved to the window, pulled the shade aside, and saw soft rain falling across the backyard. And she was soaked through. She'd been out there. Alicen searched the darkened backyard, her heart thumping in steady rhythm with the rain. She was terrified she'd see them.

You're sick. Get a grip, Alicen.

She let the shade fall closed and tried to steady her trembling hands. She was sick. She was troubled. Her mind was the cause of this. She wanted to believe that truth with every cell in her body. She wanted to pay and be free from this debt. But a small pocket of her heart had been tugged open, just enough for there to be a thin, fading feeling that maybe there was something she wasn't seeing yet. A thin, fading feeling that maybe she had once believed something that she had long since forgotten.

17

The war inside Alicen's mind was more violent than ever. One side larger, more established, combating claims of unseen children with compelling and realistic arguments. She was sick because she had let her daughter die; this was the price of shame. Her trouble. She was broken, losing all sense of herself to madness. It was normal to want to believe everything you saw was real, even if most of what you were seeing was fictitious. Then she could hide behind the lie that everything was fine. But it wasn't fine.

The other side was small and weak. But brave, enduring slaughter after slaughter. More is happening here, it told her. The things you are seeing are for a reason. Shannon sees them. Grandma Joe saw them. What if this isn't all fictional? What if there is a power that actually exists beyond what you can see? What if you know more than you realize? Had Grandma Joe known something real? Could Alicen?

She paused as she moved down the stairs from her bedroom. This was insane. The delusions had gotten under her skin, and now she couldn't shake them. But she was an adult, and she understood the way the world worked, and this was impossible.

But what if it wasn't?

Alicen cursed out loud and slammed her palm down on the stair railing. It shook all the way to the end and rattled the wall and rocked a small square picture off its nail. It crashed to the floor, the glass plate covering the photo shattering across the bottom step. Alicen cursed again, moving down the final few stairs toward the broken frame just as Betty walked around the corner, concerned.

"Alicen?" she said, her eyes dropping to the fallen picture. "What happened?"

"Clearly it needed a new nail," Alicen said.

"I'll grab a broom," Betty said.

"I can do it," Alicen spat. She knew her tone was harsher than necessary, and she made a conscious effort to reel it in.

Betty cut her eyes at her daughter. "Don't be so stubborn all the time," she said before disappearing and returning a couple seconds later with broom in hand. The two women cleaned up the mess in silence, Alicen picking up the wooden frame that had chipped and cracked while Betty swept up the broken glass bits.

"So the picture just fell from the wall?" Betty asked, her tone saying more than her words. "Odd."

Alicen bit her tongue. Anything she responded with would be from a place of anger and frustration. Betty would just end up as collateral damage. The last thing Alicen needed was to walk right into an argument with her mother.

In the kitchen, Betty tossed the broken glass into the trash, and Alicen laid the frame on the counter. The photo that had been sealed inside was one Alicen was familiar with: a Watson family photo, taken one summer when Louise was still in elementary school.

The picture held the four Watson members: Mr. and Mrs. Watson, Peter Watson, Louise's older brother, and of course Louise. All smiles, all matching in light-blue tops, standing in front of the Watson summer home, looking like the perfect snapshot of a happy family. Alicen could nearly feel the love oozing from their gazes.

"Did we ever take a family photo?" Alicen asked out loud.

"What?" Betty asked.

Alicen waved the photograph and then handed it over to her mother. Betty grasped it and gave it a momentary glance before setting it down on the counter beside the broken frame.

"There wasn't ever really a need. It was just the two of us; besides, I hate getting my photo taken," Betty said. She walked into the tiny hall closet around the corner and tucked the broom away.

"What about Grandma Joe? She was part of our family," Alicen said.

She noticed Betty pause for a moment before turning and stepping back toward the kitchen counter. "Why the sudden interest in family photos?"

The thoughts threatening to drizzle from Alicen's mouth should have been contained, but she was losing the ability to keep her words at bay. Or maybe she was just losing the desire.

"I guess I figure if I'm going to be crazy like Grandma, I should know more about her. You completely stopped talking about her after . . ." Alicen let the words *she died* shrivel on her tongue because she could see the hint of pain in her mother's expression.

"There wasn't ever any point in talking about her," Betty said.

"She was my grandmother, your mother," Alicen said.

"I know who she was," Betty snapped.

Alicen fell quiet as Betty took a deep, controlled breath and turned her face away from her daughter. The pain was familiar to Alicen. Loss, regardless of who it was, looked the same on them. Alicen knew the bitter sting and probably should have backed off, but she couldn't. She spoke softly, hoping to earn her mother's favor. "Can we talk about her? It might help me better understand what is happening to me. If we really are both . . ." Alicen let her words trail off.

Betty glanced back at Alicen, a chilly guard covering her face, something else Alicen knew well, and nodded. "What do you want to know?" Betty asked.

A flurry of thoughts shuffled through her mind. Now that the moment had come and she was being given the opportunity, she had a hard time grasping on to the right words. "I want to know more about how her illness manifested," Alicen said.

Betty wouldn't make eye contact with Alicen. Instead, she glued her eyes to the wandering wood lines in the broken picture frame between them and maintained a steady rhythm of breathing. Alicen waited patiently and, after a long minute of nothing, felt the itch to question her mother again. But she remained quiet.

"There was a time," Betty finally began, hesitantly, "before she was sick. When I lived at home, before I left for adulthood. She was funny, knew everyone in town. We couldn't go anywhere without running into a familiar face. I mean, we always had our differences, we never really saw the world the same way, but she was normal."

"What happened?" Alicen asked.

Betty nodded slightly. "I don't think anyone knows. She just changed. It happened slowly; small things at first, and then more dramatic. In the end she seemed to cause a scene everywhere we went."

"She started seeing and talking to things that weren't there?"

Betty nodded and swallowed.

Alicen could see how painful this was for her but pushed forward. "Did you ever ask her about the specific things she saw? Or did she talk about what they said? What about Grandpa? What about her family?"

Betty glanced up at Alicen, a spark of disbelief in her eyes. "How about one question at a time, dear," she snapped. "No,

I didn't ask; we were encouraged not to engage with her delusions. As far as her family, she was an only child and didn't have very much other family. When she changed, everyone turned away except for your grandfather."

"You never talk about him, either," Alicen said.

Something gentle and kind softened Betty's face for a moment before disappearing as quickly as it had come. "He always protected me. He loved your grandma in spite of how crazy she got, and he shielded me from getting swallowed in the madness for as long as he could handle." Betty shook her head and pushed away from the counter. "I should have done the same with you. I never should have brought you to this place."

"You didn't have a choice. Grandpa abandoned her," Alicen said.

"This isn't your grandfather's fault," Betty defended.

"He left you to care for her alone."

"He tried everything he could think of to get her help, and she refused. Do you have any idea what it must have been like for him all those years? A person can only take so much. I don't blame him for leaving."

Alicen felt fury rise in her chest. "How can you not blame him for that?"

"He was just a man, Alicen."

"And you were just her daughter!"

Betty huffed loudly and turned away.

Alicen shook her head in disbelief. "You always did this with Allen and me too. It was always my fault. The man was a joke of a husband, but somehow I was to blame for that."

Betty swung back around, red-hot fire in her eyes. "Well, dear, you usually were."

Alicen sucked in a deep breath as the few moments of comfort her mother had shown in the last week dissolved. They were right back where they had started. How many times would they do this? Enough that it shouldn't hurt as much anymore.

Betty realized how cross she sounded and took a deep breath, closed her eyes, and raised both her hands in surrender. "I haven't been sleeping well, and I have a pounding headache. This is a terrible time to be having this conversation." A perfectly trained excuse for beating her daughter down and shifting blame to anything but herself.

Alicen was doped up enough, and angry enough, that she didn't even care what fell from her lips now. "Of course, Mother, because me losing my mind is much harder on you."

Rage washed over Betty's face, and then she placed a shaky hand over her mouth and shook her head. As if she were holding back words she didn't want to slip out. Tears brimmed in her eyes, and she turned them away from Alicen.

Guilt racked the inside of Alicen's chest, and her anger defused. Silence stole the air from the room as she tried to think of a way to apologize. Her first reaction was always to apologize, even if she wasn't to blame. But then, wasn't she always to blame?

But Betty spoke before she could. "This is terrifying for me," she said, "watching the same thing that happened to your grandma happen to you. Knowing I could have stopped this if only . . ."

"I don't think it works like that, Mom," Alicen offered, trying to stop the spiral of self-pity that was coming.

Betty swallowed, her eyes twitching back and forth as if she were internally battling with what to say next. "Maybe I should have said . . . I didn't know if it would be helpful . . ." Betty couldn't seem to make a sentence stick.

"What are you talking about?" Alicen asked.

In a tone barely above a whisper, her eyes trained downward, Betty spoke. "She saw children too, your grandmother."

"What?" Alicen said. She could feel the color draining from her face.

"They came to her in the forms of children, she would say, her guides on a holy mission." Betty paused a beat before continuing. "You're sleepwalking. I know. I heard you come back last night. She used to . . ." Tears threatened to choke out Betty's words. "You can't imagine what this is like for me, knowing that I caused this."

Alicen's mind whirled too fast for her to grab on to a single thought, much less a response. Images of the times she'd encountered the children played on repeat, like a scary movie.

"Children, of all things," Betty said. "She put this disease in you because I let her." Betty sneered and shook her head. "Children led around by a tiny little girl with pigtails—I mean, utter nonsense."

The atmosphere in the room shifted, and Alicen's mouth went dry. "Evie," she muttered.

Betty stilled to a state that drew Alicen's eyes because it was so eerie. "What did you say?"

"That was the name of Jane's imaginary friend. She has pigtails."

Betty's shoulders trembled, her face paler than before. Her eyes were wide with horror, as if Betty herself had suddenly seen the children. A tear slipped down Betty's cheek, and she reached to brush it away. She took a deep inhale and shook off the sudden fright that had captured her. "You must have heard that from Josephine. She used to call one of them Evie—it's such a strange little name, isn't it?" Betty had dropped her eyes back to the floor as she began to fiddle with the hem of her sweater, a telltale sign that she was extremely uncomfortable.

But all that was suddenly lost on Alicen, because her brain only registered *children* and *Evie*. All the logic in the world struggled to make sense of what her soul was itching to believe.

The smaller, weaker part of herself gained ground as emotion rammed her like a train. As if she'd been standing on a silent track and then suddenly a full-speed locomotive had appeared, giving her no time to try and save her own life. Again she lost control of her words and phrases as they tumbled out on their own. "A little girl with pigtails named Evie," she whispered, her eyes fixed forward, her mind desperately trying to find some sort of footing.

"Enough, Alicen," Betty said. "She did this to you, honey. Grandma Joe put all this nonsense inside your head, and now it's coming back. What do they call it, repressed memories or something like that?"

But Alicen was ignoring her now, lost in her thoughts.

"I thought I knew that name because of Jane. How could Jane and Grandma Joe both use that name?"

"You must have said it before, and Jane heard it from you," Betty said. "That's possible, right? Does it even matter? All that matters is that this came from that crazy old woman. I should have gotten you out of there sooner."

Alicen was barely listening. Her lips quivered, tears hot but silent on her cheeks. "What if . . . ?" Alicen didn't need to finish her question.

"No, honey," Betty said as she composed herself and walked around the counter's edge to place her hand on her daughter's shoulder. "I've heard people talk about tragedy stirring up things you may have forgotten. She filled your mind with poison, and then in your greatest moment of brokenness, it's coming back to haunt you. That's all this is."

Alicen shook her head, still not looking toward her mother, still struggling to peel herself off the steel track where she'd been flattened. "All this is?" she asked. "What . . . what if . . ." Tears stifled whatever words she would have tried to say next, and a small cry escaped from her mouth instead.

Betty grabbed Alicen's other shoulder and twisted her until she was facing her mother, Alicen's eyes still lost to the ground. "Honey, look at me," Betty said. She reached out her fingers and forcefully raised Alicen's chin so that their eyes couldn't avoid each other. "Look at me."

Alicen obeyed.

"You are sick. This is not real; it's all in your head. Are you skipping your medication? You have to be very diligent about it."

Alicen nodded. "I'm taking it," she said. She felt like a little girl, standing there in her mother's grasp, being directed and scolded.

"Well then you need to do more. You need to tell that doctor to give you something else. You need to make this stop," Betty said. The softness in her tone was retreating with each word she spoke; the disapproving tone Alicen knew so well was returning.

"They make me feel so—" she started, not giving Betty the response she wanted.

"Get a grip, Alicen," Betty snapped.

Alicen clenched her teeth together and dropped her gaze again. Her mind too broken and feeble to fight back. *Yes, get a grip, Alicen.* Her mind smacked her with cruelty. *Act like an adult, Alicen. What would your mother say, Alicen?* Betty must have noticed how harsh her last statement had been, because she gave Alicen's shoulder a friendly rub.

"Honey, if you don't get ahold of this sickness, it will ruin your life. Like it did your grandma's," Betty said. "I want more for you than that. I always just wanted more for you; don't you see that?"

Alicen still said nothing. What would she say? *Yes, Mother; thank you, Mother; how kind of you, Mother,* her mind teased relentlessly. Pain thumped inside the center of her forehead, and Alicen breathed through it. Too many broken elements were swirling around in her mind.

"Alicen, do you hear me? Do you see how troubling this is?" Betty said.

Alicen nodded and turned her gaze back up toward her mother. "Yes," she replied. "This is my trouble."

"Promise me you'll stop trying to make what isn't real into something else. Talk to the doctor; don't let this follow you all of your life. Promise me," Betty insisted.

And Alicen conceded. "I promise."

Betty sighed and gave a small smile. "Good, honey; that's good. I just want you to be happy."

Alicen tried to ignore the little voice from deep within that said Betty didn't care one tiny bit about whether or not Alicen was happy. She just didn't want Alicen to be crazy. She'd rather her be numb.

But Alicen didn't want to be crazy either, and numb seemed so much more appealing. She'd hoped that she could put her mind back together. That she could reassemble a clear sense of what was reality and what was fiction. But maybe the only way to do that was to just shut it off altogether. Pay her debts.

The tiny voice whispered again, and Alicen tried to hide any fear from spreading across her expression. *But, Alicen, what if what the world believes is fiction is actually reality?*

18

Alicen managed to make it through another network session without grossly overexaggerated thoughts of violence, though it was hard every time Stew expressed how helpful carrying around an umbrella had become. Apparently his personal storm cloud didn't soak him through as often, which made him more talkative than ever.

Alicen tried to pay attention as others spoke, but her mind kept getting dragged away to thoughts of what she'd discussed with Betty the afternoon before. *Grandma Joe saw children too.* That phrase had become a permanent fixture in her mind, and she couldn't help but glance over at Shannon each time it crossed her brain. Shannon had claimed to see them too. It just didn't make sense. If Josephine had planted this poison in Alicen's mind, then how could a complete stranger—a woman who couldn't possibly have known Josephine—be seeing the same invisible force Alicen was? There had to be a connection that would help Alicen understand it. By the time the meeting drew to a close, Alicen had decided she needed to ask Shannon how she could know anything about the children.

She waited as Gina gave closing remarks and dismissed the group. People started to collect their things and move. Some chatted as they waited for their scheduled nurses to come and escort them back to their rooms. Alicen watched Shannon stand and move to the beverage table along the back wall of the room.

Alicen stood and casually drifted toward the table, avoiding interaction with anyone else. She stepped up next to Shannon and waited for the woman to notice her. She didn't. The older woman just picked through the iced crate of juice containers, passing over a couple marked orange, clearly looking for the perfect one.

Alicen cleared her throat, and Shannon gave a little jump. She turned her surprised expression to Alicen and drew her lips together in a tight line. Her eyes were worried and confused as they darted between Alicen and the plastic carton filled with juices.

"Do you want one?" Shannon asked in a tiny voice.

"No thanks," Alicen said.

"Okay," Shannon replied and then went back to searching.

Alicen racked her brain for the right way to bring up what she wanted to ask. It was pretty clear that Shannon was skittish and timid, and Alicen didn't want to scare her off. "Hey, Shannon—it is Shannon, right?" Alicen asked.

Shannon glanced up at her for a moment and then smiled.

Alicen decided to take that as a yes and a sign that the woman was listening.

"Can I talk to you about what happened between us the other day?" Alicen asked. She couldn't help but feel like she was talking to a child, even though the woman had at least two decades on her.

"What happened between us the other day?" Shannon asked, still carefully examining each juice bottle.

"You know, when you found me outside, when you talked to me about . . ." Alicen paused and dropped her voice to a whisper. ". . . the children?"

Shannon selected an orange juice bottle that looked exactly like the ten others she had passed over and turned to Alicen. She held it out. "Do you want a juice? The orange is my favorite. I can find you a perfect one if you want?"

"No, Shannon, I don't want a juice, I want to talk to you about the children. The ones you see?"

Shannon's brow dropped and she shook her head. "I don't think I want to talk to you about this. I just wanted juice."

"Shannon, please; I need to know . . ."

Shannon shook her head and started to walk past Alicen. Alicen felt her desperation take on a mind of its own, and she reached out and grabbed Shannon's arm.

The older woman whirled around, fear brimming in her eyes, and looked at the place where Alicen was holding her. "Let go of me," she said.

"Just tell me about what you saw," Alicen started.

"I didn't see anything. I don't know anything about any children," Shannon said, yanking her arm away.

"But you said you saw them that day."

"No, I didn't. I don't know anything about children."

"Shannon, you said . . ."

"I didn't say anything to you; I don't even know you. I don't talk to people I don't know, I don't go into the forest, and I don't know anything about children."

Alicen felt desperate to get ahold of the situation and could feel the eyes of a couple people now watching. "You said you had a son once," she said.

Shannon's face dropped, her skin paled, and her lips quivered. Her eyes filled with tears as she clutched the little bottle of orange juice to her chest. "How—how did you know that?"

"You told me," Alicen said.

"No!" Shannon yelled. "No, I didn't tell you anything!"

Alicen took a step back from the woman as a nurse came up to them, accompanied by Gina. "What is going on here?" the nurse asked, her eyes switching back and forth from Alicen to Shannon.

Shannon held a finger up toward Alicen, her hand trembling, and spoke to the nurse. "She attacked me."

Alicen's mouth dropped open in shock. "I did not attack her."

"You attacked my mind!" Shannon yelled. She turned back to the nurse. "She knows about Tommy. I didn't tell her, but she knows and she tried to get me to tell her about him."

Gina stepped in and looked at Alicen. "How do you know about Tommy?"

"She told me," Alicen said.

Surprise crossed Gina's face, and she turned to Shannon. "Shannon, that's wonderful that you told her."

"I didn't tell her! I don't even know her! I wouldn't tell her!"

"Okay, Shannon; it's okay," the nurse said, trying to regain control of the situation. "Why don't you let me walk you back to your room?"

"She made it up!" Shannon yelled, pointing at Alicen. "She's crazy! She made it all up."

Alicen opened her mouth to speak, but nothing came out. The entire scene was madness.

"Let's go back to your room, Shannon," the nurse said again, sending a warning look at Alicen over her shoulder, and again Alicen felt her mouth drop open. Was she being blamed for what was happening here?

Shannon nodded to the nurse, threw a final hateful glare at Alicen, and let herself be escorted out of the room, rambling under her breath about how Alicen was crazy with each step. Alicen stood frozen, completely thrown by what had just happened.

"You shouldn't make stuff up," someone said behind her, someone else from group but not someone Alicen knew a name for.

"I didn't," Alicen defended.

"Shannon has never talked about her son," Stew said to her right.

"I didn't even know she had a son," another girl said.

"Why would she tell you about him?" Stew asked.

"You shouldn't make stuff up," the nameless person said again.

"All right," Gina said, "that's enough. Everyone off now."

The room cleared out as Gina placed a hand on Alicen's shoulder and offered her a smile. "It'll be okay," she said.

"I didn't make it up," Alicen said.

Gina nodded, her eyes sympathetic. "I'm sure you didn't," she said, but she said it the way a person would when she didn't actually believe you were telling the truth. "Maybe you should share during our next session? It would be good." And with that, Gina smiled and left the room.

A single thought drifted through Alicen's mind. What if Shannon had never been there that day? What if she had simply imagined the encounter, like she imagined the children themselves? What if Alicen had, in fact, made it up?

• • •

You are failing, little Victoria.

No, Victoria thought as she paced back and forth across her dark office.

As she fails, so do you.

"No," Victoria said. "I will not fail."

Born from filth, a worm, a failure.

Anger poured through her veins, and she reached over to her desk and swept her open hands across the left side, sending its contents to the ground. They landed with a crash that vibrated under her feet as her uncle's deep laughter filled her brain. She took several deep heaves of hot air and tried to calm the tremor in her hand. She was losing control.

Victoria closed her eyes. Took her mind to a safe place. A place where she imagined she was someone else. Someone calm and sweet. Innocent and free. Where the world hadn't marked her with dirt and left her to die alone.

Vicki: Why so angry?

Victoria: Angry is better than weak.

Vicki: I'm afraid of you when you're angry.

Victoria: You're afraid of everything.

Vicki: Aren't you afraid?

Victoria: Not anymore.

Vicki: Will you protect me from the demons?

Victoria: Always.

Vicki: Don't let him get me.

Victoria: I never would.

She took a slow breath and opened her eyes as the air passed out through her teeth. Her office still again, the thundering of her heart back to a normal pace. She stooped down to collect the items that had scattered across the floor and neatly placed them back on her desk. The moment of weakness had passed.

Aren't you glad I didn't let you be weak like Vicki?

Victoria tapped the stack of files in her hand so they were perfectly aligned and then set them in the replaced metal basket where they belonged.

Like Alicen?

Yes, Victoria thought. He had taught her well, even if the lessons had come at a painful price.

Penance is due for Alicen's weakness.

No, Victoria thought. She knew what he was referring to. Her skin in the game. Stored away from inquiring eyes, hidden under a loose tile in the bathroom. She could sense the small wooden box calling to her, as if it had a tongue and were whispering her name.

Penance, little Victoria. You reap what you sow.

"It isn't my filth," Victoria said.

Her filth is your filth. Her trouble, your trouble.

The hidden scars burned along her wrists. Both beckoning her to serve and screaming at her to run. Her source of release was also her source of pain.

"No—it isn't my failure," she whispered.

All their failures are yours. You can't atone if you don't know what you are. His words crashed down over her like fiery waves. *Don't forget what demons lie within.*

The familiar statements were truths burned into the marrow of her bones. Helping her remember so she could do what was necessary to control her trouble.

Only through the admittance of our stains.

Her constant savior and accuser.

Life always comes to collect.

Again she felt the pull from the dirty secret, and it moved her feet across the office floor into the small bathroom. Without pause she removed the hidden box and held it firmly in both hands.

Release your darkness, little Victoria, so it doesn't swallow you whole.

She couldn't open the lid because she knew doing so would seal her fate. But she couldn't stop herself either.

It slipped open easily, and inside lay a single razor blade. It caught the starlight shining in through the tiny bathroom window, and Victoria felt a sense of peace begin to spread.

She'd always found the razor to be the most efficient. Knives and glass cut too deep, and she only needed small lines to release what was trapped within. A habit she'd formed in her early teens. One she hadn't practiced in a while. One she'd missed.

Victoria didn't flick on the bathroom light. She didn't need it. She could find the perfect spot with her eyes closed. She grabbed the small razor as a tremble of desire and horror pulsed through her palm.

Yes—good, Victoria. Payment is due for all she has done.

Tears already collecting in her eyes, Victoria pulled up her sleeve and lowered the tip of the blade to touch her flesh. A spark of familiarity drove her arm up as she pressed down, breaking the skin. Pain burned up through her limb and down into her fingers. Tears dripped down her cheeks as blood pooled and ran across her wrist.

And peace settled into her mind as her inner demons were exposed. Victoria closed her eyes and saw Alicen's face. She started a new line in her skin, dragging the blade up her wrist. She was paying for Alicen's weakness.

For now this will do, but she needs to atone. So you can atone.

Yes, Victoria thought as she started a third drag in her skin. Alicen would pay for her filth. If necessary, she would pay with her life.

19

The stronger dose of antipsychotics didn't take long to get comfortable in her system. The next few days passed in a slow sludge of what her reality would possibly be like from now on. A massive cloud of eternal fog that shut out most of the world. She could still see everything, of course; she could still hear the words, but everything was captured in a haze. The colors weren't as bright, and no one's words were as clear. But the children and their haunting whispers were gone, and for all intents and purposes, Alicen's mind seemed mended.

Even her senses of taste and smell were affected. The little pleasures she might have enjoyed once upon a time were now dulled. She tried not to succumb to the fact that she felt like a puppet to the medication, but it was hard to ignore the way it dictated her every move. When she slept, when she ate. She couldn't drive or be left alone, except for the hours she spent holed up in her bedroom, trying not to remember what her life had been like before Jane died.

Louise told her she'd read online that journaling her feelings might help, and without any reason to resist anymore, Alicen had started. A new page for every day, the same kinds of words and sentences on each.

I don't really feel like myself today.

I'm tired even though it feels like all I do is sleep.

I feel alone.

I think about Jane all the time.

I failed her, and this is my punishment. My trouble.

I wonder if the fog will ever clear.

I wonder if this will be the rest of my life.

Alicen wasn't sure it was helping to put her thoughts on paper, but she kept doing it, a sort of nighttime routine, because honestly she didn't have anything else to do. The days were long, the nights longer still, and every morning was the same. Reality had injected itself with staleness and a deep numbing that made the whole world seem like it was moving in slow motion. After nearly a week of taking her new medication, Alicen found herself, like she had each night before, writing in her journal the same things she'd written a handful of times.

I wonder if the fog will ever clear.

I wonder if this will be the rest of my life.

She shut the journal, tucked it away, and lay down against

her mattress. It would be another long night of empty dreams and assisted, medicated sleep that never really seemed to give her any rest. Tomorrow would come with the rising sun, and Alicen would walk like a zombie through another day of the same, and she wouldn't hear voices, or see children, or feel broken. No, she had traded her broken, chaotic brain for deadened mush, and honestly, she wasn't sure which one was worse.

• • •

Alicen had never seen the small bookstore in this state. Empty except for a few stray boxes that were still being packed, the dust on the last few bookshelves that hadn't been cleaned, and fragments of trash from all the packing materials scattered here and there.

Betty was fetching the final boxes down from the upper level, and Louise was bringing in the cleaning supplies that she'd packed into the back of her car earlier that morning. The afternoon would consist of trying to make the store clean. Wiping away the moments that had gathered across its old wooden floors and between its aging bookcases. Alicen was supposed to be taping up the last few sets of books before her, but she kept getting distracted by the memories from her childhood that danced in and out of the fog inside her brain.

She shook herself free from the accumulation of dust in her mind and tried to get back to the task at hand. All she had to do was seal a couple of cardboard flaps closed with duct tape. It shouldn't require so much focus. But the yellow morning pills mixed with the fading white sleeping tablets from the night before made every task she encountered challenging.

She'd been informed by the nurse that her transition would take some time. The body and mind needed to adjust to their new chemical balance, and while they did that, Alicen would feel abnormal. The chemical cocktail swimming in her bloodstream was much more powerful than anything she'd taken previously, so patience was necessary. It had only been six days, and the logical side of Alicen's mind, even enveloped in haze, knew she needed to give the medicine more time than that.

The problem was that this adjustment phase moved like a yo-yo. Moments of heavy emotional darkness followed by nothingness. The swing was dramatic and exhausting. She was beginning to feel like two different people.

"You okay?" a voice asked through the fog.

Alicen glanced up to see Louise standing close by, a blue bucket of cleaning supplies on one hip, a mop and broom clenched in her opposite hand. Alicen forced a grin and nodded. Waves of nausea rolled through her stomach and threatened to rumble up her chest. She closed her eyes, reached out for the nearest bookcase to use as an anchor, waited the couple of beats it took for the sickness to pass, and then exhaled. Another unfortunate side effect of her new chemical mixture.

Louise's eyes flickered with sympathy, and she smiled warmly. "It's going to get better." Her tone was comforting and full of optimism. Alicen wanted to believe her, but it was hard to see past the seemingly eternal discomfort.

Alicen nodded. "It's better than being crazy, right?"

Now it was Louise's turn to force a smile.

Alicen knew Louise thought that calling herself crazy was damaging. But of all the things Alicen had experienced in the last couple of months, calling herself insane felt like the least damaging thing there was. She hated the medication, hated feeling like she was split into two people who were both strangers to her, hated the random and frequent bouts of nausea, hated the constant worry lines on Louise's and Betty's faces, but it was all better than seeing imaginary children. Wasn't it?

The little bell over the front door dinged, and both Louise and Alicen turned to see a beautiful brunette walk through. Her skin looked soft to the touch, even with the lines of aging. Her eyes were just as bright as Alicen remembered them, even after the passing of time, and her smile was the same infectious one that drew everyone into her warmth. Alicen's heart leapt, and a genuine smile lifted her cheeks.

"Mom?" Louise said, surprised. "I didn't know you were coming up today."

Stephanie Watson walked across the room to meet her daughter, pulling off her leather gloves and scarf as she moved. "Well, I really should have come much sooner." Even her voice filled the holes in Alicen's cracked heart with comfort. Stephanie reached out and grabbed her grown daughter in a hug, placing a kiss on her left cheek, and then turned to Alicen. "Hello, sweetheart," she said. She stepped forward and took Alicen's hands in her own. Her touch was as soft and warm as Alicen remembered. It pulled at her heartstrings and stirred emotions that tried to push through her drugged state.

"Mrs. Watson," Alicen said.

"Please call me Stephanie; we're all adults now. I'm sorry I haven't been to see you sooner. I didn't want to intrude."

"I'm glad you're here now," Alicen said.

Stephanie beamed her famous smile and touched Alicen's cheek, the motion nearly fracturing the collected numbness around Alicen's heart. "You look the same as I remember," Stephanie said.

Alicen chuckled and shook her head. "Oh, I hope not."

"You really do—I've been meaning to mention it," Louise teased.

Stephanie rolled her eyes at her daughter. "I just mean, your eyes are the same. Your smile, too. It takes me back." She gave Alicen's hands a squeeze, and then gently pulled her into a hug. Alicen let the moment linger, as Stephanie held on a moment longer than she might have usually.

"Stephanie," a fourth voice spoke.

Alicen pulled back from Mrs. Watson's embrace and turned to see her mother climbing down the last few steps, a box in hand, a cautious look in her eyes. Betty and Stephanie had never been the greatest of friends. More like acquaintances who were pleasant to one another because their daughters had been thick as thieves. Alicen hadn't ever asked her mother why, but she assumed it had something to do with jealousy. Stephanie came from money and then had married into more than most people saw in their entire lives. From Betty's perspective, some people deserved that kind of luck and others didn't. Alicen knew, for a reason she would probably never understand, that Betty would categorize Stephanie as undeserving.

"Betty. Louise mentioned you'd come into town. How are you?" Stephanie asked politely.

"Fine, and yourself?" Betty responded in kind.

"Very well, thank you."

From the forced tone, Alicen wondered if Stephanie might have a hidden problem with Betty as well. Alicen had always thought that if the two weren't getting along, then Betty was to blame, but maybe there really were two sides to every story.

"Decided to come visit us in Red Lodge?" Betty asked.

"It's about time I got up here, and I thought today was as good a day as any," Stephanie said.

Betty forced a smile and nodded. She set down the box she'd been carrying and moved closer to the three gathered women. "I'd say grab a box and jump in, but as you can see, we're about done cleaning up your store."

Betty let the emphasis on *your* draw out longer than necessary, and Alicen felt another wave of nausea crash inside her stomach. She wasn't sure if it was induced by the drugs or her mother. She closed her eyes and waited as it passed.

"Alicen, are you all right?" Stephanie asked.

Alicen opened her eyes to see all three of them looking on with concern and gave a weak smile. "The medication makes my stomach a little woozy," Alicen said.

"You probably need to eat something," Betty said, moving to her daughter's side. Her new and constant concern was irritating. It was probably just the meds talking, but being watched like a hawk by her mother was nearly as troublesome as seeing ghostly children.

"I'm okay, Mom," Alicen said.

"No, she's right," Stephanie said, jumping into her comfortable mothering role. "Have you eaten today?"

"I'm fine; I just need some fresh air," Alicen said. She retreated a couple of steps to give herself space from the looming hens and took a deep breath.

"Why don't you and I go for a walk, then?" Stephanie said. "It would be great to catch up."

Alicen glanced up at Stephanie and smiled. *It would be nice,* she thought, even as she felt her mother's gaze. Stephanie must have noticed it as well and jumped in before anyone else could speak. "Unless, of course, you're not feeling up for it. I'm sorry; I should have thought of that."

"No," Alicen said. "I'm really okay. A walk sounds great." She could feel her mother's hesitation from where she stood, and turned to try to give her a supportive glance. And she caught it. A slip in her mother's carefully calculated facade. Just a twitch of an emotion flickered behind her eyes; behind the concern and judgment, it shivered and then vanished. Hurt. Betty was hurt over Alicen wanting to go with Stephanie.

"We'll grab the last couple things from here and meet you two back at the house for lunch in a few," Louise said, breaking the tension.

"Take your coat; it's getting cold out there," Betty said. Alicen thought the comment was strange and, had she been clearheaded, would have probably detected the desperation in Betty's tone not to be out-mothered by Stephanie. Instead, her subconscious grabbed it and logged it away, and Alicen only nodded and did as her mother asked.

"Ready?" Stephanie asked, her smile piercing the awkwardness filling the rest of the room.

Alicen smiled, slipped on her coat, and followed Mrs. Watson out the front door, the tiny bell ringing overhead as they left.

• • •

Alicen's mother had been right—the air carried a deep cold that made Alicen wonder if snow was coming. She hugged her coat tighter, keeping a slow and steady pace next to Mrs. Watson. They walked in silence for a few moments, putting distance between themselves and the store, Alicen trying to think of a way to start conversation while battling against the sludge that clogged up her brain. Thankfully, Stephanie intervened, and Alicen didn't need to wade further through the muck.

"How have you been, Alicen?" Stephanie asked.

Alicen shrugged, unsure of what to say. How much did Mrs. Watson know about what had been going on over the last few months? How much detail had Louise shared? How much had she heard through the rumor mill that no doubt ran strong all the way down the mountain to Billings? Was she referring to how she was dealing with the death of Jane, or the death of her sanity? Or maybe those were one and the same.

"I suppose that question feels impossible to answer," Stephanie said as if reading Alicen's mind. "Though it's probably the one you get asked the most."

Alicen nodded, thankful Stephanie had spoken before Alicen had tried to tape together broken words to explain what a mess she had become. She didn't really want Mrs. Watson to see her the way she was now. Since childhood, she'd looked up to the older woman walking beside her, and she'd always treasured the way Mrs. Watson saw the world with positivity and light. Alicen didn't want to taint her with all the darkness she was carrying.

"They say you never recover from losing a child," Stephanie said, "and I suppose maybe they're right. But then, perhaps recovery shouldn't be the focus; perhaps it's better to focus on the change that comes instead."

"I don't want to change. I just want Jane," Alicen said. She couldn't have stopped the words if she'd tried. Saying the first thing that came to mind was becoming a new, unfavorable habit of hers.

"I'm sorry not to have known her," Stephanie said, tucking her arm through Alicen's and pulling her close to her side as they walked.

"She would have loved you," Alicen said. She could feel the oncoming tears and swallowed them down.

"I bet she was a handful like her mother," Mrs. Watson said.

Alicen huffed humorously and shook her head. "I wasn't that much of a handful, was I?"

"Yes, you were."

Alicen laughed out loud, and Stephanie followed suit.

"But it was welcomed. You made our trips to Red Lodge bright and full of adventure."

"I miss those trips."

"I think my favorite one was that Christmas Eve when your mother got called into work at the last minute and you came to stay with us for the day. It was sunny for a December day, and we decided to drive up here and see the lights. Do you remember the way this little street used to deck itself out in lights? Rooftop to sidewalk, gutter to gutter, every storefront dressed in twinkling lights."

"Yeah, I remember. You made us listen to the Amy Grant Christmas CD the entire drive. I had never seen Mr. Watson roll his eyes so many times," Alicen teased.

Stephanie pinched the inside of Alicen's arm playfully. "He has always had terrible taste in music. He still rolls his eyes when I put it on."

The memory drifted through Alicen's mind—Stephanie tucked into the front seat, her legs pulled up under her, Louise strapped into the back next to Alicen, Mr. Watson trying not to mute the album as all three girls sang each song over and over. It made Louise laugh to see her dad become so annoyed. Stephanie playfully punched his shoulder every time he sang out of key on purpose. The car had been so warm and full of love, the thought of it now yanked at Alicen's cold heart.

"It was freezing," Stephanie remembered. "The sun had gone down, and all the Christmas lights lined the street. We were headed in for hot chocolate. I took my eye off you for one moment, and when I turned around you were gone.

Scared me half to death." She shook her head. "I found you outside, cheeks red, shivering, staring at the strung Christmas lights in the window. Your eyes full of tears. I thought something must be wrong, but you told me they were happy tears. You said you could see Grandma Joe in all the lights. That she had been right the whole time—that she really was the light of the world."

Alicen's heart reacted to Stephanie's words, and her throat went dry.

"She had passed away a couple months before. That was the last trip we took with you before you moved away. And I'll never forget the way you looked at those lights. It wasn't just fascination on your face; it was a kind of knowing. As if you saw something the rest of us couldn't see."

"I was caught up in the delusions of an old woman and didn't even know it," Alicen said.

"Logic says you're probably right." Stephanie slowed and stepped around to face Alicen, grabbing both of Alicen's hands and holding them tightly. She looked deep into the younger woman's eyes, her own ablaze.

"But take it from another old woman: logic can fail you. Your grandma was many things, maybe even delusional by the standards of this world, but maybe that belief gave her something the rest of us missed."

Stephanie's words sliced through the constant cloud encasing Alicen's mind and slivered down into her chest. What she was saying was dangerous for Alicen. It stirred up questions she was trying desperately to ignore. Questions she was trying to put to death so she could get back to a life without madness. But something deep inside Stephanie's eyes, the eyes of a woman Alicen loved and respected more than most, called to something deep inside her own heart that was struggling to survive. It called to her spirit. Her soul.

"I haven't known you all your life; I've missed much of it, but the little girl I knew understood something more significant about this world than the woman standing before me. Something that runs deeper than logic. Something powerful. Your grandmother used to say that unless you become like a child again, you can't see the things of heaven." Stephanie shook her head and laughed quietly, almost as if to herself, before continuing. "I never really understood that until recently. I just thought it was a funny thing she said, but looking at you now, I think I may be starting to see what she meant." She placed her gloved palm on Alicen's cheek, her warmth shocking in the bitter cold. "Maybe you saw your truth once, and maybe it's time to see it again."

Alicen didn't feel the tear slip past her bottom lip until Stephanie gently wiped it away. Instinctively, Alicen reached over and removed Mrs. Watson's hand from her cheek, but the woman didn't even twitch with offense. She continued to hold Alicen's gaze, and even though a large part of Alicen wanted to pull away, she couldn't. Stephanie had taken hold of her very core.

Stephanie reached into her coat pocket and removed an aged envelope. It was weathered from time. A deep line creased the center from being folded in half, and a tiny corner was torn away. Stephanie held the envelope tightly, shielding it from the wind as if it were treasure.

"I've thought about sending this to you at least a hundred times, but it never quite felt right. I don't know—maybe I was wrong to keep it from you all these years, but something in me says you'll need it soon," Stephanie said. She held the envelope out, and Alicen glanced down to see her name written in familiar cursive handwriting across the front. Grandma Joe's cursive.

Again her brain warned against what was happening. Her mind attempted to quash the rising thoughts that would take Alicen down the dark path to insanity, and her logic tried to keep the neatly hidden madness at bay. Alicen reached out and took the letter, her hand quivering.

"She told me to give it to you when the time was right," Stephanie said. "Of course, I don't know exactly what she had in mind, and like I said, maybe it would have been better to send it before, but something always stopped me. Call it fate, if you believe in that sort of thing. But now you should have it."

"When did she give this to you?"

"A couple weeks before she died. It was the strangest thing. I'm not sure why she entrusted it to me, but I promised to see that it got to you when you were older. Almost as if she knew she wouldn't be around to give it to you herself."

"What does it say?" Alicen asked.

"The message inside was meant just for you, so only you should know. Read it whenever you feel ready to."

Alicen kept her eyes on the letter for another long moment, Stephanie gracious enough to let her have it in silence, before she raised her eyes to see Mrs. Watson's warm stare. Alicen nodded, understanding somehow that accepting this was important, and tucked the envelope into her own coat pocket.

"I love you as if you were one of my own," Stephanie said, tears now lining her eyes. "I always saw you as part of our family, and I always will. Your sparkle is what I miss most when you aren't around. Your belief in things unseen. Don't let them take that from you."

The two women stood still, gazing at one another and sharing an unspoken moment, before Stephanie smiled, pressed up onto her tiptoes, and placed a small kiss on the side of Alicen's head.

She came back into Alicen's full view and gave her a nod. Alicen smiled and returned the gesture, as Stephanie retucked her arm through Alicen's and started walking again.

Stephanie let out a soft sigh and squeezed Alicen's arm. "Well now," she said, "I think we should head back for some lunch."

Alicen nodded, her mind still at war between old questions rising and new ones being created. "Yes," she said. "Lunch sounds good."

20

Alicen stood inside her room, the sun gone for the day, the night sky filling her window, the quiet of a sleeping house seeming to pulse as she held the letter in her hand. She hadn't opened it yet. She wasn't sure if she was going to.

The rest of the afternoon's events had moved by in a smog, clouded by her drugged state and haunted by the endless stream of questions fighting to seep through the cracks in her haze.

Stephanie had stayed for most of the afternoon before deciding to drive back to Billings for the night. Betty had hovered closer than usual, specifically whenever Stephanie was close by, and Louise had tried to keep the tension light.

All in all, by the time the sun had set, everyone was exhausted, and they'd decided to turn in early.

Alicen had been standing here, in the shadowed space of her bedroom, for far longer than she'd intended. Each moment tossed a different thought her way, and then the next tossed it back.

Open the letter.

Don't open the letter.

Open the letter.

Don't open the letter.

Her curiosity was dampened by her medication, as was her logic, so both were equally impaired, standing on opposite sides of a thin wall as Alicen tried to balance on its edge. To fall to the right or to the left was the only question now.

Stephanie was holding on to this letter all these years, Alicen thought, *because she didn't feel like the timing was right.* She'd told Alicen to open it whenever she was ready, but what if she didn't know when that would be?

It would be insane not to open it, right? Then again, would her grandmother's words only raise more questions that the drugs would have to slaughter? Would reading them only draw her further toward complete insanity? Could she even trust what was written? Yet how could she not?

Static whispers buzzed inside her ears, and dread filled her stomach. *No,* she thought, *this can't keep happening.* Her head filled with cotton, and she tried to focus on the room around her. The bed, the side table, the floor—things she knew for certain were actually there. But it was too late.

Alicen. A familiar whisper that had been blotted out by the drugs swirled around her head. *Don't you hear us?*

No, Alicen thought, *not again.* She took a deep breath and closed her eyes as the voices increased.

Don't you want to know?

Yes, Alicen thought. "No," she said out loud.

"It's all right to be afraid," a small voice said.

Alicen opened her eyes and saw Evie standing across the room. Her mind swam. She shouldn't be hearing her. She shouldn't be seeing her.

"I don't want to be afraid," Alicen whispered. "I want to be better."

"And do you feel better?" Evie asked.

No, she thought. "Yes," she said.

Silence filled the room between them, Alicen too numb to move and Evie just staring in return.

"There's another way," Evie said.

"There is only one way," Alicen replied, thinking back to her conversation with Victoria. "People just like to think there's more than that."

"But I can show you another way."

"No." Alicen shook her head and swallowed hard. "No, this is the way. The right way."

Evie looked as though she might say more, but Alicen was finished. This shouldn't be happening. She must need another dose of her meds. She stepped through the dark of her bedroom and reached for the orange bottle on her bedside table.

"Alicen," Evie softly cooed.

"No!" Alicen spun, bottle in hand. "Acceptance. That is what I need. To get a grip, to act like an adult." Blood pumping wildly through her veins, Alicen twisted off the lid and dropped two pills into her hand. It shook, and without another thought, she popped them into her mouth. "Leave me alone," she said, turning her gaze back to the imaginary child.

"Your vision is cloudy," Evie said.

"Get out," Alicen said through clenched teeth.

"Shadows are only shadows."

"Get out."

"You are the light of the world."

"Get out!" Alicen yelled.

She hadn't even realized how loud her voice had gotten until she heard soft thudding outside her door. The knob turned, drawing Alicen's attention, and Betty pushed through, rubbing her tired eyes.

"Alicen?" she said, blinking hazily at the light shining from the room's lamps. "Is everything all right?"

Alicen inhaled and looked over to see Evie was gone. Vanished as quickly as she'd appeared. Alicen turned back to her mother to answer, but Betty was already walking across the room, her eyes glued to the letter in Alicen's hand.

"What is that?" Betty asked.

Panic erupted in Alicen's chest, and she tucked the letter into the back pocket of her jeans. "Nothing," she said. "Just something Stephanie gave me."

"Stephanie? I know that handwriting, and that is not hers," Betty said. Her face had paled, and her voice quivered.

"It's nothing, Mom."

Betty dropped her eyes to slits for a moment, then swallowed and held out her hand. "Give it to me."

"What?" Alicen asked, taken aback. "No."

"Whatever it is, it can't be good for you currently. Give it to me, Alicen."

Alicen emitted a shocked little laugh. Her mother couldn't just barge into her room and demand things that didn't belong to her. Alicen wasn't a teenager. "No," she said.

"Honey, I am doing this for your own good."

"I am a grown woman; you can't just come in here—"

"A grown woman who was just talking to herself!" Betty snapped.

Alicen felt the impact of truth like a punch to the gut.

"Whatever my mother wrote on those pages, tucked into that envelope, will only be more madness. You are sick enough already; you can't afford to have more delusional garbage stuffed into your head. Now give me the letter!"

Alicen felt like the wind had been knocked out of her; she couldn't get a proper breath. Betty was right, even if it stung. Even if the delivery was cruel and painful, Betty was right. Alicen had gone nearly a week without a single delusion, and then the second this letter showed up, it all came back. How much further would it take her?

Even as she drew the envelope out of her pocket, she could hear the children's whispers telling her not to let it go. *Don't, Alicen.* She ignored them because she needed to get better.

As soon as the letter was within sight, Betty snatched it with fury, her eyes sparkling with tears, and ripped it clean down the middle.

"Mom," Alicen said.

"Enough of this," Betty said, holding the letter up in front of her. "I will not let this woman poison you anymore. You're my daughter. . . ." Tears stifled Betty's words, and she swallowed to gain control of her emotions before continuing. "You're my daughter, and I will do whatever it takes to see you get better."

Alicen watched, still shocked by the events of the last few moments, as Betty stuffed the torn pieces of the letter into her robe pocket and walked toward the door. She stepped into the hallway, then reached back and placed her hand on the doorknob.

"Make sure you take your meds, honey," Betty said, trying to sound a bit softer. "And try to get some sleep." She pulled the door shut and left Alicen alone, frozen in place.

• • •

Alicen heard Grandma Joe and her mother coming back inside, and she raced to throw her little body behind the living room couch. She'd been trying to eavesdrop on the conversation on the back porch without being caught, and if they saw her now, they'd know for sure what she'd been up to. Adults always knew these things.

Alicen crouched low, yanked her knees into her chest, and waited. Footsteps echoed across the wood kitchen floor as the two women moved toward the living room.

"Mom, we are not done talking about this," Betty said. Alicen would recognize the scowl in that tone anywhere.

"I think maybe we are, honey," Grandma Joe said, her voice much calmer, as it always was when they fought. They had been doing a lot of fighting lately. As Alicen understood it, Mom wanted to move Grandma Joe to another place. A place where people could take care of her, because Mom thought Grandma Joe's mind was sick. And according to Mom, it was only going to get worse. But Grandma Joe didn't want to go. She didn't even think she was sick.

She told Alicen not to believe everything the world said. That most of the time they got it wrong. Alicen wanted to believe Grandma Joe more than anything; she wanted to believe her most favorite person wasn't sick. But it was hard to argue with the entire world. The world was big and loud, and Alicen was just a little girl.

"Don't you understand what this is doing to you?" Betty said.

"Saving me from myself," Grandma Joe replied.

"Not this again."

"It's the truth."

Betty huffed angrily, and Alicen focused on making sure she wasn't breathing too loudly. She'd be in such trouble with her mom if they found her out.

"So becoming a raving lunatic is saving you? You can't actually believe that, and you certainly can't ask me to believe it," Betty said, her tone hushed but full of fury.

"I'm not asking you to do anything, Betty; I'm telling you I won't go to that place. That's all," Grandma Joe said. She continued to keep her tone controlled, but Alicen noticed the way it wavered. It made an uncomfortable ball of nerves form in her gut. She started to wish she hadn't stolen away behind the couch.

"Can't you see how twisted your mind has become because of this disease?"

"This 'disease' that everyone likes to continuously remind me I have has only helped me see the world more clearly. The beauty. The truth. It has shown me the light."

"Josephine . . ." Betty tried.

"The eye is the lamp of the body; when it is clear, the whole body is filled with light. My perception is clear," Grandma Joe said, her voice rising in volume. "It isn't me who doesn't see; it's you!"

Alicen gulped and then clenched her hand over her mouth to keep the sound sealed inside. She'd never heard her grandmother sound like that before. It made the nervous ball grow, and she tried to shrink even farther behind the couch. This was bad.

"After what happened on Sunday—" Betty said.

"I was trying to help them see," Grandma Joe said. "I was trying to remind them of the love they have forgotten."

"You disrupted the service. The pastor banned you from church, Mom!"

"He just doesn't see yet; I think he will, though."

"We have been over this. You're not a prophet, not seeing angels in the backyard, not walking with the Holy Spirit through the grocery store, not speaking to Jesus in your dreams. You're just sick!"

"I'm not speaking with Jesus in my dreams; I'm speaking with him every day. He is my brother, my friend, my teacher."

"Mom—"

"I thought I knew who I was before. I thought I understood the world, but I was still a prisoner to self."

"Stop, Mom."

"He showed me who I am, made my sight clear. He set me free from the condemnation of this reality."

Betty let out a long, frustrated breath as a beat of silence lingered. "I could force you, you know," Betty said.

Alicen knew that low, angry tone well. This was very, very bad.

"I could say you were a danger to yourself and others. To Alicen. Because you know what, Mom? I'm not convinced you aren't. I want to be, but I'm not! And I have to protect my daughter."

"How could you think I would ever hurt her?" Grandma Joe asked, pain overshadowing any anger there might have been.

"You think reality is different than it actually is. You see and talk to figments of your mind's invention. You believe you are on a holy mission that doesn't exist, and you refuse to get help! What am I supposed to think?"

"I love that girl more than anything, and the way she believes—"

"I don't want her to believe in fantasies. I want her to believe in what's real. In what will give her a good life!"

"A good life according to whom? You? This world? And what good does that do her?"

"The world is cruel and unkind, Josephine; it will judge her for believing in things that aren't real."

"So you would rather she believe she is limited!"

"She is limited."

"She is the light of the world! Don't you want her to know that shadows are only shadows?"

"Oh please," Betty scoffed.

Tears filled Alicen's eyes. She wished they would just stop yelling at one another. She wanted to jump out from behind the couch and distract them from fighting, but fear of her mother's wrath kept her hidden.

"Alicen is special, Betty," Grandma Joe said.

Betty huffed. "Not this again; not today."

"She is, honey."

"Yeah, well, all grandmothers think their grandchildren are special; that doesn't make it true," Betty said.

Alicen, *came a familiar whisper.* Alicen, can you hear us? *Alicen closed her eyes and listened to the voices carefully, just like Grandma Joe had taught her.* Alicen, it's okay, it's all going to be okay.

"Her ability to believe in what isn't always seen is overwhelming. I've seen it in her when we talk about Jesus," Grandma Joe said.

"I wish you could hear how insane you sound," Betty said.

The whispers reached out to Alicen again, her eyes still shut, her heart wishing to see more than what was around her. To see like Grandma Joe saw.

"She's called to the power of Christ's perfect love. She's connected with the only thing that can change the world," Grandma Joe said.

"Stop it," Betty said.

"You couldn't strip her of that if you tried," Grandma Joe continued.

"Stop, Mom," Betty said.

"It will always be a part of her. Jesus said—"

"Stop it, Josephine. Stop!"

Alicen heard Grandma Joe sniff and the crack in her last string of words. She was crying. Alicen's heart felt like it was breaking. It's okay, Alicen, *the small, comforting voices sang.* Don't be afraid.

"I should have shown you better," Grandma Joe said, her words laced with sorrow. "I'm sorry I didn't see it all sooner. I'm sorry you're in such pain."

"Don't be sorry for me," Betty shot back. "I understand the way the world works, and yes, pain is just part of it. But I use that pain to fuel me, to remind me of what the world is capable of."

"What about what you *are capable of? Who you really are? Holding on to your pain only makes you a slave to it," Grandma Joe said.*

"Pain is pain, Mom; it just is, and you deal with it. That's what I'm trying to do, and you are making it impossible!"

"There's another way, honey—" Grandma Joe started.

But Betty was finished. "No, Josephine! There is only one way. Your delusions are making you believe in things that aren't possible. Walking on water, moving mountains, prophets and spirit children. None of that is real." Betty paused and took a sharp breath. Her tone softened. "You're really sick, Mom." Alicen could hear the crack in her mother's voice and thought she might be crying too.

Don't be afraid, Alicen, *the whispers called.* You are light, and light never fears the darkness. *There was a moment of silence, and Alicen held her breath until it was gone.*

"Maybe I am sick," Grandma Joe said. "Or maybe you are. Either way, I am not going to Clover Mountain Retreat Center. I won't."

Betty let out a heavy sigh, and Alicen imagined she was probably rubbing small circles with her fingers on both of her temples like she always did. Alicen wished her little heart would stop beating so hard while the silence was so heavy.

Finally Betty spoke. "We can't keep doing this forever. I . . . I just can't."

Another moment of silence passed.

"I think I'll go lie down for a while," Grandma Joe said. Neither one of them said anything else after that. The ground vibrated slightly as footsteps carried someone out of the room, and then a moment later more steps signaled the departure of the other. The house fell silent, and Alicen hugged her knees to her chest, tears falling down her cheeks. She'd never heard them fight like that before.

"It's okay, Alicen," a small voice said beside her. Clear this time, and Alicen turned to see a sweet, familiar little face next to her. Evie.

Alicen shook her head. "I'm scared," she said.

"I know," Evie replied and wrapped her arm around Alicen's shoulders. "It's okay, I promise it's going to be okay."

Alicen nodded and turned her chin back to her knees. Evie had never lied to her before, so she felt a little bit better.

Alicen wasn't sure how many minutes she sat there behind the couch, waiting for the silence to extend long enough to assure her that leaving was safe. It felt like an hour, though. A single thought beat in her brain. If only her mom could see Evie and hear the others like she and Grandma Joe could, then everything would be better.

21

Alicen shot up in bed, her breath escaping her mouth in thick waves. The memory of Grandma Joe hung fresh in her mind. She glanced down to see her body shivering, her covers kicked off onto the floor. She swung her legs free from her mattress and tried to steady her thundering pulse. She felt a bit nauseous and stood carefully; she didn't want to lose her dinner on the hardwood floor. She moved unsteadily toward the bathroom and flicked the switch on the inside wall. Harsh light illuminated the small space, and Alicen squinted against it as her eyes adjusted.

The voices of her mother and grandmother echoed through her brain in the dead silence of night. Their anger and frustration and hopelessness. Each standing on a different side of a cavern, trying to yank the other across. The emotion of it rumbled in Alicen's chest, and she could feel their pain as if it were her own.

And then the images of the last moment returned like a sledgehammer, crashing her reality into fragmented pieces. First the same voices she'd come to dread had filled the spaces of her memory, and then Evie had been sitting with her there. Little Alicen wrapped in the arms of the child who had been haunting her.

Alicen took a deep breath. She could make sense of this, she told herself. Logic said her memory was being distorted by the psychosis ravaging her brain. Her mind had simply placed one of her delusions there to further torment her. There was no proof Evie had actually ever been there. There was no proof she had heard the whispers back then. This was just more of her diseased state.

Even as her thoughts filtered through, even as she tried to make sense of what she'd remembered, a pocket of something stronger was opening deep inside her gut.

Knowing.

That was the terrifying reality she was trying to eliminate with logic. The little girl hiding behind the couch as her mother and grandmother fought had *known* the delusion next to her. Had trusted her. Had felt comfort from seeing her face. Had seen her many times before. Those voices that had reached out to her in her time of need had been familiar.

Impossible, Alicen thought. This was just another trick of her broken mind. Another cruel side effect of letting her daughter die. She took a strong drag of air and ignored the shaking in the tips of her fingers. Her mind was imprinting her memories with her crazy. That was all this was. It had to be.

Alicen.

No, she thought, her stomach twisting into knots.

Alicen, come see the truth.

"No," she said under her breath. "No, no, no."

Do you hear us, Alicen?

Another voice echoed in her mind. *"She is the light of the world! Don't you want her to know that shadows are only shadows?"* Grandma Joe's words toyed with her heart and resounded in her chest. Alicen's mind pounded painfully as Josephine's words filled her brain.

"She's connected with the only thing that can change the world."

"You couldn't strip her of that if you tried."

"It will always be a part of her."

"Enough, Alicen," she said out loud to herself as she stood. "Stop this. You can control this." But the logic trying to pull her back from madness wasn't convinced. It was starting to feel less like she was losing her mind and more like she was discovering something that she couldn't explain. How was that even possible?

The itching curiosity and sense that she was missing something sneaked through the drugs flowing through her system. The urge to leave her room and venture toward the voices called to more than her body. It summoned her soul. Tears stung her eyes as the tone of her grandmother's lovely voice filled her ears.

"Her ability to believe in what isn't always seen is overwhelming."

A final voice bounced around inside her mind, powerful enough that Alicen found it difficult to breathe through. *"The little girl I knew understood something more significant about this world than the woman standing before me. Something that runs deeper than logic. Something powerful."* Stephanie's words from earlier lifted what was left of the stone shield Alicen was trying to maintain. She swallowed, blinked hard to wash away her tears, and turned to look at herself in the mirror. Had she once believed in more? Was she brave enough to really discover the truth? That last question struck a chord deep in her gut, and Alicen knew, even as the thought was crystallizing behind her eyes, there was only one way to find out.

Within seconds she was dressed, jeans buttoned, sweater pulled tight, coat secured, boots on, and carefully descending the stairs.

Alicen.

The familiar voice touched her as she cleared the last step and turned toward the back door. The house was covered in darkness; the ticking of the living room clock echoed through the sleeping home.

Alicen. Come and see. Don't be afraid, Alicen.

She moved softly through the kitchen and out onto the back porch, making sure to shut the door carefully. Her steps were now assured and motivated. She sought an understanding that felt bigger than the world around her. Insane perhaps, but something that felt necessary for more than her mind. She needed to know if any of it was real.

Come and see.

Halfway across the lawn, the pull seemed to have injected energy into her legs. She began to run, the chilly midnight air sweeping over her as she plunged into the thick of the forest, following her instincts toward the river. Children's laughter echoed across the wind as she ran, and out of the corners of her eyes, she saw small beings moving alongside her. The children.

A transformation was taking place as she ran. As if each step she took were shaking loose a lie that she had assumed was reality. As if each impact of her legs brought her back to a place where she didn't know the rules and instead felt open to the possibility that maybe, just maybe, she could change the world.

Alicen broke free into the clearing she'd been in before. She slowed. Her chest heaved with hard, jagged breaths, her pulse beating quickly underneath her skin. The river rushed before her, the small wooden bridge arched across it, reminding her of all the times she had sat on a similar one with Grandma Joe.

"You came," a small voice said.

Alicen whipped around and saw Evie. The two stood, locked in one another's gaze for a long beat of time, before the little girl continued.

"You felt it." Evie grinned, her eyes sparkling against the stars. "The part of you that knows me."

Emotion tugged at the frayed edges of Alicen's heart. A sense of fear began to boil in her gut while longing fingered at her soul. "Who are you?" The question slipped off Alicen's tongue before she could stop it.

"Who do you think I am?" Evie asked.

"Someone my mind created to help me cope with the loss of my daughter," Alicen's logic said through her lips.

Evie smiled. "Maybe you thought that's who I was before, but I can see something different in you now."

Alicen shook her head, her mouth gaping open. She stared forward as her mind whirled. Could she actually accept what her heart was begging her to believe? That there was a truth greater than her perceived reality? That maybe there was something beyond what she saw, beyond what she knew as fact? What if all Grandma Joe had been trying to teach her was real? Yet even as her body started to open to something new, the familiar doubt she knew too well surfaced.

Get a grip, Alicen.

Act like an adult, Alicen.

What would your mother say, Alicen?

Alicen shook her head to disrupt the flow of insults and tried to reconnect with logic. But that was nearly impossible to secure now. Belief in what logic would call insanity felt like her only path. Or the one she desperately wanted to travel. It was too tangible to erase now. The wind picked up around her and whipped through the branches that hung overhead. It was almost warm, though the night should be chilly, as it seemed to draw her farther away from her doubt.

Evie took a step toward Alicen, her face calm and certain. "Do you want to see?"

"See what?" Alicen asked.

"The truth you knew once."

She looked at Evie, who was waiting patiently as Alicen's mind battled with her soul. Her soul won. "Yes," Alicen said.

Evie's face broke into a wide smile, and she gave Alicen a playful wink before turning and racing off through the trees.

Shock made Alicen hesitate a moment before she too began running. She tried to keep her gaze locked on the little girl as Evie bounded over forest ground and around thick trees. The sky overhead rumbled, and the once-clear night sky was suddenly covered with storm clouds. Alicen ignored the fear ramming inside her chest and picked up her pace as drops of rain started to fall around her.

A small voice somewhere in her head was yelling that she had lost all sense of sanity, but her heart and soul were so fixated on discovering the truth that she couldn't have stopped her legs if she wanted to. Something else was calling to her now, something as warm as the wind, even through the icy rain.

Come and see, Alicen.

Alicen's feet landed in puddles as the rain soaked the ground, and mud splashed up her legs. Still she pushed forward, keeping her eyes on the bouncing child who seemed to still be reflecting the starlight even though the sky was covered with clouds. She wiped water from her eyes and gasped as her lungs struggled to keep up.

A crack of lightning shot across the sky, and the screaming voice of sense kicked into overdrive. Again Alicen felt the pull at her spirit and managed to keep her eyes on Evie as the child ducked around a final tree and out of sight. Alicen did the same and stumbled into another open clearing.

She huffed to a stop, twisting her head in every direction in search of Evie. She found nothing. She was alone in the clearing, the line of trees standing around its edge marking a perfect circle, her breath the only sound against the night. *Odd,* she thought. She wasn't feeling rain anymore. She glanced up and saw the sky was clear, stars beaming down, the half moon bright. Not a storm cloud to be seen.

She turned and glanced back toward where she'd just come from and saw raindrops through the darkness. She stepped toward the line of trees that encased the clearing and moved her gaze around the circle in either direction. Where she was standing it was dry, but just on the other side of the tree line, rain was still falling.

Impossible.

The laughter of children caused her to pause. She spun back around toward the center of the clearing, but still she was alone. For the first time she noticed a pool of water in front of her. Big enough to swim across but small enough that one could easily walk its circumference within minutes.

The sight of it caused Alicen to gasp, confused. Had it been there just a moment ago? Had she just not noticed it before? She took a step closer, her eyes drinking it in. The water was crystal blue, green hues swirling throughout, clean and breathtaking. Not like lake water at all, not like what one would expect to find in a body of water tucked into the forest. No, this was something else entirely.

A buzzing sensation started to work its way up her fingers as her eyes drank in the water before her. The call to her soul grew, and she could feel the pull of her body toward the pool. She wanted to touch the water, experience the way it felt on her fingers. She suddenly wanted to dive below its surface or see if she could walk across it. The thought jarred her enough that she took a step back from the strange crystal surface, afraid of what she might actually do.

"Don't be afraid," a small voice said, and Alicen froze. A voice she knew so well, as well as she knew her own, one that haunted her constantly. She turned to the right and saw Jane standing across the water, her face shimmering with the glow of the moon, blonde hair dancing softly on the wind. Perfect and beautiful. Her eyes as blue as the water between them.

Jane smiled, and it felt as if someone had punctured a new hole through Alicen's heart. Flashes of their grocery-store encounter sparked within her mind. Jane hadn't really been there then, and she couldn't really be here now.

Jane stepped forward toward the water, knelt down, and ran her small fingers across its perfectly still surface. Her touch started a small ripple effect that spread out into the center of the water and then faded into nothing. "You can touch it if you want," Jane said, her tone sweet as it ever was. "It's warmer than it looks."

Alicen wanted to respond, but she couldn't get her mind to form any words. How many times had she dreamed of her sweet girl? How many times had she begged to be able to go back to the day she'd let her die?

"I love the water," Jane said, glancing up at Alicen. "Do you remember how much I loved the water?"

Alicen nodded, tears filling her eyes. The little girl standing before her was different, though. She was more tangible, more familiar. As if she'd been plucked from heaven and placed on the edge of this pool. Alicen wanted to protect her heart from believing, but it was slipping away from her too quickly.

"I really did want to be a mermaid," Jane said with a giggle. "Would you have let me become a mermaid, Mom?" The little girl stood, removing her fingers from the water and looking up at Alicen.

"Yes," Alicen said. "You could have been anything you wanted."

"Well, *that's* not good to teach your children," said another voice. It was her own, and it drew Alicen's attention to the near side of the forest pool. There, standing a couple yards away, was herself. A living reflection. A duplicate. Dressed in the Marc Jacobs dress she'd starved for but never worn. A glass of wine in hand. Eyes fixed forward and full of mockery.

Suddenly the forest was gone, and Alicen was standing in her backyard in Santa Monica, the sky clouded and dark, their family pool before her. She turned in a circle—the trees, the small lake, Jane, all replaced by the sight she dreaded most. The place where she had killed her daughter.

"Do you remember that day, Alicen—the day she told you she wanted to be a mermaid and you told her she was just a girl?" her dress-clad twin asked, her tone maniacal.

"How—?" Alicen started but couldn't finish.

"Of course you remember," the woman spat. "It's all you can remember, and for good reason." The scary reflection took a sip from her wineglass. "Well, Jane can't be a mermaid now, because she's dead."

Pain exploded through Alicen's chest, and raw emotion choked out her words. She stumbled back a couple steps across the familiar ground, away from the swimming pool's edge.

Her doppelgänger shook her head and sneered. "Murderer."

A crack of lightning slashed through the sky. The ground shook with a roll of thunder, and Alicen felt her knees tremble with the overwhelming sense of guilt. Her legs gave out, taking her to the ground with force. She struggled to find a breath, to control the rage of shame slicing through her chest. She struggled to tear her eyes from her own reflection, the one that stared at her with judgment. She was right. Alicen had done this.

A soft touch brushed her shoulder, and she looked up to see Jane standing beside her, face bright and clear, blue eyes shining in the midst of the darkness. The backyard swimming pool was gone; the forest lake had returned. Peaceful and calm, a warm breeze licking at the surrounding leaves and pulling at the ends of her daughter's perfect curls.

Jane, who seemed to have light shining through the ends of her fingers, reached her hand down and laid it against Alicen's cheek. A comforting energy flowed from her daughter's skin, and the raging sorrow she'd felt seconds before stilled.

"Don't be afraid, Mommy," Jane said. "You are the light of the world, and the rest is only shadows."

"No, I killed you; I deserve this pain," Alicen said through tears.

"Your pain is only a shadow compared to the light inside you," Jane said.

"Oh please," the mocking version of herself countered. "Light inside you? You're just a woman, Alicen. Get a grip."

The other version of herself was back, standing close, reminding her of reality.

"Look at you," the evil twin mocked. "Act like an adult, Alicen."

Yes, Alicen thought. This was insane.

"There are always two choices," Jane said. "Fear and love. Two voices: the Spirit and the accuser. Grace and condemnation." She took her hand from Alicen's cheek and offered it for Alicen to take. "Let me help you remember what you once knew."

Her daughter's sweet words pulled the strings of her spirit that had led her to the forest and sang to the wonder in Alicen's heart that had longed to believe there was more.

Dark laughter echoed at her side. Her own laughter. "You make your bed, you sleep in it, right?" her voice said. "You actually believe there's enough grace for what you've done? What would your mother say, Alicen?"

The forest clearing disappeared again, replaced with the dreaded swimming pool. The waters dark and murky, the sky clouded. Herself standing by, pouring down waves of guilt. Alicen's fear and shame stronger than ever. As if they were heavy bags of sand draped across her shoulders, dragging her farther into the ground.

"You should have been a better mother," her voice accused. "This is your trouble; you can't be free of it."

"I didn't . . . I didn't mean . . . ," Alicen whimpered, her words getting swallowed by her grief.

"Oh stop," her reflection snapped. "Get a grip, Alicen. Act like an adult."

Alicen dropped her eyes to the ground and began to weep. Her mind battering her with shame, her chest twisting in pain. Yet through the pain a small chorus whispered.

Alicen, can you hear us?

You are the light of the world. The rest is only shadows.

When through the deep waters I call you to go.

Know the waters of sorrow will not overpower you.

The warm pulse in her soul started beating softly, but it was quickly drowned out by the cold reality of her shame. She had done this. She had killed her baby girl.

"You did this, honey; time to face reality," the cruel tone called. It was starting to transform. Originally it was completely her own, but as the words flowed from the familiar face, they began to sound like her mother's.

"You're sick, Alicen," the twisted voice echoed. "A sickness that is no one's fault but your own. Time to pay the piper."

Alicen felt her mother's tone press into her chest like fingers, wrap itself around her heart, and squeeze. And yet, even there, the children's voices could be heard.

You are the light of the world. The rest is only shadows.

"It's okay, Mom; don't be afraid," Jane's gentle voice cooed. Alicen opened her eyes, and again the forest trees surrounded her, the brilliant crystal pool was near, and the sweet beauty of her daughter had returned.

"What is happening to me?" Alicen whispered through her tears.

Jane knelt in front of her and took both of Alicen's hands

into her own. Again her touch filled Alicen with a calm that muffled the cry of her shame.

"You're being called to deep waters," Jane said, "but you don't have to be afraid. Because only when facing your fear and letting it go can you find true peace. It's a road less traveled, but it's the only way to freedom. Remember, there is no fear in love."

"I have to pay for what I've done. I don't deserve true peace," Alicen choked out, removing her eyes from the light shining through Jane's gaze.

"Don't believe the accuser, Mom," Jane said. "I can show you another way. A way where all your shame and pain have already been paid for. The light inside you is greater than the shadows in the world."

"Greater than your shame?" the haunting voice called.

Alicen glanced up, and once again saw herself, the Marc Jacobs dress clinging tightly to each curve as she moved toward Alicen. Her voice now completely replaced by Betty's. Words of accusation flowing without remorse. "What could possibly be greater than your shame? Sounds as crazy as you are, Alicen."

Looking at herself but hearing her mother was unnerving, terrifying. Her mind fought against falling into old habits. She wanted to curl into a ball of submission. Mother knew best.

When through deep waters I call you.

Know the waters of sorrow will not overpower you.

The voices sang in unison, soft and sweet, a choir of hope, and the soft beating in Alicen's heart returned. She tried to grab hold of it through her fear, but the voice of her accuser echoed around her and fired at her resolve with shame like bullets.

"There is only one way, Alicen. Accept that you are troubled. All are troubled. Time to pay your debts."

"There is another way," a soft voice echoed overhead. Jane filled with light, not to be seen but only to be heard. "Through deep waters, healing can be found. Renew, refresh, remember; see you are made of light," Jane's sweet voice echoed again.

The choir of children whispered.

When through deep waters I call you.

Know the waters of sorrow will not overpower you.

"Get a grip, Alicen," her doppelgänger warned. "Act like an adult, Alicen."

But the call was gaining momentum, enough that Alicen could open her eyes and see the forest clearly, the crystal waters before her.

"Go to the water," Jane said, and she was there across the pool, the four children Alicen knew standing beside her. Evie, Beck, Roxie, and Tate, their faces warm and full of light. "See another way," Jane continued. "When your eye is clear, your whole body will be full of light. Remember—you are light."

With havoc scraping at the insides of Alicen's chest, fear circling beneath her skin, shame swimming through her mind, but hope singing to her spirit and truth calling to her heart, she crawled to the edge of the forest pool. The waters swirling blue and green, something powerful resting right below its surface.

Tears streamed down her cheeks, and she pushed herself to standing. Without letting her mind and body give in to fear, Alicen stepped into the water.

The moment she connected with its surface, warmth bolted up her legs and into her whole being.

"Foolish, stupid girl," her mother's voice cried. "Don't give in to your crazy. What would your mother say?"

Fear threatened to destroy her resolve, but the song of the children was louder now.

When through deep waters I call you.

Know the waters of sorrow will not overpower you.

The voices rammed against Alicen's figure as she stood in the water. One side inviting her to go deeper, the other mocking her resolve. And the shame she'd been carrying over the last few months, maybe her entire life, cascaded down from the clouds.

Healing can be found through deep waters. Renew and remember. Your shame is only a shadow. Paid for by light. Shadows are only shadows.

"Get a grip, Alicen!"

She stepped farther into the water, closed her eyes, tried to block out the cruel voice of her accuser and listen to the voice of hope. Their battling tossing her mind back and forth from darkness to light.

You are light.

"Act like an adult!"

Fear and pain collided inside her gut.

Still Alicen pushed forward. For love was there too, a sense of peace gathered on the insides of her bones. She could feel the cool, dark waters splashing up over her arms but also the waves of calm, warm forest air flowing past her shoulders. Both realities crashing into one another. Her shame and her freedom yanking her in opposite directions. Two roads.

When through deep waters I call you.

Know the waters of sorrow will not overpower you.

"What would your mother say, Alicen!"

Let it go; see that you are light. The rest is only shadows.

"Foolish, stupid girl! You deserve this sickness!"

Don't be afraid. See another way.

Heart and mind at war, Alicen took a deep breath and submerged below the surface. All logic was gone; only following remained. The call from both sides pulling on her in equal amounts. Her body encased in water, her brain ignited with pain, and her heart infused with truth. And one question cut through the chaos like an arrow: What if she *was* made of light?

Something began to shift in her soul, something started to take root and grow, and the voice of her accuser began to lessen. It started to fade, the choir of children rising, the warmth of the water slicing through the chill of darkness.

And then it all changed again. A harsh grab dug into her shoulders, pulling her away from the truth she was only just beginning to connect with. She thrashed forward, away from the hold, her throat opening, still immersed under the surface, waves of water draining into her mouth. Pain pierced the back of her throat and scored the insides of her now-open eyes. It stung her brain as the echoes of the children's voices died off.

No, she thought; *no!* She pulled again, searched for the light, the warmth, but the water invading her body was yanking her deeper into darkness. She was drowning, actually drowning. Black dotted her already-muddled vision as more pain spiked through her chest.

And the single thought of truth transformed into a single thought of reality. She had been a fool to believe there was more, and now she was drowning. She tried to breathe but couldn't. A dull pain pounded through her head, and then the world went black.

22

Victoria stood in the hospital hallway, a concerned mother and best friend standing before her. She'd been called shortly after they had confirmed Alicen was going to make a full recovery and that there wouldn't be any permanent physical side effects of her recent episode.

She'd tried to drown herself. A nasty way to go and incredibly difficult to execute. To hold yourself underwater, ignoring your survival instincts. Alicen didn't appear to be strong enough for that. Her mental delusions were gaining momentum. The means with which Victoria was trying to steer Alicen should be working. But they weren't.

You're failing, little Victoria.

Victoria's face twitched at the sound of her uncle's voice. Yes, she thought, something was very wrong here.

"I'm certain she's been taking her medication," Betty said again, as overbearing mothers usually did. "I've been checking morning and night. I understand how important it is that she keeps up with these things."

"Maybe she wasn't trying to drown herself?" Louise said, playing the part of the supportive comrade.

"You yanked her from the lake, Louise; she wasn't breathing. If you hadn't gotten to her when you did . . ." Betty trailed off momentarily, refusing to say what they were all thinking. "What else do you suppose she was doing in there?"

Louise opened her mouth to say something, but Betty wouldn't let her speak.

"You heard her when they revived her. She was delirious, talking about being light, about healing waters. Mumblings about being led by ministering spirits." Betty placed her hand over her mouth and shook her head, tears lining the insides of her eyes. "She sounds just like Josephine."

She's still seeing children. Her trouble is getting worse. Victoria bit the inside of her cheek to keep her face in check.

Louise started to break in again but after a moment gave up. *What could she say?* Victoria thought. Betty was right—Alicen had been raving about being led by her delusions. Her grip on reality was anything but stable.

"I knew something was wrong," Betty continued, turning her attention back to Victoria. "I felt it. Mother's intuition, maybe. And when she wasn't in her bed . . ."

Victoria nodded politely, trying to convey that she cared

how well Betty had read the situation. She didn't, of course. In fact, she was certain Betty was probably a terrible mother. Most were. For example, her own mother had let a tyrant beat on her and her children without ever fighting back. She had encouraged his filthy habit by buying him alcohol and letting him drink himself into madness. Anger rose under her skin.

Betty was shaking her head. "She's been resistant to this from the beginning. Oh, my poor baby—how could she try and do this to me again!"

"Well, good; seems healthy to make this about you," Louise mocked.

"She's my daughter. You have no idea what it's like seeing her suffer through this."

"Yeah, Betty, I do. And I want to make sure we are doing what's best for her, not what's best for you."

"How dare you!"

Worms.

Yes, Victoria thought.

Victoria cleared her throat, and both women closed their mouths. "I think it is fair to say you both care about Alicen very much. I believe what's best for Alicen is for us all to be on the same page."

Betty looked at Victoria while Louise bit her lip and glanced down at the floor.

"I think it's time for Alicen to move onto campus," Victoria said.

Louise looked up, surprised. "I don't think that's something we should decide without speaking to her first."

"For crying out loud, Louise," Betty said, throwing her hands up in the air. "She's schizophrenic and just tried to kill herself! Do you think she's stable enough to make that sort of decision?"

Filthy worms.

"Miss Reese," Victoria cautioned, reaching out a calming hand.

"I'm sorry, and please call me Betty," she said with a small grin in Victoria's direction.

"It just doesn't make sense," Louise said. Victoria could see the sparkle of tears resting along her bottom lids and could hear the crackle in her voice. "I thought she'd been doing pretty okay recently. It just seems so extreme."

Victoria jumped in before Betty could lash out again. "I know this is very difficult, but the kind of trauma that Alicen's mind has experienced can create waves of unpredictable behavior. And unfortunately, people who have tried to commit suicide before are more likely to try again."

"So what's the solution here, then? Do you just give her more medication? She's already so . . ." Louise's words trailed off, and she rubbed the sides of her skull with both hands. "I mean, what kind of life will she have?"

"One where she isn't dead," Betty snapped.

Louise took a hard swallow and cut her eyes toward Betty but said nothing in response.

Victoria could feel the controlled expression on her face threatening to crack. She was becoming irritated. Death would be too kind for someone like Alicen. As would a return to life, as Louise called it. No, for what Alicen had done, for who she was, only the numbed state of just existing was appropriate. Anything else would look like mercy or forgiveness.

Both impossible for trouble like Alicen's.

And trouble like yours.

She swallowed and recapped her irritability before continuing. "Again, I understand how difficult this is, to see someone you love going through this, but we all want the same thing for Alicen."

Retribution.

Yes, Victoria thought, but said instead, "Recovery."

Betty was nodding again and stepped in front of Louise, who didn't object. "I'll do whatever you believe is best for Alicen."

Victoria gave Betty a reassuring nod. "As her designated family member, you'll need to sign some paperwork for me."

"Yes, of course," Betty said. "Anything."

Victoria stole a final glance at Louise, and the young woman held her gaze for a moment before nodding herself. It was good to have all the worms in order.

• • •

Victoria left the hospital, Alicen's admittance forms signed and in hand. Alicen would be transferred to Clover Mountain in the morning after a night of observation in the hospital. Victoria had requested they keep Alicen heavily sedated until she was fully transported so as to eliminate any further complications. They'd agreed.

Victoria crossed the parking lot toward her car, the lot nearly empty in the midnight hour. The longing to return to campus and release the dirt of the day was heavy. She fiddled with the end of her blazer sleeve, her finger grazing the freshly wrapped bandage that circled her wrist.

Payment is due.

Shame and want collided inside her mind. "You did this to me," she whispered.

You always did try to blame others for your mistakes.

Victoria ground her teeth in anger. She was losing her patience with her uncle's ever-present condescension.

"Leave me alone," she said.

Alone with your demons?

"You are my demon."

After everything I did for you?

"You took everything from me," she said. Her hushed tone was gaining volume, and she quickened her steps to reach her car.

No, I gave you something only I could give, and you killed it. You took it from me.

The dark memories filled her mind, and she stumbled the last step to her car, her brain throbbing with remorse. "I had no choice. The evil had to end."

You were the evil.

Victoria slid inside her car and slammed the door. The air was thick and dark around her head. She leaned back against the headrest, her breath coming in hot and heavy waves. She could feel him, even in death. Could remember him visiting her often. Pressing against her, moving over her. Talking about making her clean but only leaving her feeling like dirt.

"Children should be protected," she said.

Like you protected yours?

"I did protect him. I saved him from you, from this world of pain."

You killed him.

"There was no other way!"

Nothing but silence answered back, and her heart ached inside her chest. Behind her clenched eyes the image of his little body appeared. A picture she'd blotted out, torn down, but it was with her now. Memories of his soft skin and fine hair. Tiny hands and feet. The way he'd felt lying in her arms, sleeping beside her chest.

Created from the forced intimacy of an uncle who visited her while she slept. Who told her his acts were necessary for redemption. A man she loved. A man she hated. But not as much as she'd loved and hated what they'd created. A worm that had come from filth—as she had come from her parents, he had now come from her. A stain on the earth, destined to fail, to suffer, to be trapped in a cycle of darkness.

"I couldn't . . ." Tears snuffed out her words and dripped off her chin. She had tucked away memories of her baby, erased them from her mind, and now they hurled themselves at her like bullets. "I couldn't let our evil destroy him. Children should be protected."

The silence grew, spreading deep into her ear canals and pressing against her brain. Her hands started to tremble as sorrow and anger rolled up from her belly in equal measures.

She could still feel the pillow between her hands. There in the shadows of her room. His newborn body so small and helpless. She hadn't needed to apply much pressure; she hadn't needed much time. Smothering his life had been easy. She chased away the memories of the first life she'd taken. It had been the only way. A necessary sacrifice.

"I saved him," she whispered. "I paid my debts with his life. I was paying my debts!" Her voice rose and filled the small space, ringing in the silence, then fell quiet without a response. She huffed in fury, hot, angry tears filling her eyes. "Don't abandon me now!"

Another beat of silence passed. Victoria let out a horrid scream and banged her fist against the steering wheel. Over and over, with another loud crack of her vocal cords. And then she went still. Short breaths coming and leaving her mouth. Her eyes fixed forward through the windshield on nothing but an empty parking lot. She was losing control. She switched her anger to a different target. Alicen.

Alicen was doing this to her.

Victoria brushed back the strands of hair that had fallen in her face and took a steady inhale. This was no one's fault but Alicen's. She was refusing to be held accountable. Victoria thought Alicen could be fixed, saved. A device to help Victoria make amends for her own mistakes. But if Alicen wouldn't accept help, then there was only one road left. Victoria wouldn't continue to pay for Alicen's mistakes.

Death.

Victoria took a relieved breath. "I thought you had forsaken me."

You would never let me be free.

"No," Victoria said. "You're my trouble."

Kill her as you killed me, as you killed him.

"Yes. It is the only way."

It will not bring you forgiveness for what you've done.

"Forgiveness is a myth."

Uncle Donald's voice fell silent again as the solution crystallized in Victoria's mind. Payment was necessary. As Victoria had paid with the life of her child and the life of her uncle, Alicen would pay. With her life.

23

The moment Alicen was aware of her existence, the pain started. Deep throbbing, seeming to stem from the middle of her brain, coursed down her neck and spine. She couldn't open her eyes or move her limbs; all she could do was be still and feel the suffering of her body.

A stream of questions started to materialize, but before they could become clear, Alicen's natural defenses shooed them off. She was too weak for curiosity. Too weak for analysis. Instead she focused on breathing, which itself required labored effort.

Muffled voices rubbed at the edge of her consciousness, and she opened her eyes to clouded darkness. Light peeked through in bits and pieces, so she wasn't sure if it was actually dark in the place she was or if her vision just wasn't working. She couldn't make out any words, just mumbled tones from unknown sources.

The darkness blocking Alicen's vision started to lighten, turning a deep shade of gray and slowly lessening as images began to form. She saw movement to the side and sent a signal to her neck to turn her head. Nothing happened. She was still frozen solid, the chemical connection between thought and motion severed.

The images forming before Alicen firmed and took solid shapes. Walls, a ceiling, the railings of a bed, a bedside table, a lamp. Things close to her and easy to make out, along with two people standing across the room.

A taller woman, dark hair, dark suit, a presence of command about her. An older man standing opposite the woman, the two caught up in conversation. Their voices were strained, cottony, as if coming through a thick wall before reaching her ears.

"With all due respect," the man said, "in my medical opinion, I'm just not sure this course of treatment is best for her."

"Your concerns have been noted, Dr. Wells," the woman said, "but the call is mine to make."

Finally Alicen's brain was awake enough to communicate with the rest of her body, and she moved her chin slightly so that her eyes were directly pointed at the two bodies standing in the corner of the room. The fog and shadows cleared then, and the room became a complete picture, though she still wasn't sure where she was, or why. It was as if a stopper had been placed between her current brain activity and the memories of her past.

The man noticed Alicen staring at them and motioned toward the dark-haired woman with a nod in Alicen's direction.

The woman turned and smiled at her. "Alicen, you're awake." She took a small step forward, and Alicen noticed how perfectly even her skin was. A prick of familiarity nibbled at her mind, and even though she couldn't remember how, Alicen thought maybe she knew this beautiful stranger.

"How are you feeling?" the old man beside her asked.

Alicen wanted to reply, but she was still regaining control of her body, so her jaw seemed unusable. She racked her brain for something to stabilize her situation but came up empty. She just couldn't remember.

"Don't worry; this is normal," the woman said. She looked back over her shoulder toward the man. "That will be all, Dr. Wells," she said.

The doctor hesitated, clearly uncomfortable, but after a moment turned his attention to Alicen. "I'll come by later when you've had more rest," he said.

"That won't be necessary," the woman responded. "I'll take it from here."

Again the doctor seemed unsure what to do, but knowing his place, he finally sent Alicen a small smile and left the room.

When he was gone, the familiar woman took a step toward Alicen's bedside, reached for a chair that stood against the wall beside the small nightstand, and moved it to face Alicen. She sat, her eyes holding Alicen's face close. "Do you mind if I sit with you for a little while?"

Alicen didn't respond. She wasn't sure she could have if she'd wanted. She just watched as the woman leaned back in the chair and crossed her legs.

"You are probably a bit confused; again, that's completely normal, so let's start with the basics. I'm Victoria, the administrator here. Do you know where *here* is, Alicen?"

Alicen's eyes darted around the room, searching for something that might give her a clue, but she came up short. She felt like she should know but couldn't place the answer through the haze.

"It's all right. You're at Clover Mountain Retreat Center in Red Lodge, Montana. Does that sound familiar?"

Alicen swallowed, the muscles in her throat finally feeling normal. The rest of her body was slowly following suit. She could curl her fingers, bend her wrists, twist her ankles. Everything was sore, but being able to send the correct messages to her limbs and have them react accordingly felt like a triumph. Now if only she could get her mind on board.

She tried to push through the cloud of smoke that filled every corner of her brain but only found more smoke. She had feelings but couldn't pair them with past moments, so they just felt useless. She felt familiar with the things Victoria was saying, but she had no recollection of them.

"You've been attending sessions here for the last month but only just recently moved onto campus," Victoria said. Her tone wasn't unwelcoming, and that felt mildly reassuring. "Do you mind if I'm a bit blunt with you, Alicen?"

Alicen shook her head and cleared her throat. "No," she whispered, thankful to find a word.

"You tried to kill yourself a couple of days ago; do you remember that?"

Alicen registered a wave of surprise and searched for the sense of familiarity she'd been receiving as Victoria spoke. Nothing. How could she not recall trying to kill herself?

"I know you're struggling to remember," Victoria said. "Don't worry; you haven't lost all of your memories. You've been given a mixture of antipsychotics and sedatives for the last forty-eight hours to ensure you don't harm yourself again. The effects of this combination can result in memory blocks that should fade with time."

As if Victoria's words had an echo, they filled Alicen's head space. *To ensure you don't harm yourself again.* Pressure filled the center of her forehead. *A mixture of antipsychotics and sedatives.*

"Am I crazy?" Alicen asked.

"We don't really like to use that word around here, but it's safe to say you aren't well, Alicen."

"Will I remember?" Her voice was building in strength but still sounded rough and groggy.

"Do you want to remember? It will be very painful for you," Victoria said.

Alicen felt the wheels of logic begin to crank in her brain. "Painful enough that I would rather be dead," she said more to herself than to Victoria. The striking woman didn't respond but instead waited as the reality of Alicen's situation started to take up residence in her mind. Something had broken her enough that she wanted to die rather than live with the pain.

A heavy and sudden wave of sorrow began in her legs and rolled up her entire body until it was the only thing she could feel. Loss, strong enough that Alicen struggled to breathe, pressed against her chest like an anvil. Tears caught at the backs of her eyes, and pity filled her throat. An image of a sweet little girl danced through her mind, and in a single moment Alicen remembered her. "Jane," she whispered as tears escaped down her cheeks.

Victoria leaned forward and placed a soft hand on Alicen's forearm. "I understand, Alicen, more than you know." Sorrow flashed across Victoria's face, and her eyes seemed to look past Alicen to a different place entirely as she spoke. "I lost a child once. A son. The world is a dark place, and children should be protected."

Victoria's voice had fallen to a whisper, and she lingered on her words for a short moment before switching off whatever she was seeing behind her eyes and focusing back on Alicen. "It's all right," she said. "I'm going to take away the pain."

"You are?"

"Yes," Victoria said. "Would you like that?"

Alicen nodded and sniffed, her agony still clawing at her insides like a caged animal. Victoria smiled and pressed a large button on the end of Alicen's bed. The front half started to rise slightly as a mechanical humming buzzed through the room until Alicen was comfortably situated in a near-seated position. Victoria then reached over to the nightstand beside Alicen's bed. On top a small white cup was perched. Alicen hadn't even noticed it before, but there it was. Victoria grabbed it gently, placed it in her palm, and held it out for Alicen to see.

Inside were a handful of pills of different colors, shapes, and sizes. Alicen glanced from the medication back to Victoria, who was sweetly smiling, almost with pride.

"These will take your pain away," Victoria said. "I hand-selected each one myself. I know better than anyone what you need."

Alicen looked at the pills as more pain erupted through her senses. Whispers from the past ignited more memories that amplified her torment. Statements such as, *"You're very sick, honey,"* and *"You're seeing figments that aren't real,"* and *"We just all want you to get better"* filtered through her mind like thick waves of smoke. Words like *suicide* and *schizophrenia* accompanied the phrases, adding more fuel to her burning pain. Images of her concerned mother, her exhausted friend Louise, then a picture of Grandma Joe swept in and out like licking flames.

You're sick like your grandmother was sick, Alicen.

You think you see children like your grandma saw children, Alicen.

You're sleepwalking, Alicen.

You tried to kill yourself, Alicen.

You killed your daughter, Alicen.

You're completely broken, Alicen.

Shame and regret joined her sense of loss like thick wooden planks added to the already-billowing fire, causing the flames to explode with heat. Alicen wanted to cry out in pain as memories continued to hurl themselves at her, each one seeming to add another layer of suffering.

You did this to yourself, Alicen.

You're crazy, Alicen.

You'll never be free of this, Alicen.

Get a grip, Alicen.

Act like an adult, Alicen.

What would your mother say, Alicen?

"You don't have to feel this way if you don't want," Victoria said, snapping Alicen back to reality. "You can feel nothing." Victoria reached her palm out farther so that it was only inches from Alicen's chin.

"The choice is yours," Victoria said. "But it isn't automatic. You have to take it."

A longing for the numbed state she'd woken to fixed itself like a pillar in Alicen's gut. She didn't want to remember anything more. She didn't want to feel the agony or shame of what she had done. She only wanted escape.

Yet there was something else, too. A tickling deeper than her skin and bones. A feeling she couldn't explain but could feel. Like hearing a tune but being unable to remember the lyrics.

When through deep waters.

The rest is only shadows.

There is another way.

"They were real," Alicen mumbled, her heart invading her mind.

"Who were real?" Victoria questioned. "The children?"

"They were sent to help me remember." The words were coming from Alicen's lips, but even as she said them they sounded impossible.

"Sent from whom? A greater being? God?" Victoria let her words stand as Alicen's mind mocked the thought of such a thing. "You believe God is trying to save you? After everything you've done? A mother who failed her daughter?"

Alicen's original state of shame swept across the strange sensation that had tried to break through. Pain strong enough to cloud everything with darkness. A reality she was starting to remember, leading her toward a single truth.

"Look at me," Victoria said.

Alicen did as she was told.

"God is not trying to save you."

Alicen swallowed, a fresh wave of tears filling in behind her eyes.

"But I am trying to save you," Victoria continued. "You are troubled. Take the pills, Alicen. Stop fighting your true nature."

Victoria was right. Alicen was foolish for believing anything different. Her mind was broken, a cruel fate she'd brought on herself. And that was enough for Alicen. She reached out and took the small cup, its contents looking like freedom.

"Good, Alicen; that's good," Victoria said. "There will be some side effects, so don't be alarmed. But it will be worth it. Trust me."

Alicen downed all the pills with ease, watching as Victoria's face glowed with satisfaction. She told Alicen a couple things about her new medication regimen that seemed mildly important, but Alicen barely heard her. The moment the drugs hit her system, the world started to haze.

She could see Victoria's lips moving, could hear the mumble of words, but mostly Alicen's head was filled with the satisfying calm that came from feeling nothing. Welcoming the sensation, she let the meds take her down into a surreal state of peace.

24

Days passed slowly, like watching paint dry. Alicen barely left her room. She was hardly able to, and it was getting worse by the day. The side effects Victoria had warned her about were cruel. Piercing headaches and stomach cramps, vomiting up most of what she managed to get down. Hours would pass where she would feel like maybe she'd finally adjusted to the medication, and then she'd experience hours of physical torment and fear she never would.

On top of that, her mind was caught up in a constant haze. Like sitting behind a thick screen, knowing the world was in front of her but not really being able to experience it. It was better this way, Victoria said. She visited often, delivering Alicen's pills herself. Reassuring Alicen that soon the pain would be gone.

A couple times Dr. Wells had come and sat near the end of her bed in a pulled-up chair. He asked her how she was feeling and if she needed anything. She never responded with more than a nod or smile. He sounded concerned at seeing her in such pain. She even overheard him testing Victoria on the medication regimen, but Victoria never wavered.

At some point in the last few days, Alicen had stopped caring that everything made her vomit or ache. Physical pain was preferable to memories of Jane racking her soul. At least the numbing agony stopped the guilt and heartache. And Victoria kept promising it would be better soon. So Alicen suffered alone, in her room, wishing for the better that was promised her to come sooner.

Currently she was curled up on top of her half-made bed. She'd managed to shower and put on normal clothes that morning. At least normal for Clover Mountain. Gray cotton pants and matching gray long-sleeve top. A navy button-up sweater topped it off. She wore white socks with no slippers.

A young female nurse had delivered lunch ten minutes earlier, and the food sat untouched on the small desk across the room. There was a soft knock on her door, and after a moment's delay, the door opened, and Louise poked her head inside. "Hey," she said.

Alicen tried for a smile but gave up. She thought about sitting or even rolling over to better see her friend, but all movement felt like wading through sludge. So instead she did nothing.

Louise smiled and walked in. She was alone. The same as the last time she'd come. Alicen wasn't surprised. Betty didn't do hospitals, even if they were called retreat centers. Louise shut the door behind her and crossed the room, carrying a brown paper bag against her left side. She must have noticed it drew Alicen's attention, because she held it out and shrugged.

"I thought you could use some things from home," Louise said. "They took the face cleanser I brought—some chemical thing—but otherwise everything else cleared."

Alicen just continued to stare at the bag. Louise cleared her throat and set the paper bag on top of the room's tall five-drawer dresser. "I'll just let you go through that whenever you want."

Silence filled the room as Alicen studied her friend's face. Louise was probably waiting for Alicen to say something, anything, but nothing felt easier. Mostly Alicen just wanted to go back to sleep. Mostly she just wanted to be left alone. Louise hesitated another moment and then pulled a nearby chair over and placed it facing Alicen's bed.

She sat, now nearly at eye level with Alicen, and flashed another soft smile. "You look better today. The nurse said you had a rough night but that you seemed in higher spirits this morning. That's a good sign, right?"

Alicen tried to respond but couldn't. Somewhere deep down Alicen really did want to interact with her best friend. After everything they had been through the last couple of months, it was cruel to treat her with such numbness. But Alicen was controlled by fog. So another moment of silence passed.

"Betty wanted to come," Louise said, "but you know Betty. She's probably in bed too." Louise forced a chuckle to try and fight the silent awkwardness. "She just mopes around the house. She's driving me crazy, to be honest, but then she always has." Louise looked at Alicen and gave a small wince. "Sorry," she said. "I don't know why I'm complaining about her to you. Of all people."

The thought of Betty and Louise stuck together, alone, in the Watson summer home, was comical. Enough that even through haze it brought a smile to Alicen's lips. Louise noticed and gave a small laugh. She eased back in her chair a bit, and a comfortable silence started to settle. Alicen felt like maybe having her friend there wasn't so bad. The company might actually feel good. Or at least it might if it felt like anything.

Louise shifted in her chair, switching the position of her legs and glancing around the room. "This is nice," she said.

Alicen didn't respond. The room was . . .

Her mind decided the rest of that thought wasn't necessary, so she just continued her deadpan stare forward, listening to the steady rhythm of her own blood pumping in her skull. Had she ever been still and quiet enough to observe the way her blood pumped? She wasn't sure. Was this what ultimate peace felt like? She didn't know.

"Do you mind if I just stay with you here awhile?" Louise asked, her tone soft and almost sorrowful. "We don't have to talk; I just want to be here."

Alicen suddenly wanted her to be there as well. It wasn't a strong wave of rolling desire, just a tiny pinch in the back of her throat that mourned the idea of lying in her room alone. She managed a nod, and Louise returned her muted gesture with another classic Watson smile.

The room fell quiet once more, Louise peacefully occupying the space while Alicen's mind drifted back into the fog. They stayed like that for several long minutes, and warmth filled the room. Alicen could feel herself being dragged off to sleep, her eyelids heavy, the comfort of a friend creating a safe nook.

Alicen thought maybe she'd fallen asleep for a moment when the crunch of paper drew her attention. Louise had moved the paper bag she'd brought Alicen to the floor by the chair's front leg and was pulling a glossy magazine from its interior.

Louise must have noticed Alicen's stare, because she lifted her eyes from her task and gave an apologetic smile. "Sorry," she said. Then, as if someone had switched a light on in her mind, Louise's eyes widened. "I almost totally forgot—I have something else for you," she said. "I'm not sure I should be giving it to you, but when I found it . . . I don't know, I just thought maybe you should have it." She reached into the inside pocket of her blazer. "I didn't put it in the bag because I was afraid they might take it from me." She pulled out a thin, yellowed envelope and handed it to Alicen.

Alicen stared at the envelope for a long moment and then moved her hand out to reach for it. Her shoulder and side ached as she did. She hadn't done much moving, and the stiffness of remaining in the same position for long periods of time had worked its way into her muscles. She grasped the envelope between her fingers and turned it over to see her name scrawled across the front in a handwriting that was unmistakable. Grandma Joe's. She also noticed that several pieces of clear tape ran down the center, melding together two pieces with jagged edges. She glanced up at Louise, and Louise shrugged.

"I'm not sure what happened there. I found it in your mom's trash basket the other day while I was cleaning up the place. You know me—stress equals cleaning, so the house basically sparkles right now." Louise chuckled uncomfortably, and the room fell back to silence for a moment. She dropped her eyes from Alicen to her fingers. "It's hard to know if letting them bring you here was the right thing," she said, visibly struggling to contain her emotions. "And seeing you like this . . . I think maybe we, *I*, made a terrible mistake. And I know your mom believes that all of Grandma Joe's mess assisted in getting you here, but . . ." Her words trailed off, and there was a beat of silence before she continued. "But I just remember all the love between you two, so maybe it'd be good to be reminded of that."

Louise glanced back up to Alicen, and Alicen could see the sparkle of tears in the corners of her eyes. Alicen looked back to the letter in her hand, and two thoughts gathered at the same time. Once she could have said why her mother had torn this letter and thrown it away, though she couldn't exactly grasp it currently, and in the fumed state of things she wasn't sure she could still read.

She held the letter back out to Louise, who raised her eyebrows. Alicen mustered all her strength and said, "Read it to me?"

"Right now?" Louise asked, seeming a bit hesitant.

Alicen kept her arm extended, and Louise took the letter back. "Okay." She flipped open the top flap and pulled out the folded message, which had also been torn and taped back together. She threw Alicen another hesitant look but unfolded the letter.

She cleared her throat and started. "'Dear Alicen, As I write this letter, I am sitting inside the bay window at Grandpa's old mahogany desk, watching you dance in the fading summer sunlight.'"

Alicen closed her eyes and listened as Louise's voice was replaced by the sound of Grandma Joe's.

You're dancing to a tune only you can hear, your face filled with joy and happiness and hope. Nothing yet weighing on your shoulders, no troubles or pain, and even as I write, I want you to know I would give anything for that reality to never be dampened. But I know all too well what is coming.

Oh, my sweet, there's so much to tell you. So much that you can't yet fully understand, but I see now that we haven't enough time together. I can't explain to you how I know; it's just a feeling I get in my old bones. I won't always be around to guide you or to encourage you to find the truth. All I can do is trust in what I've seen of you so far. And oh, my sweet little girl, how great the glory in you is! It's the treasure in your earthen vessel.

There is darkness in the world, Alicen—shadows and evil. You cannot avoid it. It comes for all of us.

Remember that the world most see is only form, filled with necessary opposites. But beyond what most see is the unseen world filled with light and beauty. It took me a long time to realize that in order for light to be known, darkness must be seen for what it is: a shadow that blocks the light. Remember that shadows are only that—shadows.

Pain, shame, anger, fear—these are the shadows that hide the light, but only when you forget who He said you are. In these moments you must remember what Jesus taught: You are the light of the world. You are made of perfect love, and there is no fear in that love. You're called to it and strong enough to show it to others.

People will mock you and say you are crazy because you see the world differently. Don't get lost in the shame they will push on you. Seeing beyond what is right in front of you will save your life, as it has mine. Know this: the voice of the Holy Spirit will never lead you astray. It is a holy companion and is with you wherever you go, even if you can't always hear it.

Give your mother grace. It was my responsibility to show her different, and I failed. I believe you can succeed where I did not. Love her fiercely. As you find a different path to freedom, I pray she will follow.

People tell me the children I see are illusions. But I have always known they were sent to show me what my eyes alone couldn't see. They're real, and they speak great truth, all too often forgotten. That truth is Christ's love, full of light and power, a love that keeps no record of wrong. A love that casts out all fear, all shame, everything but itself. There is no fear in love.

The world will try to steal that truth from you. Remember they can't. You do not simply hold light but are made of light itself. All the world can do is try to make you forget who you are. At times it will be cruel. The pain will be overwhelming, and for seasons you may not be able to see through it.

When you can't see, remember that your perception will determine your experience in this world. The eye is the lamp of the body, as Jesus taught. If your perception is clear, your whole life will be full of light. If your perception is clouded, you will experience darkness, shame, and fear.

Whenever you experience fear, it's only because your perception is clouded.

To clear your vision, remember who you are as the light. Learn to forgive yourself because you're forgiven. Shame will be your accuser; it will try to blind you. Learning to let it go will be your greatest struggle and your greatest gift. I know because it has been mine. Listen to the voice of love that holds no record of wrong, and when the accuser comes to remind you of your inadequacies, hear the voice of love in the stillness singing the song of your true identity.

Even though they will try to shake your faith to its core, believe in the truth of the glory within you, which is the light of Christ. The perfect love of Him who is the vine. You are one with that vine, a branch, an aspect of the vine itself. Abide there. You in the vine and the vine in you. Don't forget where you come from. When you are called through deep waters, don't be afraid. Go to the waters that summon you. Dive deep, and be transformed.

I don't know where you will be when this letter finds you, but I am entrusting it to a woman who sees and knows more than she gives herself credit for, so I trust it will find you when you need it. My heart aches, thinking of what pain you may have already endured. Pain is not the enemy, Alicen; it is the doorway to moving beyond it. Only when we walk into the valley of the shadow of death do we understand that even death is just a shadow.

Remember, you're never alone; a part of me will always be with you. Take heart, my darling granddaughter. May you see with the eyes of the Spirit, and may you trust in the light that is Christ's perfect love. May you go into the deep whenever you are called, and perhaps even learn to walk on water. I love you with all my heart.

"'Yours truly, Grandma Joe,'" Louise concluded, her voice choked with emotion. She glanced up, tears lacing her cheeks. Alicen was sitting up. She wasn't sure when she had moved, but somewhere between the lines of her grandmother's words, Alicen's body had responded.

"Alicen . . . ?" Louise whispered but then fell silent.

Alicen could feel her heart starting to race. The most movement she'd had in days. The heavy numbness of medication seemed to be tightening its grasp on her mind, but something deep inside her gut was fighting back. "Read it again," she whispered.

Louise complied. Grandma Joe's words filled the room and bled into Alicen's chest. Every line a gentle tug away from nothingness, toward something powerful.

How great the glory in you is!

The voice of the Holy Spirit will never lead you astray.

Don't get lost in shame.

Learn to forgive yourself.

Remember, you're never alone.

The words pressed further into Alicen's body and expanded through her until it felt as if the entire room were filled with the warmth that was building from within.

"'I love you with all my heart,'" Louise read, another wave of tears running down her cheeks.

"Again," Alicen said, aware that she too was crying.

Louise began a third time, and as if her grandmother were in the very room, her tone echoed through Alicen's ears.

Shadows are only that—shadows.

You are the light of the world.

Called to it and strong enough to show it to others.

Shame will be your accuser.

Trust in the light that is Christ's perfect love.

Dive deep.

Be transformed.

Tears dripped off Alicen's chin, each word stoking a fire

inside her gut that threatened to burn through her stomach. Then something cracked open inside her skull, and pain rippled down the back of her neck. She leaned forward and placed her head into her hands, a small cry dropping off her lips. Her head throbbed and erupted with agony as another jolt of suffering exploded behind her temples. Tears flooded her cheeks as pain raced through her entire being.

Alicen, can you hear us? Not her grandmother's voice but a chorus of voices she knew.

"Alicen?" Louise said. The chair scraped the tiled floor as it moved, and Alicen felt Louise's touch on her knees as her friend dropped to a squat in front of her. "Alicen, what's wrong?"

A familiar sense bloomed and spread at a rapid pace through her body. A well of emotions that had been muted now bubbled to the surface, and all at once Alicen felt everything. Her grandmother's voice continued to echo through her drowning mind, her body filled with pain and agony, hunched over, logic screaming that this was wrong. She shouldn't be feeling this deeply; the pain would be the end of her.

But the words of Grandma Joe and the familiar comfort of the chorus echoed over the tiny scream of fear, and for a moment it was blocked out entirely. And for that moment Alicen only felt peace. Warmth from somewhere beyond her body flooded her senses and wrapped her in comfort. It didn't last, and nearly as quickly as it had gone, the aching in her mind and body returned, but the taste of such pure peace had been enough for Alicen to crave more.

"Alicen!" Louise cried, and Alicen became aware of her friend's terrified concern. "I'm going to get somebody, okay?"

Louise started to move, but Alicen reached out and grabbed her friend's arm. Louise stilled and returned her attention to Alicen. The pain was real and cruel, the shame thick and heavy, the loss terrifying and deafening, but that peace was still present, calm and quiet, waiting to be invited in. And Alicen wanted to feel it. For the first time since she could remember, she wanted to feel it all.

Pain is not the enemy, Alicen; it is the doorway to moving beyond it. It is written that only when we walk into the valley of the shadow of death do we understand that even death is just a shadow.

"Alicen, let me get you help," Louise said again.

"No," Alicen breathed out. Sobs began to pour from her mouth, shaking her shoulders, making her chest ache.

"I'm getting someone," Louise insisted and tried to stand, but Alicen's grip was strong. She tugged on her friend. Alicen stood from her bed, Louise turning back toward her, and Alicen pulled Louise in close, wrapping her in an embrace. For a split second Louise stood unmoving, and then as the shock washed away she relaxed into Alicen's arms and pulled her closer.

"I want to be free, Lou," Alicen whispered. "I want to be free."

Louise hugged Alicen fiercely, and together they wept. Alicen wasn't sure how long they stood there, caught up in the same pure moment of sorrow and joy, Grandma Joe's words seeming to echo all around them as peace began to settle throughout the room. It could have been minutes or hours, but when Alicen finally pulled back from Louise, something in her was different.

The effects of her deadening medication had lifted. Her bloodstream felt free and clean, her mind focused, her soul singing. It was mysterious and unexplainable, and Alicen knew the little girl was there before she saw her. Evie. Standing behind Louise, beside the bedroom door, smiling and ready to guide Alicen to the end. And Alicen was ready to follow.

25

Alicen stared over Louise's shoulder at the small girl and felt a tug at her soul. There was more for her yet to see, more to feel and receive. The peace she had barely touched on was vast; she wasn't sure how she knew that, but she hadn't felt so certain of anything for as long as she could remember. There was more, and Alicen had to find it.

"What is it?" Louise asked, reaching up and rubbing the side of Alicen's arm. Her face still flushed from crying, her eyes sparkling with leftover tears, she sniffed and waited for Alicen to respond.

Alicen considered her words. How could she explain something she barely understood to the woman before her?

She glanced back to where Evie had been standing, but the girl was gone.

Louise followed Alicen's eyes and turned her head to look, then refocused forward. "What?" she asked again.

Alicen returned her gaze to Louise as the sweet voices drifted through her mind. *Alicen, come and remember the truth.* Her stomach warmed, her spirit yanking at her rib cage as though it were a gentle hand wrapped around her chest, pulling her forward.

"Alicen?" Louise said with a little more force.

"I'm sorry," Alicen said, shaking her head slightly. A small gust of laughter left her lips.

Louise smiled, her eyes sparking with interest. "What is going on?"

"I need to go," Alicen said and took a step to walk past Louise toward the door.

Louise grabbed Alicen's elbow and forced her to stop. "Wait, what? Go? Where are you going?" Louise asked.

Alicen shifted around and gently pulled herself free of Louise's grasp. "It's hard to explain."

"Well, try," Louise said. Her tone was firm, filled with the kind of concern that came from deep love.

"Louise, it's all right," Alicen said. "Don't worry."

"Don't worry! Alicen, ten minutes ago you could barely lift your head off the pillow; you were barely speaking to me—"

"Louise—"

"And I know, it isn't me, it's your medication—I get that—but what, now you're fine? I mean, you were buckled over in pain, Alicen. You should probably see one of the doctors. Maybe you're having a bad reaction to the medication."

"Louise—"

"I mean, I'm not an expert, but I don't think it's normal to go from a near-vegetative state to terrible pain to this . . . whatever you are now. I really think you should get back in bed and let me go grab a nurse."

"Lou—" Alicen tried as she reached her hand forward to touch Louise's shoulder.

But Louise was working herself into a panic and yanked away. "No, Alicen," she said, her eyes filling with tears. "You need to get back in bed. You're sick."

"And what if I'm not?" Alicen said calmly.

Alicen, come and see.

Louise was shaking her head, and Alicen stepped forward and softly grabbed both of Louise's shoulders. She held the woman's eyes with her own and watched a tear slide down her cheek. "Louise, what if we have been seeing the world incorrectly? What if we have been missing the truth all these years? What if my Grandma Joe was right, and there is a different way?"

Louise's lips parted, but no words came out. Alicen could see the way Grandma Joe's words had affected her, had spoken to something deep inside Louise just as they had sprung to life something in Alicen. Something they had both forgotten.

"Look at my eyes, Louise. Something real is happening to me. Happening to my soul." Alicen could feel her own emotions rumbling to the surface. "Something beyond the pain. Something I didn't think was possible. I thought all of my life would be pledged to mourning the loss of my daughter." Tears dampened Alicen's face as she spoke, matching the ones falling down Louise's. "But what if I was wrong? Lou, something is calling me beyond what I can see right in front of me."

"Alicen, I don't—"

"I know you feel it too. I can see it in your eyes," Alicen said. "That truth deep inside your soul, the way your heart felt hearing Grandma Joe's words, the way it feels listening to me now. There is more than all of this around us, more than form alone, and it sings to me, which I know sounds crazy, but it sings, and I have to listen. Otherwise I'll get lost in my suffering, and I want to be free from it. I'm actually starting to believe I *can* be free." Alicen let a soft chuckle escape her lips because saying the words out loud stoked the flame of hope burning in her stomach.

Alicen, come and see.

"What if you're wrong, and I let you go, and I lose more of you?" Louise asked, sorrow playing across her tone. "I can't lose more of you. I won't."

Alicen smiled, salty tears touching her lips. She moved her hands from Louise's shoulders and placed them gingerly on either side of Louise's face. She swiped a tear with her thumb and felt the warmth of her friend's skin. "Look at me—really look at me. Do I look sick or confused or lost? I'm not, Lou; for the first time in a long time, I'm not. You know me, better than anyone ever has. You've believed in me more than anyone ever did. So I need you to see me now. Believe me now."

Louise sniffed, the battle of her mind and heart dancing

behind her expression. There was a sliver of silence between them as her mind churned and her heart fought. Then she whispered, "All I ever wanted was for you to be happy and well. And I never know if what I'm doing is good for you or just making it worse. I'm so afraid that all of this was a huge mistake and that it's my fault."

Alicen's heart broke. She'd spent so much time lost in her own pain that she'd never considered Louise's at all. The pressure on her friend's shoulders, the responsibility and desperation she was taking on. The blame she was carrying. She was as trapped in her suffering as Alicen was. Maybe they all were. Hadn't that been what Grandma Joe was saying? *There is darkness in the world—shadows and evil. You cannot avoid it. It comes for all of us.* Maybe everybody had their own set of shadows.

"Don't be afraid," Alicen said, repeating the words she had been hearing for months that were finally starting to take root in her soul. "Don't get lost to your fear, my dear friend. Maybe we are the light of the world, and the rest of this is just shadows."

Louise shook her head again, speechless but not resistant.

Alicen searched the room behind Louise and saw that on the corner of her bed lay Grandma Joe's letter. She stepped around Louise and grabbed it in one swift movement. She scanned it, turned back to Louise, and read aloud.

"'Learn to forgive yourself because you're forgiven. Shame will be your accuser; it will try to blind you. Learning to let it go will be your greatest struggle and your greatest gift. I know, because it has been mine. Listen to the voice of love that holds no record of wrong, and when the accuser comes to remind you of your inadequacies, hear the voice of love in the stillness singing the song of your true identity.'"

Alicen held the letter to her heart and gave a small cry of joy. The well inside her felt full enough to burst. How long had she missed what was right in front of her? How desperate she was to dive into the fullness of the truth held in Josephine's words. Alicen locked gazes with Louise again, both women teary-eyed and stunned by the way simple words written decades earlier could be manifesting through their beings. It was an undeniable charge of energy, and neither could ignore it. "I don't understand it all, but I'm certain enough that I have to follow where it calls me," Alicen said.

Alicen, do you hear us?

Louise, still in a state of awe that teetered on the edge of uncertainty, took a sharp inhale. Alicen closed the gap between them and placed her free hand on Louise's arm. "I have to go, but I need your help."

Another beat of silence passed. Another battle warred behind Louise's expression. Another deep inhale. And then she nodded yes.

• • •

Alicen knew getting out of her room wouldn't be logistically possible on her own. She was under the constant watchful eye of the nurses who walked the hallways and checked the rooms. Thankfully she had Louise. Still hesitant, but willing, and unable to deny the change in Alicen, Louise agreed to help her navigate the halls, in case they met unwanted company.

"Where are we going?" Louise asked, looping her arm through Alicen's.

"I don't know yet," Alicen answered truthfully. "But I will."

"Right," Louise said, shaking her head. "You know this is crazy?"

"Yeah," Alicen said. "But that never stopped us before."

Alicen wasn't sure where she was going but could sense the child the moment Louise opened the door from Alicen's room to the main hall. Louise led Alicen out, and there she was. Pigtails, white dress, bright smile, standing at the end of the long hallway and motioning her to follow.

Fear buzzed harshly inside her rib cage. It was such a stark contrast from the flood of peace she'd just experienced that it caused her to pause. Was she really going to do this? Follow a child that no one else could see? Risk returning to a place of insanity because of some old words written by her grandmother? A grandmother who may have also been insane? The desire to turn back and reenter her room was strong; all the longing to follow the still and quiet voice suddenly felt foolish.

Don't be afraid, Alicen.

Come and see another way.

"Now what?" Louise asked, smiling to a passing nurse and keeping her words soft so as not to draw attention.

Follow or don't follow, Alicen thought. The next step she took would set her path, and the choice was hers alone. *Follow.* She took a deep breath and started down the hallway toward Evie, her courage returning with each step. Fear still pounded in her chest, but she could feel it being shut out by the charge of her spirit. *Follow,* she thought again. Louise walked beside her, the two silent as Alicen kept her eyes fixed ahead on the child leading her.

"Alicen?" came a warm voice, and Alicen looked up to see a nurse with a familiar face. "What are you two doing?"

Louise tugged Alicen closer and interjected before Alicen could speak. "Oh, I just thought maybe a walk through the building might be good for her; is that all right? One of the other nurses—Patty, I think it was—mentioned she hadn't been out of her room much the last few days."

The nurse smiled. "Adjusting to the new medications can take some time. I'm glad to see you're out of bed."

Alicen didn't speak but just faked a half grin, and the nurse gave Louise's shoulder a soft tap. "Don't wander too far; she'll tire out pretty quickly." The nurse's tone was hushed, as if she thought maybe Alicen wouldn't hear her.

"Okay, thanks," Louise said with a wide Watson smile, and the nurse passed on.

The two women made sure to put several yards between themselves and the nurse before Louise whispered under her breath, "I had better not get arrested for this."

They walked around the end corner of the hall and into a larger walkway. Again Evie was there. A rush of tiny giggles filled the air around Alicen's head as she started toward the girl. Down a staircase, along another, thinner hallway, out a back door, across a well-laid sidewalk, into another building. Louise walking steadily beside her, never releasing Alicen's arm, never pulling her back or making her stop.

The second building was smaller, one Alicen hadn't been in before, and nearly empty. Alicen mildly remembered Victoria mentioning this building was used for physical therapy when she'd had her initial visit. The building felt hollow and stale. As though it hadn't seen much human presence in a while. They moved through its interior, across the main entry floor lined with smaller rooms for group gatherings and offices that sat unoccupied.

Reaching the back of the open first-floor room, Alicen could feel the pull on her heart drawing her down a small hall to her right. She turned and saw Evie standing at the end, a door slightly ajar behind her. Before Alicen could move, the child spoke out loud. "The rest of this you need to do alone," she said.

"Alone?" Alicen replied.

"What?" Louise asked.

Louise couldn't hear Evie, just as she couldn't see her. The familiar wave of fearful uncertainty zapped the ends of Alicen's mental resolve and began to burn away her strength. The questions returned. Was she really going to do this?

"Don't be afraid, Alicen," Evie said. "Come and see another way. The journey is yours alone to take."

Hers alone, she thought as the fear grew in momentum. But still present through her building uncertainty was the pulse of her spirit. The mysterious desire she couldn't explain, the one her logic told her was insane, beckoned her onward. Toward freedom and life. She turned toward Louise.

"What is it?" Louise asked, and Alicen could see the fear dancing behind her expression.

"Thank you for believing in me, for trusting me," Alicen said.

"Alicen?" Louise questioned. She knew her friend well and wasn't fooled by Alicen's opening.

"But I'm going to need to do this part by myself, Lou."

"No," Louise said nearly on top of Alicen's last word.

"You trusted me before—"

"Absolutely not. I am not going to leave you here!"

"This is my journey."

"Do you see me standing here? It's my journey too; you made this about me, too."

"Louise."

"Don't ask me to do this, Alicen," Louise said, her words cracking under the emotion weighing on her. It made Alicen's heart ache, but the whispers summoned her.

Alicen, come and see.

Alicen gently grabbed Louise's shoulders. "I know that you're afraid, but don't be," she said. "I need you to trust me and wait here. I have to go on alone."

Louise shook her head, shock and disbelief coloring her face.

"Look at me, Lou. I'm not confused. I'm not lost. There is more—there has to be—and I have to go see it for myself. And I'm being called to it alone. I have to go."

Alicen released her hold on her friend and took a step away. Louise stayed, her face still filled with worry, the war of head and heart waging inside her madly. Alicen knew that battle well.

"I'll be back," Alicen said and then took off toward the

end of the hall, now empty of the little girl who had been leading her. But she didn't need Evie to be there; the drag on her soul was enough. She was nearly to the open door when Louise broke the gathered silence.

"Alicen!" she croaked out.

Alicen reached the door, placed her hand around its knob, and turned her head over her shoulder. Louise was still where Alicen had left her, both of her hands placed over her heart, as if she were trying to still its beating.

"I love you, Lou," Alicen said before Louise could say anything else.

Louise paused and then gave her a small nod. "I love you, too."

And then Alicen disappeared around the wooden door and out of Louise's sight. She pulled the door closed behind her, sealing herself off from the hallway behind her and her terrified friend.

The moment she was alone, Alicen could hear the whispers strong and clear.

Don't be afraid, Alicen.

The waters of sorrow will not overwhelm you.

You are the light of the world. The rest is just shadows.

She started down the new walkway before her. There wasn't as much light here. The corridor was filled with stale air and dust. A couple yards forward, the wall to her left became windows that peered into a full-size gym. Weight racks, benches, hanging bars, cardio machines, and mirrored walls spread farther back. The room was larger than a person would have thought from the front of the building.

She continued past it, and the smell of chlorine nipped at the insides of her nostrils. Water. Memories of the forest lake pricked at the back of her mind, and her spirit flourished.

Alicen pressed forward, toward a set of double steel doors and through them. On the other side the smell of a swimming pool filled her senses. She glanced around the room covered in shadows, only a trace of afternoon light peeking in through the windows at the back walls. She was standing on a metal ledge, five feet wide, a barred railing around its edge to keep people from walking off. The ledge ran along the entirety of the room and had a single descending metal staircase to her left.

Alicen walked to the railing and looked over it. Below lay an Olympic-size swimming pool. Three-foot markers indicated the shallow end, and the depth increased steadily as it ran down toward a twelve-foot cap. A thick, blue-tiled edge outlined the large rectangular shape. White square tiles filled the rest of the surface around the pool and patterned the inside below the water and up all four sides to meet the dark-blue outer edge.

Alicen noticed all those details within seconds, and then her attention was drawn to the water itself. The pool was full to the brim, but its color was abnormal. Blue and green swirls danced in circles throughout, their clear and bright crystal appearance reflecting what little daylight was streaming in through the high windows and turning it almost gold. It was the same brilliant water that had filled the pool in the center of the forest.

Before she realized she was moving, Alicen had descended the staircase and was a couple feet from the water's edge. It lapped peacefully, which seemed odd since there was no circulating air to cause its movement. Stranger still, the water was drawing her close, calling her near, speaking to her without words.

"Beautiful, isn't it?" a small voice came.

Alicen looked up from the water and saw Jane standing on the other side of the pool. The same blue that swam through the water danced in Jane's eyes. Peace and light reflected off her skin, and a warm energy surged through Alicen's chest. It wasn't actually her daughter; Alicen knew that. Her Jane was dead, some would say by Alicen's hand. The surge of warmth was matched by the shame and horror of remembering she would never have Jane back.

"Is freedom real?" Alicen asked the little girl. "Can I actually have it?"

Jane smiled. "You already do."

Get a grip, Alicen.

Act like an adult.

Alicen's chest ached with sorrow. It seemed the moment she felt any certainty toward hope, that voice of damnation was programmed to reappear and douse it with flames.

"Shame will be your accuser," Jane began, echoing the words from Grandma Joe's letter, "and it will feel powerful."

What would your mother say, Alicen?

"It's just a shadow," Jane continued. "Learning to let it go will be your greatest struggle and your greatest gift."

Foolish, stupid girl, you deserve this sickness.

"Listen to the voice of love that holds no record of wrong."

You don't deserve to be free.

"And when the accuser comes to remind you of your inadequacies, the voice of love can be heard in the stillness."

Alicen could feel the back-and-forth pulling on her resolve. Both voices resounding in her mind, tearing it in two. The soft voice of Jane warring against the harshness of her inner accuser. One on each side of her, calling her down two different paths, one beckoning her toward heaven, and the other yanking her toward hell. She had been here before, and it had nearly killed her. Alicen could feel the powerful drag of self-doubt yearning to pull her away from the water's edge, but something was different in her spirit this time.

Something Grandma Joe had awoken and stirred. And it too drew her. Toward the water, into it. Alicen closed her eyes and searched past the voice of shame, beyond it, and felt the perfect peace that had only started to blossom. She wanted it to flourish, to consume her.

"When you are called through deep waters, don't be afraid," the sweet voice of Jane said. A small hand laced itself within her own, and Alicen opened her eyes to see her daughter standing beside her. The heat from her bright energy pulsed up Alicen's arm and wormed into her chest.

"Go to the waters that summon you," the child said. "Dive deep, and be transformed. I will show you."

Alicen could feel the heavy stir of sorrow collecting in her chest. Standing so close to Jane here, feeling her touch, seeing her hopeful expression. It was agony, and Alicen wanted to retreat.

Reading her mind, Jane replied, "Pain isn't the enemy; it's time to remember who you are."

The mother who murdered her daughter.

"The light of the world," Jane said.

A tear dripped off Alicen's chin and splashed against her collarbone. She could feel the pull to the water explode through her system. She wanted to be transformed, renewed. She wanted to find the freedom her spirit sang of.

Jane gave Alicen's hand a tiny pull and smiled with so much joy Alicen thought her own heart might burst. "Come. I will show you."

The other voice may have been screaming inside her mind, but Alicen could hardly hear it now. She was too taken with the song of the children that started to fill the room and echo off the tiled walls.

When through the deep waters I call you to go,
the rivers of sorrow shall not overflow.
When through fiery trials thy pathway shall lie,
my grace, all-sufficient, shall be thy supply.

Alicen followed as Jane led her to the water's edge and into the warm waves. The water swirled around her ankles and then calves as she waded waist deep beside the reflection of her daughter. Power surged up her body and into the deepest parts of her being. Alicen closed her eyes as the waters lapped up against her chest, moving without the pull of the elements, swishing around her on their own, warming her shoulders, calling her deeper.

The small hand that had led her this far vanished, and without opening her eyes Alicen knew Jane was gone. The waters were hers alone to walk through. As the crystal liquid licked the back of her neck, the pain began. The shame of all her perceived failures, the loss of those she'd loved, the rejection from her mother and husband, the anger of feeling used, the terror of never being enough, the lack of perfection that made her feel weak. Everything all at once surrounded her as her head sank below the water's surface.

It started in her heels and filled every cell in her body, until she was drowning in her own suffering. The desire to thrash against the painful waves, to get lost in her fear, to run from the pain, was almost too strong to resist. And for a brief moment she thought maybe she would die here in this abandoned pool, a victim of her own sorrow. It was all she could do not to open her mouth and let the water blot her out of existence. Then, through the threat of overwhelming pain, the voices cut in.

"My grace, all-sufficient, shall be thy supply."

After the choir of children, a line from Grandma Joe's letter tapped at the back of her memory and captured her heart. *Learn to forgive yourself because you're forgiven.*

Let go, Alicen; let it all go.

And with a leap of faith, Alicen let go of the pain she'd held for so long and began to believe she was more than the lies she had been taught. Just as the pain had started in the bottoms of her feet, now a swell of peace took hold. It inched upward through her body, erasing the pain, destroying the shame and agony of the lies she'd believed for so long and replacing them with truth. A truth she had long forgotten. *You are the light of the world.*

Her body eased as the peace spread up into her chest and out through the tips of her fingers, the words of truth replacing her broken cells with light. Healing her from the inside out. Freeing her from the condemnation she had thought was her eternal reality. *He is the vine. You are one with that vine, a branch. Abide there.*

Joy burst into her mind as the terror of all her gathered inadequacies fizzled out. Alicen opened her mouth and began to laugh, unable to contain the pleasure that was surrounding her figure. Water should have drained into her body, but all she felt was warmth. She was floating, caught up in the magic of the renewing waters into which she had been called. *You in the vine and the vine in you.*

Alicen's heart swelled with understanding as the light of joy, peace, and hope filled every space. She felt whole and certain of who she was. Forgiven. Renewed. Transformed. For the first time since she was a little girl, Alicen felt like light.

26

Victoria walked through the second-floor hallway of the main house, headed to Alicen's room. She absently greeted nurses and patients as they passed, her mind fixed on her destination. Her hand softly held the small plastic tube of her personally designed medication. A new dose, created that morning, intended for Alicen.

Small-enough amounts to attack her kidneys slowly without raising suspicions. Easily transferred into pill sleeves, colorless and undetectable. One of these, three times a day, plopped into the little white cup along with Alicen's other medication, and no one would be the wiser.

And the debt would be paid.

You reap what you sow.

Alicen was finally reaping.

Victoria reached Alicen's room and rapped softly at the door. No response. She slowly twisted the lever, and the door clicked open. Holding it just ajar, she looked in and paused at the scene. Bed empty, chair moved beside the bed, paper bag on the floor, magazine laid open across the chair. Victoria pressed the door fully open and stepped inside. She glanced toward the attached bathroom and saw the door open, the small room empty. Alicen wasn't here.

Victoria stepped out into the hall and called to a nurse standing a few feet away, checking the chart of another patient. "Where is Alicen McCaffrey, the patient in this room?"

The nurse glanced up from her clipboard and looked a bit confused.

"She wasn't granted permission to leave her room, and yet here it is, empty," Victoria said. "Can you explain that to me?"

The older nurse gave a slight head tilt and grin. "She was up and moving, which she hasn't done for days. Looked a lot better too."

Looking better? The words grated at Victoria's mind. Alicen should be barely holding on to life, not feeling better, not up and walking around. She was supposed to be suffering.

The best laid plans turn to rot.

"So you let her just walk out?" Victoria asked.

"She was accompanied by her friend."

"What friend?"

"Oh, I don't know her name. The only visitor she gets, something with an *L* maybe."

Worms. Filthy worms.

Rage boiled inside its prison and threatened to spill over into her guts. Victoria resisted the urge to reach out and slap the fat old nurse across her plump cheek. She stepped closer to the woman and dropped her tone to a harsh but contained volume. "The patient in this room is a high-risk resident who under no circumstance is to be out of watchful view as designated by me."

"I didn't see any harm—" the nurse started.

"Your job is not to make choices on what you deem harmful or not harmful to the patients." Victoria inched even closer, the nurse becoming visibly uncomfortable at the look Victoria was nailing her with. "Your job is to follow the orders given by those who are trained to deal with patient behavior."

"I—I'm sor—" the nurse stumbled.

"Where are they?"

"I don't know; they just went for a walk."

You tried to cut the worm in half, but it's better to squish it whole.

Victoria bit the tip of her tongue and tried to control the heat rising through her chest. "You have no idea what this patient is capable of. You've endangered her and all those around her."

She has to pay, little Victoria. If not her, then it will have to be you.

The nurse opened her mouth to apologize or defend

herself—Victoria wasn't sure which—but she didn't have time for this anymore. Alicen needed to be retrieved quickly.

"Place the campus on lockdown," Victoria said.

"I don't think that's nece—" the nurse started again.

"We are only in this situation because you *thought* outside of your pay grade," Victoria snapped. Several nurses and patients standing close were watching now, but Victoria's rage was taking on a life of its own, and she was struggling to shut it down. Another forceful inhale. "If you plan to continue working here, I suggest you begin the lockdown procedure immediately," she said.

The nurse just stood stunned for a beat, her mouth slightly open, her eyes searching Victoria's face as if she were still confused by what Victoria was asking.

You're failing, little Victoria.

"Now!" Victoria yelled.

The nurse nodded, snapped out of her dumb stupor, and moved to the half-circle desk across the wide walkway. She picked up the phone receiver and set the lockdown procedure into motion. The other foot traffic in the hallway started to move, knowing what was coming next. Within seconds a shrill alarm buzzed overhead. Three sharp shrieks followed by softer beeps that signaled the rest of the staff to return all patients to their rooms, place all visitors in the common room, and lock down the other buildings until the perceived threat could be contained.

Her failure is your failure.

"I will not fail," she said under her breath as she moved to join the search for Alicen.

• • •

Somewhere in the deep corners of Alicen's mind, a muffled shriek stirred her to consciousness. It echoed through her head and roused her from stillness. Her eyes opened, both warmth and cold registering on her face. She swallowed, uncertainty filling her brain. She rolled over, and the cold that had been on her cheek lifted.

Alicen opened her eyes fully, the distant beeping drawing closer as it sank into her reality. She was staring up at a dimly lit ceiling, lying against something hard, an alarm seeping in from the outside to fill the silence. And then, all at once, she remembered where she was. The events of her surrender to the powerful waves returned.

She shot up and looked to either side. She was lying on the white square-tiled floor that surrounded the pool. It was cold under her fingers, and she pushed herself up to standing. It took effort; her mind was groggy, and her body registered her brain's commands slowly.

Alicen stepped closer to the water and was taken aback by the normality of it. It was simple pool water. Hadn't it been filled with colors and light? Hadn't it sung to her, called to her? She lifted her eyes and scanned the rest of the room, looking for children, looking for Jane. But she was alone. She strained to listen past the alarm that was screaming overhead for the familiar whispers, the choir of angelic voices, but heard nothing.

She tucked a stray hair away from her face and then pulled her hand back. Her hair was dry. She reached down, her eyes following her fingers. Her clothes were dry. Hadn't she submerged herself? Hadn't she been transformed?

Had she imagined it all? A sliver of fear snaked along the inside of her gut, and then she felt it. The calming new sense of peace that had been awoken while hearing the words of her grandmother's letter. The hope and joy that had been ignited as she let Jane lead her to the water. The belief in the power of whose she was that had overwhelmed her below the water's surface.

Alicen closed her eyes, blocked out the warning still ringing overhead, and searched for the truth. And there she found it, swimming in her blood, melding to her bones. The light of forgiveness, renewal, transformation. The waters had washed away the broken vow she'd made with her shame and replaced it with the promise of her true identity. She was the light of the world. Connected to the vine.

Emotion rolled up through her chest, and a giggle emerged. Instinctively she reached her hand up to cover her lips and then remembered she was alone. She dropped her hand and spun in a circle, a thrill of joy twisting around her. She felt light, physically free, as though if she leaped high enough maybe she could fly.

"Wouldn't that be something?" a little voice said. "To fly?"

Alicen turned and saw the four children standing across the room. Evie. Beck, Tate, and Roxie. Ministering spirits. Sent to help her see.

"How can all of this be real?" Alicen asked.

Evie gave her a quizzical look. "You still have doubts?"

Alicen thought it through a moment and then smiled. *No,*

she thought. What had happened to her had to be real. They had to be real. They had brought her all this way to believe. Or maybe to remember. "Why children?"

"Were you expecting something else?" Evie asked.

Tears filled Alicen's eyes. She could never have expected this. She wasn't sure why, but her emotions were just too overwhelming to be contained. She believed. She saw them standing there and without a doubt believed. The pure shock of it vibrated like a shorted electric wire in her chest.

"Hold on to that powerful belief, Alicen," Evie said. "It will always set you free."

Something cracked loudly above them and drew Alicen's attention up to the railed walkway that surrounded the pool area. A large male nurse stumbled into the room, his gaze swinging back and forth until it landed on Alicen. "Hey!" he yelled.

Fear spiked inside Alicen's chest, covering the perfect peace she'd just been feeling. She took a step away from him as he moved for the stairs that descended down to her level. "You can't be in here," he said, his tone stern and unkind.

Alicen backed away farther, all of her instincts screaming at her to run. Another crack echoed behind her, and she spun to see a campus security guard walking in through a second door she hadn't even noticed before along the back wall. The guard glanced over Alicen's shoulder toward the nurse and gave a small nod.

Then he took a step toward her. "Alicen," he said, "we've been looking for you."

Panic erupted through Alicen's body, and she inched

backward away from the guard, remembering that another approached from behind. She twisted her head around to make sure the nurse wasn't too close, but either way she looked, she was sandwiched in.

"It's all right," the guard said. "Dr. Flowers wants to see you, is all."

Victoria. *No,* Alicen thought. She didn't want to be numb anymore. She didn't need to be; she'd found salvation and peace. True freedom.

"I'm fine," Alicen tried. "Really. I'll just go back to my room."

"I don't think so, Alicen. You look a little unraveled to me," the guard said.

"I'm not," Alicen said. "I'm fine; I just needed some fresh air." She backed away from the guard, who was still approaching, but found herself getting closer to the nurse.

"We're just going to help you get back, okay?" the guard said.

Alicen glanced behind her and saw the nurse pull something from his pocket. A syringe.

"No, please—I'm fine. I'll walk back peacefully," Alicen said.

"Of course you will. We're just going to make sure of it," the guard said.

"Please don't," Alicen pleaded. "I'm not crazy; I just needed some fresh air."

They were closing in on her, and she had nowhere to go.

"Don't you worry," the guard said. "We're going to make sure you get taken care of."

The nurse was only a foot away when Alicen's nerves took over and she bolted forward. Her sudden movement caught the security guard off balance, and she slipped right past his outstretched reach. She rushed for the back door he'd entered but only made it a couple of steps before large hands caught up with her.

They grabbed her shoulders and yanked her backward. An involuntary scream escaped her mouth as fear swelled in her mind. "Stop! Please don't!" she cried, but it changed nothing. The guard wrapped Alicen tightly and lifted her off her feet as the nurse quickly found an open skin patch on her arm and pricked her deeply with the syringe's needled tip.

A flash of pain cut down her arm, and then her world began to swim. "No, please . . ." But her words drifted off as the drugs took her under.

"There you go," the guard said. "See? No problems here, Alicen."

Alicen tried to fight against the medication as it sank its teeth into her brain and filled her body with lead, but it was impossible. It took her nearly as quickly as it had entered her system, and then she was gone.

• • •

Alicen roused from her foggy state slowly. Her eyes inched open as the familiar sight of her Clover Mountain room came into view. She tried to move her shoulder, but it seemed to be weighed down by bricks. Her entire body felt heavy as she painfully tilted her chin down to see that she was restrained.

Alicen shifted under the thick straps, but they held her

tightly in place against her mattress. She tilted her head back to see the world outside had faded to night; her room was dark. How long had she been here?

Her thoughts were slow as a mixture of drugs swam through her bloodstream. She tried to take in the rest of the room, tried to search for answers to questions that formed like molasses in her mind. Shadows swept across the floor and ignited an idea deep inside her brain. Shadows were only shadows, she thought.

Alicen, you can hear us, Alicen.

The whisper in her brain was familiar and soothing. Alicen reached for the voice, felt the urge to pull its power closer. She knew it well, was changed because of it, and even with the heavy dose of medication stifling her awareness, she was sure of one thing: the truth of who she was. It broke through the chemical restraints, expanded through her entire body, and set her soul ablaze with light. For a moment the room faded from view, and Alicen felt as though she were back in the waters, perfect love flowing all around her, transforming her mind and setting her free.

A soft click popped across the room, and a blip of light snuffed out some of the room's darkness. It pulled Alicen's attention back from the waters to her room and illuminated the presence of someone else.

"Hello, Alicen," the voice said. Female, soft and dangerous. Victoria.

Victoria walked from the corner where the lamp she'd brought to life stood and stepped toward Alicen's bed. "You're finally awake. I've been waiting," she said.

The hairs on Alicen's arms stood at attention, her pulse beating behind her ears as the woman strode toward her. And as her face came into view, laced with shadows, eyes filled with hate, Alicen's heart began to race. Her animalistic instincts were screaming at her to run for her life.

"I want you to know I tried very hard to help you," Victoria said. "I saw myself in you; I thought together we could offer up penance for our trouble. But at every turn you refused to accept what you are."

"Forgiven," Alicen whispered.

Victoria's chin twitched dramatically, and anger rolled across her gaze. "For what you've done there is no forgiveness," she said.

"I've seen it," Alicen said. "Touched it."

"No, you reap what you sow. You have to pay your debts."

"My debts have been paid. With grace."

Again Victoria's head twitched violently, her shoulders shaking, her eyes growing in darkness. "Stupid, foolish girl," she spat. She stepped closer, anger dripping from her expression like poison. "All there is in this world is evil, darkness, trouble. No one leaves unscathed by it. Grace is a myth."

Alicen could feel the light of her identity, could hear the chorus of truth softly humming in her soul.

You are the light of the world.

The rest is just shadows.

"You're wrong," Alicen said.

"No!" Victoria said. "You are a worm. We are all worms, birthed from dirt. Filth. Shameful and weak. As I am, so are you."

Alicen could hear the anger growing in the woman's voice, but she wasn't afraid. She was abiding in love, and there was no fear there.

You can show her the truth, Alicen.

Lead her to the water.

"There is another way, Victoria," Alicen said.

"There is only one way!" Victoria snapped back. She reached into her pocket and pulled out a thick syringe. A flash of unease jolted up Alicen's spine.

Victoria's hand shook as she reached out and grabbed Alicen's right wrist. She pulled it down so that her elbow was straight, the veins in her arm clear. Alicen tried to pull away, but the restraints and Victoria's strong grip held her firmly.

"I tried to save you slowly," Victoria said, "a little bit at a time, so that you could pay what was owed, but it's better to squish a worm completely."

She wasn't making any sense. Alicen saw only death in her eyes. "Victoria, stop," she said.

A sharp pain exploded into Alicen's arm as Victoria drove the tip of the syringe into her vein. A painful cry lurched from Alicen's throat, and the pressure from whatever was being pumped into her arm worked its way all the way down into her palm.

"A special dose for a special case," Victoria said. "Enough sedation to have you swimming, enough ethylene glycol to send your kidneys into failure before morning."

Poison, Alicen thought. Victoria was injecting her with poison. The moment her mind calculated what was happening, the sedative mixed into the deadly cocktail set in.

A heavy fog crawled up from her heels, through her legs, into her chest, and up her neck.

"I wanted to avoid death, but death seems to be my only salvation. Blood for blood," Victoria rambled. Her hands shook. Her breathing had quickened. Her pale skin flushed.

Alicen, you can show her.

Lead her to the water.

"I can show you," Alicen managed through the numbing that was overwhelming her brain.

"No!" Victoria yelled. "Payment is necessary for the sins committed. You are my payment. My skin in the game."

Through the haze taking full control of her system, Alicen heard a soft thudding. Across the room another small stream of light pierced the darkness. Muffled calls drifted into the space, and Alicen followed Victoria's gaze as she turned her head to look up at Alicen's closed door. Someone was pounding on the outside, Alicen thought. Trying to get in. To save her.

Victoria looked back to Alicen, no concern on her face. She was too far gone to care now. She had lost control. Alicen knew that feeling well. She'd experienced it herself.

The thudding continued, the muffled voices multiplying. Victoria shook her head. "Your trouble crawled under my skin, Alicen. It became my own, and it made me pay. You stole from me, and I paid for you!"

Alicen's lungs seemed slow, and she struggled to get a breath. Somewhere inside her barely functioning brain, she wondered if she was dying.

"This is your atonement," Victoria said. "Life has come to collect."

Everything felt so dull. Yet the whisper still broke through and burrowed into Alicen's heart. The voice of the Spirit calling her again to the water, but this time not alone.

Show her.

Lead her to the water.

"Grace has already atoned for me," Alicen said. With all the strength she could muster through the pain, Alicen turned her eyes to Victoria. She captured Victoria's gaze with her own, and the demons behind Victoria's vision growled at the light behind Alicen's.

"Let me show you," Alicen said as she reached her hand out, grabbed Victoria's wrist, and watched as the entire world shifted.

27

Victoria gasped as Alicen's hand clasped her wrist and the vision around her changed. As if they'd been sucked through time and space itself, Alicen's room was gone, and all around her was forest. She was kneeling, both her palms pressed down into the grassy floor. She pushed up to her feet and turned. The place where she stood was a clearing, a circle of trees surrounding it. And in the center was a lake.

Victoria looked up; a brilliant night sky shone down. Filled with stars and bright moonlight, beautiful and breathtaking. A warm breeze floated by, lifting the ends of her hair as a roll of thunder echoed in the distance. *A storm,* she thought.

"Only beyond the trees—never in here," someone said,

and Victoria spun around to see Alicen standing a couple of feet away. The woman was striking against the dark wooded backdrop. Her golden hair perfectly placed along the tops of her shoulders, her eyes piercing through the night, her skin capturing a glow that seemed abnormal and looked warm to the touch.

"Where are we?" Victoria asked. "What did you do to me?"

"I told you I would show you another way," Alicen said.

"I don't . . . How . . . ?" The shock of what had happened before her eyes was making it impossible for Victoria's brain to function.

Alicen smiled. "Trying to wrap your mind around it will only make it worse."

Victoria's mouth gaped open as she dropped her eyes and shook her head.

Careful, little Victoria, or her trouble will get you. Her uncle's voice drifted by on the wind, and Victoria clenched her eyes shut.

This isn't real, she thought.

Get ahold of yourself, Victoria, she scolded.

"This isn't possible," she spat.

"Yet here we are," Alicen replied.

Victoria took a sharp breath and clamped her teeth tightly. Her chin jerked; the place along her wrists where she paid for her failures burned. "No," she said. "No, take me back."

"Don't you want to see grace?" Alicen asked.

"Grace is a lie."

"No, Victoria, the lie is what you believe now. Your vision is clouded."

Worm. Filthy, dirty worm.

Murderer.

"I know how it feels to be tormented by your pain," Alicen said. Victoria tried to shake the hold Alicen had on her gaze, but the woman seemed to be reaching into her chest and drawing her closer. "I believed, like you do, that I could never be rid of my shame."

Victoria's heart thumped quickly, ramming the inside of her chest. Her brain spun, her stomach ached. The grass seemed to be reaching up into the soles of her feet, hot and electric, as if the ground itself were infused with Alicen's words.

"All I saw was the darkness in the world. And then I was led back to truth. Renewed. You can be as well," Alicen said.

Lying, filthy little worm. There's no forgiveness for what you've done.

Remember what you are, little Victoria.

"Remember what Jesus taught: you are the light of the world. Forgive yourself because you are forgiven," Alicen said.

"Stop," Victoria commanded. Her demons rose up through her chest again, heating the inside of her throat. Rage ignited her bloodstream. Her uncle's mocking laughter filled her brain.

Foolish, worthless girl.

"I can show you," Alicen said, taking another step forward and extending her hand between them. "I can show you how to access grace."

Born from filth, the weakest of all worms.

Thunder rumbled close, and hot light from strikes of

lightning flashed in the distance. Victoria's trouble roared, her memories soaked in, taking her back to that place. To the nights when he'd come for her. To the places where he'd reminded her of what she was. The living nightmares of her past. *No,* she thought. *No—get control, little girl.*

"Let me show you," Alicen said. A strong, wild wind swept across the clearing and ruffled the top of the still water. Then a new small voice whispered through the madness collecting in Victoria's brain.

Victoria, do you hear us?

The voice of children, coming from her right. Victoria turned to peer across the water but saw nothing. *Children?* Her eyes fell to the water filling the small, round pool. It drew her attention as it swirled in brilliant colors of blue and green. The wind fingering across the top, drawing circles that rippled up to the water's edge and lapped peacefully out onto the grass.

Something about the sight stirred Victoria's feet, and she nearly stepped toward it. For a split second everything else stilled as her eyes drank in the reflections of light playing off its surface.

Victoria, do you hear us?

And then the voice of chaos returned.

Pathetic, weak child.

I tried to save you, but you were never worth saving.

Pain erupted through her skull as a screaming newborn's wail filled the sky. She cried out, waves of hot pain piercing her, shutting out the comfort of the breeze. It shook her bones, boiled her blood.

Worthless, evil girl.

I tried to love you, but you were never worth loving.

"No, no, no," Victoria rambled as her demons spread out through every inch of her being. Images of her newborn son flooded her mind. His screams rattled inside her brain.

Murderer.

Children should be protected.

"I did protect him. I protected him from you. From all the evil you were!"

Stupid little Victoria, the evil is you.

The baby's screams grew, thundering down against her skin. Guilt and sorrow pounded into her bones like nails. "He had to be protected from our evil," she cried. "I paid for your sins against me with his blood. Blood for blood."

You failed. Your blood is still dirty and worthless.

"No, no!" she screamed. She glanced up at Alicen, still serene and untouched by the horror exploding through Victoria's existence. "I paid what was owed!"

"When the voice of the accuser comes, don't be afraid," Alicen said.

Be very afraid; your trouble will eat you whole.

His voice scorched through her system, leaving fires of agony in its wake.

"For there is another voice in the stillness," Alicen continued, "the voice of love, and it calls you to the waters."

There is no love for a murderer. For a worm.

"Stop!" Victoria cried.

Victoria, do you hear us?

Again the soft childlike whispers tickled at the back of her mind. The collision of forces around her dragged Victoria to her knees. Her chest threatened to burst open, the raging fire blistering in her seemingly strong enough to burn the ring of trees that circled the clearing to the ground.

"Listen to the voice of love; follow it to the water, dive deep, and discover grace," Alicen said.

"Stop," Victoria said, her shoulders shaking, her mind being split in half.

From her knees, Victoria watched as Alicen walked to the lake's edge. She dropped low, placed both hands in the water, and scooped them together, collecting a small amount in the bowl of her palms. She then stood and walked to where Victoria was. The water stayed in place, not dripping through the slits of her fingers, not splashing up and over her thumbs. It just rested in the center, and then it was inches from her face. Victoria tried several gasps that turned sharp and painful, her lungs and throat on fire.

"When called to the deep waters, know the sorrow will not overwhelm you," Alicen whispered, her hands outstretched, her eyes shimmering with light. Victoria couldn't tear her gaze from the blue-green magic that spun inside Alicen's palms.

"For you are the light of the world, and your pain is just a shadow," Alicen said. As she spoke, the water seemed to transform, light spilling from its center, drifting off Alicen's hands and down into the ground between them. The wonder of it once again stilled the madness inside Victoria's head as it stretched across the ground toward her knees.

"The only way to be truly free . . . ," Alicen whispered.

Victoria's eyes remained locked on the light creeping across the grass.

". . . is to walk into the shadows and remember who you are."

Then the transformed water touched Victoria's skin. It warmed a place in her kneecap and pressed up her legs. It swam through the anger pumping in her blood and chilled it with ease. A new sensation of peace inched into the pit of her stomach as the grass beneath her swayed to the choir of soft voices that barely floated by on the wind.

When through deep waters you are called, don't be afraid.

You are the light of the world; the rest is just shadows.

Victoria felt a tear plop against the back of her hand, more following, streaming down her face. Her heart ached for more, but just as soon as the peace and light had begun to fill her, the agony of her past returned.

Darkness crept over the place where the light had been, and hot rage broke the cool sensation of peace.

Foolish little Victoria, you reap what you sow.

Pain and sorrow ripped through her chest, bursting across the clearing and knocking the trees together like bowling pins. Victoria cried out again, toppled forward, and grabbed at her heart, which felt like it was being squeezed out through a fissure in her rib cage.

This is what you are.

This is what you've done.

Don't forget your filth.

Terror and anger erupted like lava. Hot and deadly, spewing out from her every pore, melting her bones, turning her skin to ash. The words of her uncle mocking her.

This is what you're worth, child.

I tried to save you, but you weren't worth saving.

I tried to love you, but you weren't worth loving.

Tearful agony washed her face, drenched her cheeks with regret. Somewhere in the depths of her pain she heard Alicen's voice. "Don't believe the lie of the world, Victoria; you are more than what he says."

Don't listen to her, Victoria; you know exactly what you are.

Another spasm of torment ransacked Victoria's body. She cursed, pressed her forehead into the cold ground, and begged for it to be over.

"Forgive yourself, for you are forgiven," Alicen said.

Worms don't get forgiveness; worms get eaten.

"Grace can be yours; all you have to do is accept that it is," Alicen said.

Eaten by their trouble. Accept that, little Victoria.

"Don't be afraid; there is no fear in love."

You can't be loved.

He was right, Victoria thought; he was always right. The pain, the memories, the tiny cry, the raging sorrow, the rippling anger, the abuse, the guilt, the shame, the abandonment, the loss, the heartache—all of it attacked her at once. And she knew that if she stayed here, she'd die.

Squirm away, little worm, before your trouble eats you.

Victoria pushed herself away from the ground and took off, away from the clearing. Out past the tree line and into the pouring rain. It hit her like icy picks drilling down from the sky.

Run, run, little Victoria.

This is what you are.

This is what you've done.

Don't forget your filth.

Branches slapped against her body as she moved. She had to get away from the memories, from the pain, from the trouble that had risen up to swallow her. The cries of her murdered son still spilled across the sky, and no matter how fast she pumped her legs, they followed her. She had saved him, she tried to rationalize; she had only been saving him.

Victoria's foot caught a thick root and she started to fall forward. Suddenly the forest was gone. She was back in Alicen's room, Alicen lying on the bed in front of her, her eyes rolled back into her head, her body seizing.

Victoria's heart crashed inside her chest as the door to the right swung open and chaos ensued. Voices took over the room as large hands were on top of her, pulling her backward and away from Alicen.

"Get her back," a familiar male voice called out. It was Dr. Wells, accompanied by a handful of nurses. "What did you do to her?" he demanded of Victoria, but she couldn't speak.

Pieces of reality were falling into Victoria's mind, but the emotional rampage of her forest experience was still too heavy to push past. The pain and terror she'd fled the clearing with remained brimming under her skin.

"Get her on her side," a voice called. "Someone get me a crash cart."

"What did you give her?" Dr. Wells asked. "Victoria!"

She still couldn't speak. Shock had taken over her body.

"Dr. Wells, I need your help." The room was busy with motion to try and save the woman lying on the bed.

The room became muffled. Voices called out commands as people moved about, but Victoria only heard the sound of her heart beating.

And then his voice returned.

Filthy little worm. They'll fire you now.

You'll pay for this.

She closed her eyes, her lips quivering, but before she could conjure another thought, something else whispered through her reality. Something she'd only just discovered.

Victoria, can you hear us?

The voices made her still. The entire room seemed to slow to a snail's pace. Even her own heartbeat. And then their voices returned. Children's voices.

Victoria, can you see us?

She opened her eyes; the nurses and doctors still surrounded Alicen's bed, working feverishly. In the corner, standing in a row, were four children. A young boy, two smaller twins, and a little girl with pigtails. Their eyes sparkled with wonder, staring right at Victoria. The one with pigtails smiled.

"Good," she said with a wink. And then they vanished.

• • •

Alicen's eyes blinked hard to life. She inhaled harshly and struggled to get another breath. Unknown faces filled her view, their mouths moving, their eyes directed at her, but all she heard was silence. All she felt was pain.

Then the world broke through, as if someone had yanked the cork from her brain, and the sounds of the room crashed in.

"Alicen," a strange man asked, "can you hear me?" His eyes danced across her face looking for signs of life, and she blinked in acknowledgment. He smiled, and another face came into view. Dr. Wells's kind eyes filled with relief.

"You had us worried," he said, and gave her shoulder a gentle squeeze.

She didn't understand, and she tried to grasp the memories of what had just happened as they drifted in and out. She moved her eyes back and forth, watching the nurses read her vitals and check her over. Her heart started to feel as though it was beating normally again, allowing her to inhale oxygen at a steady pace. She let her head fall softly to the right, keeping her eyes open, and took several deep breaths.

A nurse moved out from her line of vision, and Alicen saw her. Victoria, standing in the corner of the room, her face ashen, eyes wide with wonder, tears streaming down her face. Her whole body frozen, but also shaking. She was being detained by security, questioned but not giving any response.

Clarity of her situation blossomed peacefully in Alicen's mind. Victoria had seen the water, and it had opened her soul. The demons she'd been taught to believe were having to contend with a powerful truth. Alicen knew the effect opening up one's spirit had on a person. She imagined Victoria would never be the same again.

Alicen wondered if Victoria would ever be able to forgive herself. If she'd be able to return to the waters and be transformed. If she could let go and accept grace.

Victoria's eyes shifted and met Alicen's. The movement in the room slowed for them both, and for a brief moment they were connected. Two different women, both slaves to the way of the world, to the shadows they'd been taught defined them, to their shame. They were the same.

Two police officers came into view then, stepping up to take Victoria from campus security and escorting her out of the room.

Exhaustion fell over Alicen like a heavy wool blanket, and as she drifted away from consciousness, she thought of Victoria and prayed the woman would find freedom just as she had.

28

Alicen stood in her Clover Mountain Retreat Center room and looked across the beautiful front lawn that stretched out below her window. The grass seemed greener these days, the sky more blue. Would it fade, the light she saw everywhere in the world? Alicen smiled to herself. She hoped not.

"You should be in bed, Alicen," a warm voice called from across the room.

Alicen turned to see Louise giving her a don't-make-me-use-my-mom-voice look and rolled her eyes. "If I have to spend another afternoon in bed, you'll have to just leave me here, because I'll actually go crazy."

"You shouldn't joke about those kinds of things," Louise said.

"What, too soon, you think?" Alicen teased.

Now Louise rolled her eyes with a halfhearted sigh. A sharp rap sounded at the door, and it swung open. Betty stood in the doorway for a brief moment, as if she were contemplating whether or not she could catch Alicen's crazy from just crossing the threshold, and then she stepped inside.

"Hey, Mom," Alicen said, surprised to see her. She threw a look at Louise, who just shrugged.

"Alicen, shouldn't you be in bed?" Betty said.

"Good luck," Louise warned.

Betty's eyes traced the outline of the room quickly and then landed back on Alicen. "It's cute. Seems comfortable enough."

Alicen nodded. "It's fine. I'm not going to be here too much longer, though."

"So that worked out then?" Betty asked Louise.

"Yes," Louise said. "I'm picking up her release papers this afternoon."

"Well, who would have thought it was so simple," Betty said. Alicen recognized the disapproval in her voice, and she tried not to let it dampen her mood. It had been nearly a week since her interaction with Victoria. Though it felt like a lifetime.

Victoria had admitted to injecting Alicen with enough ethylene glycol to kill a horse, yet after she had recovered from her seizure, not a single trace could be found in Alicen's bloodstream. A medical miracle, they said. Enough so that a couple superstitious nurses wouldn't visit her room anymore, while others couldn't help but constantly peek in. The entire campus was talking about her.

The woman who should be dead.

And about Victoria. The woman who had tried to kill her.

After her arrest, it didn't take long for Victoria to admit to the crimes, including poisoning her uncle Donald. A full-scale investigation into Clover Mountain Retreat Center and its practices was thrown into action. Alicen had heard a couple nurses whisper about transferring all the patients to other facilities, along with staff, as it would be several months before this place was up and running again. If that ever happened at all.

The hidden secrets of Donald Flowers had also come to light. A very strict, physically and verbally abusive uncle who had sexually assaulted Victoria for most of her teen years. Most incriminating was the child he'd impregnated Victoria with, a child she'd smothered only a couple weeks after giving birth.

The whole situation sounded like something straight out of a crime novel, and people were generally shocked. Many of them had worked on campus through the entirety of the happenings, never having any clue what was going on in the modest cabin at the back of the property.

There was guilt and sympathy toward Victoria from some, and Alicen overheard that she planned to plead insanity. She hoped the woman would be able to accept forgiveness one day. But the world would still expect her to pay for her crimes. She would likely spend the rest of her life in a facility just like this one. Getting help she actually needed.

Betty was outraged. She wanted Alicen to sue. It was well within her rights to press charges, a suited lawyer she'd been required to talk with had told her, but Alicen had no interest in that. Why would she? Yes, Victoria had tried to kill her, but Alicen felt more alive now than she ever had. This only infuriated Betty more.

Betty cleared her throat and moved over to Alicen's side. She sent Louise an eyebrow raise, and Louise gave a corny grin.

"You know," Louise started, reading Betty's signal, "I'm going to double-check with the nurses that I don't need to do anything else. I'll be right back." She stood and left the room, pulling Alicen's door closed behind her.

The room fell quiet for a moment. Alicen could sense her mother's discomfort. She was struggling to process how she felt about Alicen's situation.

"So you're feeling better, then?" Betty asked.

"Yeah, I cleared all my medical checks, and my strength is back, so I feel really good," Alicen said.

"And your—" Betty struggled for the right word—"mind?"

Alicen smiled. "I'm not seeing little children anymore, if that's what you're asking." And she wasn't. Alicen hadn't seen them since the pool. No Evie, Beck, or the twins. And no Jane. Alicen had spent hours sorting through all the events of the last few months, cataloging memories and conversations, organizing dreams.

Had the waters been real?

Had she actually drowned?

Had she transported Victoria to a place of power and healing?

Had the children been her ministering spirits all along?

They were questions she knew her mind couldn't answer. Some things the brain couldn't completely understand. But a deep knowing was so ground into her bones that she always returned to the belief that it couldn't have been anything other than real. The children had been her helpers, and they had brought her back to seeing what she couldn't see with her eyes alone. She couldn't explain it to herself, much less anyone else, but it had been real.

It had *all* been real.

"Don't worry, Mom," Alicen said with a smile. "My mind feels very clear."

Betty sighed. "I'm happy for you, really; I'm just having a hard time understanding it. Of course I get why you don't want to be in this place—you should be burning it to the ground—but to go back to living with Louise . . . I mean, maybe you should come back with me, and we can get you checked in somewhere else."

Clover Mountain couldn't legally keep her on campus after everything that had happened. But at the heartfelt request of Dr. Wells, Alicen had stayed the last few days for observation. He'd visited often, and they'd talked very openly about what had happened to her, about the way it had changed her. He'd listened, interested, without judgment, even though she was pretty certain he still believed it was all in her mind.

Either way, he'd concluded that she seemed well enough to go back to living with Louise as long as she promised to continue speaking with someone. She'd been thrilled to hear that Dr. Wells was planning a sabbatical and would stay in

Billings while he thought out his next move. Alicen had convinced him to see her once a week while he was around. She'd grown rather fond of him, and the idea of trying to start over with someone new was unappealing.

"I really am okay, Mom. I've got Dr. Wells, and I'll have the constant eye of Louise," Alicen said.

Alicen believed she was healed but understood that the world would still have reservations about her. She had, after all, still seen *imaginary* children. It didn't bother Alicen anymore that the world would see her that way. She knew this "disease" had saved her. She knew now that it had never been about what she saw, but rather how she saw herself.

A small shiver rippled across Betty's shoulders. "Well, one good thing—I won't have to come visit you here anymore."

"Because you did so much of that."

Alicen saw the way her words pricked at Betty, and she wished she could take them back. She hadn't meant to cause her mother guilt. Or maybe she had, but she was trying to learn how not to. She was trying to let go of brokenness between them, trying to give her mother grace, trying to love her fiercely, just as her Grandma Joe had asked.

"I'm sorry about that," Betty said.

"I didn't mean—" Alicen started.

"No, I should have come more. I should have done a lot of things differently with you."

Alicen reached out her hand and wrapped her fingers inside her mother's. Betty turned to meet Alicen's stare, and Alicen could see the forced control Betty was trying to mask.

Behind years of pain and shame, she was a prisoner too. It broke Alicen's heart.

"Please don't blame yourself for any of this," Alicen said. "It was a journey I had to take. I was called here for a reason. I had to walk through these shadows to discover who I am. To find peace with the world and with myself."

Alicen saw her mother's gaze flicker, and Betty swallowed to control her emotions.

"And I am at peace, Mom," Alicen said. "Real, authentic peace. So please don't worry about me. I'm more ready for the world than I've ever been. I see it clearly now."

They held each other's eyes for a long moment, a warm connection passing through their joined hands, before Betty sniffed and yanked back. She wasn't ready to face her shadows yet, and that was fine. They were, after all, only shadows.

Betty forced a smile and nodded. "I'm really happy for you," she said. "Peace is hard to find."

Alicen returned her smile. "What's next for you?"

"Oh," Betty said with a wave of her hand, "I'm going to head back to Santa Monica for a while. I have a flight first thing in the morning; it'll be good to see the girls. Martha has a new *friend* who has a handsome brother, apparently."

Alicen laughed.

"I mean, after all this I could use a nice man with a vacation home."

Alicen laughed even harder, and Betty joined. The two giggled together for a moment before the bedroom door opened and Louise walked in.

"Well, I'm sad I missed whatever happened here," Louise said. Alicen smiled at her and Betty shook her head.

"Everything squared away?" Betty asked Louise.

Louise nodded. "She's all set to leave tomorrow afternoon."

Alicen watched another bout of anxiety quickly cross her mother's expression, and she reached out to give Betty's hand another gentle squeeze. Betty glanced to Alicen and shot her a soft half smile.

Alicen wanted to give her mother peace but knew accepting peace was a step Betty would have to take on her own, just as Alicen had. She smiled at her mother and then at Louise, who had become her rock. The three of them had been through something that would uniquely hitch them together forever, and Alicen knew none of them would ever be the same.

• • •

Alicen walked arm-in-arm with Louise across the long front lawn stretching toward the Clover Mountain parking lot. The night had passed peacefully, Louise only leaving when forced and then returning the next morning as early as was allowed. They'd finished packing up Alicen's things and had them transported to Louise's car while Alicen had attended a brief session with Dr. Wells.

Now the sun was warm on their shoulders as the cool winds of the final days of spring were turning to summer. Sometimes when the breeze picked up, she felt like she was back in the forest, beside the lake. Even the memory of the water's touch was strong enough to rouse the comfort of truth in her gut. She wondered if that would fade. She imagined the world would try to block it out, but Alicen knew it couldn't change who she was, only trick her into believing differently.

To be so certain of the truth was radical, Alicen thought—transformative, like the waters in which she had drowned. It was a singular battle everyone fought.

Be free or be a captive.

Abide in love or in fear.

Be in light or be in shadow.

"What are you thinking about?" Louise asked beside her.

Alicen had slowed without realizing it, and now the two friends stood staring back at Clover Mountain Retreat Center. Alicen inhaled deeply and then exhaled with a smile. "I was thinking about how differently I see this place now."

"Well—" Louise shrugged—"you're different."

Alicen looked at her friend and nodded. "Remind me of how I am now, if I ever start to go back to the way I was before?"

Louise's eyes gleamed with compassion as she smiled. "I still can't believe all that happened to you in there. I mean, I want to, but . . ." Louise's words trailed off.

Alicen looked back toward the campus as a ray of sun shone behind the main building's roof, casting brilliant light through the nearby treetops. The wind whirled across Alicen's shoulders and neck, pulling her attention toward the trees. She turned her head and there, standing just across the tree line, she saw them. All four children. Alicen's heart leapt, and a sense of wonder filled her chest.

Alicen felt the still warmth rumble into flames, and she smiled. She turned back to Louise. "It's okay, Lou; I just need to believe."

Louise pulled Alicen closer as they turned and continued down the path toward the parking lot. Alicen's mind swirled in awe with the belief of what she had experienced.

Her logic would question what her heart knew was true. Ministering spirits had been her guides, and she'd followed them to the waters of salvation. And below the surface she'd discovered that she was the light of the world. Able to forgive herself because she was forgiven.

And through that forgiveness, she was free.

1

Carrington felt as though she'd collided with a moving train.

The room around her echoed with sweet laughter and flirtation. Handsome men softly led blushing young ladies around the dance floor while other girls looked on from corners, smiling with gleeful exuberance, all of them too consumed with their personal victories to notice the dread filling Carrington's face.

She should run. Maybe she could get away before they came for her. But how many girls had successfully escaped from the Authority? None.

Her hands trembled at her sides as bits of reality began to crash against the inside of her skull.

How could things have gone so wrong? This was not supposed to happen to her.

Panic pricked at her legs, and that voice of self-preservation shouted at her to stop standing there like a corpse and *move*.

Carrington turned toward the massive Capitol Building doors and saw the horde of CityWatch guards enter. Silently they spread out across the room and headed for Carrington and the other girls who stood in fearful recognition.

The guards' black uniforms fit their forms tightly enough to punctuate how impossible it would be to overpower them. Their faces were fixed in stern focus on the task of collecting the Unchosen and escorting them to the Exiting Room.

Fear filled Carrington's chest like a balloon. Sweat bled through the skin on her forehead. The room felt as if it were being pumped full of hot air that wilted her lungs. This wasn't right; this wasn't the plan. She should be looking on others with pity, not feeling it for herself. All the hours spent; all the learning and dreaming and wishing. Her entire childhood had been consumed by one singular thought, preparing for a single moment. This wasn't right.

Before Carrington could form another thought, a CityWatch guard was standing inches from her. He stretched out his arm in the direction he wanted her to move. Still dumbstruck by her situation, she hesitated. His brow folded, his soulless eyes narrowed to slits, and the corner of his mouth began to twitch. He thought she was being defiant.

Carrington swallowed her panic and found her feet. Her legs felt like gelatin and the ground swayed beneath her. It was impossible to ignore the slight glances from girls she knew, girls she had grown up with, girls from her practicing classes, girls now standing beside the men who had chosen them.

The Exiting Room was through a large set of mahogany double doors along the far east side of the Grand Capitol Ballroom. There were at least thirty other girls moving throughout the room, each one with a CityWatch escort.

Carrington kept her eyes on the marble floor, studying the shimmer of her red ball gown reflecting in the polished shine. How many hours had she spent dreaming about wearing this dress? This gown had represented a perfect moment. Now it would remind her of how worthless she really was.

As she passed through the doorway into the Exiting Room, a shudder crawled down Carrington's back. Surely there had been a mistake. If she could just have a couple more minutes . . . he would be there; he would choose her. She turned to rush back into the room that held all her hopes and dreams and watched as two guards pushed the doors closed. The sound echoed to the ceiling above her, and she fought to keep from collapsing.

Carrington heard whimpers from the girls around her as the reality of where they were spread through the group like a contagion. The realization that everything they had worked for since the moment they understood their purpose was gone. They were nothing without that purpose.

As was customary, the families of the girls were brought in for their good-byes. They had only a few moments before the CityWatch would round the girls up and transport them by train across the river to live and serve as Authority Workers. As "Lints." They would no longer be daughters or sisters, no longer attached to the families that had raised them, no longer a part of the world they had known. Now they would submit to the Authority, receive a low-level trade, and remain loyal to that trade until death. This was the law, given to them by God, set into motion by the Holy Robert Carson many years ago during the Time of Ruin.

Carrington closed her eyes and tried to focus on the pounding of her heart. She had been taught since childhood that everyone had a place, everyone was called to serve, and all were summoned by God to obey the laws of the *Veritas*. She'd hoped for a different future, prayed for a different path, but this road was now hers to walk. She could not change it. She opened her eyes and hoped that a small sense of comfort would begin to ease through her clenched muscles, but it didn't.

A small hand tugged on the side of Carrington's dress and she glanced down to see a familiar pair of deep-set blue eyes. She forced a grin and was greeted with a crooked smile. Tears welled along her bottom eyelids and she choked back the swell of emotion.

"Did you get picked?" he asked.

Carrington softly lowered herself to his level so she could look into her baby brother's eyes. She gently ran her fingers through his golden hair and it flowed across them like silk, thin and soft like her own. He looked very much like her—round face, tiny nose, unwanted scattered freckles that still looked adorable at his age—all but his striking blue eyes. Those he had gotten from their mother.

No. The word sat in her mouth like a foul taste. Even at four years old, Warren would understand that this was not the desired outcome. She leaned forward and placed a kiss on his forehead. Fighting back another round of tears, she stood and was confronted by her mother's glare.

Some mothers were embracing their daughters, spending their last moments together reassuring them that even from afar they would always have their mothers' love. Carrington knew that she would not be granted this kind of comfort from the woman before her.

She could see the disapproval twisted in the angry lines around her mother's mouth. Cold eyes bored into Carrington with utter disappointment, casting a chill through the blood in her veins. She balled her fists tightly at her sides, her pale skin now ghostly white.

Her mother drew closer, grabbed for Warren, and pulled him away from his sister. The boy's small face changed; he knew something was wrong. He clutched the side of his mother's dress with tiny, fearful hands.

"Mother, I—"

"One thing, Carrington; only one thing was required of you." Her mother's voice was harsh and tight. "After everything I have done for you, how could you fail me so gravely?"

The strength to hold back her tears was fading as her mother's words crashed against her like physical blows.

"How is it possible you were not chosen? Girls half your worth were chosen while you just stood around and watched like a fool."

"Mother, I tried."

"Well, clearly you didn't try hard enough or we would not be standing here!"

"Vena," a comforting voice interjected.

Carrington's father appeared like blanketing warmth. He laid his hand on his wife's shoulder in a firm but loving grasp that seemed to defuse her momentarily. Then he stepped around her toward Carrington.

The urge to throw herself into his arms was overwhelming, but Carrington knew she would crumple into a ball of hysterics if she did. His eyes were green like hers. His face and hands had aged beyond his years from working long, hard hours in the Cattle Lands, but his smile was youthful, and the sight of it amplified what she was losing.

He gently pushed a loose strand of hair from Carrington's face and placed a warm kiss on her cheek.

"Remember, we all have our place," he said quietly.

Her mother let out an aggravated huff.

"Vena . . ."

"This is not supposed to be her place, Seth. She was supposed to be chosen."

Tears gathered in her mother's eyes, but Carrington knew her mother was crying for herself, for the way people would look at her now that her only daughter was an Unchosen. It was a mother's duty to raise daughters whom men would be proud to take as wives. And the truth was, she had failed as much as Carrington.

She wished her mother could cry for her, mourn this day as it would be the last they had together; yet it was foolish to think her mother could be anything other than who she was.

"But she wasn't chosen, Vena," her father said. "So this is her place now."

A loudspeaker creaked to life overhead and the room fell to a hush.

"Good evening. This is Ian Carson, Authority President. I want to greet each of you as you make the transition from being children to assuming your roles as contributing members of society. Though this day may be clouded with grief, you must remember that we all have a place and a purpose. You are still a significant part of our growing city.

Remember what the book of *Veritas* says: 'A man's heart plans his way, but God directs his steps.' On behalf of the Authority, I wish you well in your new responsibilities. As God set forth the law, so the law must be obeyed."

The room echoed in unison as the girls all recited the phrase as familiar to them as their own names. "As God set forth the law, so the law must be obeyed."

"The train has now arrived. The CityWatch will escort you to the platform. Please conclude your farewells and make your way to the exit. Authority Workers, may you take pride in your service," Ian said before another screech bounced around the room and then fell silent.

To the right, several guards pulled open another large set of double doors that let in the chilled night air. Carrington could see the side of a steel train car, and a pit formed in her stomach. This was it.

She dropped to her knees and pulled her little brother to her chest. She wasn't sure if he completely understood what was happening or if the entire situation was just too overwhelming, but tiny tears streaked the sides of his face.

She squeezed him until she thought he might pop and then pulled away, took his face in her hands, and pressed the end of her nose to his. "I love you, Warren. Never forget that."

A small whimper left his lips, and tears rushed down Carrington's cheeks. Her chest cramped with pain and she struggled to breathe.

"Assemble," a guard yelled from across the room.

Carrington stood and stared as the CityWatch guided girls quickly into a line to head toward the train.

Her father leaned over and hugged her tightly. She could feel the dampness from his chin on the top of her head.

Once separated from her father, she turned to face her mother. The woman was rigid and aloof, but she reached out and wiped the tears from Carrington's face. "Be good," she said, and her voice quivered with a hint of emotion.

"It's time to go," a guard said.

Carrington hadn't noticed him approach. She nodded and moved with the man. A hand reached out and grabbed hers and she spun back around. Warren held her hand tightly, his eyes wide with fear.

"Stay," he said.

"I can't, Warren. But don't worry. Everything will be fine."

"Now," the guard said.

Carrington yanked her hand away and watched her brother erupt into wails of confusion. Raging sadness threatened her balance, but she managed to remain steady as she followed the guard away from her family.

"Carrington!" Warren yelled.

She didn't dare turn around for fear that her legs would stop working.

"Carrington!"

She could hear her mother and father trying to console the child as she stepped onto the train platform. Drawing one last breath of the air that held freedom, Carrington moved onto the train filled with weeping girls. Even as the CityWatch guard slammed the door shut she could still hear the heart-wrenching cries of the little boy she'd never get to watch grow up.

ACKNOWLEDGMENTS

There are dozens of people who deserve acknowledgment for helping me walk through this novel. More than I'll probably remember, and more than I have time or space to name. Beautiful souls that were brought into my life specifically for the moments of struggle that came with writing this book. Because it was a difficult road, with turns I didn't expect, and heartache as the characters led me into places where I really had to examine the view I had of myself.

I could list names, but at this point I'm sure all those involved know the role they played and how impactful they were. So instead of the normal listing of each, I'm going to say only this:

To my heavenly Father, my brother Jesus, and the Spirit that softly held my hand, I would have struggled without purpose if not for you. In the moments when I was unaware of you, you were with me. Letting me discover and fall so that I would end up back in your light. Loving, leading me to the truth of who I am. Showing me how to see myself without shame or fear, as you see me. Teaching me to trust the call given, the Spirit leading, and the story that is always unfolding in me.

I rest in your light, a light that lives in me, that I see in others, and that reminds me the rest is only shadows.

DISCUSSION QUESTIONS

1. Alicen and Victoria both have strong ideas about what they deserve. Contrast this with what each of them receives in the story. What is the right balance between grace and consequences? When should people receive what they are due, and when should we give them grace?

2. In this book we see some characters who suffer from mental illness, others who have spiritual vision, and possibly a few who fall into both categories. How can Christians approach the subject of mental illness with dignity and respect? How can we become advocates for people who suffer from it?

3. In your circles, do you find there's a stigma regarding mental health? How can you learn more about this issue? What books can you read, or what professionals can you talk to?

4. Mental health and spiritual health are distinct matters, both of them crucial to a person's overall well-being. What kind of help does Victoria need for her mental health? For her spirit?

5. Though this is a work of speculative fiction, there are people who think they receive messages from angels or other beings that people around them can't see or hear. If you

knew someone who claimed to see and hear angels or other voices, what steps could you take to get appropriate help?

6. Think of someone in your life who faces a mental health challenge, large or small. How can you be a supportive friend as they manage this condition?

7. Jesus said, "I tell you the truth, unless you turn from your sins and become like little children, you will never get into the Kingdom of Heaven. So anyone who becomes as humble as this little child is the greatest in the Kingdom of Heaven" (Matthew 18:3-4). Why is childlike faith so important? As we grow up, what changes make it harder to maintain this childlike faith? How can we become like children again?

8. Alicen and Victoria both are tempted to think they are beyond forgiveness. What causes Alicen to finally accept it? Why does Victoria refuse? What in your past makes it hard for you to forgive yourself?

9. Alicen endures a heart-rending tragedy in her life that nearly breaks her. When you recall the most difficult moments of your own life, where do you turn for hope? Are there any passages of Scripture that you find particularly comforting?

10. The Bible records people seeing messengers from God. Do you think this happens still today? What evidence should we look for when people make such claims? How can we discern among delusions, deceptions, and true revelations from God? (See 1 John 4:1.)

ABOUT THE AUTHOR

The oldest daughter of *New York Times* bestselling author Ted Dekker, Rachelle Dekker was inspired early on to discover truth through storytelling. She won a Christy Award for her critically acclaimed debut novel, *The Choosing*, which was followed by two more books in the Seer series: *The Calling* and *The Returning*. Rachelle graduated with a degree in communications and spent several years in marketing and corporate recruiting before making the transition to write full-time. She lives in Nashville with her husband, Daniel, and their diva cat, Blair. Visit her online at www.rachelledekker.com.